Books by Lola White

Magic Matched

Betrothed
Married
Motherhood
Sovereignty

Sovereignty

ISBN # 978-1-78686-128-3

©Copyright Lola White 2017

Cover Art by Posh Gosh ©Copyright 2017

Interior text design by Claire Siemaszkiewicz

Totally Bound Publishing

Published in 2017 by Totally Bound Publishing, Newland House, The Point, Weaver Road, Lincoln, LN6 3QN, United Kingdom.

Magic Matched

SOVEREIGNTY

LOLA WHITE

Dedication

In loving memory of my grandfather, a patriarchal man who appreciated strength in the women around him. And for my aunts, who not only showed their strength in his final days, but grace, as well. Also, to Jennifer Douglas who brought the quartet to this point, and to my editor, Jamie Rose, for bringing it the rest of the way. Thank you all for teaching me so much.

Chapter One

Georgeanne

"Concentrate." Encouragement resounded in the low voice of Georgeanne Davenold's new, not-quite-wanted husband. "You can do it. You've done it before, just let it happen."

Silver ropes of magic wound through the ballroom of the Davenold coven's English estate, ruffling Georgeanne's hair. But what had been a sturdy, smooth ribbon of power before Silviu Lovasz-Davenold had broken her heart now felt to Georgie like a frayed thread—still powerful, but carrying a hint of the unexpected, as if it could snap at any moment. She reached for it, anyway.

"Yes. Feel our strength, my love. We are Magic Matches, aligning and merging our talents in ways non-Matches could never understand."

As she drew the cool, silver current of Silviu's talent into herself, it turned gold and grew in power, as all Matched magic did. Georgeanne let the untamed force channel through her and flood her senses. It filled a void inside her—to the brim, but the brim of the vessel she was, the container she was born to be, rose in proportion to the magic being pumped into her. She would never be overfilled.

"Our bond has been there since birth," Silviu intoned. "Our betrothal set our futures on this path, and our marriage has only solidified our connection."

"Our accidental marriage," Georgie muttered. "Who knew combining sex and blood could result in a life-long union?"

"The ties of magic are unbreakable. I am your husband, now and forever."

A fortunate circumstance for Silviu, considering the way he'd betrayed her. Georgie huffed. "And thanks to this morning's surprise ceremony, my whole Family has accepted you as such."

"They've already seen our connection." Silviu raised his hands as if in surrender, but the gesture didn't fool her. "Please, concentrate on the task at hand."

Georgeanne glared at him. "I am trying."

"Try harder."

Concentrating as her groom demanded, Georgie made an effort to tighten her grip on the slippery threads of his magic. Power swept through the room, rustling the long velvet drapes, rattling the humongous windows. Golden light burned like a small sun. The chandelier swayed, and Georgie swore she heard the wainscoting groan under the pressure of the force she and her husband created between them—a force they would use to rule over all the covens of their insular world.

"Perfect," Silviu called out. "Exactly like that, Georgie."

She tipped her head back and relished the power flooding her. Having none of her own, Silviu's magic eased an ache and healed a loss Georgie felt every day. She could almost believe his was her own magic. She could almost believe she was normal.

But she wasn't. She was a Bane-born witch who'd pinned her hopes of inheriting her Family's power on being blooded and named as heir by her grandmother. She was a warrior, trained in combat and politics, because magic had not been gifted to her upon birth. She was a woman who had been banished after committing an indiscretion with Silviu when they had been teenagers.

He, of all people, should not have been the one who had stolen her inheritance.

"No," Silviu warned. "You must keep concentrating, my love."

"Your *love*," she whispered, suddenly hating the endearment.

He should have understood. He knew how she'd spent her life pressured by her Family's aspirations, alienated because she was different. He should have talked to her the moment he'd begun to doubt her ability to host her Family's magic, so they could make their plans *together*.

With those thoughts ricocheting through Georgie's mind, the magic wavered wildly. Even as she reached for more and greedily pulled it into her, the light around Georgie dimmed—darker and darker, until the gold was swallowed by the purest black, exactly as it had done when she'd battled her cousin for the right to lead the Davenold coven.

"Damn it, Georgeanne! *Concentrate!*"

Untamed arcs of power shot from the previously controlled flow. Black ropes whipped the walls, tore at the drapes and made the chandelier's dangling crystals tinkle. A gust of wind lifted Georgie's short hair and tangled her curls above her ears. Silviu widened his stance, braced his legs and leaned into the powerful breeze. As he pumped more magic through her, she felt him struggling to exert enough dominance that the black light contracted into an impenetrable ball in the center of a golden sea.

"Get it under control, Georgeanne!"

"I can't!" The magic was too wild. Georgie made a desperate attempt at containing it, but she didn't have the skills she needed. While every other witch had learned how to control their magic, those lessons had been pointless for her. She was disadvantaged.

"You *can*," he screamed. "Stop being so damned stubborn!"

His anger sparked against her own. The black ball exploded. Raw power streamed around Georgie, tearing at her hair before it sent Silviu staggering. Not far—his Reap strength saved him, erupting in a torrent of silver flares bright enough to have her squinting. Anyone else might have been knocked off their feet, but Silviu caught his balance quickly.

He cursed. His lips moved in a spell Georgie didn't know and could barely hear. He waved his arms until silver sparklers trailed through the air, slicing through the black mass intent on destruction. A harrowing moment later, the magic cut off abruptly. Georgie swayed.

Silviu worked his jaw and planted his hands on his hips. "We are Magic Matches and our magic will only grow more unstable if you don't move past your distrust."

"I'm working on it. I realize—"

"We balance each other," he interrupted harshly. "I love you and you love me, so there should be no impediment to our talents merging completely and strengthening into the force we need in order to accomplish our goals and keep ourselves safe. The only obstacle is you."

"Me?" Georgie reared back. "You think it's only me?"

"I've explained what happened and why I did the things I did. You—"

"When trust is broken—"

"I trust you implicitly, Georgeanne."

"Well, isn't that nice," she sneered. "My head understands why you stole my Family's power, Silviu, but you're simply going to have to give me more time to wrap my heart around everything that's happened—"

"We don't have time!" He threw his hands up. "We leave for the Council Palace in a matter of days."

"What do you expect me to do, then?" She lifted her chin as frustration prompted her to step toward him. "You're not explaining yourself very well. You only tell me to *reach*, and I do. I try! But you've never told me how to control all this!"

"I want you to do what you did at the Ngozi wedding and again when the dark magic spell found us in the sitting room a few days ago." Silviu rubbed his eyes and shook his head. "I know you can do it again. You just need to concentrate."

Georgie felt hostility clawing at her restraint. "Maybe I

just *need* a break. A funeral and a wedding all in one day is a little hard on the mental faculties."

"Yes, I know, my love, but we can't afford a break. We can't afford for you to blow witches up with wild magic. That would definitely put a damper on our political aspirations."

"Moderate your attitude, Silviu. I've been able to access this magic for approximately three days. You've had nearly three decades to learn how to do this."

Until he'd stolen the power of the Davenold bloodline and become the new Mother, Silviu had been a member of the magically dominant Lovasz coven. He'd also been born at the height of the Reaping Moon, which only magnified his talents. He'd always had an excessive amount of magic at his disposal while Georgie, being Bane-born, had spent her life believing she had none at all.

Things had changed so suddenly and now Georgie could also access Silviu's magical power — though she still wasn't quite sure how to use it. It had been a little easier to do what Silviu requested when he'd physically touched her, but with him across the room and pushing her to try a long-distance connection, Georgie had barely known where to begin, and had no hope of keeping the flow stable.

Silviu's eyebrows lowered, not marring the prettiness of his face at all. "You are a fast learner, Georgeanne, when you want to be."

"I'm tired."

"We can't afford to be tired, either."

"I just buried my grandmother, Silviu." Georgie closed her eyes and willed away the pressure behind them. She was tired of crying. "I need a little break, then I'll tackle this puzzle with a fresh outlook."

He heaved a sigh as he glanced away from her. "Georgie, I don't know what you did in your battle against Suzette. I don't know why your magic is turning black and I don't know how you turned your cousin Bane with a single word. These are things we must figure out before we travel to France and meet with the Council."

As the Davenolds believed she was the new Mother, Georgeanne had had no choice but to meet her cousin's challenge for the right to lead the Family. At first, Georgie had resisted, knowing her Bane imperviousness would shield her from Suzette's spells, but the faces of her relatives had grown too confused and suspicious to stand firm in that tactic. She'd used Silviu's magic to launch a counter-attack, but whatever she'd done had been dangerous and abnormal, with the golden glow typical of Matches turning black and stripping Suzette of all her abilities.

"I don't know what I did, either." Georgie turned to stare at the massive double doors leading out onto the wet gardens. The rain that had been near constant for the past two days pelted the inset glass. It was fitting weather for both her sad excuse for a wedding and the funeral of a beloved Matriarch.

The pain Georgie felt at having to bury her grandmother was stronger than the grief had been when the old woman had died. It was almost as if the unthinkable had suddenly become more real — as if Georgie were now truly alone, with no wise guide to lead her through the pitfalls of witching politics and no maternal advice on how to move past the betrayal Silviu had inflicted upon her.

Georgie sighed and let her shoulders slump for a brief moment. Then she straightened, smoothed her clammy palms over her black dress — the one she'd worn to her wedding that morning and her grandmother's funeral that afternoon — and glanced around the ballroom. It was clean, no cobwebs or dust, and the still-swaying chandelier sparkled under its own light, but there was a definite air of disuse clinging to the room that had made it perfect for their exercise.

"Fine," she finally sighed. "Let's try it again, then."

"It won't work until you learn to forgive and forget, Georgie."

She dragged oxygen through her flared nostrils. "I guess

I'm not very good at living up to the standards set by old proverbs, Silviu."

But she was trying. She was trying hard to move past old suspicions that everything Silviu had ever done had been nothing more than a ploy to gain power. She empathized with his desire to put them both into secure positions, including the highest in the witching world. She'd faced the demon within herself that whispered she'd have taken desperate measures, too, if their situations had been reversed—but doing and having it done *to her* were very different things.

She felt Silviu move behind her a moment before he wrapped his arms around her stiff body. "My love, when you were caught in the spell at the Ngozi residence, our magic merged perfectly. I felt it. But when Suzette challenged you for Davenold Motherhood, I also felt the distance you tried to maintain between us."

"I was trying to figure out how to pretend to use something I don't even have. I'm not the Mother. I don't have access to the Davenold magic."

"Yes, you do." He tightened his arms around her. "You have access to all the magic at my disposal. When you used it against your cousin, I felt the instability. Your distrust might as well be a brick wall between us. I believe that is why our gold magic turned black."

"Maybe it's just what I do." Georgie slipped from Silviu's arms and turned to face him directly. "I break magic. I break witches, just like I did to Suzette when I bound her talents so completely that she lost all her power. Now she's Bane-made because I am Bane-born. I am a creature of nightmare, just like those old stories said."

He shook his head. "It's within your ability to control. Your distrust of me is what's weakening your concentration, and I am sorry for that, Georgeanne. Your magic—"

"I don't have magic!" Georgie threaded her fingers through her hair and tugged, wishing she could get off the merry-go-round. They continued to have the same conversation with the same results—Silviu's disbelief.

"Still?" He slapped his palms together, making her jump with the loud, unexpected noise. His voice dropped into a low tone that warned her of his growing anger. "Still, you deny your abilities?"

"I didn't use my magic. I used yours. I am the absence of magic and I consume it." Georgie crossed the space between them in a rush and pressed her palm to Silviu's sternum. "You fill me up with all the extra you have and with all the natural power you can draw from the world around you when we're linked. But *none* of that is mine. I'm just a convenient container to put your power into so that its force doesn't rip you apart."

"My father said you—"

"Your father was wrong! Vasile read some fucking fairy tales and figured they were as good as real life."

"He's been right—"

"He's been half-right," she argued. Georgie took a step back and rubbed her temples. "We can't depend on legends alone, Silviu. We have to face facts."

"My father believed you would be an extremely powerful witch. He believed that all your magic is locked inside you, hidden by your Bane shield, but that my magic held the key."

"It's the other way around," she whispered.

"No. Magic Matches take the heft of the stronger witch. You access my magic, but I can't access yours. That means you're more powerful than I am, and we just have to unlock what you have, stabilize it and learn to use it."

"I have no magic for you to access." She held up a hand to forestall his argument. "Whatever I am, Silviu, and whatever we can be together, it's not what your father expected."

He stared at her for a long minute, the silver hue of his eyes darkening, his lips pulling straight. Just when Georgie was about to simply leave him to his thoughts and find a quiet place to organize her own, he moved. Silviu was lightning quick when he wanted to be, and she didn't have a chance to register his actions before he'd caught her in an unbreakable embrace.

"My love." His breath feathered over her ear and made her knees melt. "We'll figure out what we can do, but only when this wall of doubt between us comes down."

Not giving her a chance to reply, Silviu captured Georgeanne's mouth with his own. He dominated and conquered, letting the full force of his authority bear down on hers. Reacting without thought, she fought back with slick thrusts and wet parries, doing her best to combat his patriarchal arrogance with her own feminine pride.

But the kiss dragged her under his spell—a different kind of magic. The enchantments of want, need and desire fed into the alchemy of the schoolgirl's crush and became the woman's greatest pleasure. The magic of sensuality between two lovers who fit each other in every way had the room spinning, swirling with gold, controlled without effort.

Silviu broke their kiss, but his lips moved against hers as he said, "I'll teach you to trust me again, Georgeanne, the same way I taught you before—with pleasure, patience and love."

Silviu held her to him as her bones liquefied with the stress of too many tragedies in too short a time. Georgie had rarely had anyone to lean on in times of trouble, but now she was in Silviu's arms, and it felt like a safe haven, in spite of his crime. He felt like home.

It hurt.

As he made to take her mouth again, Georgie turned her head. "I can't do this right now, Silviu. Let me go."

Chapter Two

Costel

"Well?" his sister demanded.

Silence descended, lengthened and finally grew weighted before Costel Lovasz realized Ileana expected an answer from him. He jolted and turned from the view of the pretty French countryside beyond the wavy pane of glass in time to see Ileana stop next to Eliasz, her betrothed and the son of the tertiary branch leader of the huge and influential Levy Family.

Eliasz sat on the bed and wrapped his arm around Iley's hips. Costel's chest warmed at the sight, at the energy crackling between the pair and the obvious affection they shared. They made a beautiful couple, with Ileana's trademark Lovasz looks—dark hair and silver eyes—contrasting beautifully with Eliasz's blond-god genes. Like a fairy tale, but Costel felt his sister deserved happiness after all she'd been through.

A wedding was just a formality between the two witches. Their betrothal had been sealed in blood, making it binding and permanent, as good as married. But, in the witching world, formalities were highly valued and, without a ceremony, everyone would simply consider Ileana undeserving of the proper rank equated with being Eliasz's wife. Costel couldn't let his sister be disparaged any further than she had been during the tyrannical reign of their grandfather, and he had already begun to make plans for an enormous wedding, one that would show the world that the Lovasz Family was ready to move forward and heal.

If he were any less cowardly, Costel knew he'd be planning his own wedding instead.

Ileana clapped her hands. "Costel? Are you still with us?"

"Yes." He cleared his throat and dragged his thoughts back to the conspiracy of the day. "Daniel Levy, the only Family Father who nearly every witch on either side of the Schism holds in high esteem, is your prime suspect."

"No." Eliasz rubbed his temples. "We think Daniel is involved, but we're looking for a very powerful dark magic witch. Daniel has virtually no talent of his own, so it can't be him."

Costel sighed and leaned back against the windowsill. Crossing his arms over his chest, he took his time ordering his thoughts, a habit he'd been forced to acquire first against his father, then against his brother, as the two were always quick to jump on any inconsistency in his statements. He'd found it more advantageous to force them into waiting while he marshalled his opinions and evaluated any potential arguments contrary to his.

As time ticked on, Ileana and Eliasz donned matching expressions of exasperation and frustration. Costel elevated his chin but said nothing. He hadn't been prepared for the conversation, but how could he explain that his entry to their room had been nothing short of a desperate evasion tactic? Bijoux Laurent had been coming down the hallway and Costel had avoided her by ducking into the closest room—which happened to belong to Iley and Eliasz, assigned to them when they'd arrived at the Council of Covens' headquarters two days ago.

"Our apologies," Eliasz finally drawled, narrowing his eyes. "I didn't realize we were boring you."

Costel shrugged. "Perhaps it is easier than you realize to hide truths about one's abilities and intentions."

He gritted his teeth as his sister rolled her eyes. For years, he'd watched her make that same action so often when he spoke, and for years, he'd been fighting the irritation it caused him. He knew what she thought of him, what their younger brother thought of him too, but his hurt feelings were a small price to pay to keep the peace and ensure their safety as much as possible.

"Trust me," Ileana said with more steel in her voice than Costel had ever heard her use before, "I'd know if he were powerful."

"He's in league with someone," Eliasz added. "We just need to figure out who."

"I can't imagine your Family Father obeying someone else's orders, especially not when the plan results in the death of the reigning High Seat." Costel exhaled noisily. "I still can't quite wrap my head around the idea that Madeleine Davenold, a witch powerful enough to rival Grandfather, has been felled."

"By a dark magic enchantment cast by a dangerous and unknown black magic witch," Ileana said. "She had been formidable as the leader of her Family, as well as the Council of Covens, but now she's gone and—"

"You're all determined to solve the mystery. I know." Costel nodded.

"The point is"—Eliasz glared—"Daniel doesn't have enough magic to cast the spell that targeted Madeleine."

For a moment, Costel wondered about his brother-in-law's honesty. Eliasz was the strongest witch of the Levy bloodline and could very well be in league with his Family Father. But Costel quickly dismissed the suspicion. He knew of the scandal from generations past that had resulted in a rift between the two houses. He'd been told how Eliasz's grandfather had been passed over as heir to the Family and given the third branch instead.

Costel only said, "I suggest you be careful in your investigations, Eliasz. Accusing your own Family Father of this level of treason will not be taken lightly by him."

The other man lifted a blond eyebrow. "Have you spoken to Bijoux? If we can get a peek at the paperwork Daniel filed here, then maybe we can get an idea of what—"

"I have spoken to her, and she assures me that her father

has been made aware of my request. I know he has, because I also asked him directly. We must wait for his decision."

"Costel," Ileana's voice took on a persuasive tone, "Bijoux's father indulges her, and she seems to have a soft spot for you. Take the opportunity to talk her into speaking to her father again."

A wash of cool magic trailed over Costel's skin. His sister was manipulating him. He knew it. Costel had years of practice at recognizing her influence, not that recognition did him any good. She rarely targeted him directly, but, occasionally, she tried to bend him to her will, and it almost always worked, much to Costel's displeasure. His weakness was yet another vulnerability in a long list of them.

Unable to fight against his sister's talent—a talent shared by both their brother and father—Costel felt the influence at work. It slithered over his skin and burrowed deep, sneaking upward to root itself in his brain. The last thing he wanted to do was spend more time in the Council Palace, or in Bijoux's company, but Ileana's magic had grabbed hold of his intentions. He knew from experience that the manipulation planted in his mind would only grow until he was sleepless, restless and ready to do anything asked of him just to make his brain stop clamoring for his obedience.

Costel pinched the bridge of his nose. "Emeric Laurent takes his responsibilities as Council Administrator very seriously. He won't just hand over the documents."

"Bijoux can ask," Ileana suggested. "She seems to be able to get her way frequently with that man."

"Why don't you just talk to Emeric yourself, Iley? Surely you can be as *persuasive* with him as you are with me." Costel heard the bitterness in his voice but he couldn't help it. Just as he couldn't help the brief flash of triumph that flared when his sister's cheeks flushed.

Then the guilt set in, pulling Costel's lips straight and stiffening his stance, even as it weakened his resolve. Every time he began to feel a hint of self-pity at their treatment, brutal memories of how much lonelier his siblings' upbringing had been raced through his mind.

His brother and sister had never understood how much Costel cared, but that was his secret to keep and he knew he couldn't hold their ignorance of it against them.

"This situation is difficult and dangerous." Ileana's eyes widened and she bit her lip. "We need your help."

He grimaced. "Caught between a rock and a hard place."

"Yes," his sister agreed. "I am. Silviu, as well."

Costel hadn't been talking about his siblings.

He treasured his sister and loved his brother. Costel steeled himself to spend more time in Bijoux's company. Silviu and Georgeanne would soon travel to the Council headquarters and Bijoux was an unworldly recluse trapped on the Council Palace estate. Surely he could hold out against temptation for a few more days.

Keeping his face perfectly blank, Costel ignored the knotting of his stomach and gave a quick nod. "Fine. I'll see what I can do."

Without waiting for the couple to say another word, Costel strode from their bedroom. Though tense and paranoid, he stepped into the corridor boldly, only to sag a little when he saw it was empty. He moved toward the stairway at the hall's end, his thoughts so overfilled with his wish to be back home, working on tasks he knew how to handle, that he followed the sharp curve of the stairwell blindly.

And ran directly into the bane of his existence.

Soft, generous curves imprinted his senses. The subtle scent of lavender filled his nose and an electric pulse plucked at his nerves. Pleasure and pain mingled as his heart squeezed and his dick hardened, a mixed response he had yet to grow used to in all the years he'd known — and loved — Bijoux Laurent.

She blinked up at him with eyes so blue they rivaled the nearly purple Jacaranda blooms on the tree he'd planted in the greenhouse back home. Costel immediately pictured Bijoux naked, pale skin flushed with pleasure while he hammered into her wet, willing body. Not that his mental images were helpful to his resolve, but Costel had been an eyewitness to the full force of magic at his brother's command and he was desperate to keep that fact from the telepathic witch before him. He could only hope his lusty thoughts were enough of a distraction.

"Spying, Bijoux?" He narrowed his eyes and prayed for her denial. She was a particularly gifted witch, intuitive and accurate in her power—an oddity, considering most intrusive talents were rarely as reliably precise as hers.

"Lying in wait," she admitted. Her high, clear voice sounded like bells to Costel—a beautiful carillon playing his favorite song. "You are fascinating, you know. I've never met anyone whose mind works quite like yours, but, then again, I've hardly met anyone at all. No wonder I'm so lonely."

He drew himself up and lowered his eyebrows. "I'm sorry. That's a shame."

"You're lonely, too. I know you are. I've seen it."

"Keep your magic out of my head, Bijoux."

She grinned, the Christian devil's mischief dancing in her eyes, though her face was angelic—a work of art. Bijoux Laurent was Botticelli's ideal come to life—and Costel's too, a knowledge that was hammered into his soul every time he glimpsed her smile or heard her laugh.

"You leave me no choice, Costel. You've barely even had a real conversation with me since your arrival. I'm not used to that."

Since he always came to the Palace early to prepare for the Council meetings, Costel was used to seeing Bijoux. He was used to the way she searched him out whenever he was in residence, accustomed to the stress of avoiding her and familiar with the mental challenge of hiding his feelings from her, especially his regret at not being able to claim her as his own. Her accuracy with others was nothing compared to the insight she had a habit of gleaning from him—probably because they were Magic Matches. As Costel refused to accept such weakness and vulnerability, and, most especially, refused the weapon Bijoux could become under his grandfather's manipulation, the nature of their connection was a cold and terrifying truth.

"Things are a little different this time. More...serious."

She cocked her head. "More secretive, you mean."

"Nonsense." Costel redoubled his efforts to distract her. He immediately pictured himself stripping her of the nearly indecent clothing she wore. He had no idea how she managed to look so innocent while dressed like a sex industry professional, but the incongruous mix left him hard as a rock. He focused on her generous curves and long legs, imagining how they would look wrapped around his body. He ran his eye over her bountiful breasts and pictured her nipples rising for his mouth. He imagined her blonde hair wrapped around his fist as he took her from behind.

For a moment, Costel forgot about all the ways his murderous grandfather could hurt her, forgot about how much more vulnerable he'd be to his father and siblings if a woman who held his heart was involved. For a moment, all Costel knew was that he loved Bijoux and had loved her for as long as he'd known her.

With a small gasp, she raised a hand to his chest. "Costel."

Pain caught his heart. Lust and loneliness stormed through him so ferociously his skin became sensitive to the subtle air currents whispering through the ancient, drafty Palace. He flinched back from the temptation of dragging her hips against his and taking everything he wanted from her.

"Please, let me by." Costel fought to keep his hands to himself. He barely glanced at her flushed cheeks and sparkling eyes, but he was entirely too aware of her quickened breathing as he tried to push past her.

"What are you thinking, Costel?"

"Why ask when you already know?"

"The things that go through your head intrigue me." The innocence fell from her face, leaving hunger behind. "The things I see when you're nearby, especially lately.

The things you make me curious about." Her voice was an enticing purr.

The muscles in his back pulled tight. "Whatever ideas you might steal from my mind are simply illusions for my imagination to play with, but—"

"I don't *steal* them. You broadcast."

"There is a reason I haven't, and won't, act upon them—ever, Bijoux."

If he'd hoped she would be discouraged, Costel was disappointed. Bijoux laughed in his face.

"The dirty things filling your thoughts are begging for action. You'll surrender one day, *mon lapin*. I just have to find the proper provocation."

Chapter Three

Bijoux

"Don't try to play games you're not experienced enough to win," Costel warned her in a dangerous tone that curled her toes.

Bijoux grinned hard enough to emphasize her dimples. "I'm a fast learner."

"Find a different teacher," he snapped.

Not in a million years — Bijoux was having too much fun. With the new Lovasz Father in residence at the Council Palace for so long, she was, in fact, having the best week of her life, no matter the glare he currently bent on her. Costel's face could hold any expression he felt like pasting on to it, but the horrified look in his eye didn't stop the dirty fantasies from racing through his mind, just as it didn't stop the quickly banished image of a bucolic scene — a rolling green pasture Bijoux knew had to be his home in Romania, populated with hard-working witches and fluffy sheep, a place he saw her occupying by his side, an environment of idyllic beauty.

And freedom. Her chance to escape the loneliness and isolation of the Council Palace.

She would have preferred a politically savvy witch. Bijoux would have liked her Magic Match to be powerful, influential in the wider witching world and not someone others believed was stuck in his own arrogance and pomposity. She would have chosen someone who was invited to parties and celebrations, and didn't choose to bury himself in the hills of Romania in a crumbling castle in the midst of craggy acres stretching halfway across the country. But a witch had no control over whose magic would Match their own, just as a woman had no control over who she would fall in love with.

At least Costel was handsome, with his thick, dark hair and silver eyes. And at least there were people on the Lovasz estate—women she could speak to, villages she could tour and shops she could visit. As a bonus, Costel was the leader of his Family, which *surely* had to hold some merit for her father.

Intent on seduction, she dragged her finger over the low neckline of her tight dress. "Why should I look to someone else, when all the wicked things rolling through your mind seem perfectly suited to the lessons I want to study?"

"Don't try it." Costel's spine stiffened further. "Hold yourself in higher esteem, Bijoux. Surely you should be worth more than a hard fuck?"

"Mmm, hard, huh?" Bijoux's lower abdomen gave a curious jolt as Costel cursed. Rarely did she hear real people swearing in her presence, so the word *fuck*, spoken in Costel's deep voice, caused a reaction she couldn't have predicted. Just as she couldn't have predicted the turn of his thoughts toward the pornographic over the past few days, but she was determined to exploit the new situation. "I'd say that's a good start."

His expression darkened. "That's all I would give you. I'll still leave you here when I go, trapped in your ivory tower, because I don't want you with me."

But Costel's naughty mind made another detour to a bucolic vista of the Romanian landscape—the mountains, forests and rivers, and her, sitting in a shaft of sunlight, smiling at him and growing big with his child, a new generation for his bloodline. Costel strangled the image in seconds, at nearly the same instant some shadowy thing took hold of his memory and filled the pretty scene with nightmarish screams.

Bijoux shook off her unease with the simple act of stepping

closer to Costel's heat. "You want me and we're both here. I don't see the problem in indulging."

He backed up, but she followed, undeterred. One more step put Costel's back to the curving wall of the ancient stairwell, and Bijoux took advantage. She pressed her entire body to his, rising to her toes to fit better against him, then closed her eyes to relish his heat, his scent, his presence.

She loved him. Since the moment she'd met him, years ago, the very first time he'd ever come to the Council, when his Family's seat had been forced upon him, she'd been head over heels. Bijoux had taken one look at Costel, one look *into* Costel—into his mind where fear and anxiety circled like vultures, where the pressure of being the heir weighed him down and where the excitement of all the possibilities of the future lifted him up. More than any other witch she'd ever met—which was admittedly and regrettably too few for her liking—he was such an easy read.

Just then, his mind had seized on the image of her lips and all the ways he'd taste them, if he ever got the chance. She decided to assist his goals. "Ah, Costel, I love the places your brain has been taking you lately."

"Nowhere good," he murmured. "Let me by."

She tipped her face up and brought her lips within a breath of his. "We were made for each other."

"No."

"You're my Magic Match. I know you better than anyone else ever can, Costel. I see you, and all the things you try to hide from everyone else."

"No." His muscles were unyielding. "You don't see everything. You can't or you would stop this insanity. You would realize that I am not the man for you."

"You're a wide-open mystery, a fascinating contradiction." For all the things Bijoux knew about Costel, all the things she'd seen in his head—his frustration and distaste for politics, his soul-deep need to stick his hands in rich, dark earth and find peace in the energy he manipulated there—there was so much more he kept back. There were whole chunks of his life he deliberately refused to think about or envision, but she didn't mind. "I think that's so intriguing. Sexy."

Costel's lips thinned. "You're enraptured in a fairy tale of your own imagining, complete with a happy ending and salvation from your lonely life."

She refused to listen to his bitter speech. There, in the stairwell, Bijoux was physically closer to Costel than she'd ever been, in spite of what they'd both wanted over the years. She didn't understand why he always held himself apart from her, but she was ever optimistic and determined to grab the advantage before it slipped away.

She slid her hands up the width of Costel's chest and traced her fingers over the column of his throat above his dress shirt. Need and desire unfurled in the deepest parts of her body and soul. Hope and heat raced the length of her, shoring up her wobbly audacity and encouraging her to push on, no matter what Costel pretended to want. Even as he shook his head in denial of her touch, she grasped the hair at the nape of his neck and tugged him down.

He refused to kiss her. He tensed, though she could sense his struggle against temptation. His breath fanned her lips and set off a chain reaction in her muscles that didn't stop until her thighs were trembling. Bijoux was so close, hanging off his neck, balancing on the tips of her toes, her body flush against his, but she was still a half inch too short. The tension swelled until the air between them crackled with emotion. She gritted her teeth.

Costel would not close the distance.

His rejection hurt. Pain shafted into the center of her being and threatened to expand. Bijoux dug her nails into his neck and pushed away all fear, all doubt. She would not settle for anything less than victory — not when her whole future was on the line.

"Please, Costel." She squirmed against him. "I know you want me."

"More than anything." His whisper was reluctant, torn

from his lips in a rush and nearly inaudible, though he exhaled the words over her mouth.

"Kiss me, then."

The world stilled. He was so close to surrender. She could feel it. She could see it. Costel's imagination grew fiery with the detailed images he projected — the softness of lips, the taste of pleasure, the slick glide of tongues and bodies as he deepened the caress, took it further, all the way to full possession and a claiming that wouldn't end until death found them in old age. Bijoux wanted that with every fiber of her being.

With a shudder, Costel pushed her away.

She fought. Ignoring the hands holding her back, Bijoux twisted and arched, fighting without pride to regain the advantage. The narrow confines of the curving stairwell worked counter to her goals — until her foot slipped off the step and gave her the catalyst she needed to win.

For a moment, fear screeched in her head. Bijoux hung, suspended in time, her body battling for balance. Just when she tipped backward, Costel snatched her to him and spun, planting her spine against the wall, supporting her with an intimate press that flattened her to the old stone.

With desperation and fear surging through his mind, he lodged his body between her legs, her short hemline rolling up as her thighs parted to make room for the intrusion. She was squeezed tight between a panicked man and rough stone, but Bijoux didn't mind. Shaken but triumphant, she wound her arms around Costel's back and held on tight, relishing the feel of his chest pressed to hers. He was solid and thick, muscles born of hard work beneath the slight give of his top layers. He wasn't a soft man, though he wasn't lean either, and there was real strength in his biceps, telling her all she needed to know about his preference for working in his Family's fields.

From hope to pain to horror to joy, Bijoux's moods were changing too fast for her to process. So she stopped thinking and simply held on to the man she loved.

Costel stiffened then groaned. Before Bijoux could figure out what that meant, his hips arched forward. The pressure of his erection had Bijoux gasping and lifting for more. She'd never experienced such a sensation, not even on the loneliest of nights when she touched herself and pretended she had a boyfriend. Tingling heat spread out from the point of contact, pulling at her nerves, even as her muscles seemed to loosen. Bijoux needed him to do it again.

"Shit." Costel froze. With his hips jutting forward, the thickness rising inside his pants was plastered to a place Bijoux had begun to wonder if any man would ever access.

Too eager to push on, to get what she'd longed for before he stole it away again, she writhed. The pleasure doubled, expanding beyond the region Costel filled. Bijoux lifted a thigh and anchored it to his hip, moaning when his weight pressed into her more firmly, losing her breath altogether when the hard bar of his cock slid over the thin fabric of her panties.

She could feel that fabric growing wet at an alarming pace. Usually Bijoux had to spend several minutes stroking and fondling to get any sort of moisture between her legs, even when she put on the movies her father never suspected she'd ordered or used the toys that had been conveniently delivered to the Palace in anonymous brown boxes. Often she thought about Costel when she played with her clit, but she'd never been so turned on so fast.

"You… We can't… I don't want…" Costel lowered his head and licked a hot, wet line up Bijoux's neck.

Pleasure seared her. A shivering, electric jolt raced down toward her collarbone at the same time it shot up to prickle her scalp. The breath she'd lost came rushing back on a sharp gasp that echoed in the stairwell. Costel rocked his hips forward.

"Please," she managed.

"You feel…perfect." Costel panted, warm breath puffing over a too-sensitive spot located behind her ear. "You smell so…sweet."

In the corner of her eye, Bijoux thought she saw a flash of gold light, but when she forced herself to concentrate beyond the lust overriding her senses, she couldn't see it anymore. She let the oddity slip from her awareness as she fought to assimilate Costel's emotions into her own.

He *wanted*. His lust was that of an experienced man — one who struggled to contain himself and release her, one who refused to get involved with her, but one who had been involved with others, had taken part in pleasurable pursuits and knew what the two of them could achieve together. Sensory memories of pleasure stormed through her brain. Bijoux bit back her jealousy and focused on manipulating the need Costel couldn't help but pour into her.

"You want me," she whispered. "Here I am. Take me."

"No." A storm of bleak thoughts rolled over the lust in his mind.

Fear and regret whipped Bijoux's heart, stemming from the source of all her frustration.

Costel shuddered. "I don't dare."

He slammed his palm to the wall and pushed off. Bijoux bit her lip as his bicep bulged next to her head, her mind racing to find a plan to get his acceptance, his consent and participation. It was difficult for her to do, with the riot taking place in Costel's head overwhelming her own concentration.

"What? What, Costel?"

He shook his head. His voice like broken glass, he told her, "This won't work for me."

Bijoux knew she had to do something before the opportunity slipped away. She had no example to follow but the dirty movies she'd watched, the only things she'd ever seen that were overtly sexual in nature. Boldness seemed to work for those women.

With her sauciest smile, Bijoux reached out and placed a finger against Costel's chest, then dragged it down over the buttons of his shirt. Hitting the waistband of his slacks, she didn't stop to evaluate what was — or wasn't — under her fingers, just as she didn't measure her words when she spoke. She was simply trying to be as sexy as the women onscreen.

"I've been a bad girl." She gripped his waistband and repeated a line she'd heard on a movie she'd watched just a week ago. "Perhaps you should spank me...with your belt."

Costel was a man. He should like it, but he didn't. Bijoux was left reeling as he stumbled back. His eyes blanked and horror stole over his face, and only then did she realize he wasn't wearing a belt. Once she thought about it, she realized she'd never seen him wear a belt.

The fog of regret in his mind parted in a sudden shockwave of pain. Images invaded Bijoux's cooling desire fast enough and strong enough to have her gripping her skull. Vivid, appalling pictures of Costel on his knees, a belt ripping into his back over and over. Sometimes a younger boy who looked just like him was next to him on the floor, and sometimes Costel was wrapped around the boy, protecting him from the blows. Sometimes Costel was by himself, but he was taking the beating meant for the boy—or the girl, who Bijoux immediately recognized as the youthful image of Ileana.

"Oh, my gods," Bijoux grated.

A man too old to be the father, though his appearance was so much like Costel's that he had to be some sort of forebear, wielded the whip. Pain spread out. Costel's knees ached. He never made a sound. Costel, a little boy, bit his lip and did not utter a peep or a groan or a wail. He hardly flinched as the leather sung through the air.

Bijoux's throat closed. With startling suddenness, the images cut off, no longer penetrating her mind without restraint. She pried her eyes open and stared at the still expression Costel wore—no emotion, no signs of life. His lips were stiff when he spoke.

"Now you know. You can't come with me. There is nothing for you with me, Bijoux."

"No, I..." She cleared her throat and stepped forward, but Costel backed into the hallway beyond the stairwell. She held out her hand in a silent plea for him to stop running away. "I'm sorry. I didn't mean it, about the belt. You don't have to—"

"This isn't about a fucking belt!" Costel clenched his fists, his chest expanded on a massive breath. "This is about life as a Lovasz. I can't save you, Bijoux. I couldn't save any of us."

Costel turn on his heel and stormed away. Bijoux blinked back her tears and panted through the residual pain. She didn't feel it physically, as the little boy had so long ago, but deep in her mind, she now held a memory of abuse she could never get rid of.

And in her heart, more determination than ever to make Costel hers. If he couldn't save her, then she would save him, and together they would find happiness.

Somehow.

Chapter Four

"Milo."

Silviu paused in the doorway of the dingy little room Madeleine had used as her office while in residence at the estate of the Family's secondary branch in England. Vivid, sensual memories of the time he and Georgie had nearly consummated their accidental marriage on the desk almost took Silviu to his knees, but he gripped the jamb's wood trim and fought for composure—something he'd been short of since his new bride refused to share his bed.

Once Milo Ivanov-Davenold looked up from the papers he was perusing, Silviu stepped farther inside and pushed the door closed behind him. With a wave of his hand, the new Davenold Mother cast a silencing spell before taking a seat in the straight-backed chair in front of the desk.

"I want you to come to the Council headquarters with us."

Milo, newly appointed advisor to the Matriarch and therefore the second highest-ranking Davenold male after Silviu, blinked his bright green eyes owlishly. Then his face took on a more arrogant expression. "I beg your pardon?"

"I need your help."

Milo slowly sat back, letting the paper he was reading fall from his fingers. For a moment, he took on the look of a deer caught in the headlights of oncoming traffic, but then his eyebrows lowered and his lips thinned into a suspicious line. "I'm rather busy here."

Silviu gritted his teeth at the cool reception and glanced at the cluttered desktop. "What are you doing?"

"Looking through Madeleine's business accounts."

Irritation at Milo's abrupt reply tightened Silviu's neck muscles. He clenched his fists on his thighs and reminded himself that he was a diplomatic man and that Milo was a member of a matriarchal Family that had just lost its old Mother and now followed a new Mother, currently at odds with her husband.

Never mind that said husband was, in fact, the new Mother. Silviu couldn't admit to such a thing without putting everything he'd worked for—including a happy marriage to Georgie—at risk, but not being able to set the Family straight when their behavior warranted it was beginning to infuriate him. He had little choice but to be patient as his bride came to terms with what had happened, and when she finally remembered her affection for him, Silviu was confident the wider Davenold Family would treat him with more respect.

"Why are you looking into Madeleine's business accounts, Milo?"

"Georgeanne asked me to." The reply was terse to the point of belligerence.

Silviu worked his jaw. "May I remind you that your own marriage has been fraught with disagreements? And may I also ask how you felt when the Davenolds treated you with less respect than was your due, simply because you'd had an argument with your wife?"

Again, Milo looked up to meet Silviu's gaze. In less than a heartbeat, the man's shoulders slumped and his cheeks took on a dull, reddish hue. He exhaled and shook his head, his regret and empathy soothing Silviu's temper a bit. "My apologies."

Silviu elevated his chin. "I understand we're putting everyone in something of a difficult situation, but, at the end of the day, Georgie is my Magic Match and my wife, and I have every confidence that we will work things out. I suggest the rest of the Family keep that in mind."

"It's awkward for us." Milo pinched the bridge of his nose. "None of us know exactly why she's suddenly become so… cool toward you, but we… That is to say, it seems…"

When Milo's explanation petered out, Silviu completed the thought for him — with a thin smile. "I must have done something to her. Is that it, Milo?"

The man nodded. "Christiana told me that you've done something to betray Georgeanne's trust, that you broke her heart. But none of us know what, so we are left to speculate —"

"Whatever you're imagining is probably far worse than the truth." Silviu spoke the lie as he slid to the edge of his chair. "And I intend to fix it. It's simply a matter of expectations and not getting what she wanted. Both of us must learn to compromise."

"Both of you?" Milo looked disbelieving. "Well, for what it's worth, I will do my best to remember how, when Chris and I argued, I was not always the villain her Family believed me to be. I will consider that, perhaps, you aren't either."

Silviu winced. Then, in a rare showing of self-doubt, he dropped his head into his hands and rubbed his forehead. Hunching forward over his own lap didn't ease the sudden, slight ache in his stomach, but neither did it change his mind about what must be done.

"No, Milo, I'm not the villain everyone currently thinks, but I'm not exactly Georgie's hero, either. Not yet, at least, but sometimes actions must be taken that are… controversial, but for the greater good and for the safety of the one you love."

"You're planning on doing something Georgie won't be happy about, aren't you?"

Silviu jumped to his feet, the need to pace overwhelming him. Normally he was very adept at hiding every ounce of emotion. For too many years to count, he'd been watched and evaluated by his father and grandfather — and even Madeleine Davenold. He'd begun stepping into the world of witching politics, as well, and had gained the notice of others, which required him to appear unruffled at all times. Silviu prided himself on his restraint, but the subject he was about to embark on had him restless, impatient and terrified.

"Do you remember after the attack came on Madeleine while you were with her, Milo?" Silviu glanced his way. "Chris, Georgie and I came to help you?"

"Yes." The other man shuddered. "It was horrible. I doubt I'll ever forget—"

"I was able to use your magic," Silviu admitted. "I manipulated your talent with my own, and it lent a measure of healing toward her convulsions. I did it again when Christiana was hit by the dark magic spell—"

"I think I knew that," Milo interrupted. "I remember feeling like my magic was being taken, streamed into a new pathway, one that brought a massive well of peace."

Silviu nodded. "That's your gift—an amazing ability, and one I could use in the coming days."

"For what?"

"For the Council." Silviu rubbed his jaw and turned his gaze toward the small, rain-streaked window overlooking the night-shrouded lawn beyond. He took a breath to center himself, though he didn't look Milo's way when he continued. "For Georgie, too."

Milo's chair squealed, giving Silviu the impression that the man had slid it back and the legs had scraped the hardwood floor. "What does that even mean?"

"It would be beneficial to...allow the Council representatives a sense of calm during the upcoming session. I wouldn't think electing a new High Seat would prove any less contentious than other pursuits undertaken in the witching world."

"*No*," Milo clarified, "I meant about Georgie. She's my Mother now, and my wife's favorite cousin, and we've always had a friendship. I'm not sure I'm comfortable manipulating her for any reason when the situation could prove dangerous."

"I would never willingly hurt her or place her in danger." Silviu focused all his attention on the slide of the raindrops down the pane of glass in front of him. "She's my Match. Unfortunately, while we are…in disagreement about a particular subject, our magic is unstable. You saw it for yourself, when Suzette issued her challenge and Georgie… had difficulty narrowing the path of her talents."

"It didn't seem difficult to me," Milo muttered. "Suzette is now Bane."

"Yes, and we can't afford for that to happen again. Witches like Georgeanne are already considered dangerous, creatures of nightmare. I will admit that I never truly understood why before, but obviously their abilities have been hidden by time and an understandable unwillingness to speak about it. Still, some deep part of our collective psyche must realize how atrocious such a talent can be, in the wrong hands."

"Ah, Silviu—"

"Georgie should be calm during the Council meetings, Milo. We can't afford for her unhappiness to spark an outbreak of magic no one will be able to control." Silviu rushed on as he closed his eyes briefly, wanting nothing more than to say his piece, gain Milo's agreement and set about planning his line of attack on the Council—and his wife. "That's all I ask of you. Help me help her."

Silence reigned for a full minute. After so long, the tension tugged at his curiosity, and Silviu turned to look. Milo sat like stone behind the desk. Silviu wasn't certain the man even breathed. His skin was nearly gray, his eyes wide and locked on the doorway. Ice slithered down Silviu's spine. Dragging in oxygen, he spun the other way, already knowing what he would find.

Georgie would have filled the doorway, but the presence of her cousin, Christiana, had forced both women over the threshold. They stood with identical postures—backs straight and arms crossed—with matching expressions of outrage on their faces.

"Georgie," he murmured, "I didn't hear you open the door."

She lifted her chin. "It wasn't closed all the way. Really, Silviu, if you're going to conspire to use your magic against the new Family Mother, you should at least check to make certain the door is closed."

He heard the sarcasm in her voice and couldn't help but reply in kind. "I'm not acting against the new *Mother*, my love, so much as *my wife*."

"You should employ the same theory when plotting against your wife."

"What's the point? No one could hear, except you, after you no doubt walked right through my silencing spell. Didn't you?"

"No, I broke it completely. I'm surprised you didn't notice, but, then again, you did seem pretty well wrapped up in your plans to take over...well, everything you possibly can."

Suddenly exhausted, Silviu rubbed his eyes. "Georgeanne, this isn't about plots or power. I just want you happy, calm and ready to face the Council. And, *yes*, I'm afraid of what all the recent stress on you has wrought. I'm terrified that our magic will get away from you again and the mobs will ready their pitchforks."

Georgie's lips thinned. "I've always hated how melodramatic you are, Silviu."

He glanced at Christiana as she laughed behind her hand. "My love," he told his wife, "I believe we should finish this conversation in private."

"Why?" she challenged. "You involved my cousins in the first place. You've already tried to get Milo to use his magic on me. *Me*! The Bane witch. It won't work, by the way."

"My magic gets through to yours."

"You're wasting your time and pissing me off, Silviu."

He sighed and reevaluated. Almost from the beginning, he'd done very little right where Georgie was concerned, and he was starting to recognize that fact. While he knew there were several events that had taken place over the past three weeks that he had no control over, Silviu had to admit there were also things he could have handled differently.

For one, he could have been more invested in working with Georgeanne. He could have been more open with her, more honest, although the one occasion where he'd let down every guard for her had resulted in the rift that left him frustrated in his lonely bed night after night. She'd allowed him to seduce her on the beach beyond the estate grounds. She'd let him take her and hold her and consummate their marriage. She'd told him she loved him.

But Georgeanne had also taken a profound piece of herself back, well away from his grasp. Her trust. Silviu hadn't even known he'd had it until it was gone.

"I'm making a mess of everything, aren't I?" he whispered.

Georgie barked a bitter laugh. "Maybe you just can't help yourself."

"I love you." Silviu paid no attention to their small audience as he made his claim. He didn't care who knew, so long as Georgie was among them. "All my life, everything I've ever done has been for you, for us and our future. I've told you, Georgeanne. No matter what I have to do, no matter who I have to fight, including you, I will."

"Yeah, you're a romantic." She uncrossed her arms and gestured sharply toward Milo. "So fucking sweet of you to enlist my cousin's husband's help in manipulating me."

"I'm afraid of what's going to happen at the Council meeting." Frustration sent Silviu stomping several steps toward his wife before common sense drew him up short. "With a dark magic witch—"

"I think I've already proven that there is no need for me to fear that witch, Silviu. I haven't fallen to his attacks."

"You almost did. You almost died when Graves Ngozi hit you with that spell that was enhanced by the dark magic witch. I'm afraid to lose you!"

"But now I can break magic. I can protect myself."

Silviu's heart pounded and his stomach cramped, but only the truth would do, from there on. His wife was right. He'd spent too much time protecting her and not enough time trusting her to help him achieve his goals. To get trust, he had to give it, and he knew their future rested on his ability to be honest with her.

Silviu made his confession around the lump in his throat. "I'm afraid of your magic, too, Georgeanne."

She staggered back a single step. Her face lost color and her eyes grew wet. Then she blinked and raised her chin.

"Good. Everyone should fear me." Turning on her heel, Georgie swept out of the room.

Silviu groaned and dropped back into the chair before the desk. "If I could just calm her down, I'm certain that she would listen to me and hear my truth."

"I wonder," Christiana said quietly, "if your truth is different than everyone else's truth."

Her tone was surprisingly gentle. Silviu and Christiana had not always gotten along and the distrust between them was often palpable. But since the death of her grandmother, Christiana had been much more accepting of Silviu and his patriarchal ways. For those reasons, he did not take offense at her words.

"I don't know anymore," he admitted. "I thought I'd done the only thing I could. I thought my actions would be understood and that she would forgive me."

"Well, Georgie's only been angry at you for a few days." Chris shrugged. "Maybe she just needs time."

He shook his head. "We don't have time. The black magic witch murdered Madeleine, forcing the Council to convene quickly so they can elect a new High Seat. Over the past few weeks, there has been too much chaos and danger. I hardly catch my breath from one thing before another starts up, and I don't know where the trouble will come from next."

"A black magic witch." Christiana moved to stand next to her husband and shrugged as if the answer she gave was obvious. "That should narrow the options down."

"Graves Ngozi is dead and Suzette is Bane now," Milo added.

"Wonderful," Silviu sneered. "Two down, a thousand more to go."

Christiana rolled her eyes. "No, I believe Milo's point is that, so far, my cousin has done very well combatting the threats against her."

"Really?" Silviu raised his eyebrows. "She still has some faint bruising on her cheek from where my grandfather punched her the night he tried to kill her with his bare hands in Poland."

"But she's alive," Chris pointed out.

"Poland." Milo nodded as if to himself. "Yes. It seems to me this whole thing started in Poland."

"I doubt my grandfather is the black magic witch in question," Silviu scoffed. "My brother is now the Lovasz Father, and he would surely have noticed. He would have told me."

Christiana met Silviu's glare directly. "Would he?"

"I trust my brother." Especially since Costel was working on his behalf at the Council Palace. "The threat isn't from my Family."

"No," Milo agreed, "I was thinking more along the lines of the Levy Family."

Silviu slashed the air with his hand, frustrated at the cyclical argument they'd been having for days. "They don't have enough magic, maybe not even if you combined them all."

"But they have far-reaching influence."

"He's right, Silviu," Chris said. "Daniel even managed to influence my cousin, Suzette, and she's a matriarchal witch, former heir to the secondary branch and this house, before she lost her mind and tried to challenge Georgie for Motherhood."

Silviu felt a stab of remorse for the woman. In all honesty, he believed she'd gotten nothing less than she'd deserved, but, as a powerful witch himself, Silviu couldn't imagine the horror of having his magic taken from him. For a moment, he relived the attack where Suzette had hurled insults and spells until Georgie had finally had no other choice but to engage.

With a single word. *'Bane.'*

Georgie's will and their combined Matched magic had changed the course of Silviu's future in that very moment. Now he was desperate to temper the danger that had sprung up as a result.

Milo stood and put his arm around his wife's shoulders. "I believe that whoever Daniel is in league with will be at the Council meeting. They'll want to see their handiwork."

Chris disagreed. "That would risk exposure."

"I think Milo is right," Silviu thought out loud. "They won't be able to resist seeing the Council in action, manipulating them, maybe endangering them to make certain they get their way."

Milo frowned. "Do you think they want Daniel in the High Seat?"

"I think it very likely." Silviu nodded. "But it's also just as likely the black magic witch will do something to put themself in the High Seat."

"But that can only happen if the witch is already a member of the Council," Chris said.

Silviu grimaced. "Daniel filed paperwork. My brother and sister are trying to figure out what's in the documents, but it should be a motion assigning his Family's seat to a new representative. The old one retired."

"Still, that would be a Levy."

"So many possibilities." Milo straightened his shoulders. "All right, I'll go with you."

"Me, too," Christiana added.

Her husband immediately protested. "Oh, no, *krasavitsa*. You are pregnant and have already come too close to danger for my liking."

"If you're going, I'm going." Christiana lifted to her toes, but only managed to plant her kiss on her tall husband's chin. "I'm a strong witch, powerful, excellent with spells and, at the very least, I can research the vaults or whatever is there, while the meetings are in session."

"*Krasavitsa—*"

"I'm sick of not being near you, Milo. Where you go, I go."

"Excellent," Silviu interrupted. "Then it's settled. I'll go find my wife before she retires for the night and let her know you'll be joining us."

Christiana winced. "Maybe you should wait until tomorrow to tell her?"

Milo glared at him from beneath lowered eyebrows. "And make certain she knows I will not be manipulating her for any reason. You will simply have to gain her trust in the way the rest of us mere men gain the trust of our wives. Be charming."

"Yes," Chris stated with a smirk. "Surely you have some charm, right? After all, how did you get her to fall in love with you in the first place?"

Chapter Five

Georgeanne

"Good goddess, what is that smell?" Georgie covered her nose the moment she stepped into the appropriated storeroom. It was too early in the morning to deal with such an odor, in her opinion.

Her cousin, Adam, looked up with a grin, his eyes appearing comically large behind the magnifying goggles he wore. "Truth serum."

"Huh. You need a better ventilation system."

"What do you expect from a third-floor linen closet?"

Both of Georgie's twin cousins hunched over a rough wood table holding numerous glass beakers filled with a variety of things she didn't want to think too hard about. She shuddered, realizing this was where the stereotypical idea of witches cackling over cauldrons as they dropped in newt eyes and frog toes came from, except the twins were much more scientific about it—with Bunsen burners, measuring cups, and not a single amphibian anywhere nearby.

Georgie focused on the other half of the dynamic duo, Christiana. Identical to her brother but for the femininity that came from being a woman, her eyes were just as large as Adam's, but her goggles were also crowded with thick, dark lashes. She wielded a wooden spoon gleefully, stirring the unnaturally orange contents of a large glass tumbler that was set over a burner on full blast.

"Should you be breathing in that stuff, in your condition?" Georgie asked.

Chris put a hand to her belly and shrugged. "It's not harmful to the baby. It just stinks."

"Truth stinks," Georgie agreed. "Tell me about it."

Adam sent her an evaluating glance. "Still fighting with your husband, are you?"

Georgie winced and nodded, grateful her cousin had jumped to an odd conclusion about her argument with Silviu. Adam thought she was irritated at not having a lavish wedding. The day Silviu had stolen her birthright for himself and become the new Davenold Mother, Adam had overheard Silviu confess his suspicion that they'd been married in the old way and had witnessed Georgie's shock.

She'd been beyond angry but also deliriously relieved on a fundamental level. She didn't understand herself—how one minute she could be spitting mad, and the next weeping in gratitude at the thought of having the man she loved by her side forever.

"Maybe you need to give the guy a break," Adam suggested.

"Maybe you need to mind your own business."

"Georgie." Her cousin lifted his magnified eyes to hers and pinned her with a meaningful glare. "A lot has happened, honey, and I get why you'd be frustrated—or maybe even feel cheated—"

"Yeah, you can say that again—"

"But I think he's trying," Adam finished in a hard voice. "It can't be easy."

Offended, Georgie stuck her nose in the air. "What is that supposed to mean?"

"He's patriarchal, honey, and he's turning himself inside out to fit in with the Davenolds. And we aren't making it easy on him, either." Adam's eyebrows dipped under the weight of his unspoken thoughts. "He's doing everything he can to bite his tongue around us and make things easier for you."

"Anything he does is for his own benefit. You can believe that."

"Oh, yeah? Is that why he lets you sleep alone?"

"He's not going to force me, Adam."

"Finally, a point in his favor from you." Adam cocked his head and shot her another odd glance. "But I'd say he's never forced you to do anything, has he?"

"He married me against my will."

"Through sex and blood, Georgeanne. You've heard the old cliché. It takes two to tango."

Georgie crossed her arms over her chest. "Since when did you become such a fan of my husband?"

"Since he pulled you back from the brink of death at the catastrophe that should have been the Ngozi wedding."

Georgie's throat suddenly felt too dry, though her eyes seemed more than able to make up the deficiency. Blinking rapidly, she dropped her gaze, wishing they could all be transported back to that moment in time—a moment where she'd felt such a soul-deep connection to her betrothed, a man she'd already married, but she hadn't known that yet. She wondered if he'd known and had no choice but to assume he did.

He was always two steps ahead of her and doing his damnedest to keep it that way.

"I wish I had a time machine," she whispered. "I would give a great deal to go back and change the outcome of the events."

Constance Gage-Levy had been seconds away from becoming Mrs. Graves Ngozi when the Ngozi Family Father had done the unthinkable. The magical battle that ensued had ended when Georgie stepped into the line of fire to save Adam's wife, Tulah. Being Bane, Georgeanne hadn't thought it would have affected her, but somehow the dark spell had blown through her shields and sapped her of life.

Until Silviu's essence had filled her up. At the moment of her death, his anguish and desperation had filled her to the brim with all the magic he could call to his command.

His power was vast—infinite. He just needed her to

unlock the full potential.

"I wish we'd never gone to the wedding," Georgie choked out past the constriction in her throat. "If we hadn't, Madeleine would still be alive."

"She'd have gone anyway, Georgie." Adam's voice held a quaver, too. They'd all been close to their grandmother and grieved her passing. "As the High Seat, she had to go to perform the Bestowal Ritual."

"But I threw the germ of that damned effigy on the flame and burned it! I'd been told the results would be unpredictable, but I did it, anyway, so certain that I'd broken the magic." Bitterness flavored her words. "My arrogance is what brought her down."

Christiana glanced up from her potion and shook her head. "You don't know that. The spell that infiltrated Grandmother was a nasty piece of work, enhanced beyond all natural boundaries. Whoever cast the spell was much stronger than either her or Silviu, otherwise they would have been able to eradicate it."

"We searched for a cure," Adam reminded Georgie. "Chris and I are very good with spells, you know, and we couldn't find anything strong enough."

Georgie knew her cousins were possibly the best at spellcasting anywhere in the wider witching world — or rather, second best. "But it was a dark spell, and that's not where your gifts lie."

"True," Adam conceded. "But it is where Suzette's talents were focused. So, as soon as the serum is ready, we'll be able to get some answers."

"How does this work?" Eager for a new topic of discussion, Georgie jumped on his words, not caring whether or not they showed her lack of witchcraft know-how. She'd been trained in politics rather than magic and usually tried to gloss over the weakness. Until recently, she'd never needed to know more.

She waved her hand and immediately wished she hadn't. The motion seemed to encourage more of the vile scent her way. "I hope you don't expect her to drink it."

Christiana blinked up at her. "Why?"

"How can you force her to drink?" Georgie reared back as an evil grin crossed her cousin's mouth. "Chris."

"That woman tried her best to ruin my life." Christiana stood up straight and pushed away from the table with enough force to rattle the hodge-podge of potion ingredients spread across it. She planted her fists on her hips and bared her teeth. "I don't care if I have to sit on her to make her drink this shit. I will happily do whatever it takes to get it down her throat."

"I don't think it will come to that," her brother protested quickly. "We could always just compel her to drink."

"Compelling her hasn't worked so far," Christiana sneered.

Georgie shrugged. "I couldn't care less what needs to be done to that bitch. I agree that she's tried to hurt too many of us to forgive her."

"Yes, honey," Adam drawled, "and we all know how much trouble you have forgiving people."

"You have an objection?"

"*I* don't. Talk to your husband."

Gritting her teeth, Georgie looked from twin to twin. "How much longer is this going to take? I thought you sent for me because it was all set to go. If I'd known I was going to have to listen to Adam's opinions on my marriage after I refrained from criticizing his—"

"It's almost ready," Chris announced. She picked up a vial and dumped a portion of the revolting brew inside. She added a few drops of liquid and the whole mess turned bright purple. Smoke rolled from the beaker as Chris swirled the potion and took a deep whiff. "Perfect!"

Georgie gagged. "That is noxious."

"This will pry the truth right out of Suzette." Chris' smile held a wicked edge. "She won't be able to hide anymore and she'll tell us everything we want to know about Daniel, the disgusting plot to have a child together and the black magic witch."

"Are you sure?" Georgie didn't think she kept the nervousness from her voice. Too much was at stake and her anticipation was making her insane. The Council meeting was looming and her grandmother's murderer had yet to be punished, and that, combined with the aggravation that was her marriage, made Georgie itch with the need to expend her frustration *somehow*.

Punishing Suzette, to her mind, was a fine way to start.

"Let's go." Her tone chipper, Christiana waved everyone toward the door.

As a group, they tromped down the hallway toward Suzette's bedroom. Conveniently close to their target, the room they'd just vacated had been stuffed with a wide variety of linens, pillows, bathroom necessities and carpet cleaning appliances until they'd been relocated to other smaller closets, so less than a minute passed before the trio stood in front of Suzette.

Georgie looked her unlikeable cousin over very carefully. Suzette had been the original heir to the secondary branch of the Family, Madeleine's niece and all-around Family nuisance. She'd spent her time ignoring her own husband while seducing everyone else's and perfecting her dark magic. Suzette had often been dismissed as a weak witch, but to the Davenolds, power was a relative term. Georgie didn't dare underestimate her.

Even then, when the woman was without magic, Georgie knew that didn't mean her cousin was helpless. She'd have rather held the woman elsewhere—a dungeon, for example—but Aunt Margaret had put her foot down, insisting her granddaughter should be allowed to stay in her own room. That room had become a prison, but it was a soft confinement, with Suzette's personal things easing her discomfort.

The woman sat on her bed with her arms behind her back.

Georgie's gaze zeroed in on her fist. "What's in your hand, Suzette?"

She said nothing, but that wasn't unusual. Since the moment Georgie had broken Suzette's magic and made her Bane, the woman hadn't spoken a single word. They'd all tried—Suzette's husband, mother and grandmother going about the task more delicately than Georgie, Chris and Adam. With the Council convening in less than a week, the time for gentle persuasion was past.

"Show me what's in your hand, Suzette."

Georgie moved around the bed to see better. The spell that kept Suzette inside her bedroom was strong enough to send streaks of color over the windows, and so bright that Georgie could almost imagine it as light. Christiana and Adam had outdone themselves with the enchantment, and Silviu's added boost made the whole room nearly hum with energy.

"Suzette! Open your hand."

The woman jolted and spun. Her movements were slow and uncoordinated, lacking any sort of practice or athleticism. Georgie had no trouble avoiding the highly polished knife Suzette thrust toward her. The attempt was almost laughable, until Georgie realized Christiana was taken off-guard, having never trained in any sort of non-magical combat.

Suzette leaped off the bed, swinging the knife. Adam jumped in front of his pregnant twin and received a shallow slice across his shoulder for his heroic efforts. Suzette bounded toward the door.

Instinctively, Georgie grabbed for her. Even as she heard Adam claim the spell would stop their prisoner from leaving, she scrambled across the mattress, her hand outstretched. Suzette lurched forward.

And passed through the spell decorating the doorway unharmed.

Georgie sprinted into action. She was fast and well-prepared. She caught up to Suzette three steps down the hallway and jumped on her back, taking her down to the floor.

Suzette made no sound as she struggled. Kicking and rolling, she fought to dislodge the person on her back, but Georgie held on and finally took immense satisfaction from the punch she landed on her cousin's jaw. The bitch deserved a hundred more just like it. One strike would have to do, however, because Suzette went limp. Georgie checked, but her cousin was simply dazed and out of breath, not unconscious.

Cursing, Adam stomped down the hall. Normally he was a man who revered women and treated even the vilest female with a measure of respect, but, when he reached Suzette, he grasped her ankles and dragged her back to her room. Georgie assumed sliding over the hall runner had brought her cousin back to herself, based on the way Suzette began to struggle again. She gripped handfuls of the carpet, bunching it as she was towed farther, but Adam was relentless in his determination.

"Good goddess!" Christiana screeched. "How did she get out?"

Only slightly out of breath, Georgie shook her head. "I don't know, but the knife is from the kitchen, and she must have gotten it recently. They polished the silverware yesterday, in preparation for Grandmother's wake."

"She must have been able to come and go," Adam pointed out. "And we never knew."

"How did she break the spell?" Chris whispered furiously. "With the help of the dark magic witch?"

"Let's ask her."

Doing exactly what Christiana had threatened, Georgie sat on Suzette and clamped her fingers around the woman's jaw. Adam tightened his hold on her ankles while Chris crept forward until she stood next to Suzette's head, staring down with such hostility that Georgie suddenly wondered if the serum was for truth or purposes much darker.

"Chris?"

She snarled. "All the lies you've built your life on will start to crumble now, bitch."

Christiana tipped the vial of foul-smelling potion over. Georgie rushed to angle Suzette's head, prying open her lips so some of the colorful liquid would reach its target. Then she held her hand over Suzette's mouth and nose while her cousin sputtered and gagged, until Georgie felt the woman swallow.

Suzette glared at her with hatred burning in her eyes — and triumph.

"You want truth?" she spoke in a voice rusty from days of disuse. "Here's truth for you. You took my magic, so I'm without. Just. Like. You."

It took Georgie a minute to catch on. As the twins watched the clock and counted the seconds, waiting for the serum to work, Georgeanne came to understand just what her cousin had meant.

"She's Bane."

Chris' gaze jerked toward Georgie. "What?"

"She's Bane now," Georgie repeated. "Magic can't work against her anymore. Your potion won't work. That's why you couldn't compel her to speak, either."

"I'll beat the truth out of her, then!" Christiana lifted her foot, clearly intending on kicking the woman in her head.

"Not yet!" Georgie levered herself up so that she could look directly into Suzette's eyes. "Tell me what you know or I'll let her kill you. Tell me who the dark magic witch is."

Suzette smiled. "Never. You might as well kill me now."

She meant it. The gleam in her eyes told Georgie everything she needed to know about her cousin's decision.

Leaning down, Georgie smiled back, her anger sharpening with the gesture. "Death is too easy for you. You are hereby banished from this coven. You can spend the rest of your miserable existence contemplating your choices, outside the protection of this Family. For the rest of your life, however long that may be, you will know regret and isolation, hunted by those who believe Bane witches are abominations who must be destroyed."

Victory rang in Christiana's laughter. "You don't stand a

chance. Justice will finally be served."

Chapter Six

Costel

"Harvest the remainder of those plots quickly and take the surplus over to Dominic." While the rest of the residents slept in, Costel used the quiet hours of the early morning to check on his agricultural endeavors back home. "The fields under his watch were flooded when the river rose and they won't have enough to feed their people this winter if we don't reallocate supplies."

Just because politics wasn't his strength didn't mean Costel was weak in all arenas. He'd been well-trained for his role as Lovasz Father—in everyday practicalities of his Family's needs, rather than the petty intrigues plaguing the witching government. He couldn't wait for the Council session to begin so he could formally hand over all the responsibility to his brother and get back to what truly mattered.

Using his shoulder to press his phone to his ear, Costel shuffled papers on the desk he'd claimed for his use during his stay at the Council Palace. He found the spreadsheet he'd been searching for and confirmed the facts for his foreman.

"The trucks should be there today. I'm sure we can co-opt a few to take the produce to the northern villages."

His foreman asked a question, but Costel's concentration suddenly abandoned him. A roll of warmth worked over his body, nape to heels, and his nerves buzzed and stretched. His groin pulled tight. A hot tingle stroked over his skull, letting him know he was being mentally prodded. There was only one reason his senses would react in such a way. He looked toward the door and saw Bijoux leaning against the jamb—watching him, evaluating him, reading him.

He immediately pictured her peeling off the tight dress hugging her generous curves. His mental leap offered self-preservation in equal measure to self-torture—maybe for them both, considering the way her violet eyes deepened into amethyst.

The voice on the other end of the phone demanded attention, but Costel had difficulty holding on to the conversation. He watched Bijoux walk toward him with an extra sway to her curvaceous hips and wondered what she was about to do. The woman had a mind as devious as his brother's, which was not a compliment, in Costel's opinion.

He covered the phone with his hand. "What do you need, Bijoux?"

"You." She smiled.

There was nothing he would love more than to take Bijoux up on her offer, but she deserved better than anything he could give her. His father and grandfather were too dangerous to allow a relationship of any kind, and she was the sort of woman a man should treasure and protect forever. The previous week had been the hardest of Costel's life, denying temptation and unsuccessfully avoiding the woman he loved. After their meeting on the stairwell, Costel's resolve had remained frayed.

Finally answering the question he'd only vaguely heard repeated through the phone, he said, "No, you'll have to ship in salt for the winter. That village has recently seen an increase in the non-witching population. We can't be caught casting spells to clear the snow from the streets, so we'll have to do things the slow way."

"You worry too much," she whispered as she drew closer to the desk.

Costel didn't know if she was referring to the measures he took to hide magic on his property or if she was commenting on his feelings toward her. It could be either, as his thoughts had unwittingly filled with both concerns.

Then Bijoux took over all his thoughts. He tensed in his chair as she smoothed her small hands down her body, following the dips and curves in a teasing, tempting glide. Costel would have loved to do that to her, if she were any other woman but herself. Unfortunately, the stakes were too high where Bijoux was concerned.

Through the roar of his own lust, Costel struggled to listen to the man handling the Lovasz estate duties in his absence. When Bijoux skated between him and the desk, his concentration faltered. Then she pushed her hands down her body to her hemline and pulled her skirt to her waist, hijacking his attention completely.

Her boldness was breathtaking. She wore nothing beneath but a narrow path of blonde curls, boldly directing his eye to her pink folds. Pretty. Every inch of Costel's skin prickled painfully as a hot wave of desire coursed through him.

Bijoux slid onto the desktop. In a move worthy of any quality stripper, she lifted and spread her legs, her high heels digging into Costel's chair on either side of his thighs. Without pause, Bijoux's fingers traced a path through that narrow strip of curls and circled her clit.

"Just a hard fuck, right?" she murmured. "Isn't that what you promised?"

It had been a warning, not a proposition, but he couldn't take his eyes off her hand, and the longer he watched her, the better the idea sounded. Costel became mesmerized with the drifting pattern of her fingers as they traced around her clit, flicking and rubbing. Watching her folds swell before his eyes and flush a deeper pink under her growing passion hypnotized him.

"I'll have to call you back." He ended his phone call abruptly. Rudely. He didn't care.

"Like what you see?"

Her voice overflowed with mocking confidence. Costel jerked his gaze up to hers and saw calculation lurking behind the gleam of lust. Anger mixed into the need setting his veins on fire, making him hotter, but also more determined than ever. There were precious few places outside his fields where he was freely given the respect he'd earned through years of sacrifice and hard work. He was tired of that.

He refused to let her manipulate him. Sitting back in his chair, Costel adopted a bored expression and indicated things lower than Bijoux's clit. "I'd like it better if you fingered yourself for me. If you want a hard fuck, little virgin, you better prove you can take my cock."

Stilling her fingers, she blinked. But they shook against her clit as Costel deliberately envisioned her doing exactly what he'd demanded. He let his imagination flood hers, picturing her fingers wet, shining with her cream, stroking through her folds and deep into her pussy. He pictured her working her own body until she was saturated, dripping and writhing.

"Well, little virgin?"

"How do you know I'm a virgin?" Her voice trembled but still held an edge of defiance.

He smiled. "Who else would you fuck around here?"

"There are guards."

"Kept to the outer perimeter of the property. Besides, your father probably had them castrated before they ever stepped foot onto the Council grounds."

"They'd still have fingers and tongues."

"No one's ever touched you." Costel leaned forward, gritting his teeth against overwhelming need, and stroked between her folds with a single finger. He relished Bijoux's gasp. Then he sat back before the sound could tempt him any further. "Show me how many of your small fingers you can take, and maybe I'll show you how many of mine will make you come."

She licked her lips. "I want more than your fingers."

"Prove you can handle it."

Costel gave her credit for her nerve, though he wasn't surprised by it. She was everything he couldn't be—bold and daring, eager to experience all the things Costel imagined he would do to her. Bijoux tossed her head, her long blonde hair swaying just above the desk as she leaned back and braced her weight on her elbow. She kept her other hand between her thighs, her fingers moving again, slow and tortuous.

And Costel watched. He knew hunger filled his eyes, though he struggled to keep the bored mask on his face. He forced his spine to relax against his chair and ignored the pounding plea in his cock that he at least set it free from its tight fabric prison. He settled into agony watching her flick her clit, tug and rub before slipping a single finger down through her folds.

"Spread your legs farther, Bijoux."

Her breath caught but she didn't protest. She had little balance to do as he'd ordered until he helped her lift her feet to the arms of his chair. Costel was given a grand view to every secret between Bijoux's legs—her pink folds, her peaked clit, the dampening entrance to her body. His gaze zeroed in on her finger as she drifted it lower to stroke and retreat, back and forth.

Finally dipping her fingertip into her pussy. Bijoux stilled.

Costel looked up and fierce satisfaction raced through him. There was not a single hint of calculation in her eyes, not a single spark of manipulation. There was nothing but nervous excitement and womanly desire. She wasn't sure what he was doing to her—or what he was going to do to her—but she was a curious thing, intent on finding out.

Costel waged war on the protective instincts sneaking through his lust.

"One finger, Bijoux—all the way in."

She waited for him to drop his eyes before she complied.

Gritting his teeth, Costel held back his groan and watched her forefinger penetrate and enter—a slow slide, more than hesitant, nervousness rather than a tease, though the results in Costel's cock were the same.

"Are you wet, Bijoux?" He couldn't help the bass vibration in his voice. "You look tight."

Her throat moved as she swallowed. "Yes."

His lips quirked. "Yes, what, little virgin?"

But she didn't answer—or maybe couldn't answer. A fine tremor worked over her body as she held her finger perfectly still and squeezed her eyes closed. Costel didn't know if it was nerves, lust or the need to adjust to her penetration that paralyzed her, but the anticipation was killing him.

Telepathy had its drawbacks. He used that against her. Costel's imagination erupted with every lurid desire he could call forth—images of his mouth in action, his touch all over her body, his cock sliding deep into her slick, hot pussy. He let his thoughts tumble them both deeper into lust, driving them higher into physical need. And Bijoux responded as if his fantasies were her own, her body quaking and her eyes widening.

A delicate pink flush stained both her cheeks and her thighs. Her breath broke and her legs stiffened. Bijoux jerked on the edge of the desk and Costel watched, riveted.

She put on a private show, one perfectly calibrated to suit him since her actions mirrored his thoughts and what he envisioned her doing. When he wanted her to add a second finger, she did so without any words needing to be spoken. He watched her acclimate, impatiently waiting until she thrust and stroked and arched in time to his mental demands. She was beyond beautiful, the reality of her pursuit of pleasure unequaled by any fantasy Costel could ever dream up.

"Three fingers, Bijoux." He spoke the words aloud because, when he'd tried to form the picture in his mind, all he could see was his cock filling her over and over until they were both limp and exhausted with satisfaction.

She no longer shook with nervousness but with a need Costel felt echoing in his own body. The arm she braced behind her on the table developed a dangerous tremor, her hips lifted erratically and her flushed thighs seemed cramped. Bijoux's breath fractured, coming too fast while her tongue flicked over her bottom lip. Errant thoughts overtook Costel's mind—him replacing her hand with his mouth.

The mental image drove him forward in his chair. Before he could stop himself, he reached for her wrist and dragged her fingers from her pussy. He licked them clean.

Costel watched her face as her eyes popped open. He sucked her fingers into his mouth and swirled his tongue all over, sucking the sweet taste of her need from her skin. His cock jerked in his pants. Bijoux jolted on the desk. Costel maintained the suction even as he pulled back, scraping his teeth over the pads of her fingers until he finally released them from his mouth.

And he knew, in that instant, that he'd just done himself in.

Costel looked down at Bijoux's wet, swollen folds and inhaled her sweet scent. He wanted to taste her pleasure directly, to thrust his tongue past the clenching muscle at her entrance and lick from the inside out. He was shocked at how badly he wanted to eat her up, though with the flavor of her passion still teasing his taste buds, he knew he shouldn't have been.

His desire was out of control.

Bijoux read his thoughts before he could give them voice and lay back across the desk. Her pussy beckoned him with a triumphant gleam and a steamy, seductive perfume. Costel leaned forward, breathing her in as he trailed his hands up the inner surfaces of her thighs. She had the smoothest skin, the softest curls, the hottest flesh—the sweetest taste.

Costel licked her, back to front with a slowness that denied the need clenching in his gut. His balls squeezed and his dick ached to be set free and given a chance to pound into Bijoux's hot sex, but he denied himself that pleasure. Instead, he took in her taste, loved her with his mouth and tried to give them both a beautiful memory to carry into the future.

Because it was all he was willing to give her.

He refused to think about what else he could teach her,

what else he could do to her. He refused to imagine what she would look like waking up in his bed — for the rest of their lives — or how she would smile at him every night before they went to sleep. He couldn't give her any more fuel for her optimism and couldn't risk going too far in the current situation.

He took the moment without pushing for more. He appreciated the spread of her legs, the drape of her body across papers emblazoned with his letterhead. He loved the taste of her, the smell of her, the feel of her. He pressed his nose to her clit and his lips to her folds and tried to remember not to be too rough or too greedy.

Bijoux writhed and arched beneath him. As Costel sucked her lips into his mouth and bathed them with a leisurely lick, she tugged hard enough on his hair that his scalp seemed to catch fire. She gasped, cried and pleaded, one moment twisting away from the torment, the next pressing closer. Costel followed her every movement.

"Please." The word ripped from Bijoux's throat.

Lust burning him alive, he lifted his gaze. Costel stared over the plane of Bijoux's abdomen, her muscles visibly clenching inside the tight confines of the dress she wore, her bountiful breasts heaving with her struggle for breath. He met her gaze. Her eyes were misty, unfocused, the pupils nearly obliterating the irises until all that was left was a thin ring of purple. Her legs quivered at his shoulders. Costel thought she was the most beautifully erotic creature he'd ever seen.

He licked her clit before pulling back to breathe over it. "What do you need, Bijoux? Tell me."

"I need… I need you to touch me. I need…something harder, Costel."

He put his fingertip on her lower belly, far above her curls. "Here?"

"Lower." She panted and moaned, wriggled her hips and sobbed. "Play with my clit."

"Ah." Costel flicked his finger over the peak a single,

gentle time. "You think you can give me orders, do you?"

"Oh, gods. Harder, please."

Instead of giving her what she wanted, Costel traced random designs over her flesh, all while keeping his touch nearly nonexistent. "But if I touch you harder," he whispered against her shaking thigh, "you'll come, Bijoux. And I don't want that—not yet."

"You don't want me to come?" She shook her head, making an effort to lower her chin to look at him, rather than at the ceiling. "Costel, I'm so close. Please. I've never… only by myself…and I love you…so much."

Her words infected him. They swept through his nervous system and pulled his taut muscles even tighter. Costel's scalp prickled and his spine tensed. His cock was hammering inside his trousers and his balls were tingling with his need to possess her. He felt tortured, and he loved every minute of it.

Looking down, he knew Bijoux felt the same. Her honey slipped from her pussy, her flesh trembled and her entrance contracted rhythmically. He hardly knew what he was saying when he told her, "Yes, I want you to come for me."

He slipped his finger lower and gently pressed against her. A broken moan flew from her mouth and Costel held perfectly still, letting her nerves settle—letting his nerves settle, too, as her heat licked over his fingertip and tempted him beyond reason. Scalding and soft, Costel couldn't wait to feel Bijoux's pussy clamped around his dick.

He bit his lip until he could banish the thought.

When her hips stopped writhing so hard, he pushed in farther. A single finger sliding deep and stroking silken tissue that flexed in time to her ragged breaths. Another low groan poured from her mouth, adding a new note to the ringing in Costel's ears. He held still, perfectly immobile as her pussy clenched and released around his knuckle. He waited, ignoring both her broken pleas and the pulsing demand in his dick. Only when he felt Bijoux's inner muscles ease did he add a second finger.

Slow and gentle. He didn't want to hurt her. She was so tight that his fingers were pressed together with no wiggle room between them. He waited an interminable moment for Bijoux to relax. Her muscles unclenched in mind-numbing degrees, in tiny increments that had Costel worrying for the integrity of his pants. He was damn close to finding his own release just from the searing stranglehold of her pussy on his knuckles.

When her inner grip finally eased, he pulled back and stroked in farther. He felt like he was touching liquid fire, with her pussy flooding anew and her delicate tissues heated to a scorching intensity. He gritted his teeth and gave her all the care she deserved, letting her grow used to his touch, letting her adjust to the repetitive thrust of his fingers.

After a few moments that Costel felt certain qualified him for the Christians' sainthood, Bijoux lifted her hips. She caught his rhythm in another two strokes. With a groan that spoke volumes of the sensations storming through her, Bijoux stiffened and her inner walls tightened in a rippling contraction over Costel's fingers.

He dipped his head and sucked her clit into his mouth. She exploded with a scream. The inner confines of Bijoux's body provoked a faint ache in Costel's fingers, but he pushed them deep anyway, forging through the ferocious contractions ripping through her channel. He licked her clit then dove down to catch her honey on his tongue, his own fingers in the way as her body locked down on them.

Costel's torture lasted an eternity, then Bijoux's body finally relaxed in a rush. Tempted beyond sanity, needful beyond human endurance, Costel pulled from her as quickly as he could without hurting her.

"Come here," she whispered.

"No."

Contradicting his own intentions, Costel stepped between Bijoux's spread thighs. She reached for his waistband with tenuous coordination and questionable muscle control.

Costel felt like a conquering hero when he saw the dazed expression on her face.

He grabbed her wrists and pinned them above her head. Then he leaned down and licked her lower lip.

"That was it for us, Bijoux. The best I could give you."

"It's not enough."

"I know." He straightened.

Then Costel walked away, before he kept her for all time.

Chapter Seven

Bijoux

"I don't want to go." When it came to getting what she wanted from her father, Bijoux had long ago learned that it was better to start off with a single, bold statement relating her intentions. Usually, her opening sally had Emeric Laurent's thoughts spinning before he could stop them, and she was able to glean a fair amount of insight as to what tactic might work best in the situation.

This time she had an ace up her sleeve, but old habits died hard. Already confident she'd won the skirmish, Bijoux barely paid attention to the swirl of mental images that would give her clues to her father's sudden anxiety.

"It will be so boring, my treasure." Emeric opened his eyes wide in a show of sincerity that didn't fool Bijoux at all. "Why would you wish to stay?"

She wondered how he could ask that question and briefly pondered what answer would best gain his cooperation — inconvenience, loneliness or stratagem? Beyond her curiosity to rifle through the minds of Council representatives so far sunk in their own intrigues they couldn't even remember what truth was, and even greater than her need for company in her lonely world, was Costel Lovasz.

She couldn't tell her father the whole truth, certainly not about what they'd done that morning. She couldn't explain the way her heart felt — as if it floated five feet above the rest of her. And with her body still humming with pleasure and excitement hours after Costel's intimate kiss — his licking of her, sucking and stroking, the pleasure his mouth gave her… Her cheeks felt too hot and she struggled to control her thoughts and the physical reactions they inspired.

Her father would not take that truth very well at all, and Bijoux did not feel like sharing such a new and special experience with others, anyway. She wanted to keep it all for herself until she got used to the sensations, the emotions and the hope that had buoyed her all day long.

So she only said, "I can help you."

Emeric lowered his bushy eyebrows until they were a slash of gray over his long nose. His nostrils quivered. "My treasure, you know the rules."

"I know Madeleine's rules." Bijoux met her father's gaze directly over the mile of desktop between them. "But she is tragically gone now. Her rules no longer apply."

His eyebrows continued to lower to an alarming degree. "The Council representatives expect you to remove yourself."

For years, every time the Council was in session or Madeleine Davenold was in residence, Bijoux was forced to pack a bag and move into the little house at the far end of the Council property. Well away from everything and everyone, isolated even more than the Palace, the cottage's only saving grace was the warmth. The castle, filled with numerous arcades, high rounded arches and stone walls too thick to even contemplate was a nightmare to heat.

The autumn weather was turning wintery. However, Bijoux had no intention of leaving the drafty Palace this time.

"I could be useful to you, Papa."

A flash of fear sparked in both his eyes and his mind. "But if you use your talent, then the representatives will learn how powerful you are, and they will fear you."

"They already know, and fear is not a bad thing."

"It is, if they decide to punish you for what you may learn." Emeric rubbed a hand over his face. "I can't take the risk of losing you. You are all that I have in this world — my treasure, beyond price."

"I would see the danger coming." She used his overprotectiveness against him ruthlessly. "If someone is set on doing me harm, wouldn't it be better—*safer* for me, Papa—to confront the villain in front of all who gather, rather than by myself at the back edge of the property?"

"These times are too troubled and about to get more so, with the need to fill the High Seat. You must go where it is safe, and you will be much safer in the cottage, where I shall post guards for you. Out of sight means out of mind."

She crossed her arms. "I won't go."

"There is a reason you are not to be here, Bijoux."

"Because Madeleine did not want her secrets plucked from her mind. I was sent away to protect *her*, but if she could have found a way to block me from hearing her thoughts, she would've gladly had me present to look into everyone else's!"

"Please maintain some respect for the lady."

Bijoux forcibly reined in her tone. It was too important for her to stay and outright petulance wouldn't get her what she wanted. "Yes, of course, Papa. I only meant—"

"She was very good at ensuring your safety and we owe her a debt we can never repay." Emeric's lips tightened. "But that protection has now been lost and it is safer for you at the cottage."

"I don't want to be by myself." Loneliness was a deadly affliction. Bijoux kept her face blank out of love for her father, but there were far too many days she wished her mother had taken her, too, when the woman had left. Emeric's marriage had been arranged for money, and not enough money had changed hands to inspire Bijoux's mother to reside in obscurity at the Council Palace after bearing a child.

Bijoux adored her father, but she hated the Council Palace as much as her mother did. And while Bijoux enjoyed the gifts her mother sent so frequently, she would have preferred to have received a train ticket and an offer of hospitality, instead — not that her father would ever let her go. He wouldn't even allow a trip into the nearby village. It was the one topic Bijoux could never sway him to give in on, but that had been before the current opportunity had dropped into her lap.

Costel Lovasz was finally giving her something she could exploit, an inroad to his steely, aloof refusal to acknowledge their connection. She wasn't about to lose her new advantage.

"I'm not going to the cottage, Papa. Not this time."

Emeric's train of thought often took odd turns and delved into shadows Bijoux sometimes had trouble following. Just then, a montage of frightening images flicked through his head. He envisioned angry leaders offended at being vulnerable to her talent and elder statesmen bringing harsh judgments and penalties down on their heads, and not just Emeric's and Bijoux's, but their wider Family — the Laurent Coven, who Emeric shouldn't have felt such attachment to, but did. Bijoux couldn't understand why he pictured all he did, or how her presence could result in the widespread destruction he anticipated, the terrible wars between factions fighting to use her magic for their own gain. The jumble of pictures was horrifying.

And from the chaos, a single image rose. Stronger than the others, more developed and vividly colored, trailing a cloud of such loneliness Emeric's eyes watered as he thought of it. Bijoux on Costel's arm, walking away from the Council Palace toward a life that was worlds away — worlds away from Emeric, who feared he'd never see her again.

"This is really about Costel Lovasz, isn't it, Papa?"

His nostrils flared in obvious irritation. "You can't help yourself, can you? You simply must use your talent at all times."

"How else am I to learn anything?"

Emeric's eyebrows knit together again. "How many times have I told you to stay away from him?"

"Many times, Papa." Bijoux met her father's gaze boldly, though she tried to keep her expression contrite so as to lessen his pain. "But I can't stay away from him. I'm going to marry him, as soon as he comes to his senses and asks me."

Clearly fighting for patience, Emeric rubbed his temples. "Why him, Bijoux?"

She lifted her chin and took a deep breath. "He's my Magic Match."

Emeric jolted in his seat, his spine slamming back into the cushion behind him hard enough to move the chair several inches away from the desk. His mouth dropped and his eyebrows merged with his hairline. His throat worked for a full minute before he could gather his tumbling, disorderly thoughts.

In all, Bijoux thought her father had taken the news rather well.

While every witch had a Magic Match, finding one was fairly rare, unless a Family went out of their way to search. Bijoux knew that Emeric would never have looked for her Match, and had certainly never expected such a witch to walk through the front door. However, she also knew he'd never allow her to leave the Palace grounds for any other reason than to be with her Match. Unlike other witches, who could only have a single child, Magic Matches could have many, and had a duty to their bloodline to beget a dynasty.

The one ray of hope in her campaign was Emeric's belief that witches should be married before they reproduced. Otherwise, Bijoux doubted he'd have ever saddled himself with his own wife and would have, instead, paid her to be his brood mare, just as he would have encouraged Bijoux into Costel's bed to fill the Palace with children, without giving her permission to marry — or leave.

"Nonsense!" he finally yelled. "You are much more... *more*, my treasure. You are simply *more* than he will ever be. To be his Match is...impossible."

Bijoux kept her voice calm, in spite of the need to defend her future husband. "To be a Match has only to do with magic, Papa. It doesn't matter what I am or what he is, though I will remind you that I can read Costel more easily than I can anyone else, and I promise you that he is a better man than he first appears."

"*Better?*" Emeric shot to his feet and swept a hand out in a grandiose gesture. "He needs a head start in the most basic principles of politics and is obnoxious about making it known that he wants to return home almost before he even arrives."

"But he does his duty for his Family and, therefore, you can't fault him," Bijoux argued. "I've seen into his head, and I know he's pushing against his anxiety to try to socialize and network—"

"With disastrous results. He is not popular, Bijoux. Certainly you do not want to be tied to such a man for life?"

"He is a good man, and—"

"He is a pig. I see the way he looks at you, and you... The way you've thrown yourself into his path is not helping him improve himself."

She lifted her shoulder. "You accepted the idea—"

"Of you learning why nearly every Lovasz in creation has taken it upon themselves to grace us with their presence," Emeric interrupted. "Yes! That is why I allowed you to be near them all."

Bijoux gave him a slight frown. "It is only two Lovaszes, so far."

"How many does it take to transfer a Council Seat?"

"I don't know, but I am doing my best to figure it out."

"You have learned nothing of value," Emeric shouted. "You've admitted that you see nothing in Costel's head but his desire to hand over his Council seat to his brother and return home to prepare his land for the coming winter."

She hadn't gone into great detail about what she'd gleaned from the eldest Lovasz in residence. The last thing Bijoux had wanted to tell her father about was the flow of wickedly interesting pictures concerning her own naked body in a wide variety of poses. When Ileana and Eliasz had arrived in the Palace, Bijoux had hoped they would offer a bit more insight. They had not.

"You say," her father continued, "our cousin Eliasz and his fiancée have few thoughts beyond each other and the happiness they've been blessed to find. Therefore—"

"Doesn't that strike you as odd, Papa? How often can people think of romance?"

"Our cousin is newly betrothed," Emeric spat. "That, and he probably inherited a romantic streak from his mother. She was the same as a child."

"Oh, come on, Papa!" Bijoux planted her fists on her hips and glared.

Emeric was politically astute, a necessity in his job as Council Administrator. Bijoux knew full well that he did not truly believe the new couple was so enraptured with each other that there was no room for anything else in their heads. Emeric was simply being difficult, stubbornly refusing to agree that there was a very good reason for her to have begun spending so much time in the Lovaszes' company.

"You have seen nothing of value," he repeated in a calmer tone of voice. "Therefore, there is no use in continuing to search for that which they will not present to you. Trust me, my treasure. I have ways of learning what I need that do not involve using telepathy. I will uncover the truth in my own fashion."

"The new Davenold Mother is a Lovasz, and her husband wants to represent his former Family on the Council. Papa, you've told me there is no precedent for such a situation, and I am only trying to help you gain some insight as to what plans the Lovasz Family is embarking on."

"Yes, yes." Emeric waved his hand and sat back down. "I shall take it from here, leaving you plenty of time to pack your things."

"That won't be necessary." Momentarily sidetracked,

Bijoux tapped her chin and mused out loud. "Costel, Ileana and Eliasz are occupying their minds with things that are completely inconsequential."

Emeric straightened a stack of papers and pursed his lips. "You have only a few days to remove yourself to the cottage, my treasure. You had best prepare for a long stay, as I have no notion of when the Council will settle on another High Seat. Good gods, it took nearly a month for them to choose Madeleine."

"There hasn't even been a single, drifting thought about the *architecture* of this place, and it's all we can do to keep ourselves out of the tourist guides."

"Because they are here for politics, my treasure, not a vacation. Go pack."

"Their control will falter, and I can easily penetrate their thoughts when they do. No one can keep their guard up all the time."

"I believe the cottage will be too far away for you to read anything more of their intentions."

Bijoux blinked, bringing her father's scowling face back into focus. "I'm staying here. You need me, Papa."

"Not for this meeting, where representatives from every coven will be vying for the greatest power, a position many would — and have in the past — killed for. It's much too dangerous."

Fighting a growl of frustration, Bijoux folded her hands in front of her chest and widened her eyes again. "As you say, we find ourselves in troubled times. The High Seat is dead, and a new one must be elected. The peace of witches everywhere is threatened by the vacancy. We, *you and I*, as the guardians of all the knowledge this Council has accumulated over countless generations, have a *sacred* duty to ensure, with all the strength of our talents, that a proper candidate is chosen for this *great* position we so *sadly* find ourselves having to fill."

She laid it on thick, but she knew her father would appreciate that. He took his responsibilities to the Council very seriously. It also helped that Madeleine Davenold had been the only High Seat he'd served under, and as the woman had proved very effective and surprisingly fair, Emeric had given his utmost loyalty to her in that role.

His eyebrows had risen with every word. "No."

Bijoux was flabbergasted. She'd rehearsed her speech over and over until she knew she could hit the right tone, had practiced her facial expressions in her mirror. Emeric was being more stubborn on the subject than she'd ever seen him before.

"Why?" she wailed.

He pinched the bridge of his nose. "I have had terrible premonitions, my treasure. All I know is that I want you away from here."

Bijoux played her trump card. "Georgeanne has asked me to stay and help her."

For a long moment, Emeric stared at Bijoux with horror in his eyes. His face paled, but otherwise he was completely still—not a muscle flickered, not a thought appeared. Then he put his elbows on the desk and buried his face in his hands.

His groan was beautiful to Bijoux. It sounded like surrender, and the murky pictures in his mind confirmed it. She leaned forward and kissed his head, just below his receding hairline.

Emeric's implicit permission came several moments later. "I can hardly refuse the new Mother's request, after all Madeleine had done for you. I owed that woman a great debt."

"You can repay her by aiding the new Mother, then."

Emeric glared up at his daughter. "But will Georgeanne keep you as safe as Madeleine did?"

"I don't doubt it." Bijoux smiled. "But I can also take care of myself."

"No, you can't. Therefore, you will remain out of sight as much as possible. If there is any danger, I expect to be told immediately."

"Of course," Bijoux lied. There was no way she'd tell her father she was in danger unless she had no other choice. One vengeful thought from a Councilman would have Emeric sending her off into total isolation for the rest of her life, and she couldn't bear that.

Emeric's jaw hardened. "If the representatives make a scene, you will immediately be taken to the cottage, no matter what the new Mother desires. Do I make myself clear?"

"Yes, Papa." Bijoux put a bit of a tremble into her lower lip. "I will go…so far away, all by myself where no one will be nearby, should danger present itself."

Emeric stared at his daughter with bleak eyes. "You will not call attention to yourself. Do you understand me?"

"I will be very careful."

"And you will stay away from Costel. Do not let him touch you."

She leaned over the desk and gave her father another light kiss on his cheek. "I promise that I have no intention of allowing Costel to seduce me."

Not when seducing him should prove to be so much fun.

Chapter Eight

Silviu

Silviu knocked on Georgeanne's door in nearly the same instant he entered her bedroom. He didn't want to give her a chance to refuse him entry, as she appeared ready to do when she looked up from her vanity. She placed her brush on the countertop with a hard click that told him all he needed to hear about her mood.

The sharpest pang Silviu had ever felt traveled the length of his body and nearly tore his knees out from under him. For a moment, life was extraordinarily commonplace, a husband and his wife together after a long, hard day. An intimate setting, a feminine ritual played out before Silviu's eyes, giving him the sense that every night could be exactly like this, and it would be perfect, in spite of the bulky flannel pajamas Georgie seemed to prefer. Then he remembered he still slept elsewhere and was hardly welcome in her domain. His short-lived satisfaction was quickly followed by regret.

"The Shimizu Family was extremely unimpressed at the discovery of their long-lost cousin, Tulah," Silviu said before Georgie could order him out. "That changed once their Council representative learned she'd married Adam, however."

Georgie lifted her chin. "The Davenold name holds weight. And Adam is a very high-ranking male."

"A patriarchal witch would consider him more than fitting for such a lowly member of Tulah's bloodlines, yes." Silviu winced, wishing he had a better way of phrasing such a sentiment, but his tact had worn thin over the past several hours. He'd been calling the Fatherhouses, one after the other, speaking to the highest ranking male he could get on the phone, as well as each coven's Council representative.

"Which bloodline?" Clearly intent on ignoring the prejudice the patriarchal covens held toward the matriarchal Families, Georgie picked her brush up and attacked her curls. She met Silviu's eyes in the mirror and quirked her eyebrow. "Ngozi or Shimizu?"

"Currently, my love, both are extremely important to us, but Ngozi gave me his support at the wedding. I wanted to see where the Shimizus stand."

"You trust Muso Ngozi?"

"He knows better than to retract his agreement." Silviu clenched his fists as the possibility infiltrated his confidence.

He'd warned the Ngozi Father at the wedding. After defeating the spell that had almost taken Georgie from him forever, Silviu had denied his instincts to kill the son of a bitch and had, instead, wrung a promise of support from him. When Silviu made a run for the High Seat at the upcoming Council meeting, Muso would back him one hundred percent or he'd suffer Silviu's wrath — and there was plenty of it, bubbling up every time he thought of just how close he'd been to losing his wife to Graves' deadly spell.

"He knows that Graves' death did not placate my temper in the least," Silviu said. "If Muso does not support me, Georgeanne, he will die for his crimes against you."

Again, she put down her brush with a resounding clack. "He wasn't exactly at fault, Silviu. I agree with the tactic to utilize his vote, but murder should be considered very carefully, don't you think?"

"He did enough on his own to deserve my hostility, not least of which was instigating Graves' attack. A Father is responsible for his Family's actions."

She took a deep breath. "Is that all you came to tell me? You've garnered the support of two patriarchal Families?

Excellent. Three matriarchal covens have also pledged to give you their vote, and I'm certain the others will, too, once I speak with their Council members face to face. Good night, Silviu."

"No, that is not all I've come to speak with you about." He was torn, wanting to pace but needing to stand his ground. It made his muscles bunch and hum with an energy he didn't dare release. "My love, about earlier... I'm not trying to manipulate you."

"Of course you are. You're always trying to manipulate me, trying to gain the upper hand. Isn't it enough that you're the new Mother, and I am your wife and, therefore, subservient?"

"No one knows that."

"How long do you think that will last? Even if I were the Mother, the patriarchal houses would still expect me to scrape and fawn on bended knee before you."

"I won't ever admit to my new position, Georgie."

"I would say that sounded like a promise, but you lie so well that I can't be sure."

He couldn't continue to meet her narrowed gaze in the vanity's mirror. Silviu closed his eyes, even as he stepped forward. "Nothing but truth now, my love. I swear. Everything that came before was to protect you, to protect us, and we need as much authority as we can possibly get to stand against any potential threats."

"You know, except when I was actively engaged in the fight to end the Indian witch hunts, I've never felt I was in danger. And yet, that's all you go on about."

"Madeleine and her reputation protected you. Please do not be so stubborn as to pretend that all will still be right in our world." Silviu rubbed both hands over his face. "Your grandmother is gone, and with her, all the security she'd offered."

"Don't underestimate me. I have a lot of friends and allies."

"You're about to have more enemies, too. You can break

magic now, you're married, and we will have powerful children one day. You've made a witch Bane, Georgie."

Looking up, Silviu saw the glimmer of emotion his wife quickly tried to hide. She wasn't fast enough, and the pain in her eyes was magnified and reflected by the mirror of her vanity. She had deep regrets, shadows that hadn't been in her gaze before, fear that lent her anger strength, and unspeakable sadness.

"My love." He dashed toward her.

"Don't!" She stood so fast that the vanity's bench seat tipped over. Holding up her hand, she met his gaze in the mirror. "*Don't.*"

Silviu kicked the bench out of the way and stepped closer, pressing his chest to her back in blatant disobedience to her command. He wrapped his arm around her waist and ignored her struggles as he leaned down and ran his lips along the outer curve of her ear. He wanted to replace her agitation with pleasure.

"Let me make love to you, Georgie."

"No."

But he saw the flicker of need in her eyes. He understood perfectly. They were two halves of the same whole, after all, both different, lonely, isolated their entire lives. Only they had understood what the other felt, and even that company had been denied them for a decade. She was hurting, grieving, afraid and unsure of what their future held and needed some sort of physical contact — pleasure and connection — to bring her a moment's peace.

Silviu trailed gentle kisses down the side of her neck. "Let me love you, Georgie."

"I'm not in the mood for —" She bit her lip, closed her eyes and shook her head.

"For what, love?"

Her reply was nearly inaudible. "Intimacy."

Silviu pressed his face to the curve of her shoulder. Hiding — he knew it and admitted it to himself. Regret stabbed him in the heart and he suddenly wished he had the magical talent to turn back time so he could make an effort to include her rather than working around her desires, but that wasn't an ability any witch had ever possessed.

He'd been patient enough to make gains with her before, and while he resented being back to square one with her, he was determined to win Georgie over again. Just then, he knew a slow seduction was the last thing she'd agree to, and part of him wholly supported his Plan B. She wasn't ready for intimacy. She wasn't ready to forgive him and open her heart to him again, but she was tempted. He could work with that.

"Tell me what you want, then, Georgie."

Her reply came after a tense moment where neither of them seemed to breathe. "Fast. Hard. Just sex."

She was crazy if she truly thought they could separate the sex from the intimacy, but Silviu wasn't about to argue the point with her—not then, when he was already sliding his hands under the flannel she wore, with her light fragrance filling his nose and her soft skin under his lips. She could believe whatever she wanted, and in the morning her own emotions would set her straight.

And he knew they would, eventually. Silviu glanced at the mirror and caught the faint signs of her confusion, the futile battle she waged to keep things physical with the man she loved. Her brow bore the slightest furrow. Her teeth pinched her bottom lip. Her beautiful dark eyes were tightly closed, but Silviu took that as a good sign. That gave him a chance to study her, and gave her a chance to simply feel.

He didn't want to leave her any room for thought, so he poured every ounce of his emotions into physical touch. He didn't just smooth his hands over her torso, he savored the texture of her skin. Silviu made certain Georgie understood just how much he appreciated the feel of her, filling his senses with bold strokes and gentle sweeps. He absorbed the heat of her and the tingle of their Matched magic into his fingertips, then increased the flow of his own talents until a soft, golden sheen radiated through her pajama top.

A tremor ran through her. She writhed and shifted, then caught the edge of the vanity in a white-knuckled hold. Silviu kissed her nape as he caught her breasts. Her nipples were swollen, begging for his touch, her back arching subtly so that the sensitive mounds pushed into his palms. But Georgie jerked her chin, nearly dislodging his hold on her.

"Don't kiss me. I don't want your kisses, Silviu—just your cock."

Again, he was torn. His lower half jolted with a spurt of lust so great he was surprised he didn't ruin his pants right then. The woman his heart had always been set on, the woman his body responded to so effortlessly, wanted him—boldly, maybe desperately. Her lust was a heady thing. Yet, his heart clenched, because he needed her arms holding him close, their magic melding into a cohesive whole and her body receiving him with a hot, wet welcome.

He could have one of those things. "All right, Georgie. No kisses. What about teeth?"

"What?" Her eyes flew open.

He bit down on the curve her neck, just above her shoulder, with more pressure than he would have otherwise. Repayment in the smallest way for her stubbornness, yet he was careful not to hurt her. At the same time, he clamped his fingers around her nipples. He pinched them tight and held them, relishing the moan that broke from her lips.

"Fast and hard, Georgie. I hope you can handle it."

"I can handle"—her voice cracked under a fierce shiver—"anything you dish out."

He put his lips against her ear and breathed, "Let's test that, love."

He tugged on her nipples and Georgie gasped. Silviu called his magic to his palms in a steady stream and sent it out to sweep over her, silver turning to gold and pulsing along her skin, pushing over the dips and valleys of her body. He let his hands follow the flow of goosebumps trailing toward her bulky waistband, then ripped at the bow she'd tied. The fabric fell to her ankles and a matter of shifting her weight freed her completely.

Silviu let his gaze fill with all the lust Georgeanne had always inspired within him as he took in the sight of her in the mirror—her long, smooth legs, her lacy black underwear, the hideous flannel top covering her north of her waist. A blast of magic ripped all the buttons off the shirt, letting it sag open to drape her torso and reveal her straining breasts.

Patriarchal dominance rose like a flood inside Silviu's soul. Georgeanne was his—his woman, his wife, his prize, the only thing that had kept him going in his youth, the only thing that had ever truly been his. He would prove to her they belonged together, he would conquer her fears as he conquered her body and they would finally have the peace and connection he'd craved for the past ten years.

He was not gentle, but she hadn't asked him to be. Silviu pushed his hands up to her chest, cupped her breasts and fondled. He squeezed the tempting mounds, shot a bolt of magic into the tightly drawn peaks and flicked them with his thumbs. He watched his hands at work while he scraped her nape with his teeth, rising until he caught her earlobe in a punishing bite.

Then he licked the shell of her ear. "You like this?"

Georgie made a soft sound of encouragement and arched her bottom, rubbing his groin. Silviu ground his dick against her ass at the same time he dragged his palm down her body. Fast and hard with no lingering touches or meandering forays, he angled straight for the apex of her thighs. He surged beneath the lace panties and caught her clit as he'd caught her nipple.

"Fast enough, Georgie? Hard enough?"

She cried out and bucked on his hand. "Yes! More. Faster."

Rolling the swollen nub under his fingertip, he zapped her with magic. Her gasp echoed off the mirror and urged him on. Another bolt of magic had her panties disintegrating, scraps of lace fluttering to the carpet.

"I'll buy you another pair," he promised.

"You owe me a lot already."

"I'll buy you a fucking store full." Silviu bit her earlobe again. "And spend the next week ripping them off your body with my teeth."

He lifted his eyes to the mirror to gauge her reaction. Silviu wasn't even certain Georgie heard him or cared. Her gaze was glued to the fingers he pressed between her legs. He looked too and experienced a scorching wave of lust so strong he struggled to remain upright against it.

Visually, his hand was nearly obscured by the flickering corona of light produced by his magic, but his tactile impressions of Georgie's soft, hot flesh overwhelmed his senses. The sight of his wife caught in the throes of passion burned into his retinas. He saw her flushed face, noted the hunger in her eyes as they darted from the hand he'd placed on her breast to the one he occupied in stroking her clit. She arched and swayed, the muscles of her abdomen working hard, her rib cage laboring harder. A fine, golden glow covered her body like dust, but swirls of jet snapped out in random places.

Her desire rocked him. The evidence of their combined magic, stable or not, the way her body blushed with need, her muscles quivering and her legs shifting all drilled into a protective core only she had ever fully mined in him. He couldn't lose her — wouldn't lose her — and he would take whatever opportunity she gave him to reconnect. His pleasure and his pain combined, merged and became one in that instant.

He had to find a way past her defenses, even if that meant using her own tactics against her. A lifetime of manipulation came to his defense, and Silviu remembered that Georgie's sexual experience was predominantly limited to him and what he'd taught her. He set about overwhelming her, disarming her, as she'd done to him all too often.

He shifted his hand farther between her legs. Circling and stroking, he pressed into her folds, followed the curve of her body down and found her heat. His bride lost her breath on a shivering gasp that filled him with smug delight. Wet, soft, welcoming—her pussy seemed to suck in the two fingers he used to invade her depths. Soft walls closed around his knuckles, tight and clenching, tempting him beyond all reason.

Silviu worked his hand with shaky finesse. His wrist brushed Georgie's inner thighs, his fingers pushed into her depths and his thumb rolled over her clit. The feel of her and the sheer strength of his need had him gritting his teeth, fighting the urge to rush. It had been days since the one and only time he'd gained entrance to her body, and that occasion had been hurried and desperate, too. He wanted a moment to drag out, to take his time and make a memory sweeter than anything that had come before.

Georgeanne wouldn't allow him to, however. "Now!"

Her eyes were bright, her chest labored. A grimace that couldn't mar her beauty crossed her face as she gripped the vanity and twisted against him. Her pussy was creaming all over his hand and their magic burned him alive. Silviu hoped it would be enough.

He withdrew his fingers from the hot clasp of her body to unzip his pants. She only wanted his cock, and he determined that was all she would get that night. Silviu liked the idea of having her exposed before him, vulnerable and stripped in more ways than she might immediately recognize. The gods knew he'd felt too naked lately, and he was eager to even the playing field just a little.

He angled his cock under her ass and pushed forward until his shaft rode the damp edge of her sleek heat and rammed her clit. George bent forward with a moan, shifting as if she didn't know whether to widen her stance or draw her thighs closer together. Silviu used his hand on her breast to haul her upright, forcing her to see it all in the mirror.

"Look, love, there it is," he growled near her ear. "That's my cock—what you wanted, isn't it?"

"I want it in me."

"Ah, my mistake. Like this, then?"

Silviu angled just the tip of his cock against her. Georgie moaned. He lost his breath. His crest lodged in the depression created by the ring of soft, tight muscle, her entrance just parting around the barest of intrusions, driving her wild and threatening his sanity completely.

But now, more than ever, manipulation was key. Silviu used the moment, Georgie's emotions and even the sensations he prayed were enough, as weapons, in the vague hope that something of what he did would snap through the walls she'd thrown up between them. He would use her body against her. He would orchestrate her need until she'd seduced herself into forgiveness, if that's what it took. He couldn't bear thinking of any other outcome.

He held still and met her gaze in the mirror. As she watched, he brushed his fingers over her clit, hardly a touch at all — a tease, instead. At her breast, his grip on her nipple tightened further, calling a startled cry from her throat, but he knew by the way she'd bucked that it hadn't been pain that slammed through her.

With her sharp movement, a little more of his dick slipped into her body. Her pussy gushed, taking him by surprise with the sudden surge of slick heat washing over his shaft. Georgie gasped and squirmed, but the look in her eye told him of her satisfaction — of her need.

"What do you want, Georgeanne?"

"You, inside me. Now."

"I am." He grinned and shook his head. "I don't know what else you mean."

Her cheeks flushed and her eyes narrowed. Silviu held her stare as he rubbed her clit, rolled it and tugged until Georgie bared her teeth and groaned. The magic flowing over their bodies was cleaved in half by a dark vein, but that only added to the excitement roaring in Silviu's balls. He would master his Bane wife and her magic through the sheer simplicity of surrender.

His little spitfire would never be able to resist.

"Let me lean forward," she whispered a moment later.

"Just a bit," he agreed, loosening the granite hold of his caging arms.

Cocking her to an angle where she could reach the vanity only emphasized the contractions of her pussy. Silken tissues just kissed the crest of his cock, but the rhythmic clenching of her entrance was wholly enticing. Silviu used all his willpower to keep from shoving balls-deep into Georgie's tight depths. That would defeat his goal.

Georgeanne widened her stance and braced her weight on the tabletop of the vanity. Their eyes met in the mirror as Silviu flicked her clit. She took a deep breath and rocked back, slowly taking more of him into her body.

Gods, she felt so good around him. Pleasure beyond the physical, a sense of finding his home, his Match.

Inch by excruciating inch—Silviu clenched his jaw and let his bride lay claim to his flesh. He remembered when he'd taught her to pleasure him with her mouth, the satisfaction she couldn't hide, the flush of power she couldn't fight. Now he gave her the same opportunity again, but encouraged her to use her pussy to take him, to own him and to teach him a lesson neither one of them would ever forget.

And she did. She watched his face closely as she pushed back onto his cock, taking it all until there was no room left inside her. Silviu gulped oxygen, desperate to hold on, his struggle translating to an iron grip on her clit and nipple, a brutal hold Georgie almost squirmed free of, moaning and tightening around his dick as more cream flowed between them.

She shimmied and rockets flared in Silviu's balls, warning of an impending explosion. He groaned and bit Georgie's shoulder, simultaneously lodging himself deeper in her body and bringing her more securely into his embrace. She gave him a smug smile in the mirror as if she knew what she'd done, what damage she'd caused to his control, then flung herself into action.

She took him. Back and forth, gripping the shaking

vanity for leverage with a strength Silviu couldn't deny. He didn't even attempt to help hold the mirror steady — his hands were locked on his wife's body, pulling and tugging, stroking and flicking the two peaks he'd claimed and refused to let go of. Her nipple was berry red, the skin around it pink and swollen with abuse, but Georgie licked her lips and rode him into oblivion, her moans of pleasure ringing out all around them.

Hot, wet silk slammed onto his shaft over and over, swallowing him in slick honey, sucking him into paradise. Georgie's pussy clamped down tighter, and she damn near drilled her fingers through the vanity's top. Her ass bounced and her legs shook, but he held her up with the hand he'd wedged between her thighs, so that she still managed to rock back hard enough to have Silviu gasping.

He started helping, just a little. This was her claiming, but Silviu couldn't stop his hips from jutting forward. He couldn't prevent the small push that had his pelvis trying to bury itself in her soft ass. Breathing was a forgotten ability as need swept him away and stilled his heart. All he knew was animal desire and a driving instinct to hold his woman and keep her, however he could, no matter what he had to do to achieve it.

Georgeanne wailed and shook. Her body stilled and tightened, her muscles knotting and locking. Silviu managed to pry his fingers from her breast to grip her hip, but it wasn't enough and he had to use his other hand, too. He tugged her back onto his dick and flattened her against the vanity, grinding deep and hard until the pleasure spiraled out of both their control.

She fractured. Her shoulders jerked. Her inner walls contracted and held him tight. Her scream ripped from her chest, the sound wrapping Silviu's spine with satisfaction. He pulled from her slick embrace and slammed back in, hauling her onto his shaft in a futile attempt to bury his dick inside her for all time. Spurting and panting, Silviu surrendered to the drag and draw of the tremors inside

Georgie's pussy.

Body to body, he struggled to restrain his emotions, though he couldn't find strength within himself to hide them completely. She knew… She had to know, because the love she held for him shone from her eyes and became a beacon of pure gold magic in the single moment they'd come together as one. Light blazed around them. They'd loved before they were old enough to know better, and no force on Earth could change that. Silviu just needed to remind her.

But as he opened his mouth to do just that, a whip of black light snaked through the glare of the Matched magic. Uncoordinated, Georgie shivered and shifted, pulling from his hold awkwardly. Keeping her eyes downcast, she slipped from between him and the vanity, then waved toward the door.

Pain, anger and resentment nearly stole his vision when she said, "Thank you and goodnight, Silviu."

Chapter Nine

Georgeanne

The setting sun painted the sky with vivid tones of orange and red which, if it weren't for the picturesque quality of the French hills beneath, would be taken as an ill omen by many. Georgie tightened her fingers on the steering wheel as she rounded a curve in the drive toward the Council Palace and risked a glance at her passenger. She'd have preferred the company of one of her cousins, but Christiana's overly protective husband had refused to let her drive, and since Milo utilized chauffeurs and Tulah had always relied on public transportation, Adam was left to man the wheel in their vehicle. Georgie was stuck conveying Silviu.

She'd been to the Council headquarters many times before, but this was her husband's first trip to that region of France. His nose was practically pressed to the window, and she suspected the only reason he didn't have it down was because of the shockingly cold weather they'd run into. As they'd gained altitude, the thermometer had dipped even further.

"It's pretty here," he murmured.

"I'd expect you to say so. It looks a bit like the Lovasz land." Georgie remembered Silviu's Family estate extremely clearly, in spite of only having stayed in the area once. He'd grown up on a series of hillsides that were wild and free, a place that had greatly appealed to her on her brief visit—a little more than a month ago.

"Maybe." He shrugged but didn't look her way. "I don't know. I was hardly allowed out to roam the property. There were too many lessons yet to be learned."

Georgie did not reply. She knew what his childhood had been like, but she didn't need any reminders to help soften her heart while she was still busy being angry. The moment of sexual weakness she'd indulged in back at her Family's English estate had nearly done her in, with not even a minute passing after Silviu had left her to her cold and lonely bed before she'd wanted to race after him. She hadn't, because her willpower was strong, but it had been a near thing.

It was amazing how, in such a short time, a woman could grow so used to having a particular man around that it almost seemed as if her entire happiness depended on his presence.

Silviu made a strangled noise. "The postcards don't do the place justice."

Georgie blinked the world back into existence, thankful she hadn't driven the car into a ditch as her thoughts had wandered. Directly ahead was the Council Palace, and the vision it made at the end of the drive was fantastic. A medieval castle built in the heyday of such structures, it was still small for its purpose, but grandly designed with rounded turrets and square towers, flying buttresses and even a few gargoyles. Pale-gray stone was complimented by the wild backdrop of majestic mountains and a forest losing the last of its foliage in a bracing breeze.

Georgie drove through the open gates, the thick walls containing the property briefly blocking the dying light of the sun. Following the paved path around to a spot designated for vehicles, Georgie parked and got out of the car quickly, without waiting for Silviu.

She'd spent enough time in his company, in her opinion. She needed space—and air that wasn't saturated with the scent of his intoxicating cologne.

Just as Silviu exited the vehicle, Adam pulled up next to them and parked. The Davenolds tumbled from their car and stretched, then huddled together for warmth. Looking over the castle and the view, Milo gave a low whistle. Tulah seemed shell-shocked. Adam had been to the Council headquarters before and Christiana had grown up with unmatched opulence, so neither were as impressed as their spouses.

"Remember to guard your thoughts," Georgie warned them, "and your words, your actions, your tempers, your theories... Be careful."

"None of us are novices at intrigue," Christiana reminded her.

Beyond the car park, a door in the wall opened and a handful of strapping, strong women tumbled out. Many waved at Georgie cheerily, calling out greetings in Occitan, French and English. Some women spoke a single sentence of condolence in all three languages at the same time.

Silviu blinked. "Who are these women rushing toward us, Georgie?"

"They work here, at the palace. They'll take our baggage. I'm sure Emeric is already aware that we've arrived and has our rooms ready. There is a decent lookout in the northern tower than has an excellent view of the road, and someone is always at the post."

"There are no men?"

"Only a few. Emeric doesn't allow many men to stay here full time."

Silviu shook his head and smiled as the women bustled to the car and hauled out the luggage. "Why, Georgie? He's a patriarchal witch, so he should have men—"

"But Bijoux is female." Georgie turned away from her husband at the sound of her name.

Emeric Laurent threw himself through the doorway and hurried in her direction. He called general greetings to them all, with an old-fashioned bow thrown in for good measure, though she worried the gesture would tip him over as he never stopped moving forward.

Reaching her, he grabbed for her hands and held them tightly. "My dear, I'm so sorry for your loss. Please accept my sympathy. It was a shock, a terrible, terrible shock."

Georgeanne had a knack for languages. Her native English was a given and her husband's Romanian was necessary, but of the other languages she spoke, French had been the most useful. As the Council of Covens met in France, a witch who couldn't speak the language was at a disadvantage, so she had no trouble following her host's rushed greeting.

However, Georgie switched to English for the benefit of everyone else. Her throat nearly closed around her response. "Yes, it was a shock. Grandmother became ill so quickly, and there was nothing anyone could do... Silviu tried everything."

Elevating his head the moment Georgie waved toward her new husband, Emeric also replied in English, "Silviu Lovasz. Welcome to the Council headquarters."

"Thank you, Monsieur Laurent. I'm just sorry that we're meeting under such circumstances." Silviu slid forward to take Georgie's hand.

She allowed him to squeeze her fingers for a good showing of their relationship before disengaging. She gestured toward the Palace. "Shall we go in? It's chilly out here, especially with night falling."

"Yes," Milo agreed. "Let's go in."

"Of course, of course!" Emeric waved toward the building. "Please do. Follow the women and they will show you where your rooms are. They've been assigned in haste but, Adam, I'm sure you remember where you belong?"

"Of course." He reached for Tulah. "And my wife will stay with me."

"Ah, then we need one less guest room." Emeric gestured at the women, but Milo stopped him.

"We're all paired up. We'll only need three rooms."

Georgie could have killed him and scowled to let Milo know he would receive retribution for such slander. The very last thing she'd wanted was to share a room with Silviu, but once it was made known they were a couple, it would be imprudent to request separate quarters.

Emeric's next statement, however, made it clear that the damage had been done long before Milo's unfortunate admission. "Yes, Father Lovasz told me the happy news of your wedding, Georgeanne. I would say I was surprised at the speed at which your betrothal was ended, but I suppose Madeleine's illness made such expedience necessary."

"Something like that." Georgie took a step forward. "Let's go—"

Emeric moved to block her and his voice took on a formal tone. "A moment, if you will, Mother Davenold? Everyone else may find their rooms, of course."

"Georgeanne needs to go in, as well." Silviu placed his hand at the small of her back. "My *wife* is getting cold and I would see to her comfort."

"The Council Administrator has need of Mother Davenold's time. Consider this a formal request." Emeric pretended not to notice the sudden tension as his gaze veered out over the mountains beyond the property. No one moved except the women bearing their bags.

Georgie shook her head in exasperation. "Everyone should get themselves ready for supper."

"It will be served soon," their host confirmed. "Even though the cook is busy adding to the menu as we speak, I'm certain all will be settled in good time. When you did not arrive this morning, we figured to expect you tomorrow."

"We had a late start. Go in, everyone. I must speak with our host, but I'll see you all at dinner and explain, if I can." Georgeanne shooed them all inside, but the Davenolds walked away unwillingly. Silviu, unsurprisingly, remained at her side.

Emeric lifted an eyebrow. "Why don't you go with them, Mister Lovasz?"

"Lovasz-Davenold," Silviu corrected. "And I'll stay with my wife."

Emeric shook his head. "I have placed you in the yellow solar at the top of this very tower. Georgeanne's customary accommodations. Very easy for you to find. You simply go up the steps until you can't go any farther. The room is just below the top level of the castle with an excellent view."

"I'll wait."

"This is a private matter, Mister Lovasz."

For a moment, Georgie was close to gnashing her teeth. She lacked proper authority to demand anything—either that Silviu go inside or that they all did. She could not command Emeric to relent, and she couldn't order her husband, the Family Mother, to leave. She was stuck in the cold, standing between two patriarchal witches eager to engage in a pissing match.

And yet, she wanted her husband by her side for this meeting. She trusted Emeric more than she trusted most, but she needed Silviu's input. And she didn't feel like questioning that instinct.

"My husband is stubborn and won't go."

Emeric rolled his lips between his teeth. "This is a personal matter, Georgeanne."

"I take it this is about Bijoux, then?" Georgie gathered her patience and her fortitude, suddenly understanding why their host would delay his hospitality. She marshalled her arguments in favor of her goals. The sound of the door closing behind the women and the Davenold entourage spurred Emeric into action.

"Mother Davenold, my heart is breaking, *oui*. Madeleine was a woman I respected and admired. Your grandmother…" He leveled Georgeanne with a glare just shy of hostile, but most definitely demanding answers. "She was my friend, but Bijoux is my daughter, and you will tell me why you've demanded her presence here."

"I need her help," Georgie said. "With the Council convening soon, I need—"

"*Non.*"

"Emeric—"

"My daughter, Georgeanne." He straightened, his broad shoulders going stiff as he lifted his chin so that he looked down his long nose at her. "My treasure, my only child, my companion in this isolated world."

"What happened to your lady-friend in Limoges?"

Emeric growled at her, even went so far as to snap his teeth. "You are playing games. Davenolds are always playing games, and I will not have my Bijoux involved in dangerous plots when you do not have Madeleine's strength of will to keep my daughter safe from those who would exploit her talents."

"We have magic to keep her safe," Silviu said calmly, without inflection. "More magic than Madeleine ever had."

His words were so dry, so even, that Emeric appeared momentarily stymied. The man's mouth worked, his nostrils quivered and his cheeks flushed. He stood in the brisk wind shaking his head.

Georgie added her own thoughts, "I would argue that I have nearly as much influence as my grandmother did, Monsieur Laurent."

He didn't listen. "Magic? You are Bane! What magic could you have that would keep my daughter safe?"

"We are Magic Matches," Silviu told him. "Together, we are much stronger than even Madeleine was with her Match. Georgie needs your daughter's help. *I* want your daughter's help, and, in exchange, I will personally guarantee her safety."

Georgie gritted her teeth but said nothing. She let her dominant, patriarchal husband speak to the patriarchal Council Administrator. She thought perhaps Silviu's words carried some sort of promise her own couldn't—that of a man, that of a witch with magic, that of a high-ranking male born and raised in the same traditions as their host, and, therefore, more weighted than anything she could offer.

But Emeric's fears were deep-seated. His face paled and he seemed surprised by the idea that a Bane witch had a Magic Match. His expression grew ever more terrified. He turned to Georgie directly and asked, "What do you need my daughter for?"

Georgie took a deep breath, knowing that saying the words out loud would hurt more than she could anticipate. She already felt the acid roiling in her throat. She swallowed, but it did no good, so she explained in a rush. "My grandmother was murdered by a black magic witch. I need Bijoux to help me figure out who."

Emeric reeled backward. "*Non*! You have lost your mind if you think I'll let my treasure do such a dangerous thing for you."

Silviu stepped forward and gripped their host's shoulder. Georgie saw magic blaze and spark before sinking through the man's clothing. "Let's go inside and discuss all the reasons why you'll give my wife exactly what she wants."

* * * *

"Graves made an effigy of your grandmother?"

"Yes, and I burned it." Georgie winced as Emeric propped his elbows on his massive desk and sank his head into his hands. "The spell rebounded, and there was nothing we could do to stop it."

"You burned it?"

"I'd thought I'd broken it."

"Ah, so you know your talent."

Georgie took a breath and willfully hid her surprise at her host's familiarity with her magic. "I found out, but not in time to use it effectively, I guess."

"I'm so sorry," Emeric murmured. "I told your grandmother so long ago to share the histories of the Bane witches with you, Georgeanne, but she refused. If she hadn't, perhaps you could have saved her."

Georgie suddenly felt as if her muscles compressed her bones and her bones confined her lungs. Her spine stiffened, making the chair she occupied twice as uncomfortable, and she looked toward Silviu in reflex. The same questions burning her tongue smoldered in his eyes.

"What histories?" the words nearly choked her.

"We have a whole room full of documents. Not the *legends*," Emeric spat the word as if it tasted foul. "Real accounts, biographies. Your condition is rare, but not so unheard of that the world has not been able to gain an idea of what to expect from such a witch."

Some indefinable emotion seared Georgie's veins. "I want to see them."

Their host nodded. "For you, I will make an exception. For my daughter and her safety, I will make an exception. You shall have access to the Documents Chamber."

"What did you mean, though?" Silviu moved to Georgie's side and placed a hand on her shoulder. "What could we have done to save Madeleine?"

"Bane-born witches break magic." Emeric sighed. "You could have broken the spell."

"We tried that." Silviu's fingers tightened on Georgie. "The spell that had taken root within Madeleine couldn't be broken."

"Nothing I did had any effect on my grandmother's health," Georgie confirmed.

"It was a dark spell," Silviu added.

Emeric waved his hand. "That is the specialty of the Bane witch. They use dark magic themselves."

The small hairs on Georgie's arms lifted, and she might have thought the tension strumming her nerves actually belonged to her, if her husband hadn't hardened into a statue. Silver magic crackled and snapped in the air around him, piercing deep into Georgie's chest and begging for a reply she refused to give.

"Ah. I see." Silviu turned a considering stare onto Georgeanne, making her more than anxious. "Yes, it makes so much sense, doesn't it? Your magic is black."

She got to her feet and paced, wriggling her shoulders in an attempt to negate her husband's regard. "We didn't know I was a dark magic witch, though perhaps we should have."

"All things considered," her husband drawled.

"At any rate, I couldn't break the spell. It was enhanced."

Emeric shrugged. "Any spell is subject to be broken, no matter who cast it or to what ends. A witch only needs the proper tools to do so."

"Any magic..." Georgie lifted her chin, debating the possibilities and coming to the conclusion that Emeric was trustworthy enough to reveal a few secrets to in exchange for some answers. Plus, she saw merit in letting her talent be known, especially with a potentially volatile Council meeting approaching, as it could act as a warning against harming her and her Family. "I broke my cousin's magic. She's Bane now, too, and... I didn't exactly mean to, it just..."

"Happened." Emeric again waved his hand. "So say witches anytime an outcome is different than what they expected their magic to accomplish. You, at least, have a good excuse for such a thing. I told your grandmother to let you be what you were meant to be, even though she thought you were too young."

"Young? Most witches are using magic by the time they're ready for school." Silviu's eyes narrowed. "Why did it take so long to develop her talent, Emeric?"

"She needed a key." He glanced at Silviu. "But you threatened her gradual unlocking and terrified her Matriarch."

Old fears clogged Georgie's head. She glared at her husband suspiciously. "What is that supposed to mean, Emeric?"

"The answer to your question lies in your relationship to your *Magic Match*," their host said. "Now that I know you are Matches, so much makes sense. That confession tells me more than you think, Monsieur Lovasz."

"Lovasz-Davenold," Silviu corrected. "What do you think you know?"

"I know of your history, your youthful indiscretion. There is a reason Madeleine moved Heaven and Earth to preserve your union, even as she prevented it."

"What do you mean?" Silviu demanded.

"To Match a Bane, you must be Reap." Emeric slouched back in his chair and regarded Silviu warily. "That fact of your birth was hidden from Council records, but, I suppose, not from Madeleine?"

Silviu nodded. "She knew."

Emeric smirked. "She also knew that a Reap witch is a significant enough catalyst to bring a Bane witch into their power. Just being near each other would be enough to begin the process, but you compounded the problem by adding in sex — too early to handle the consequences, I might add."

Georgie thought about her host's statement for only a moment before enlightenment dawned. "The punishment is finally making some sense. I wasn't ready to handle such...power, at that age."

Emeric raised his eyes to the ceiling. "Sex is the oldest form of communication, the greatest connection a Match can forge. The bond grows because people share vulnerabilities and weaknesses as they share their bodies. It is an enhancement of its own variety."

"The magic of life?" Georgie slid another glare Silviu's way. "Like sex and blood for marriages?"

Emeric shook his head indifferently — neither a yes, nor a no. "When you had sex, the Bane's full potential was unlocked."

Silviu shifted the slightest amount, but Georgie knew him well, and the gesture was as dramatic as if he'd fallen to his knees. "That was all it took?" he asked, his voice rough.

"For you, as her Match." Emeric's eyebrows lowered.

Georgie pressed her hand to her stomach. "You know an awful lot about it."

Emeric lifted a shoulder. "She never told me all the details, but I knew Madeleine had wanted you to grow into your power more slowly, Georgeanne. Your actions as a teenager must have worried her tremendously. I'm surprised you both got off as lightly as you did."

Georgie cleared her throat, desperate to move to another

topic. With any luck, she could read all about sex and magic in the Bane histories, rather than talking about it with Emeric. The discussion was beginning to feel too close to the interrogations she'd suffered when she'd been a girl, after she'd been caught in Silviu's bed. There were some things she would rather not relive.

"Why couldn't I break the spell that killed my grandmother? Because I don't have practice?"

"I doubt you need practice. The full force of your talent, along with being a Match, should have been enough to overwhelm the spell." Emeric rubbed his forehead. "I suppose the offending witch is simply…stronger."

"Impossible." Silviu made the statement in a tone hard enough to prevent Emeric's argument, but Georgie *felt* the waver in her husband's resolve.

His emotions surged, and somehow she sensed them almost as if they were her own, yet distinctly separate from how she felt. It was a sensation she'd been starting to get used to, until Silviu had betrayed her so terribly. Thoughts spinning, Georgie fell into the thick silence that followed her husband's pronouncement and fought to get her resistance to his turmoil under control.

"Not impossible," she finally murmured once she'd succeeded. "Clearly, not impossible, which brings us to our mission here. Emeric, we want the High Seat."

"Not least because Georgeanne's safety depends on us inhabiting a position of power," Silviu interrupted.

Georgie took a deep breath. "I also want to find the witch who killed my grandmother and make the bastard pay. This person wields dark magic and appears to have set up some sort of coalition with Graves and my cousin Suzette."

Emeric gasped. "Patriarchal and matriarchal, both?"

"Yes, so long as they used dark magic, it didn't seem our villain cared what side of the Schism they came from." Silviu nodded. "Daniel Levy is involved somehow, and he's been donating money to various endeavors, projects and policies, both in the witching world and in global politics.

Not limited to patriarchal strongholds, either."

"*Merde.*" Their host closed his eyes for a moment, but when he opened them, he locked his gaze on Silviu with an intensity that made Georgie nervous. "Father Levy is the only Council representative who has yet to sign your brother's petition to assign his seat to you, Monsieur Lovasz."

Silviu's sudden anger was palpable. "What right does he have—?"

Georgie answered for the Council Administrator. "When a new representative is nominated, the other covens on that side of Schism, patriarchal or matriarchal, have to sanction the change. It's a formality of recognition, and, to my knowledge, there hasn't been a single dissention in over four hundred years."

"No coven wants to deny another's right to choose a politically influential representative for fear the same would be done to them," Emeric agreed. "However—"

"Daniel is the Father," Silviu protested, "but he isn't the rep—"

Georgie shook her head. "The Levy Councilman retired, Silviu, remember? Daniel represents his Family until he chooses a new delegate for the job."

"Yes, I understand, but as he's not really—"

Emeric cut him off with a harsh, guttural sound. "He's the Father. It doesn't get more real than that. And I must tell you that others may rescind their signature as soon as they learn you're married to the Davenold Mother. A witch can't serve two Families at once."

"Well, that's another reason to have Bijoux stay close to the Council." Georgie returned to stand in front of Emeric's desk, squaring off with him over the wide top. "I need information on all the representatives, but *especially* Daniel. He might try to influence the others—persuade them. I want to know what he's up to and I want to know who he's working with."

"But Bijoux—"

"Will be protected with everything I have in me," Georgie promised. "My influence, my magic, anything I can offer. I swear to you that I will keep her safe."

"What you ask of me—"

"I'm not *asking* you. You owe my grandmother, and Bijoux already agreed to help." Georgie stared at him until he understood that she would not back down. "I know Daniel Levy knows who the dark magic witch is, Emeric. And I want to know, too."

Chapter Ten

Costel

Exhaustion slowed his steps, but Costel kept plodding down the hall in the hopes of finding Bijoux and finally talking her into letting him have access to the information his sister needed to know. He swore he'd be persuasive. He vowed to throw himself on Emeric's mercy as well if he had to — anything to find peace from Ileana's compulsion.

When his sister's suggestion had first taken root, Costel hadn't thought to fight it. There was hardly any point, and he knew the need to persuade Bijoux into helping him would only grow until he surrendered. But that had been before he'd touched her in the stairwell. That had been before he'd laid her back over a desk and tasted her sweet honey, listened to her cries of pleasure and felt her tighten around his fingers. That was before he'd had to marshal the strength to walk away from the only woman he'd ever loved, the one woman he'd never dare to keep.

He'd avoided her since, a nearly impossible feat that had sapped the remainder of his mental energy. Costel had had less sleep in the past month than any man should — between his issues with his grandfather, taking over as the Lovasz Father and coming to the Council — and Ileana's magic was only making everything worse. He felt out of sorts, lacking patience and dangerously close to taking everything the woman he loved had offered. He had to do something to set things right.

He found Bijoux just outside her father's office, idly caressing the brown stem of a nearly dead houseplant. Her head was cocked and her eyes were blank, though her brow furrowed as she stared at Emeric's door.

"What are you doing, Bijoux?"

"Georgeanne Davenold has just arrived. I was waiting for her to finish with my father. I believe your brother is in there, too. Or, at least, my father thinks so, but it's a little harder to get a good read this far away."

"You're using your magic right now? How close do you usually need to be?" Costel would give almost anything to have a truthful answer, but Bijoux merely smiled.

"Depends on the witch. From here, all I know is that my father thinks there is something Georgie needs to know about being Bane that may have saved her grandmother."

"Well, what does Georgeanne think? Or my brother, for that matter?"

Bijoux scrunched her nose, sending a warm flicker of some soft emotion swirling through Costel's chest. She shook her head. "I've never been able to read Georgie, and apparently your brother is…problematic, too."

"That's actually not surprising." Costel leaned against the wall on the other side of the dead potted plant and absentmindedly began digging in the dirt. Just the feel of the soil, dry though it was, gave Costel a deep sense of peace. A quiet stream of magic wended through the contents of the pot, a flicker of life left within the dying vegetation. Without thinking, Costel started playing with it.

"Why not?" Bijoux asked quietly.

"After Silviu and Georgie were married, I stopped being able to feel him within the Lovasz magic. I suppose her Bane shields extend to him now. Unlike the ritual transferring of power — which I've felt twice since becoming the Father — my brother's wasn't a slow loss, but a sudden absence."

"You were worried about him."

"Of course." He glanced at Bijoux but quickly realized she hadn't asked a question. She knew because he knew. He was surprised, however, that all her attention seemed focused on the hand he'd driven into the dirt.

"You're doing something, Costel." Lifting her violet eyes to his for an instant, she then returned her attention to the plant, reaching out to touch a swiftly growing nub on the lowest part of the brown stick. "What is this?"

"A flower." He shrugged, knowing what he'd done was hardly special, but as the bloom unfurled and Bijoux gasped and laughed, he felt as if he'd accomplished something incredible.

"That's amazing, Costel! I had no idea you could do such a thing."

"Influencing magic is a Family talent," he murmured.

His father, brother and sister may have cornered the market on manipulating people, but Costel had always had a greater affinity for growing things. The presence of the small flower gave him a measure of joy, a brief jolt of energy to counteract the dragging exhaustion he'd come to rid himself of.

The idea of a second wind motivated Costel as little else could just then. He wanted to sleep without being awoken every half hour with a compulsion to track down Bijoux and make her unlock the Documents Chamber. He wanted to rest without dreaming of making her reveal the secrets to be found in dusty piles of biographies and boring descriptions of Council agendas.

"I wanted to ask for your assistance in getting your father's permission to look at the paperwork Daniel Levy has filed." Just saying the words brought immediate relief.

Bijoux cocked her head the other way, her pretty eyes losing their intensity in a way that told Costel she was rummaging through someone's thoughts. As his own skull was devoid of the slight tingle he felt every time she went exploring in his mind, he assumed she was listening to Emeric's inner dialogue.

As if to confirm, Bijoux nodded. "My father has agreed to let Georgie into the Documents Chamber. She'll have access to everything while she's here, but only until a new High Seat is elected."

"It's a very good deal for her."

"If she can read fast." Bijoux's dimples made an appearance as she smiled.

Heat rolled down Costel's spine so that it took a great deal of effort to keep his voice steady. "She won't have to read fast. There are a lot of us here to help."

Again Bijoux's nose scrunched and her eyes developed a faraway glaze. "Oh, including four more Davenolds. It seems my father put them near your sister."

"Four?" Costel hardly heard her and hardly cared what she was saying. He was too busy remembering the picture Bijoux made as her body had tightened around his knuckles — her eyes twice as dreamy as they had been then, her dimples nonexistent but her mouth slack, lips moist, breasts heaving while she'd panted and squirmed. The taste of her was seared into his tongue for all time.

"I do love the way your mind works." Bijoux moved around the houseplant, her gaze caught on Costel's lips. "You are...fascinating."

He swallowed hard, but it didn't clear the tightness from his throat or ease the band constricting his chest. He struggled to breathe as Bijoux stepped close enough that her body heat seemed to singe his skin through his clothes.

Need and desire raged. Trapped by a moment's insanity, he fell victim to his own lust. Now he knew what she looked like in the throes of passion. Now he understood what would build between them in times of intimacy. But Costel couldn't afford another weakness and he'd be damned if he put Bijoux in harm's way.

And anywhere close to his grandfather would most definitely be considered *in harm's way.*

He stumbled back, but he was already pressed to the wall. Elevating his chin to deny the temptation of her pouting lips, Costel attempted to merge into the cold stone behind him. Bijoux placed her hands on his chest and lifted to her toes, sliding against him sensuously as she rose. Tension swelled and thickened.

"Costel—"

Emeric's office door opened. Bijoux flinched and stepped back quickly. Costel dragged in as much oxygen as his knotted lungs could handle. Gritting his teeth and willing his erection away, he turned his head to meet the suspicious glare of his younger brother.

"Silviu." Costel cleared his throat. "I'm glad you're finally here."

Silviu's eyes bounced between the pair in the hallway. "Yes, we arrived just a little while ago."

"Have you met Bijoux Laurent yet?"

"No." Silviu held out his hand. "A pleasure."

Bijoux dimpled. "Of course."

As his brother stepped farther into the hall, Georgie pushed past him. Immediately, Costel stiffened. Over the years, his reaction had become reflex, an uncoordinated motion he couldn't prevent. Feeling awkward and inadequate, knowing she was judging him to be inferior, Costel didn't know how to keep his lips from thinning or his chin from elevating.

She enveloped Bijoux in a hug that spoke of an old friendship—perhaps a friendship Costel had previously underestimated—before turning to him with a haughty nod. "How are you, Costel?"

He wondered if he'd ever grow used to the disdain and distrust that always filled her tone. It had been different ten years ago when Vasile Lovasz had taken his three children into the matriarchal lion's den, to allow Georgeanne and Silviu to meet in person. There had been the potential for friendship and affection then, but years later, when the two heirs had been reintroduced after both had been appointed to represent their Families at the Council, there had been a distinct chill between them.

For his part, Costel conceded that he'd been less than tolerant after the way Georgeanne had hurt his brother. Even their grandfather had never been so cruel. Silviu had spent the better part of a decade searching for her, then writing to her, begging her to see him, to talk to him, to meet with him—but all he'd met with had been a silence Costel knew had damn near killed him. That, and the way Georgie constantly lorded her superiority in all things pertaining to politics and social expertise over Costel, made it nearly impossible for him to behave with anything more than restrained detachment.

"Georgeanne. My condolences for your loss."

"Thank you." Her civil reply dripped with icicles. She turned to Bijoux and spoke in rapid French. "Your father gave me the key code to the Documents Chamber, and I was hoping you'd come with me?"

"Of course," Bijoux replied in English. "Costel has wanted to ask me for days, but his mind has been…preoccupied with other matters, hasn't it? Now is your chance, *mon lapin*."

Georgie's eyebrows flew upward. "Costel is your rabbit?"

"He runs like one." Bijoux gave an unconcerned shrug and started off down the hallway. "Come."

Georgie set off in her wake at a fast clip, but Silviu waved Costel to a more sedate pace. Clearly believing they wouldn't be overheard, he said, "Things look promising between you and Bijoux. I assume the seduction is going well?"

"She can hear you, Silviu."

"She speaks Romanian?"

"She knows when I think about your words, no matter what language you speak, so I'd suggest you go about your business as if she were always next to you." Costel sniffed. "And I told you, there would be no seduction."

"It seemed like there was a seduction."

"You're wrong."

"Am I?" Silviu turned his head just slightly, but it was enough to let Costel know he was being evaluated, much like their father did so often. "Hmm, then why do you look as if you haven't slept for a week?"

"Probably because I haven't slept for a week," Costel shot

back. "The past month, really, when you add up traveling to Poland, all the bullshit I've been dealing with at home, grandfather, the flooded fields, then the trip here—"

"All right, all right!" Silviu rolled his eyes. "Perhaps you *need* to get laid, then, so we are back to the seduction of Mademoiselle Laurent."

Costel fought his outrage. "You don't just *get laid* by a woman like Bijoux, Silviu. Her father is protective. She is innocent—"

"You were a breath away from kissing her when I stepped into the hallway, Costel. Don't deny it."

"No, she was trying to..." Costel's inhalation sounded loudly through his nose. "Never mind. I had come to ask her help in getting a peek at Daniel Levy's paperwork, because Ileana asked me to."

Costel slid his brother a sidelong glance to see if he'd understood what he was trying to say about their sister. His siblings were close and they always protected each other without fail. Unfortunately, Silviu was even better than Costel at blanking his features into an impenetrable, emotionless mask. He appeared completely bored with the conversation, so Costel had no way of judging how entangled his brother and sister were in the plot, but he guessed they were fully in tune.

It was difficult being on the outside looking in, but Costel knew his separation from them was simply the price to be paid for everyone's well-being. Someone had to protect them both when they'd proved themselves too stubborn to modify their behavior.

"You know how determined our sister is. I knew I wouldn't get a moment's rest until I'd done as Ileana begged me to do," he continued. "But it all fell together, didn't it?"

"Yes, so it seems."

"Hopefully, I'll get some sleep tonight."

"You do look like you need it," Silviu agreed blandly.

Costel arched his eyebrow. "Then we must look alike. What's happened to you?"

"As you said, a stressful month."

Just ahead, the women disappeared through a doorway. Not having the code to punch into the keypad, Costel jumped to catch the door before it closed. Silviu stopped at his side, still in the hallway but staring in at the rows of floor-to-ceiling bookshelves lining the walls. Both men hesitated, but somewhere in the stillness between them, Costel sensed a change. He braced himself.

Silviu rested his hand on Costel's shoulder. "I do hope you get a good night's sleep, brother. I don't want you to think I'm uncaring. I realize I've asked a lot of you, a lot that's gone against what you've wanted or believed. I'm sorry to have put you through that."

With the words came compulsion. Costel stifled his sigh of defeat, momentarily unable to decipher the command hidden inside his brother's friendly words. But from the swirl of magic sinking into his brain, the need to sleep emerged as a promise, and he understood his brother was trying to help. It didn't make the experience any easier to accept, however.

"I would do anything to assist you, Silviu. By now, I would hope you know that. All you have to do is ask."

Silviu smiled without speaking and stepped into the Documents Chamber. Costel followed. Instantly, the smell of leather and lemon polish consumed his senses, reminding him of his grandfather's library back home. The Lovasz collection was largely untouched, while a long survey told him someone had clearly read and reread all the tomes housed in this chamber. Having spent the happiest times of their childhood immersed in books, the two men took their time wending their way deeper into the room.

"Silviu?" Georgeanne called out from behind a free-standing group of shelves. "We're back here. Come look at this."

They rounded the bend and found the women standing by an ordinary metal filing cabinet. Costel found it jarring that, in the middle of a space filled with leather-bound books and ancient documents outlining the history of their society, a centerpiece of modern office equipment was arranged in ugly companionship. While the honey-wood bookshelves gleamed in the light of the pendant lamps overhead, the garish aluminum desk reflected the glare harshly. The books offered a sense of adventure and discovery while the computer screen glowed with a heavily stylized word.

Costel squinted. "Witchapedia?"

"My father's little joke," Bijoux murmured. "It's everything to do with *everything* in here. He's been compiling the histories in one program."

She dug through a drawer in the filing cabinet, quickly flicking through folders before finding the one she wanted. The file she put on the table was several inches thick.

"This is Daniel Levy's?" Costel opened to the first page — the summary.

As the document was used to record every petition to the Council, he was intimately acquainted with the format, especially having just filled one out himself. Costel had only needed to write a single sentence conveying his desire to transfer the representative duties of the Lovasz Council seat to his brother. Daniel had needed every line available and he'd written in small script.

"These are the motions he filed a little more than two weeks ago." Bijoux pulled the sheet of paper from Costel's grasp and handed it to Georgie. "This is the bare-bones summary. It's the same on all the documents. What comes after is the detailed — "

"I know. I've filled out enough of these myself," Georgie interrupted absently. Already scanning the page, she widened her eyes farther and farther until she looked up at Silviu. "Daniel designated himself as the Levy Family's nominee for the High Seat."

Costel watched his brother's expression darken, and yet knew he wasn't surprised. "So that *was* his game," Silviu practically purred.

"You knew he would do this?" Costel glanced between

his brother and Georgie.

Both shook their heads, but then Silviu said, "I suspected he might, when he showed up at the Davenold estate while Madeleine lay on her deathbed. I thought he might have been prodding for weakness or judging Madeleine's ability to recover, anticipating just such a move."

"But then we thought we were perhaps wrong, after we discovered he was having an affair with my cousin," Georgie added.

Costel blinked to hide his surprise. "Well."

"And yet" — Silviu planted his fists on his hips — "we know he's in league with a powerful dark magic witch, so there was something going on. As you pointed out when we had our webchat, Costel, Daniel filing paperwork was highly suspicious."

"I assumed he was transferring his seat to Eliasz."

"It appears not." Georgie went back to reading the document. "He claims the Levy Council seat for himself and nominated himself for the High Seat...and... Oh, my gods, that bastard."

As she lifted her head, she glared at Silviu. Thrusting the paper toward him, she left him no choice but to take it. Silviu read the page much more calmly than his wife had before handing it over for Costel's examination.

"He doesn't state his objection outright."

"I think we can guess what he meant," Georgie spat.

"It is disheartening, my love, but we had to figure the truth would come out after the events of the Ngozi affair."

"He petitions the Council to disqualify you from ever being nominated to the High Seat." Costel stared at Silviu, his thoughts racing though he couldn't seem to make any sense of them. "Do you even want that position? You're just now getting the Lovasz seat, after all."

Silviu blinked, his lips straightened and his answer was devoid of inflection. "I wouldn't turn it down, but only a member of the Council can hold the High Seat."

Costel narrowed his eyes at his brother's suspicious turn

of phrase, but only said, "Daniel claims he has evidence that would prohibit your leadership, documented in the more detailed section of his submission. He says there is a historical precedent he wants to bring to the Council's notice."

"I don't know about any *historical precedents* that may be alarming." His brother looked at Bijoux, grimaced, then sighed. "Have you read the rest?"

She shook her head. "No. I'm not allowed to see the full petitions."

"Really?"

Bijoux's innocent expression never wavered in the face of Silviu's skepticim. Costel believed her, as, apparently, did his brother, who sighed again.

"So you don't know what his claim is against me?"

"It's most likely he's trying to disqualify you for being a Davenold, now that you've married Georgie," Bijoux pointed out. "After all, no Family can hold the High Seat for consecutive terms."

"And there must be a hundred years between the terms, yes." Silviu nodded. "But we've hyphenated. We are Lovasz-Davenold."

Georgie held up a finger. "Or Davenold-Lovasz."

"Either way, we should be eligible. There is nothing in the histories that suggest a" — Silviu quirked an eyebrow at his wife — "a witch like me can't hold the position, is there?"

"Well, that depends." Bijoux transferred her glare to Costel, who thrust his vague suspicions of his brother's intentions aside and pictured Bijoux naked just in time to hide from her next question. "What kind of witch can't hold a position on the witch's Council? What else could Daniel hold over you except being the Davenold High Male?"

Chapter Eleven

Bijoux

It was now or never, and Bijoux knew it. She felt the urgency of her situation as she snuck into Costel's bedroom. The arrival of the Davenolds hammered home just how short their time was growing.

Costel had been at the Palace long enough to have Bijoux's frustration mounting—not to mention her impatience and her terror at the thought that he would soon return to his home and never come back. He was, after all, giving his seat to his brother. He wouldn't have a reason to visit the Council headquarters again.

He'd been quiet, his demeanor more reserved than usual at dinner, and he'd retired early, giving her an excellent opportunity to make her own excuses and go to bed.

Just not *her* bed.

She turned on the light. Her future husband slept on his stomach, his cheek pressed to the pillow and a fall of black hair hiding his forehead. He looked younger and more peaceful than she'd ever seen him, though she was vaguely surprised that he didn't wake up. From all she'd witnessed in his thoughts, Costel didn't seem the type of man to sleep so heavily. He was constantly on alert, as a matter of fact, though Bijoux suspected most didn't realize it.

She moved to the bed. "Costel? Wake up."

There was no response. Bijoux frowned down at him, watching the even rise and fall of his shoulders and wondering what she was supposed to do with a man who was fast asleep. She rifled through his mind but only found an adamant need for slumber spinning out on a silver wave of magic that didn't feel quite like Costel's — close, but not exact.

For a full minute, Bijoux was stymied, but optimism soon came to her rescue. She placed a hand on Costel's shoulder and shook him. He didn't even flinch, yet a hazy impression of her began to form in his mind. Along with her image, a nebulous desire to undress her and drag her naked body against his infiltrated Costel's dreamscape. Encouraged, Bijoux tugged the covers off the man she was determined to marry.

"Well, I can certainly use this opportunity, Costel," she whispered as she climbed onto his bed. "At least asleep you can't send me away, and in your dreams you can't deny you want me."

Her plan solidified in her mind. Without a qualm, Bijoux made her decision. The advantages were many, and she relished the idea of having the time she wanted to explore his body, as he was the only man she'd ever touched and she'd been dying of curiosity — and need. A terminal case of loneliness.

Bijoux hiked her nightgown up and threw a leg over Costel's waist. Beneath her thighs, his flannel pajama pants were soft, but the cotton shirt he wore was rough under her fingertips. She pushed it up, making contact with the warm skin beneath. Sliding the fabric higher, she paused in shock and confusion when she revealed a network of ugly scars, some deep and red, others shallow and white — all glaring and unexpected, spreading across his skin.

The memory of the whippings he'd suffered ran through her mind. Bijoux traced the ridges, then dropped a series of kisses over each one, until Costel moaned in his sleep and shifted on the mattress. Bijoux paused, but he didn't awaken, though his dreams turned a touch hotter.

She poked through his mind without hesitation or guilt. Some things he dreamed of she didn't understand, and some she knew *had* to be impossible. She was as used to dreams as she was to thoughts. To her, they weren't all that different, with both jumping track often or becoming jumbled and confused. The mind worked too rapidly for any witch to process completely, and no one ordered every thought in a rational, logical sequence.

She tried to take Costel's unspoken suggestions in the hopes of ensnaring him in his own lust. She prayed blending his fantasy with her reality would ease his eventual transition from sleep to wakefulness so smoothly that he would be too busy making love to her to regret, to stop or to deny her.

Her strategy demanded his nakedness, so Bijoux set about gaining that very accomplishment. She pushed and pulled his shirt up his body, briefly confounded by the breadth of his shoulders until she shoved Costel's arm up and ordered him, "Take it off, *mon lapin*."

Still sleeping, Costel shifted and rolled. Bijoux had to scramble to keep her balance as he moved onto his back, but another minute saw him stripping off his shirt and flinging it to the floor. Costel began to snore.

"No, no, none of that." Bijoux adjusted the pillow beneath his head and his breathing settled into an even, steady draw that thankfully wasn't loud enough to hear downstairs.

From her position on her knees next to him, Bijoux looked her fill of the man. He was heavier than when they'd first met, telling her he had been spending more time behind a desk and less time in the fields, as she knew he used to do. Beneath the top layer of softness, however, his body still bore the hallmarks of great strength and scars, though fewer than were on his back. Curiously, he had no marks on his arms, neck or face.

From his waist down, Costel remained clothed. Bijoux's mouth went dry at the thought of getting him out of his pants, but his dreams encouraged just that. She hesitated another few moments, taking the opportunity to stroke his chest, discovering that his nipples could rise as fast as hers when she rubbed them, learning the feel of his crisp chest hair and the width of his rib cage—the warmth of his skin, the texture of it, the resiliency of the muscle beneath.

Then she took a deep breath and reached for his elastic waistband. Beneath the fabric, the outline of his cock had her heart pounding. She knew it would only get bigger, harder, once she began to touch it. She'd seen the movies and the photographs. Theoretically, she knew what to do, but his was about to become the very first real-live penis she'd ever seen with her own eyes.

His skin was warmer below his waist. She could feel his heat before she even touched him. The hair from his chest kept going, angling down his body and growing crisper the lower it got. Bijoux licked her lips and ran her fingers over the grooves at Costel's hips, his muscles tightening so that a V shaped her travels, directing her toward her main goal.

She leaned over and kissed his lower belly. Costel's reaction was immediate and fierce—he lifted, arching and groaning, as a wicked picture of her mouth swallowing the length of his cock infiltrated his dream. Liquid heat flowed down Bijoux's spine at the image.

With shaking fingers, she pulled his pants down. He lifted when the fabric got caught on his backside and Bijoux tugged too hard—the waistband jerked low and his cock sprang free. Bijoux's chest tightened and her pussy contracted at the sight of him, half-hard and lying across his upper thigh. She studied the thick length greedily, surprised at its darkness considering how pale the rest of his skin was. She liked the contrast.

Biting her lip, she tried to focus on getting him out of his pajama pants before reaching for his dick. Anticipation had her palms itching. Bijoux wanted to touch him so badly that a fine tremor worked all the way up her arms. Oxygen was in short supply, and the way Costel gave a low groan every few seconds wasn't helping her willpower. The dirty pictures infiltrating her mind made the cool bedchamber seem twice as hot.

Finally, she touched him. Trembling and hesitant, Bijoux

palmed his shaft, completely surprised by the softness of his skin and the heat burning her fingers. As she moved her hand, his cock lengthened and flushed. The more she stroked him, the higher it lifted, until it was no longer lying across his thigh but swaying against his lower abdomen. She traced the thick curve down toward his balls and cupped them, flinching when Costel arched and gave a strangled grunt.

She lifted her gaze, but his eyes were still closed and his brain still demanded he sleep under the slippery stream of foreign magic. Bijoux wondered about it and its source, but it was becoming harder to concentrate on anything beyond Costel's body and the naughty images flowing through his dream.

Her hands and her mouth, her lips and her hair — there seemed to be no rhyme or reason to Costel's fantasy, and the whole thing became a blurred montage of lust. Bijoux tried to sift through it all, but in the end could only catch snatches of what he wanted in the overwhelming mix, so she decided to do what she wanted, instead.

She ran her hands over him from knees to shoulders and back down. She closed her eyes and catalogued the difference in skin textures, in muscles and forms. Her own body grew heavy as she explored his, her heartbeat speeding up to match the pulse she could feel pounding in Costel's dick, her breathing as labored as his, though she managed to hold her moan behind gritted teeth, while Costel voiced his loudly.

She dropped kisses everywhere she could reach. Leaning over him, bracing a hand on the mattress beyond his hip, she dragged her lips down his body, flicking out her tongue to taste him. She learned the flavor of the skin in the hollow of his throat, felt the coarseness of the hair surrounding his nipple, the smooth plane to the side of his navel. The delicacy of his cock's shaft and the velvety curve of the tip.

Bijoux sucked the crest of his dick into her mouth, but Costel gripped her hair and her nervousness surged beyond her lust. Heart pounding, she bolted upright, relieved when he released her. His eyes were still closed, and the images in his head told her what his sleepy intention had been.

She wasn't ready for that—not yet, not until she figured out how their bodies could fit together or how far his strange compulsion to sleep would allow her to go before breaking and letting him awaken. She was unsure of herself and wanted something more binding to hold on to than a blow job she wasn't certain she could do with any sort of skill. Needing the assurance of his body against hers, she had the uncontrollable desire to press her full-length to Costel's and take comfort from his presence, his heat and his unique smell. Bijoux wanted her future husband to open his eyes and tell her he loved her, but he remained nonverbal in his communication.

So she levered her nightgown up to her hips and straddled his waist as she'd done a moment ago, but this time she flattened herself to his chest and buried her nose in his neck. Before she could find ease for her nervousness, his hands swept down her back, caught her hips and dragged her lower, pulling her so that his cock lodged between her folds and her ear rested over his heart.

And just like that, Bijoux relaxed. Though new sensations rocketed through her—the compression of her flesh around his shaft, the heat and moisture flooding the space between her legs and the feel of his skin, hair and muscles beneath her thighs—Bijoux had never felt less lonely in her life. She blinked back tears and fought for breath.

"This is what I want," she whispered.

As if he'd heard, Costel wrapped his arms around her and held her for a long moment. Bijoux started wondering if he'd finally come awake, but the coercion to sleep had only faded a little. She realized he was simply absorbing the feel of her in his arms into his dream, the hazy swirl of jumbled needs solidifying into a soul-deep impression of having the woman he loved in his embrace, savoring her and protecting her simultaneously.

Warmth spread through her chest. Bijoux felt validated, loved and treasured. She knew, in that instant, that she would do whatever it took to keep Costel, to love him for all time and make his life a happy one they could share. In the darkest recesses of his mind, he admitted to loving her, and that was all she needed to know. That was all that mattered.

Without warning, Costel rolled, taking her with him and putting Bijoux's back to the mattress. Before they'd come to a stop, his lips were on her jaw, sliding down her neck. He teased her with his tongue and rocked his cock over her clit. Bijoux gasped and arched, the heat between them growing until she was certain she'd burn alive.

He overwhelmed her. Suddenly, everything was at the extreme end of sensation, pleasure and emotion. Her heart felt as if it could burst, her body seemed as if it could fly. She arched and wriggled, lifting her knees and wrapping her legs around Costel's hips. The images in his mind turned scorching and intriguingly detailed.

The tip of his cock notched against her entrance and her body rippled in welcome—nerves contracted, honey flowed. Excitement had her arching. There was nothing she wanted more than Costel's possession, his dick thrusting deep into her pussy and bringing them both pleasure. Bijoux lost her breath at the unique and novel feel of a man—this man—at the point of breaching her body, then lost her ability to breathe as his hips shifted.

Costel slammed in. Deep. Without warning. A strangled scream clawed its way from Bijoux's arrested lungs.

The sleep magic spinning through his brain lessened, frayed, snapped. All in a rush. Costel's eyes flew open. Silver darkened to lead in a rapid slide of dismay.

"*Gods.*"

He stared down at Bijoux in dawning horror as she looked up at him in paralyzed pain. Every inch of her lower half felt impaled, too tight and raw with the need for escape. The mounting heat of a moment ago had turned to an icy regret in less time than Bijoux could handle. She thought perhaps Costel felt the same, as his face was drawn into agonized lines, teeth gritted and jaw clenched.

"What the hell are you doing?" Costel's voice was shaky, breathless, strangled — as pained as her body, surely.

"Seducing you," she gasped.

"*Foolish* virgin."

"Not a virgin anymore."

Costel closed his eyes just as Bijoux caught a glimmer of tears. His exhale trembled violently. "I hurt you?"

"It's okay. Just…just finish."

"*Fuck.*"

He panted. His nostrils flared and he bared his teeth. Costel's entire body shuddered, making Bijoux wince. She couldn't stop the small moan from slipping free, but, because the pain was lessening, she hoped Costel believed it to be a good sound. He didn't.

"I never wanted to injure you, Bijoux." Eyes still squeezed shut, Costel pressed his forehead to hers hard enough to hurt. "Hold still and I'll make it better. I promise I'll make it better."

Bijoux didn't think that was possible, but she did as she was told and held totally still. She concentrated on breathing and was surprised to find out that she could, and that the pain which had stolen her breath in the first place was nearly gone. Just the memory was left behind, but that was enough to keep her tensed in preparation for more discomfort to come.

Still, she sighed, "Don't stop."

"No, I can't. My foolish little virgin," Costel whispered against her jaw. "Only you would think getting into my bed would be a good idea, Bijoux. Only you—"

"I love you." He had to know. Bijoux *needed* him to know.

His inhalation echoed between them, but Costel did not give her the words back.

Instead, he used actions to share the truth of his emotions. He kissed her mouth softly, sweetly. He caressed her lips from corner to corner, dragging his over hers, back and forth as she slowly — *slowly* — relaxed. Costel's cock seemed to fit inside her a little better, though his body shook as if he were straining under great exertion, and Bijoux's pussy seemed to soften. Only then did he venture inside her mouth with a gentle glide of his tongue that left her wanting so much more.

He withdrew before giving it to her. He teased her mouth with quick kisses while he drew circles on her hip. Costel braced his weight on one elbow while he stroked her skin beneath her nightgown, drifting his fingers higher and higher. The fabric led the way, rising up her body as Costel explored through touch. Gently, carefully, he helped her shift so he could tug her nightgown off.

Sliding his lips down her throat, he then pushed up on both hands so that he could continue farther. Licking her collarbone and kissing her breasts, Costel painted sensations onto her skin with his tongue, closer and closer to her nipple until her nerves prickled and the peak tightened to the point of pain — a new brand of pain, achy and restless. Throbbing softly.

He licked her and breathed, "Do you like this, Bijoux? Tell me what feels good."

"Um, yes. Yes, that feels…nice."

"Nice?" Costel tasted her skin again. "How about this?"

He closed his lips over her nipple and sucked. The action was neither gentle nor rough, but some perfect combination of the two that lifted Bijoux straight off the mattress. Fire streaked from her breast and exploded just under her ribs. Her lungs tried to turn themselves inside out and her spine sizzled with sensation.

"Yes! Good," she yelped.

"Excellent." His voice was strained, grating, but his actions remained gentle. Costel slid one hand between their bodies, flattening his palm to her belly and reaching lower. He rested a finger on her clit. "What about this?"

He sucked her nipple and stroked her clit at the same

time. The fire in Bijoux's breasts shot straight down to her hips, where it mingled with the sharp pleasure she felt under the touch of Costel's calloused fingertip. Her pussy relaxed and tightened again in nearly the same instant, but softer somehow, as if Costel's dick suddenly fit inside her *perfectly*. Bijoux's body moved without her permission, lifting her knees higher.

With a harsh groan, Costel settled more fully inside her with her action, but the pain she expected never materialized. Instead, his touch was emphasized, the feeling of him lodged inside her – thick and hard and shaking – and the inexplicable need to have him *move* vexed her. She wanted him even deeper, but she wasn't certain she was quite ready. Bijoux felt torn and a little cowardly, so she put her arms around Costel's back and pulled him closer.

"It's okay," he murmured against her collarbone. "Tell me if this feels better, love."

His hips shifted and he withdrew. Bijoux panicked at the sensation of his loss, the way her pussy ached in loneliness without him to fill it, the maddening glide of his retreat. And she worried about more pain, knowing he would return. She murmured in protest, bit her lip and clutched his shoulders, but he brushed his mouth over hers and soothed her fears with a barrage of mental images designed to comfort.

Slow and steady, Costel drove back into her body with an unhurried thrust. Heat and lightning raged in the small of Bijoux's back. A fierce shiver shook her spine and raked her thighs. Her pussy adjusted to the gentle filling with a warm stretch that shocked Bijoux down to her toes, which immediately curled.

"Better, my love?"

"Yes. Yes, I liked that, Costel."

"And this?" He did it again, but a little faster. When he was as far inside her as Bijoux believed he could go, Costel gave an extra push that truly ignited all of Bijoux's senses.

Nerves tightened and magic flared. Bijoux closed her eyes

at the explosion of gold that encompassed them. She'd never seen such a thing before, but she knew what she felt and all the empty, neglected places within her soul suddenly seemed full and alive. Electric currents ripped through her, dragging over her scalp and zinging in her toenails.

"My Match," Bijoux gasped and arched, tightening her arms around her lover.

Costel groaned a moment before taking Bijoux's mouth in a searing kiss she knew would mark her forever. For the first time, all his defenses crumbled in her presence, and the avaricious thrust of his tongue had her head spinning, conquered and ravished between one heartbeat and the next. He was patriarchal dominance at its most elemental, and Bijoux was a woman raised in a household that held to such traditions.

She felt intensely female under the onslaught of Costel's kiss, under the driving possession of his cock. She surrendered without a fight, already having known the only place for her to exist was within his control. She softened, he hardened, and pleasure built between them with greedy speed.

Bijoux followed his lead, letting him guide her and teach her until they moved together. The magic swirled and sparked, heightening all the sensations, all the emotions. Bijoux's head spun, both with her own musings and with Costel's, and she struggled to obey all that his thoughts demanded of her.

He wanted her to come with him, he wanted her to enjoy herself and he wanted her to remember that night for the rest of her life. Beyond that, he refused to think of anything, and Bijoux was too busy experiencing her first intimate encounter to prod further.

He drove her on, his thrusts growing bolder, harder — more erratic. Eventually, they both lost their coordination and settled in to strain and thrust, grinding one moment and pounding at each other the next. Desperate to get closer, Bijoux arched, Costel slammed deep, and the heat and magic erupted, streaking through her in rivers of gold light. An unexpected orgasm took her by surprise because she hadn't known it was coming. Unprepared as she was, the sensations destroyed her.

Lost in the twisting, roaring pleasure, Bijoux didn't know when Costel followed her into the void. She only knew that he met her there, holding her close as she shivered and screamed, keeping her safe while her body melted around him and her heart reformed. For long, long moments, he wrapped her in his arms and held her until she remembered how to breathe. Slowly, as time ticked on, she regained the ability to see into his mind.

It was a hazy landscape, thoughts only half-understood. "Costel?"

"You shouldn't have come here," he said. Since he began to nibble on her neck while he scolded her, Bijoux didn't pay too much attention, until he told her, "This night is ours. Beyond is impossible."

"What does that mean?"

Costel shifted his hips. Bijoux gasped as she felt his cock harden inside her. A new kind of filling that had nothing to do with his driving body and everything to do with the driving need he felt for her. Images flowed past in her mind's eye, and she struggled to understand what he was telling her without words.

"The Lovasz life is not for you, my love. But tonight, you're here and I'm here." He brushed his lips over hers. "And no one else is."

"Costel—"

"Shh, let me love you, Bijoux, just for tonight."

Sadness had settled into his heart. She didn't like that and refused to allow it to happen while he was in bed with her. So Bijoux held her protests back, kissed him and let him make love to her again.

Chapter Twelve

Silviu

"Oh!"

Georgie stumbled to a stop in the bedroom doorway. Silviu saw her jaw clench, the barest hint of tendon running the length of her neck. The flash of annoyance and perhaps a glimmer of panic in her eyes told him she hadn't expected him to already be ensconced in the bed they would share while at the Council headquarters.

He was impressed when she admitted, "I thought you'd still be with your brother and sister."

"I haven't seen Costel since he finished dinner." Silviu shifted higher on the pillows. "And there's only so much I have to speak to my sister about. We've only been out of each other's company for a few days."

"Yes, that's true." Georgie cleared her throat and looked all around their room, obviously avoiding his gaze. "What are you doing?"

"Reading over Daniel's paperwork."

"In bed?" She waved weakly. "Shouldn't you do that at a desk or something?"

"Want to show me where one is? I haven't exactly had time to explore my surroundings, Georgeanne."

"Well, feel free to do so. I'd like to get some sleep, so now is a good time to give yourself a tour of the Palace."

Silviu studied his petite wife with surprise coloring his view. She wasn't put out over the idea of his bedside lamp shining while she tried to sleep. She was unnerved at having to share his bed. He would never have thought Georgie would look so uncomfortable and awkward, fidgeting on the threshold, in a situation that shouldn't have caused her distress. After all, it wasn't as if they hadn't been intimate before. He knew what every inch of her naked body looked like. He'd tasted her and touched her and felt her pussy clamping down on his cock in the moments she'd found her pleasure.

And she knew he'd never force her. Perhaps Georgie doubted her own restraint?

"Do you think I'll seduce you in the night, my love?" Silviu couldn't stop his voice from dropping into a low, husky register. "Or are you worried that you'll roll over seeking my heat and wake all wet and bothered, needing my magic and my —"

"Don't be ridiculous!" Her chin shot up. "The thought would never give me a minute's worry. If I wanted to fuck, I'd just tell you to get hard. It's bodies in motion, and I can admit you give me pleasure."

"How generous of you, love. As you say, I'm at your service, should you need my body."

Her lips pinched and her cheeks flushed. Silviu watched her, utterly fascinated with his bride's reaction, enthralled anew with the woman who had already captivated him years ago. She was stubborn and proud, desperate to hold on to her anger, but he could see the lines of stress around her mouth, and the bitter pain in the black abyss of her eyes.

He wasn't the only person responsible for her sorrow and probably wasn't even the cause of most of the emotional chaos. But he *was* the one closest to her heart. Silviu took pity on his bride and changed the subject. "Daniel knows I'm a Reap witch."

Georgie immediately lost much of her tension and released a breath Silviu hadn't realized she'd been holding. Her chin lost its defensive angle and she sighed. And yet, he knew the importance of that news wasn't lost on his astute wife. Politics was her forte. Georgie had been born and bred to lead, to strategize and to manipulate.

"Like you said, that was to be expected, after the Ngozi wedding," she muttered.

"Yes. A small price to pay to save your life."

"He witnessed the full force of your magic, Silviu. I felt its power, heard the strength of it rebounding in your scream." She shivered. "It was…a lot."

"You handled it easily enough." He fought to keep his eyes from narrowing but didn't know if he'd succeeded since his lips moved of their own accord. "When you trusted me."

Once again, Georgie's chin inclined. "I can still handle your magic."

Part of him wanted to simply agree and settle down for the night, pretend that the woman sleeping by his side was happy with him, strong in their Match and would soon find forgiveness for his supposed crimes. His fear whispered that he should ignore the tension between them until it went away. Silviu wondered if all married men felt that way when their wives were unhappy with them.

But another part of him—the slight majority—wanted him to confront the issue and work the tangle smooth. Fear had been a constant weight in his gut, his chest clenched every time Georgie turned away from him, and he was tired of it. He wanted what he'd fought so hard for—Georgie's respect and love—and he felt reckless enough to fight for it.

"No, you can't handle it," he spat, just to get her riled. "Now whatever you do with our magic turns sideways. It's unstable because you're insecure. Without trust, there is no solid foundation to shore up the magic."

"I beg your pardon?"

"You should." With a sharp flick of his wrist, Silviu launched Daniel Levy's file toward the bedside table. "You should be telling me you're sorry for doubting me. You should be apologizing for ever thinking all I wanted from you was the big chair at the Davenold dinner table—"

"You *bastard*." Georgeanne's eyebrows lowered and her dark eyes glowed with anger. Silviu remembered the last time she'd become enraged with him and wondered if he should be on his feet in case he needed to get away from her flying fists.

He remained in bed, pretending enough cockiness to fold his arms behind his head. "Come on, love. Isn't that what you've always thought?"

He was impressed when his bride bit her lip and stiffened, rather than launch an attack—either physical or verbal—that would have been heard in Paris. Her temper had always been her downfall, and Silviu had witnessed the weakness himself, the times she'd railed against his grandfather fiercely enough that she'd provoked his attempted murder of her. Georgie was diplomatic to a fault, until her emotions were brought into the mix—then her mouth got her into trouble.

But not this time. Silviu's stomach twisted as her chin notched higher and her voice turned icy. Her anger was hot and so was her passion, and he loved that about her, because he didn't know what to do with a cold woman, or how to get through to her.

"That's right. That's exactly what I thought. Why should I trust you?" she asked frostily. "After all, you're just a man who seduced a child and left her to the wolves. You're the man who got me sent away to a war while you remained in Europe gallivanting around with whoever took your fancy."

"I was a child myself—"

"Hardly!"

"And we've been over this before." Silviu jerked upright and tore the blanket off his lap. Leaping to his feet, he glared at her. "I wanted you. I wanted you then and I want you now, so badly I can't even *breathe* with the need to have you next to me, against me and wrapped around me. Then and always, Georgie, and I will never deny that need. I will *never* lie about it."

"That *need*"—she quoted the air with her fingers—"is a lie, in and of itself. You can fuck anybody you want, but they couldn't give you the Davenold Motherhood, could

126

they? No! You needed me for that."

"If that's all I'd wanted, I could have taken Suzette up on her offer."

Georgie growled and snarled. "But that would have lost you the Family, wouldn't it? They wouldn't easily have accepted your presence among us with another woman on your arm—or in your bed."

"With my magical talent, I could have anything I want, but I don't want another woman, Georgeanne. I didn't want the Davenold Motherhood, either, but you couldn't take it on your own and we'd be as good as dead if Suzette had gotten the power."

"With your magic?" Georgie purred dangerously. "*Please*, and I'm Bane. I made her Bane, and I doubt the Davenold magic would have stopped that from happening if she were the woman wielding it."

"But would it have made your whole Family Bane, too?" Silviu slid forward on his toes, shooting one arm out in a frustrated gesture. "If you break the magic of a Family leader, will you make the whole Family Bane?"

That brought her up short. In an instant, her anger drained away, leaving behind confusion and the pain Silviu wanted so badly to banish.

Georgie shrugged. "I don't know."

Silviu rubbed his head. "I have never betrayed you. You think I have, but everything I've done has been for us, for our success and our survival."

"Just *stop*." Georgie's face screwed up, with her eyebrows drawn together and her eyes closed as if she simply couldn't bear to see him anymore. She quickly composed herself and moved toward the dresser holding her clothing. "You can't tell me that you've been testing my limits with your magic in preparation of gaining the High Seat. To what end? When will I ever have to use your magic, Silviu?"

"You needed it at the Ngozi wedding."

She paused in rummaging through her drawer to send him a disbelieving glance over her shoulder. "You gave it to me. I didn't need to know how to use it. You used it for me."

He tried again. "When you broke the effigy's spell—"

"It was the connection between us, the way magic just"— she waved a pair of pajama pants—"happens, when you're around. Otherwise, no magic was needed to break the spell. It snapped when I touched it."

"Then put it down to my instinct, Georgeanne. I feel it's important."

"Oh, you're a seer now?" Georgie turned to him and folded her arms over her chest. "You know what I think? I think there's a pathway you're trying to open between us. I think there is some way you can use some part of my Bane… whatever it is, to your advantage. That's what I think."

Guilt nearly took Silviu to the floor. Bitter acid filled his throat, though he tried to clear it away. "That had been my father's plan," he admitted, "but he was wrong."

With halting words, Silviu told her what his father had asked of him. Vasile Lovasz had outdone even himself with his last request to his son. He'd believed Madeleine would honor her promise to make Georgie her heir and had encouraged Silviu to marry in the old way, combining sex and blood, in order to gain access to his wife's magic and absorb the Davenold power into the Lovasz bloodline. Vasile had underestimated what it meant to be Bane, however, just as he'd underestimated Madeleine's devotion to her Family as a whole. Georgie had never been named heir, and the Bane witch had turned out to be much stronger than the Reap.

"Wow. I didn't expect you to confess so easily." Georgie shook her head. "I suppose that means you either failed, or it was a wild success and there's no longer any need to hide it from me."

Silviu took a deep breath. "My father didn't think you would be the stronger witch. I suspected, and now I know it's true. Matches take on the heft of the stronger witch, my love. You can use my magic, but I can't use yours."

"Great. But did you fail, Silviu? Where is my Family's magic?"

He thumped his chest. "In me, where you can reach it whenever you want, with a little bit of practice. I want *you* to rule your Family. I have no interest in—"

"*Where* is my Family's magic, Silviu?" she interrupted him in a strangled scream, the color in her cheeks deepening again and her eyes too wide. "Costel is your Father, your magic is his. Where is the Davenold magic that is now yours?"

"Costel's not my Father, Georgie. When the Davenold magic came to me, it broke my ties to the Lovasz bloodline. I'm a Davenold now."

"But Costel—"

"Doesn't know what happened." Silviu rubbed his chest. "He felt my absence from the bloodline and called me to ask. He thinks we got married and your Bane shields covered me."

"And the betrothal agreement that says I'm a Lovasz now?"

"Merely a technicality. We're Lovasz-Davenold, anyway, so the point is moot."

"For who?" She closed her eyes. "All these lies, all these plots—for politics, leadership, whatever…but a marriage? How can you expect me to trust anything you say or do?"

Silviu was tired of arguing. That fast, the need to directly confront the issues between them faded, leaving him sinking into despair. "You never trusted me, Georgeanne. Not since we were children."

"Too much has happened," she agreed sadly. "Please excuse me. I'm going to get changed into my pajamas."

"I should have listened to you in Poland when you told me you'd never trust me again. You thought I'd set the whole thing up when we were young, that I purposefully did something to make them find us. I didn't."

Her slouched shoulders snapped straight. "When did I—?"

"You were punished for the crime of loving me, Georgie — by your Family, not by me. I'd have kept you by my side, but they sent you away." Silviu got back into bed and hugged the edge, his back to his bride. "Them, you trust. Me, you suspect of every foul thing under the sun."

The silence between them grew weighted. Floorboards suddenly creaked and Silviu heard the door close. A few minutes later it opened again. He'd already turned out the light. The mattress dipped and swayed as Georgie got into bed. She did not inch closer to him. He couldn't feel the heat of her body across the expanse of emptiness between them.

"I love you," he whispered.

But there was no answer.

* * * *

In the middle of the night, Silviu awoke when a warm weight landed against his side. As if her instincts couldn't rest until she'd wrapped herself around him, Georgie shifted and wriggled into place. Her cheek dragged over his chest and one sleek thigh slid over his hip. Silviu angled toward her and pulled her closer, wrapping his arms around her body until he was sure his pounding heart would wake her.

He felt Georgie smile and sigh. Heat and hope filled Silviu's chest in equal measure. When her guard had been at its lowest, she'd turned to him. He breathed in her scent and held her tight, closing his eyes on a wave of well-being.

They slept, entangled and in peace.

Chapter Thirteen

Georgeanne

Adam opened Georgie's bedroom door after a quick knock. "There are two limos coming up the drive. Thought you'd like to know."

She dropped Daniel's file onto the duvet and rubbed her eyes. With Silviu stalking the halls of the Palace, she'd decamped to their bedroom. Considering her resistance to sharing it with him, Georgie figured it was the last place he'd look for her, should he get it into his mind to search her out. She'd been alone all morning, however, and she was tired of her own company.

"Who's here, Adam?"

He shook his head. "I don't know. They aren't flying flags emblazoned with their Family crests."

Georgie narrowed her eyes at his sarcasm but let it drop. She got to her feet and stretched, glancing at the clock as she yawned. "They're just in time for lunch."

"Chris and Tulah are already by the door waiting to pounce on the new arrivals and gain their vote." Adam grinned. "Who would have ever thought we'd be actively campaigning for a patriarchal witch to take the High Seat?"

"Who indeed?"

"Silviu is our best bet for a fair shake in the next reign," Adam continued. "At least he's Family, and you can sway him to our side whenever we need something."

"Can I?"

Adam gave her a questioning glance as they stepped out into the hall and moved toward the curving stairwell.

"Still fighting with him, honey? Okay… Well, it's not the best start to a marriage, I'll grant you, but considering other witching alliances, it's not the worst, either. You love him and he loves you, so, yeah, he's our best bet."

Georgie shook her head. "Love isn't a guarantee of outcomes in political matters. Grandmother loved us but rarely gave us anything we asked for."

"I'm going to go out on a limb and say it's different between a husband and a wife." Her cousin shrugged and smiled wickedly. "Never underestimate the persuasive power of a good blow job."

"Adam!"

"Just saying. Oral sex opens a lot of doors. Take it from me."

Georgie groaned, though she gave merit to what her cousin suggested — not because she expected to use such tactics with her husband but because Adam made a good point and had a great deal of experience to back up his observations. Georgie suddenly wondered how pleasure would play into the intimate politics between her and her husband.

Silviu definitely gave her pleasure — physical and emotional, sexual and the simple, basic need to have someone close by. Her husband's understanding of how badly Georgie craved company — though she'd never admit it by thought, word or deed — went beyond mere recognition. The loneliness they'd both experienced as children had carried far into their adulthood.

Silviu had proven that he was willing to use his body and her vulnerabilities against her. As Georgie reached the bottom of the stairwell, however, she wondered if she'd also done the same to him. She'd dismissed his declarations of love on the grounds that they'd both changed over their ten-year separation, but perhaps he *did* know her. Perhaps he would always understand, simply because they'd been so similarly restricted in their lives. And perhaps Georgie had used Silviu's weaknesses against him, too. After all, there had been several occasions where he'd acted counter to his natural inclinations in order to make her happy — dealing with his grandfather and again with Father Muso Ngozi.

Christiana's voice interrupted Georgie's reflection of her marital relationship. Her cousin called out, "Limo just pulled in. Hurry."

Georgie crowded up to the narrow window set beside the door leading to the car park. Tulah stepped back to give her a view just as the first limo came to a stop outside. A man got out.

"Father Laurent," Georgie announced. "Not surprising that he'd be among the first to arrive. The Council Administrator is his cousin, after all."

"Eliasz's, too, isn't he?" Adam reached for his twin sister and forcibly removed her from her position so he could look out of the window with Georgie. "Perhaps you can use Eliasz's help?"

"He's already offered and we've already accepted. Eliasz has excellent connections all over the patriarchal world."

"Better than any Lovasz, that's for sure. Eliasz has been active and he's well-liked," Christiana said. She turned toward the door. "Ready to get this show started?"

"Silviu has a decent reputation in the witching world," Georgie protested. The surge of defensiveness took her by surprise, but she let it shape her words as she continued. "Those who know him like him very much. Even you've come to like him. Those who only know *of* him still look on him favorably, especially since they considered him more a Davenold than a Lovasz."

"He's a novelty." Chris shrugged and opened the door. "He's a decent guy, as good a man as any patriarchal Family could produce, in spite of the insanity of his grandfather, but Eliasz is more charming, Georgie."

Adam added his two cents. "Eliasz is active in many different aspects of our society. He's an excellent host. He's perfect to chat up any number of patriarchs, and I believe we were simply advising you to make good use of your ally, so there's no need to bite her head off."

"Yeah." Chris scowled. "He's a strong ally. Isn't that why Silviu wanted him onboard with your plans so badly?"

"My husband and I know what we're doing." Georgie hoped she spoke truth, but it was just as well that others *believed* she spoke truth, even if she didn't. She hoped the arrogance she'd injected into her tone helped their perception of things, but she immediately sweetened her voice as she stepped outside and called a greeting to Father Cyril Laurent.

"Ah, Georgeanne!" The older man's face lit up at the sight of her, then immediately scrunched into a mask of regret. "I'm so sorry for your loss, *ma cherè*."

Georgie steeled herself for such condolences many times over and gave him an even smile that said nothing of her pain. "Thank you, Father Laurent."

"She was—surprisingly, for a Matriarch—a very good High Seat. One of the best in over a century, certainly."

"Emeric feels the same."

"Ah, yes, of course he does. Madeleine was very fair." Cyril's graying eyebrows dropped down over a nose very much like Emeric's. "It is a shame you aren't from a Fatherhouse—or a man. I believe you would also be as fair as your grandmother."

"High praise. As to that..." Taking an inconspicuous breath, Georgie launched into her political persona, all personal loss, pain and turmoil pushed to the side in order to accomplish her goals. She was determined that not all would be in vain. "Silviu Lovasz and I are married now. We've decided to hyphenate, but, of course, our betrothal agreement had conceded kinship to the Lovasz Family."

Cyril's expressive eyebrows winged upward. "You are not a Davenold?"

He glanced toward Christiana, still waiting closer to the door, immediately recognizing her as Madeleine's other heir. He studied her for a moment, and anyone other than

134

Georgie would have missed the speculation in his eye.

"Motherhood is mine," she lied. "But we are a brand new breed of Family, now. As expected, once the Schism was crossed by such high-ranking members of both Family's primary branches, we've had to create a new path."

Cyril rocked back on his heels. "Yes, most unusual. Whatever had your grandmother been thinking?"

It was a better opening than Georgie could have hoped for. She needed to plant the seeds that Silviu and even Eliasz would nurture into full growth by the time the Council election took place. There was so much material Georgie could work with, too.

"She was thinking we could take the High Seat when she stepped down," Georgie told him bluntly. "I'm technically a Lovasz, and my husband is still eligible."

"And how does that work for your Family?"

"I am their Mother. My husband could be your High Seat, however." Georgie met Cyril's gaze directly. "Are you aware that Costel Lovasz and your cousin, Bijoux, are Magic Matches?"

Georgie prayed Bijoux would forgive her, but desperate times called for desperate measures. Neither of the pair had ever admitted their Matched relationship to Georgeanne, but her Bane gifts had brought her the ability to see magic in action, and on the few occasions she'd seen Bijoux and Costel together, Georgie had been blinded by the flash of gold light between them. Now that she was used to seeing the same thing develop between her and Silviu, there was no denying its source.

Georgie took a bold path. "You want influence over the High Seat, Cyril. Every Family leader wants the same thing. As Costel's wife, Bijoux would gain you a larger advantage than her father ever could, because the Lovaszes are a fairly tight-knit group, all things considered."

"Ah, but then, very few witches have brothers or sisters, so it always seems as if siblings are loving."

"The Lovaszes are." Georgie watched the Laurent

Father's eyes and followed his thoughts well enough to see the emotion in his gaze turn from caution to greed.

"You are suggesting Bijoux could intercede on my Family's behalf?" Cyril shook his head, preparing to play hardball. "But that is a matriarchal way of thinking, *ma cherè*. Bijoux would have no power over her husband."

"Every wife has some measure of power over her husband," Georgie argued quietly, Adam's words still echoing through her head. "And the Lovaszes are used to engaging with strong and opinionated women, more than any other coven on your side of the Schism."

"But we are speaking of Costel. He does not have any softer sentiments for females."

Georgie held back her grimace and tried not to think of all the times her brother-in-law had been casually dismissive of women's intellects. "But a Match is different, isn't it? Besides, I am also a friend to Bijoux and can take her suggestions to my husband, as well. I'm merely pointing out that he is more likely to take her needs into account if she is his sister-in-law."

"But will she be?" Cyril's eyebrows once again descended.

"You're the Father. You have the final say."

"My cousin is most attached to his daughter, and he won't give her up easily. Especially to a man who may not treasure her as he does. The Lovaszes are not known for treating their women well."

Georgie lifted her chin. "*That* has changed. I give you my word."

"Perhaps, Mother Davenold." Cyril was suddenly cool and businesslike, all hints of greed or political astuteness wiped from his expression. "It is something to consider, *non?*"

"Indeed." Georgie smiled and nodded, and let her argument drop. She would not be the persuading factor for a Father, but she certainly had planted the seeds for his support. It would be up to Silviu and Eliasz—and possibly even Bijoux—to bring Laurent the rest of the way.

He stepped away from Georgie with words of greetings and condolences for the other Davenolds waiting for him. Tulah, as a former patriarchal Family member, looked to be most equipped for bringing the Laurent Father the welcome he seemed to desire. She lowered both her gaze and her chin and Cyril's face lit up. Georgie hoped she was working some sort of useful wiles, but then Adam hauled his wife against his side and glowered at the other man. A second later, Emeric came bustling through the door and Georgie stopped paying attention.

The second limo pulled up next to her. A swarthy man popped out of the front passenger's side. Immense relief swept through Georgie as she recognized him and only the bracing wind kept her from falling to the ground. Once he approached the back door, he bowed to her before opening it, then reached in to help out an older woman Georgie regarded in the most affectionate terms. The lady was regal, dark hair piled atop her head, honey-brown skin luminescent in an orange sari, rings flashing and bracelets jingling as she lifted her hands toward Georgeanne.

"Mother Choudhury." Georgie welcomed her embrace. "I am so happy to see you, but what are you doing here?"

"I came to help you through such a dark time, of course. Georgeanne, *beti*, how are you? Your grandmother's loss must be painful."

A sudden, hot surge of tears took Georgie by surprise. When she'd been exiled for her indiscretion with Silviu, she'd been sent to the Choudhury Family and taken under the wing of their powerful, intelligent leader. Tanmayee had been reserved but very kind. Most of what Georgeanne had learned had been at the knee of the woman before her, and, in Madeleine's absence, Tanmayee had become the matriarchal role model George aspired to be.

"I'm glad to see you, Mother."

The Matriarch's face folded into sympathetic lines, but Georgie quickly blinked to clear her eyes. With a deep breath, she looked past her foster mother when Tanmayee's daughter exited the vehicle and came forward. As the Council representative, Aditi Choudhury was the one Georgeanne needed to persuade, and so, in spite of their awkward relationship, Georgie greeted her with just as much affection.

"We're so sorry for your loss," the other woman said politely.

Georgie took another deep breath. "Thank you, Aditi. It still doesn't feel quite real."

"How are you holding up?"

"I'm married now."

"Ah, Silviu Lovasz finally caught up to you, did he?" Tanmayee's lips curved into a secretive smile. "Your grandmother had once asked me to keep him far from you, and I had a great deal of fun pulling strings in the non-witching world to keep him out of my country."

"Yes, he told me about that." Georgie managed not to grimace at the recollection of Silviu's anger, frustration and possibly even pain during his explanations of how he'd failed to find her during their decade-long separation. "You caused him some trouble back then, Mother, but perhaps you can reimburse him now?"

"What do you mean?"

"We are here to elect a new High Seat."

"He wants the position? The High Seat must be on the Council already," Tanmayee reminded her.

"Yes, Silviu's brother has already filed paperwork to that end, therefore no such impediment exists." Georgie turned to Aditi. "We have combined our names, but our betrothal agreement states that I am a Lovasz, so that will not be an obstacle to nomination, either. Davenolds may not be eligible for the next century, but Lovaszes are."

The younger woman lifted a perfectly arched eyebrow. "Is he not the Davenold High Male, then? Did your Family's Motherhood go to your cousin?"

"No, it did not. My Family regards my husband as the High Male," Georgie conceded carefully. "The situation is as complicated as my grandmother foresaw. We are calling ourselves Lovasz-Davenold."

"That still makes him matriarchal." Tanmayee glanced at her daughter and pursed her lips. "You know the Fatherhouses will resist another matriarch in the role of High Seat after Madeleine held the position for so long."

Georgie protested with a shake of her head. "That's not a hard and fast rule. Besides, my husband was raised in a patriarchal coven. In him, there is a unity of our traditions, a blending of beliefs, and I don't think any Fatherhouse would be displeased with his nomination."

"I see." Aditi looked at her mother, then back at Georgeanne. "And what do you wish us to do?"

"Support him. Support *me*." Georgie lifted her chin. "Remember all I've done for you, and know that my heart resides with your Family on a great many issues, so you won't find a better champion than me outside your own bloodline."

"What an interesting prospect." Mother Choudhury straightened in much the same manner Georgie always did when she contemplated complex plots and their various consequences. "Such a thing would put us in a wonderful position for yet another reign of the High Seat. Madeleine was always very good to us, after we took you in."

"It was a great debt my Family owed you, and I can see to it that the return on your investment continues to pay off in the future."

"All right." Aditi nodded, already having come to her decision. "Our Family has no suitable candidate to put forth, and I assume the Gholamis will support you, as your uncle is the father of their future Mother."

"Yes," Georgie murmured. "All I need now is the support of Mei Lan Cen and I'll have all the Asian covens on my side."

"That is excellent news for our goals in the East." Aditi's eyes flashed and her lips tightened into a line speaking of her suspicion. "But what does your husband bring to the table, Georgeanne?"

"Africa and Romania, at least. Possibly the Laurents, as well."

"He's a shoo-in, then. Cyril will command the Seriks to vote as he does, and that will give you the majority of patriarchal Families."

"Not quite a done deal, however. He's still needs to get through the largest Family of all, which could be a problem." Georgie winced. "Let me tell you what we've learned about the Levy Father."

Chapter Fourteen

Costel

Almost all of the Council representatives had arrived by dinner. As was customary, Emeric ordered a great feast for everyone and a string quartet to hide the fact that all and sundry were roaming around the grand ballroom making deals and double-checking strategies with their alliances. The whole thing made Costel vaguely ill and always had, so he was more than happy to leave the politics to his brother and escape outside.

The wind had died down, but the chill in the air had grown sharper. Though his suit jacket held enough residual warmth to keep him comfortable for a little while and the castle walls blocked much of the leftover breeze, Costel wished he'd had the foresight to grab his coat. Where he stood on the grassy expanse angling westward, the scent of pine and livestock carried from the surrounding peaks and valleys, but that was an aroma that soothed some caged beast inside Costel's soul. Being outdoors and surrounded by living, breathing *things* that had nothing to do with politics or intrigues also made him feel calmer. Costel braced his fists on his hips, leaned back and breathed deeply.

"I was wondering where you'd gotten to." Silviu's voice traveled from the shadows, quickly followed by the soft crunch of his shoes over the gravel path. "There's so much happening inside. What are you doing out here?"

"Breathing," Costel muttered. "You are far more capable of achieving your goals in there than I am, so I assumed I wasn't needed any longer."

"I know mingling isn't your strongest suit, but you could at least escort Bijoux Laurent through the room."

"Why?" Costel spun to meet his brother. The look on Silviu's face, the deep scowl, with the moonlight making the angles of his cheeks seem demonic, had Costel's heart pounding. He lifted to his toes, ready to race back into the ballroom and fight for Bijoux's honor, if necessary. "Is she having trouble?"

"No." Even in the dark, Silviu's eye-rolling was apparent. "She does better with people than you, which is surprising, considering how few she's seen before. A trifle awkward, but many expected that and are helping her find her way."

"Then why does she need my escort?"

Silviu waved a hand. "Because it's obvious the two of you have a connection. You should be with her, encouraging her to use her talents and tell you everything she learns. That would be a tremendous asset to me, Costel."

Amazement held him hostage for a breath of time. Costel had the sinking feeling that he must appear as a fish out of water – lips opening and closing, throat working, gasps ripping from his lungs in sheer surprise – and in outrage.

"Have you lost your mind?" Without thought to the consequences, Costel slid forward in a wholly intimidating manner that had zero effect on his brother. "Bijoux's talent is enough to strike fear into the hearts of everyone here. They're all probably mentally reciting their respective alphabets in the hopes that she doesn't overhear anything of importance inside their skulls!"

"Wonderful. We should use that."

"If she is blatant about using her magic, the other witches will come after her."

"I'll protect her" – Silviu shrugged, then arranged his features into a stern mask – "if she helps me."

"*Good gods.*" Costel wheeled backward, gripping his hips to keep from reaching for his younger brother's throat. "Could you be any more like our father?"

Silviu flinched as if Costel had struck him. "I beg your pardon?"

"You would throw her to the wolves, risk her *life*, for a political advantage you could get without her help at all?"

"She is useful. Whether or not I could achieve the same ends myself is beside the point, Costel. The whole process would be so much more efficient with her assistance." Enthusiasm crossed Silviu's face. "I could specifically tailor each proposal, each promise and each assurance to individual witches or their Families, without guessing or hinting. I could give them what they want, and, therefore, get what I want. I could get what the Lovasz coven *needs*."

Listening to his brother, Costel raised his hands and pressed his palms to his eyes, hoping the pain could keep him from exploding with rage. Silviu was more powerful than him, which was saying something, as Costel knew without modesty. Costel was strong. He wielded his personal magic as well as that of his bloodline, but so had his grandfather, and Silviu had taken it all away from the old man.

"I won't put her in danger," he finally gritted out. "And I won't allow you to, either, Silviu."

"Costel…"

His name on Silviu's lips resounded with magical influence. Costel clenched his teeth as he felt the tell-tale tingle of his brother's talent. Ileana was bad enough on the rare occasions she grew so desperate as to manipulate him, and Costel usually gave in quickly to stop the mental torment, even on issues he truly opposed. But there was little hope of holding out against Silviu. Previously, he'd never even lasted a day before surrendering to his younger brother's demands.

Still, Costel tried, latching on to his anger to help him combat the cool slide of influence. "Use your magic, you bastard. Go ahead! Make me gain her help. Make me put her in danger, and then what? *Maybe* you'll protect her? Maybe you'll stop another witch from returning here to slaughter her when no one but her aging father is around to help?"

"She has a talent I need."

"Just like our father," Costel spat. "This is what I meant. Vasile will bend over backward to assure someone all is well, and, meanwhile, he's constructing the gallows himself. That's you! You disparage our grandfather, but at least his tactics are straightforward. You don't care what you have to do to get what you want. You don't care who you lie to, who you hurt or who you might betray, so long as you gain power."

Costel didn't know which part of his wild accusation hit its mark, but Silviu's entire body shuddered and his magic cut off abruptly. In the moonlight, his brother's face twisted, and despair was the only thing Costel could read in his expression. Silviu dropped his chin and stared at the ground, his shoulders stiff, his back tense.

"Shit," he whispered. "I just wanted — "

"Leave him alone!"

The command came in Bijoux's voice, in French and in a rough and unsteady tone. Costel could hear her panicked fury and could also see it on her face as she burst from behind a hedge and sprinted down the gravel path. He and Silviu had been speaking in their native tongue, and, as he knew full well that Bijoux didn't speak Romanian, Costel assumed she only knew what was happening based on his limited, mental point of view. He had no idea what she'd seen in his mind, and he hadn't thought to try to guard his thoughts from her.

"How dare you?" she shrieked at Silviu. "How dare you act as if he's never done anything for you. As if he owes you."

Silviu jumped backward as Bijoux struck out at him. Costel rushed forward to seize her and pull her away from his brother. Beyond that action, he was at a loss as to what to do or how to stop whatever might be coming.

As Silviu's French was barely passable, Costel wasn't

surprised when his brother transitioned to English. "What?"

Bijoux followed suit, her command of the foreign language equal to their own. "After everything your brother has done for you? You are ungrateful."

"Do you even know what we're speaking about?" Silviu pushed the question through clenched teeth.

Costel leaned close to her ear. "Bijoux."

"Yes," she screamed, ignoring Costel's vague command. "Yes, I know! You want something from him. You always want something."

"But you don't know what?" Silviu cocked his head. "And how could you know, unless you speak Romanian?"

"Specifics don't matter. You are asking too much of him, as always. I feel it. I feel his frustration, the powerlessness you try to impose on him, and why? He is the Father, not you."

Costel tried again. "Bijoux, that's enough."

Silviu's face darkened. "He's my brother—"

"And how do you treat him?" With a quick movement that took him by surprise, Bijoux twisted from Costel's hold. "After everything he's done for you, after the beatings and the abuse he's suffered so you and your sister wouldn't have to—"

"When we were children, he protected us," Silviu protested, "but since—"

"*Still*," Bijoux screamed. "He still protects you. He's traded the skin on his back for your peace of mind many times after you've grown up. Your grandfather enjoys testing him in such ways."

"*What?*" Silviu's eyes flew wide and he staggered back another few steps.

With triumph and gratification etched onto her face at his reaction, Bijoux grabbed Costel's suit jacket and hauled it up his back. He jerked, but she'd already taken advantage of his surprise and ripped at his shirt. In just a few seconds—less time than Costel needed to wrap his head around what she was doing—Bijoux had revealed all. She forced the material higher on his back until the moonlight shone down on the network of scars Costel had always been so careful to hide from his siblings.

He froze. Even his heart stopped beating before it began again, much harder, louder and hotter than anything he'd ever known previously. Something beyond rage stormed through him and Costel briefly wondered if it was the same driving force that had stolen his grandfather's sanity.

"Oh, fuck." Silviu covered his mouth with the back of his hand. "Costel—"

Bijoux's chin shot up. "And you have the gall to *rape* his mind any time you want something."

"*Stop!*" Costel lifted his hand as if that action alone would keep all the pain from dragging him beneath the waves of the terrible emotion burning him alive.

There was too much chaos to hold back. Something deep in Costel's chest seemed to break open and bitterness flooded his lungs. He couldn't breathe. He was drowning in pain. He didn't know who he was angriest with—Silviu or Bijoux or himself.

For years he'd taken the beatings in silence. That was the price he'd paid to keep them all safe from Alexandru's insanity, because he would be Father, and Costel was determined to be the best damned Father the Lovaszes had ever known. It didn't matter that Silviu was more powerful or that Ileana was so reckless. It didn't matter that 'headstrong' was a Family trait. Costel was their shield, allowing them to do what they needed or wanted, giving them some semblance of normalcy in a world stripped of all laughter and joy.

But that was his choice, his burden. His duty. It was never meant to inspire their guilt. He'd never meant for his brother and sister to find out the abuse had been ongoing, and Bijoux's unwarranted defense of him had his stomach boiling with acid. She'd seen too much within him and hadn't been able to keep his secrets to herself.

He turned on her. "You had no right."

"He needed to know, Costel."

"*No,*" he shouted.

Costel had no idea what she saw in his face, but whatever it was had Bijoux backing up and Silviu snapping to full alert. Costel saw red when his brother half-stepped in front of Bijoux as if she needed shelter.

"Now you offer her protection?" he sneered. "You're the one who wants to use her, to dangle her before the wolves, uncaring of whether or not they take exception to her *fucking* intrusiveness. But now you stand by her side as if *I'm* the one who would hurt her?"

"Calm down, Costel," Silviu urged, though there was no evidence of influential magic in his voice. "Why didn't you tell me what has been going on?"

"It's not your business. I am the Father. I am the heir and the eldest. It is my duty to see to your safety, *damn it*, and you had no right to know."

"How many times — ?"

"*Enough.*" Costel couldn't contain himself. He couldn't bear to confront the pity in his brother's gaze another second, and he would rather burn at a witch hunter's stake than look upon Bijoux's beautiful face, her expression formed from some unholy mix of defiance and regret. Her eyes shimmered with tears — so did Silviu's — but Costel couldn't handle thinking about the pain he may have caused them just then.

Not when his own agony was threatening to kill him.

Forcing his legs to function in spite of the lack of oxygen in his lungs, Costel stormed off.

Chapter Fifteen

Bijoux

Bijoux fidgeted, denying her sudden need to be ill as her brain finally acknowledged the awful expression that had been on Costel's face. Shock and revulsion, horror, denial and a rage Bijoux had never seen in him before. And profound sadness. She had a nagging fear that she'd somehow reached the root of who he really was and had lacerated it.

She took a massive breath. "I don't know if he'll forgive me for that."

"He will." Silviu staggered off the gravel path and sat down hard on the cold ground. He rubbed his head and eyes, then glanced up at her through his fingers. "I think he loves you."

"He loves you, too."

"Yeah." Silviu's eyes seemed to sheen and he cleared his throat. "I just didn't realize how much."

"Well..." Bijoux didn't know what to say, and fear at Costel's reaction made it difficult to think. "Now you do."

"Why would my grandfather do that to him? I mean, long after childhood? Costel was his heir, treated better than anyone else in the whole Family...I thought." Silviu turned his head and rubbed his face onto his sleeve. "Why hurt him?"

"To make him stronger, perhaps? That's what Costel thinks. To instill in him a sense of duty, Family, protection." Bijoux bit her lip then continued in a rush, "Maybe your grandfather wanted to see how far he could push before

Costel broke."

"But he never did. *Gods*," Silviu exhaled. "I had no idea…"

A moment passed in awkward silence until she asked, "What, exactly, were you arguing about?"

He looked up at her warily. "You really don't know?"

Bijoux thought of the emotional swirl she'd gotten from Costel's mind. Anger and protectiveness — she'd felt his distress from the ballroom and had excused herself to search for him. As Bijoux had walked down the garden path, she'd felt the terrible weight of Silviu's magical command over his brother, recognizing the sensation as the sleep compulsion Costel had been under the previous night. This time, however, Costel had been fiercely prepared to resist, resentment and fear giving an edge to his willpower and aggression.

That, in turn, had led to Bijoux's aggression.

"Not…exactly," she finally admitted. "With what Costel said, I know you want me to do something for you, but, before, I only knew that you wanted something from *him* and were going to use your magic to get it."

Silviu's jaw stiffened. "What do you know about my magic?"

"I know you use it against Costel whenever you want something. I know he feels debased and humiliated by it." Bijoux clenched her fists at her sides as a fresh wave of anger shook her. She fought to contain her emotions. "He can feel when you do it, you know. And so can I."

"You… I…" Silviu's mouth opened and closed, giving Bijoux a small measure of satisfaction. "I didn't know that."

"Now you do. Tell me what you wanted."

Silviu rubbed his eyes. "Your help. I wanted your help in learning what the perfect thing to say to each witch would be, to gain their vote for High Seat."

"You want me to be your spy?" Bijoux's extreme confusion slowed her words. "Why would you two argue over that?"

"My brother doesn't want you to use your magic. He's afraid someone will hurt you because of what you learn or how you may go about learning it."

The worried knot in Bijoux's chest eased the slightest amount at Silviu's words. Costel might be angry with her for sharing his secrets, but she was suddenly a great deal more confident that he would forgive her and also take her with him when he returned home.

"He loves me," she whispered.

Silviu heaved a sigh. "So I gather."

"But," Bijoux shook her head, still confused, "I have already agreed to do this for your wife. Georgie asked for my help before you two even arrived in France."

"I'm aware, but I wanted to ensure—" He stopped speaking abruptly, and Bijoux didn't have to be able to read his mind to guess how he would have finished his statement.

"That I told the truth," she finished for him. "You don't trust me."

Silviu stared down at the grass between his knees for a full minute in silence. Then he sighed. "Go to him. My brother will need someone to... He needs someone to love him, right now."

* * * *

Bijoux didn't bother to knock on his bedroom door. She entered unannounced, blinking at the sudden transition from the brightly lit corridor to the dark bedroom. Costel stood by the tall window, overlooking the gardens in a muted swath of moonlight. His silhouette was tense and his shadowed hand seemed to be clenched in the heavy curtain. His mind was empty of everything but anger.

"I'm sorry," she whispered.

"You had no right." As quiet as hers, Costel's words still rang with violence.

"I understand that now."

"You have no idea what it was like, Bijoux. No matter what you think you've seen in my head, you can't have any idea—"

"Tell me, then."

"No!" Costel's back got straighter. "Why? So you can run downstairs and tell the first person you find? You think my life is there for everyone to gawk over and laugh at? Poor, naïve, *stupid* Costel? Don't you think I've heard enough of that over the years?"

"That's not—"

"You think I can't fight my own fucking battles, Bijoux? Think I can't stand up to my own brother?"

"His magic, though..." Bijoux took a few tentative steps forward. "I know you never fight his compulsion."

"He wasn't using magic when you decided to tell him—" Costel cut himself off with a harsh growl.

She waited a moment, but when he didn't continue, she asked, "Why is it a secret? Why can't your brother and sister know what you've done for them? They *should* be grateful."

"*Grateful?* My gods, I didn't protect them for their *gratitude*, Bijoux."

"You shouldn't have had to protect them at all, Costel. If they had known what you had to go through for them, they could have, and *should have*, modified their behavior. There was no reason for them to misbehave and make you pay for it."

A bitter laugh echoed in the dark. "Is that what you think? Is that what you've seen in my mind?"

From the void of anger filling him, images rose. Distorted and darting, they were hard for Bijoux to see or understand—a first for her, where Costel was concerned. She did, however, catch snatches of both sadness and laughter, the image of a hazy woman who smiled and smelled like gardenias. Joy burst through a young child's heart, followed by beating, shadowy wings belonging to a terrifying presence.

"I remember my mother," Costel murmured. "Not a lot, but enough. She was...spirited, like Ileana and Silviu. Made for laughter and love."

"Did your...?" Bijoux took a breath and swallowed past the constriction in her throat. She'd heard the rumors — or, more accurately, her father had made certain she knew. "Did your grandfather kill your mother?"

"I don't know if he killed her, but I know he did not mourn her death." Costel flinched in the dark. "I remember them fighting a lot, arguing. I remember my mother being sad, begging my father to take her to live anywhere else, but he couldn't, just like I can't. We can't leave Alexandru on his own, for fear of the consequences."

"And later...you couldn't take the chance that your grandfather would hurt your brother or sister?"

"They knew how to laugh." Costel's voice broke. "In spite of all the ways he and Vasile found to lock them up, all the strategies they attempted in order to steal their childhood, then their adulthood, Iley and Silver smiled and remembered how to love."

"But, what about *your* childhood?"

"I was the heir. Heirs aren't supposed to have a childhood. We have responsibility, instead." His breath shuddered from him. "It was us against the world. I'd have died for them. I still would."

"Oh, Costel." Bijoux ran to him and flung her arms around his middle, holding on tight as the sound of tears filled his tone.

"I'm the one who is grateful to them, Bijoux. Without them, I would have become like *him*."

"No," she replied fiercely, knowing he spoke of his grandfather. "Never! I've seen what he's done, Costel. I've seen it all in your mind, and I know how different you are. You are a good man, even if others can't recognize that. You're protective and courageous. You care about people, and you've tried so hard to be honorable, even when you couldn't take credit for being so."

"I'm afraid that one day I'll wake up a bitter old man, alone and insane, just like him."

Bijoux pressed closer to Costel's back. "I won't let that

happen."

"You won't be there to stop it." Costel turned in her arms and gripped her elbows. "I can't take you with me, Bijoux. I know what you want, but I told you the other night. I can't. I can't take you to live with him."

"Of course you can."

She'd seen Costel's thoughts on the matter. Beyond everything else, they were the easiest for her to read. Filled with an incongruous mix of fear, hope and desire, he'd wanted her to come home with him. Even then, in his dark bedroom with words of denial on his lips, he pictured her on his land, pregnant with his child, a family of their own making. He pictured her smiling, he imagined them loving each other for many years into a happy future.

But the shadowed presence of his grandfather was a blight on the bucolic fantasy Costel favored.

Bijoux was determined to get her way. She could be ruthless—she was sure—and she could certainly use whatever she saw in the old man's mind against him. She knew Costel simply had to have his fears settled. He had to see her as someone he didn't need to protect, someone who could make his life easier and more joyful. And, from the moment she'd stepped into his bedroom to apologize, he'd given her all the ammunition she'd needed to win the battle she waged.

"You need me." She lifted to her toes, stretched as far as she could and breathed over his mouth, "You love me."

Costel's hands tightened on her. His words were tortured. "I do love you. That's why I can't take you to Romania."

"Maybe it's your turn to be happy."

"I told you"—he shook his head—"just one night. That's all we could have."

Bijoux shimmied against his body. "Well, this is one night, Costel. This is just one night, too."

He put his forehead against hers and sighed. There was too much defeat in Costel's thoughts to decipher, so Bijoux took matters into her own hands and tilted her face, pressing her lips to his, even as she tugged her elbows from his grip. As soon as she was free, she threw her arms around his neck and used her hold to lever herself closer.

He opened his mouth for her and she swooped in. He'd taught her so much the last time they'd been together, but she still relied on the mental images that were rising fast in Costel's imagination. She tried to do everything he wanted with her mouth, regardless of how desperate it made her seem.

She *was* desperate. That night was a fight for her future, and with the Council session drawing ever nearer, Bijoux knew this moment was her last stand.

All or nothing.

She licked into his mouth and demanded he participate. He allowed her the control with an indulgent, if sad, turn of thought. Their tongues slid together in a wet, velvet glide and hot need twined around them both, making them moan. Bijoux wrestled with Costel's necktie and he slid his hands down her back. He gripped her bottom and hoisted her to her toes. Bijoux immediately widened her stance and rocked over the swiftly growing bulge pressing into her.

Breath mingled, as did hopes and dreams. For that moment, Bijoux saw Costel putting all else away, his thoughts narrowed to concentrate on her and them, as if it really were to be their last night together. She let him think what he would, so long as he agreed with her by morning. She kissed him harder, ravenously, trying to set the foundation for his capitulation.

But Costel was a patriarchal male, and he only let her have the upper hand for so long. She'd gotten him out of his coat and shirt. His tie was a crumpled splash of silk on the moonlit floor. With a final lick to his lower lip and a few biting kisses down his chest, she clawed at his waistband, wrenching them open. Costel grabbed her wrists.

"Why the hurry, my love? If this is to be our last night, I want to slow down and enjoy it."

She shook her head and struggled to draw air. The

pleasure he'd given her before was too new to dissuade greed. She wanted him, and everything he could share with her, but she also wanted to please him in return — enough that he would never again speak of leaving her behind. Bijoux was certain the force that grew between them when they were intimate would help hold him to her side later.

"Why slow down, when fast means we can indulge in each other many times through the night?" She pressed against him again, suddenly needing to feel him — his heat and the thump of his heart — in a way she couldn't have explained if she'd tried.

He seemed to understand — and she suddenly wondered if he could read her mind as she did his, before she dismissed the thought as nonsense. Telepathy wasn't Costel's talent, and most would go so far as to claim he was the opposite of perceptive. Yet he fitted Bijoux's body to his with a hard press down her back that seemed to soothe the strange disquiet that had taken hold within her.

"Easy," he murmured. "I've got you. It's all right."

Costel brushed her lips with his own. He traced his tongue over the lower curve of her mouth. He fondled her ass. With slow movements, he turned the tables on her, gently reclaiming the reins and leading her where he wanted them to go. Bijoux surrendered sweetly.

Within moments, her clothes were on the floor. The cold night air swept over Bijoux's skin, but Costel's heat kept her warm enough. He backed her across the room toward the bed. When the backs of her knees hit the mattress, Costel gave her a little push. Bijoux willingly collapsed to the covers and waited.

The last time they'd been together and the first time they'd been intimate had both been well-lit events. The lamps had been burning bright, allowing Bijoux to see a range of emotions cross Costel's face. She could evaluate the way his muscles flickered under his skin and measure the rampant hardness of his cock.

But in the dark, their relationship took on magical tones

Bijoux never expected. Unable to see, she listened—to his thoughts and to his breathing, to the sigh of his zipper and the soft slide of fabric against skin. She heard when his pants hit the floor, and it seemed electricity arced through her body at the sound.

The air grew weighted as lust thickened the atmosphere. Nearly blind, Bijoux learned to feel. She felt the quiver of his muscles and the texture of his flesh, the indrawn breath he took as he ran his hand down her body in a possessive slide that set her nerves humming. She learned to understand what each of his touches meant and to obey his mute commands, dancing to the tune his mouth and fingers played on her skin.

In her peripheral vision, a soft, golden glow formed between them and around them. Her lover's harsh expression was revealed in the radiance, the flush of his face and, lower, that of his ready cock. Bijoux closed her eyes, preferring to *feel* what Costel gave her. Everything was so much more intense without sight. Deeply guarded emotions ascended to the surface and actions followed the images running through Costel's brain until reality and fantasy blurred together.

Costel sucked her nipple into his hot mouth. Lightning seared her and desire shot down her spine, laying a path he followed with his hands. Adding to the trail of sensation, he sent his calloused palms sliding over her breasts and belly, circling her navel before reaching farther. He delved into her curls and found her clit, rolling it beneath his thumb as he sought even more contact. He cupped her, pressing into her folds until she ached with need.

Bijoux lifted her hands and ran them over his chest as he drew closer. He stilled for just a moment, but the pleasure he'd gotten from her touch told her how rarely he'd been petted in his life. She vowed he'd never go another day without knowing he was loved. She lifted as best she could and kissed his throat.

"I love you, Costel. I love you because of all the things

you keep hidden, all the things you never let anyone else see, and not just because you're my Magic Match. Not even because you're one of the few men I've ever met, either."

He huffed, but she knew she'd amused him. The tension filling the fingers he still pressed between her legs drained away, and he groaned. Like laughter, affection had been a rarity for him, too, so she kissed him again and lifted against his hand.

His whisper warmed her nipple. "I've loved you for years, Bijoux."

"You should have done something about it, then."

"How could I, knowing there's no future for us?"

"You're wrong, love," Bijoux murmured, "but we can discuss it later."

She took it as silent agreement when Costel stopped speaking and started stroking her folds. With a busy hand, he manipulated her flesh until she was running with honey, slippery and hot, panting and begging for more. He curled his fingers into her pussy, stretching her, preparing her until her body rippled in anticipation. She planted her feet flat on the mattress, but it didn't stop her inner thighs from shaking.

Bijoux lifted her hips, driving his fingers deeper. Moaning, creaming, she did it again and again, while Costel bent his head to her breast and sucked her in. She was awash in sensation, from her chest to her knees, her nipples and clit seemingly linked by a hot ribbon of pleasure. Her pussy rippled, encouraging Costel to press harder, thrust more forcefully, until Bijoux teetered on the edge of her climax.

She fell into the abyss.

Costel's thoughts rioted in her mind. His wishes and desires, his pleasure becoming hers. There was no room for his sadness, however, as he held her close while she shuddered and screamed. Feeling his fingers pressing, still moving in her pussy, dragged out her orgasm, stretching it and weaving it into something new.

Bijoux tried to catch her breath, but her body still pulsed

and Costel still played. "Come in me," she begged. "I need you."

"I know." His tone was satisfied, though she knew he'd yet to achieve his own release. "I will fill you, Bijoux, so well you'll never forget me when I'm gone. But this is our night and I won't waste it. I will bring you pleasure many times before I find my own."

Costel withdrew his hand, leaving her empty and needing his return more than she needed her next breath. Then he shifted, sliding between her legs and notching his cock against her clenching pussy. Bijoux moaned and arched, tempting him with a hot, wet glide over the tip of his dick. She heard his inhalation.

He pushed forward in a slow, smooth slide that allowed Bijoux to feel every single inch of his shaft as it forged deep. Her pussy took him in with an expectant shiver, her inner walls giving way with heated welcome. He reached his limits inside her body and still rocked forward another half inch, humming a sound of approval at the delighted noise she made.

Costel put his lips to her temple. "Tonight, you'll come around me, my love, until you're weak and exhausted, then you'll come again. I will fill you, and you'll fill me."

"I'm all yours, to do with what you will."

She felt him smile. Then he said, "I know."

Chapter Sixteen

Silviu

Silviu shivered in the wind but refused to return to the ballroom. He was no longer in the mood for a party, after Bijoux's revelation. His brother's secret had cut him deeply, and he needed a minute to set his emotions aside before he refocused on the political games at hand.

Therefore, Muso Ngozi's voice slicing through the night was absolutely unwelcome. "It surprises me to find you out here, Silviu Lovasz."

The thick West African accent had Silviu gritting his teeth, but the animosity in the other man's tone was truly galling. After all, the man's lies and misuse of magic had done a great deal of damage over the course of many years and may even have played a part in the mess Silviu currently found himself in with his marriage. If Muso's greed hadn't spurred him into a criminal conspiracy with his brother, Graves may have never turned to dark magic and Madeleine Davenold might still be alive.

And Georgie wouldn't be angry at Silviu.

"Good evening, Muso." Silviu stiffened and half-turned toward the Ngozi Father as he stepped from the path, eyeing the man with a great deal of well-earned distrust.

"I would have thought you would be inside, with the female you seem to prize so highly." Muso grinned. "Yet, you hide in the shrubbery while she does all the heavy lifting."

"Heavy lifting?"

"She's all but turning herself inside out to get you enough

votes to take the High Seat." Muso waved. "And you stand in the cold, admiring the view."

"Perhaps my goal in the endeavor has been met." Silviu quelled a shiver after a particularly icy blast of air swirled around them. He took perverse pleasure in the expression that crossed Muso's face—the man was used to much warmer temperatures than the central highlands of France offered at that time of year.

"I wonder that you feel comfortable enough leaving your future to a female."

"Careful," Silviu warned, sudden anger spiking his blood pressure. "As you say, I prize that particular female above every living person on this earth. I would suggest you find a good deal more respect for her yourself, Muso. The last time you tempted my anger in regard to Georgeanne, you nearly paid for the transgression with your life."

The Ngozi Father huffed and dismissed Silviu's threat with a flap of his wrist. "She has you on a leash."

"And you should be *glad* of it." His temper snapped. Silviu slid forward over the grass, putting himself into Muso's personal space before he'd even developed a plan for intimidation. He simply acted on instinct.

At the Ngozi-Levy wedding celebration, Muso had pushed Silviu to the very limits of his patience and tolerance. Before the ceremony, the man's magic had come dangerously close to Georgeanne, and the fact that she couldn't be hurt by it had done nothing to ease Silviu's outrage. Then, at the failed ceremony, Muso had backed Graves into a corner, challenging him until the man had been provoked into recklessly throwing around his dark magic.

Georgie had almost died, until Silviu had poured all his Reap strength into her, filling her and overfilling her until her heart had restarted and their souls had fused together. Not enough time had passed for him to get over his fury, however. Eternity wasn't long enough for that.

"She begged for your life, Muso."

"She—"

"You lied to me," Silviu growled, unwilling to hear anything the Ngozi Father had to say. "Over and over, you abused my trust and destroyed any hint of charity I might have held for you. Georgeanne's *leash*, as you call it, is the only reason you're still alive. But that can be changed."

Muso scoffed. "You're melodramatic for a patriarchal son."

"Let me show you *melodramatic*." Silviu's voice softened into low octaves of a rage that burned white-hot in his gut. Georgie, too, had called him melodramatic, but Silviu took grave offense at being labeled so by a man such as Muso.

He lifted his hand and called his magic—not a small amount, either, but a brilliant ball of silver light easily controlled in his palm. A cheap trick every witch learned at a young age, except Silviu's magic had weight and density, a mass no other witch in the world could claim. Reap strength stretched out in solid silver bars to twine around Muso's body and hold him prisoner.

With only a thought, Silviu set his magic into motion. Little flashes flicked out from the bars to land swift, pinching strikes against Muso's body. From his face to his ankles, silver flared and bit down, through both clothing and the meager magic Muso struggled to bring into existence as a defense. The Ngozi Father writhed in his prison, but there was no escape.

"You lied to me. Blamed heinous crimes on your brother." Silviu circled the magical cage. "To feed your ambitions, you had your own son killed and drained of his magic. But Graves stole it. In revenge, you tried to start a magical war while my wife and her matriarchal Family were present— people I feel a great responsibility toward. My sister was there too, Muso."

"You're crazy! Let me out of this contraption!"

"You may not care about your Family, but I cherish mine"—Silviu grimaced—"for the most part."

"Lovasz, listen to me. I am the Father—"

"Not my Father. My Family was put into harm's way,

Muso, because of you." Silviu lifted a finger and the silver bars turned red, magical heat racing their length until the whole cage sizzled and smoked. Muso grunted. His breathing escalated.

"*Lovasz.*"

"I find I'm having a rather bad month," Silviu said conversationally as he paused before the Ngozi Father. "You played a very large role in my terrible mood."

"Please! My apologies, Lovasz. I apologize."

"For what?" Silviu cocked his head and watched the strange, shuffling dance Muso performed in the cage. "For hurting my Family? Perhaps for agreeing to allow the Davenolds to take Tulah with them, then attempting to renege on that promise at the moment we were to depart the wretched hospitality of your coven?"

"She went with her husband. She went!"

"But you've proven yourself entirely untrustworthy, and, therefore, expendable."

Except for the fact that he needed the Ngozi coven to vote for him for High Seat, Silviu almost wanted Muso to step out of line, just so he could work out his aggravation. He was terrified that his wife would never forgive him, irritated with the new responsibilities of being Mother and frustrated by his inability to find a dark magic witch intent on murder. His political aspirations were in peril, with the leader of the largest patriarchal Family in direct opposition to him and harboring secret goals of his own.

"I'm your ally," Muso squealed.

"Are you, though? What are you doing out here? Why have you come to make offensive statements about my wife?"

"I haven't. Please!"

In an instant, Silviu's anger diminished to a low simmer in his chest. The sport was poor and Muso was still useful, no matter that Silviu could hardly stand the sight of him. The Father was a powerful witch with a moderate amount of influence in the world, and, more importantly, he owed

Silviu.

Silviu decided to remind the man of that fact. "Then you must have come out here to assure me that I do, in fact, have your vote for High Seat?"

Muso twitched his chin downward. "Yes, of course. Most definitely."

Silviu dispersed his magic with a wave of his hand. "I'm happy to hear such a thing, Muso. I believe Daniel Ngozi also wants the High Seat. Have you heard anything about that?"

"No," the Ngozi Father panted. He patted his clothes and straightened his cuffs with a hard yank on his sleeves. "I've heard nothing, but he won't approach me after what I did at my brother's wedding."

"No, he wouldn't. He was very disappointed when you stopped the ceremony. Still... Keep your ears open, will you? Let me know if you do hear anything."

"Of course." Muso's wide eyes reflected the moonlight as he nodded jerkily. "Of course."

* * * *

Long after the soiree had ended, Silviu and his allies gathered in one of the many small sitting rooms made available for political intrigue at the Council headquarters. They were perched on all manner of chairs — Iley and Eliasz, along with Christiana and Milo, on a pair of couches facing each other over a small table. Georgie had hopped up onto the drinks cabinet while Adam lounged in a chair by her side, with Tulah balanced on the padded arm. Silviu hardly paid any attention to what they were discussing.

"Perhaps Bijoux has more input," Eliasz suggested, breaking into Silviu's wandering thoughts. "Where is she?"

"And Costel," Ileana added. "Silviu, didn't you tell them to come, too?"

"They are..." Silviu blew out a breath and rubbed a hand over his head. His emotions were in such turmoil that he'd had to forgo the rest of the party. He was feeling much too violent for polite society. "They're busy."

"Doing what?" his sister demanded.

"What is wrong with you?" his wife asked at the same time. "Silviu, you've hardly paid attention to anything we've said, have you?"

He elevated his chin, in much the way she did so frequently. "My thoughts are occupied elsewhere."

Georgie stiffened, her posture straightening into a nearly impossible perfection. The expression that crossed her face slammed into Silviu's gut, stealing his breath. He could read her thoughts in that moment as well as Bijoux Laurent had ever read his brother.

Georgie was furious—and hurt. He knew why. After all they'd gone through, after he'd taken the Davenold magic as his own, she was still campaigning with all her heart to get him into the High Seat, and he was too distracted to help.

"I thought you'd like to know that we've secured nearly every matriarchal coven's support and several more of the Fatherhouses, too. I thought you'd like to know that Muso Ngozi made a public declaration of endorsement in the ballroom while you were outside *taking the air*."

"After the conversation I had with him," Silviu murmured, "that doesn't surprise me."

"You never came back inside."

"I was distracted, my love. I still am, so perhaps we should continue this discussion—"

"I'm sorry"—Georgie jumped off the table—"I had no idea there was something more important than your quest for power."

She pushed past him, stomping toward the door. Silviu caught her elbow and spoke in a low tone that didn't carry beyond her, his sister and Eliasz, who were sitting on the near couch. "A lot has happened tonight. I learned my brother was beaten every time any of us did something wrong. He took whatever whippings Alexandru doled out, for me and Ileana, in our stead."

Iley gasped, Eliasz cursed. Georgie's eyes widened the smallest amount, but she rolled her lips between her teeth and took a breath deep enough to flare her nostrils.

"Well," she finally rasped, "at least now I know I haven't been the only victim of your selfishness."

The pain and renewed anger brought by her words took him by surprise and he let her go. Georgie fled the room. Silviu cursed and looked around, his full attention caught by the speculation in Adam's eyes.

"My cousin," the man immediately said, noticing Silviu's glare, "has a stubborn streak that few really run up against."

Silviu fought for patience. "I know."

"It's a defense mechanism, of course," Adam continued. "She shuts down like that when she's hurt. She used to, at least, when we were kids and the other cousins were mean to her."

"She said you broke her trust." Christiana folded her arms over her chest.

Silviu spoke through clenched teeth. "I'm trying to fix it."

"I would suggest doing whatever it was you did that gained her trust in the first place," Adam said slowly. "At least, that's a good place to start."

"I'm trying."

"Are you?"

His anger surged higher. It was on the tip of Silviu's tongue to tell the Davenold male that he'd gained Georgie's trust by giving her more pleasure than her senses could process, all while holding himself back from fucking her into the closest mattress. He'd lived by Madeleine's ridiculous command for abstinence, and his restraint had won Georgie over.

In the nick of time, Silviu swallowed the harsh words, but his silence fractured the rest of his strained temper. "You're right," he gritted out instead, already striding toward the door. "Enough is enough."

He left the others behind and moved through the hallways

of the Palace like a predator. A rampaging bear, perhaps. Hearing Georgie's footsteps echoing up ahead in the high-ceilinged stone corridor, he lengthened his stride. Muscles stretching and burning as he chased her, he caught up to her just a moment after she stepped into their bedroom.

Silviu slammed the door behind him. "I've had enough of your attitude, Georgeanne."

Her eyes flew wide. "Oh, have you?"

"I have been patient. I have been nice. I accepted that you are grieving for your grandmother, that my actions took you by surprise and even that you were disappointed at not being able to claim your Family's power yourself, but your childishness is going too far."

"Excuse me?" His wife's cheeks turned red. "How dare you—?"

"How dare *you*?" He was in her face before she could finish her statement. "All I've done and gone through for you, all the years I searched for you and was turned away when I found you. Fighting my grandfather and forcing him to relinquish his power, for you! Do you think I did that for me, Georgeanne?"

"I have no idea—"

"I took his magic from him so that you would be safe." Silviu grabbed her shoulders and barely managed to keep his grip from hurting her. "I have apologized for becoming the Mother of your Family and I have explained my reasoning for doing so."

"But you still made sweeping, life-changing decisions without bothering to ask me," she snarled. "Your patriarchal dominance is not—"

"*Dominance*?" Silviu let her go and yanked at his tie. "An excellent idea, my love, and exactly the reason I followed you to our room. I am your husband. You've become a patriarchal wife, according to our betrothal agreement. I am also your Mother, the leader of your Family."

"You're an asshole."

"Now there's another idea. That, too, requires trust."

Silviu spun Georgie around, taking her by surprise. In spite of her fast reflexes, she hardly had time to flinch as he grabbed her wrists and pulled them behind her back. He wrapped his necktie around her forearms, securing them, though he made certain he didn't cut off her circulation.

"What are you doing, Silviu?" Georgie immediately tried to free herself. "Let me go."

He leaned down, licked her neck and breathed into her ear. "No, my love. Not until I've reminded you why you trusted me in the first place."

"What... What are you doing?"

Silviu slid his hands up the front of his wife's dress, curled his fingers into the fabric and used a quick bolt of magic to shred the garment down the center. He pulled the dress from her body and went back to stroking — this time touching her soft skin directly.

"I'm pleasuring you, Georgie."

She shook her head, gasping when his fingers worked over her nipple as it hardened inside the lace cups of her bra. "I...don't want you to."

"You will, as you always do," he assured her. "In no time at all, you will be begging to be fucked. But, my love, this is an exercise in trust, yes? So tonight, I will teach you patience, anticipation, surrender."

Silviu pushed Georgie forward, onto the bed. She was petite — no trouble at all to manipulate and move onto her stomach. Her bound hands made getting to her knees difficult without help, but Silviu admitted to a dark thrill at watching her try.

"Silviu! What are you doing?"

"Regaining your trust. This will help you remember, my love." Silviu grinned. Then he snapped his fingers, and the lights went out. Darkness enfolded them.

Chapter Seventeen

Georgeanne

With the heavy drapes pulled across the window, the darkness was complete. Georgie's stomach gave a nervous flutter as the silence thickened and still neither of them moved. She could feel Silviu — she could *always* feel Silviu — but trying to pinpoint his location and identify his motives while she balanced on her knees in the center of the mattress, blind and bound, had all of Georgie's senses in a jumble.

"Silviu?" She'd tried to make her voice firm and exasperated, but his name escaped her on a wobbly sigh that she knew had revealed too much.

"Georgeanne," he whispered in response.

His anger beat against her senses — the four he'd left her working overtime to compensate for her lack of sight while her magical perception stretched as far as it could. She could have sworn she even tasted the bitterness of his claim on the Davenold Family power, and she winced at the sharp regret that filled her. She'd hurt him. She knew it and had even done so deliberately, determined to make him as miserable as he'd made her.

Except the harshest misery she'd felt came at the thought of leaving him, of never seeing him again. She couldn't bear the idea of never again breathing in the unique scent of the only man she'd ever loved or feeling his arms close around her to offer strength in her weakest moments. She would never again feel part of something special and precious, one half of a rare Match that joined so much more than just their magic.

A blaze of heat swept along her chest. Her bra and panties disintegrated. She caught her breath, momentarily nervous as she'd never been with Silviu, never having felt such a disconnect in the way he chose to undress her. A blast of magic that left her naked without even a touch of his finger was something new.

She bit her lip then rallied. "You keep this up and you'll owe me an entire store full of lingerie."

"In any other circumstance, Georgie," Silviu intoned from behind her, not rising to her bait, "I would allow you time to get used to things. In any other circumstance, I'd never have been forced to take the actions I took, and you wouldn't even be angry with me."

He paused, and she would have rushed to fill the gap with words—angry accusations were already rising and filling her throat, pure reflex and deep-seated fear making a wild grab for the betrayal she'd felt when he'd stolen her Family's magic. But Silviu ripped the breath from her lungs with a light stroke over her shoulder, making any noise but the soft whimper that pushed through Georgie's lips impossible.

Surprise filled her. Her skin tracked the feather-light touch of her husband's fingertip with a warm ripple that extended far beyond the path he stroked. In spite of the way he'd removed her clothes, she felt his care of her in the spark that flared between them as their magic met. The connection they shared didn't allow for insincerity in that moment.

Thoughts and feelings tumbled through her head—profound love, profound rage. Desperation and greed found their counterpoints in protectiveness and devotion. Georgie's mind went temporarily blank, long enough to let Silviu touch her again without reproach—and again after that.

And again.

His was a sensual onslaught, a sexual blitzkrieg that

left Georgie wrecked and gritting her teeth to keep from revealing it. His gentle touches were unpredictable — quick or long, coming fast or slow — but they all trailed heat in their wake and left Georgie's muscles quivering with expectation. From her collarbone to her calves, he claimed her. She swayed under every stroke, gasping at every glide of his hot palms over her skin. Silviu's pleasing, vaguely spicy scent filled her nose and muddled her thoughts, just as his hands sweeping over her body pushed her farther than ever from her anger.

Silviu slipped his fingers over Georgie's thigh, again trailing heat and also a touch of ruthlessly controlled magic. Small silver tracers spread over her legs, melting into gold as they landed on her skin. Tiny flashes of subdued light, radiating pleasure.

"But this isn't another circumstance," Silviu finally rumbled. "We are in a fight for our lives."

"Melodramatic," she managed to say.

Georgie heard a low snarl, then her husband calmly told her, "I'm sick of hearing that word, my love. Take the threat we are up against seriously, please."

"A dark magic witch."

Silviu slid his hand down her hip. In a move so quick she wasn't even certain she hadn't simply imagined it, he delved beneath Georgie's ass to caress the soft flesh guarding the entrance to her pussy. She felt the brush of his fingertips, then his touch was gone — so suddenly.

"Yes, my love. Dark magic. Witches have died, power has been transferred, magic abused and corrupted. I need you to trust me, because we are all that stands between the combined covens and a villain treacherous enough to murder the Council High Seat."

Harsh words, spoken in a gentle tone and accompanied by the heated glide of hands over parts of her body only he had ever truly touched. Georgie struggled for breath as her fear and grief battled the lust her husband called forth.

With grief so close to the surface, she focused on the lust.

Sometimes, a woman needed to be touched by a man who loved her. And, no matter how she pretended otherwise, despite her distrust of his motives and manipulations, she did believe Silviu loved her as much as he claimed. With the magic flowing between them, no matter how hard she tried to shut it off, she could feel it.

On behalf of them both.

She relaxed and spread her knees for better balance. "This is your way of regaining my trust?"

"Can you see?"

"No."

"Then you must feel." His murmur became another caress. "In the dark, you must trust me."

A hot, wet streak trailed down her neck, not rushed, but quick, teasing. Velvet. Georgie's breath broke and she realized her husband had licked her, which reminded her of other things he'd licked on her body. Her pussy contracted and flooded.

"Silviu—"

Georgie choked on his name. With his lips, he searched for, and found, her nipple, closing his mouth around the hard peak, pulling it tighter than it had ever been as scorching waves of sensation spread out from under his tongue. He licked her, sucked hard and nipped softly. Tremors raced toward Georgie's collarbone and she arched, dangerously close to falling back on the covers as she tried to push her breast deeper into his mouth.

With a strong suction that had her groaning in need, Silviu pulled back from her nipple. "Read the truth in my tone, the honesty in my touch. Tonight, Georgeanne, you will remember why you trusted me in the first place."

She wasn't quite certain she wanted to play Silviu's game, but her body seemed too heavy to wriggle her way off the mattress and her breathing was too labored to contemplate the struggle for freedom. Her senses held her in thrall—as did her husband, who reached from the dark to pet and caress her body in unpredictable ways.

A drifting touch down her arm. A slow swipe around her navel. He flicked her nipple, brushed her clit. Silviu traced the cleft of her ass before palming the globes, quickly squeezing and releasing her. Her nerves sparked and her head spun, wondering where the next sensual assault would target.

The mattress shook, telling Georgie that Silviu had climbed onto the bed with her. Her blood heated with anticipation and her skin tingled, waiting for contact. Oxygen shivered through her lungs. He blew a breath over her back.

Hot, then cool. His exhale whispered over her skin and goosebumps erupted. Georgie shivered and gasped, trembling a little on her knees and lowering her head to better feel the unexpected sensation traveling down her spine.

"Release my hands, Silviu."

"No. You are at my mercy, as a good, patriarchal wife should be."

A zing of anger had her straightening, even more so when he chuckled. "Silviu, I've told you before that I won't be just a patriarch's wife, no matter what the agreement between our Families stated."

"But that's exactly what you are, my love." He spoke with his lips against her hip, brushing a soft caress over her skin before he licked her. "And tonight, I will finally teach you what that means."

"I don't—" Georgeanne's words were cut off as Silviu pushed her forward. Surprised, she couldn't stiffen her muscles in time to save her balance and with her hands behind her, she couldn't catch herself. Her cheek landed on the thick bedspread.

Silviu's palm pressed between her shoulder blades. "Almost perfect, wife."

Georgie's mouth worked, but no sound emerged as her husband stroked down her back and over her bound hands in a move so outrageously possessive that it sent a shiver through her whole body. She chose to think of her reaction as indignation, but, deep inside, her pussy gave an excited tremor and flooded anew. Juices leaked from her depths to begin a slow slide down her inner thigh, but Georgie bit her lip and denied the need to shift on her knees.

Silviu caught her hips and tugged them backward, lifting her ass as he pulled. Georgie's spine curved in a severe arch. Silviu spread her knees a little more, then he blew over her folds. The nerves hidden in Georgie's flesh quivered madly, desperate to free themselves from her control and bask in the pleasure her husband heaped upon them.

"Are you wet?" he crooned.

She bit her lip and fought to inhale. "Fuck me and find out." Though strangled, she'd managed to inject a bit of brazenness into her words.

"Oh, I will, but not yet." He licked a blazing path around her pussy. "Mmm, I love the taste of you."

There and gone, he licked and withdrew. Georgie bared her teeth to the dark but swallowed her growl of frustration. Her clit hummed and swelled, and she knew her husband's position by the heat radiating over the backs of her thighs. She figured that if the light was on, Silviu would have an excellent view of the vibration that seemed to wrap the little peak straining for his attention. Georgie turned her face into the bedspread and exhaled roughly.

"What's wrong, my love?" He swept his fingers over her clit with unerring precision, as if Silviu did, indeed, have a spotlight focused on that area of her anatomy. At the same time, the mattress shook and his lips found her ear. "Frustrated at not getting your way, Georgeanne?"

"Who says I'm not?" she grated.

His chuckle tickled her nape and he shifted his legs to press forward, slipping his thick cock between her thighs to bathe in her cream. His shaft ran over her hot, swollen folds, slicking through her softest flesh until the tip of his dick bumped her clit, making Georgie rear back and grind her ass against his thighs.

Silviu's rumble of approval had electricity clawing up

Georgie's spine. Forward and back, he teased her. He was a welcome presence between her legs, and her pussy wept for his entry. She was slippery with need, but he only thrust against her—not into her. The deepest parts of her body twisted and cramped with blatant demand.

"Fill me," she demanded. "I want you inside me, *now*."

Silviu pulled away from her completely. He kissed her knuckles where her fingers curled, resting in the small of her back as her wrists were still bound. "You are impatient. For all your predatory ways in every other aspect of your life, you've never been good at waiting for pleasure."

"You must be joking. That's *all* I've been doing since I met you."

"Gods, how you please me, wife." Again he gave a low laugh, but this time from a few more inches behind her. He cupped her ass, fondled and squeezed, pulling her cheeks apart until the space between her legs seemed stretched and entirely too empty. Needy.

He scraped his teeth along the bottom curve of one buttock and set her scalp to prickling. Silviu's lips moved on her skin. "There is little build-up for you. I give you just a taste of pleasure, and you start creaming all over me. Passion floods you and you become wild under my hands, under my mouth."

He buried his face in her folds, his tongue stretching along her skin to lick at her entrance. Soft, wet heat, a gentle pressure at the entry to her pussy, had Georgie rocking on her knees, unashamedly pressing her temple to the covers for leverage. Silviu groaned, laughed and licked, sucked and bit.

"*Goddess*." Georgie muffled her screech in the bedspread. The length of her body blazed with greed and magic, desire verging on ecstasy.

In the next instant, Silviu disappeared. The mattress shuddered, but Georgie didn't know if that was because of her or because her husband had gotten off the bed. She struggled to catch her breath and quell the need burning her alive, but she knew both were losing battles.

"See, my love? No patience."

She panted as she searched for understanding. "I thought the goal was to get each other off."

"If that were the case, your grandmother wouldn't have demanded abstinence from us. Think on that, love, while I take you past your limits to a place where all you can do is trust me to bring you fulfillment."

"Force?" She tried to make it an accusation and not a kinky game request, but the heat in her pussy shuddered through her too vibrantly.

He licked the back of her thigh. "Never. I will not take you until you are *quite certain* you will welcome me into your body."

"You want me to beg?"

"Knowing you," he bit her ass quickly, sending lightning up her spine, "your plea would come in the form of a command."

Silviu put an end to Georgie's ability to have a conversation by ripping away her wits and taking control of her body. With every touch, every breath and every kiss he pressed on her skin, she felt his patriarchal dominance in a way she wouldn't have if he'd beaten her into submission instead. Her husband was a sneaky bastard, choosing his weapons with care.

Georgie realized what he was doing. On a deeply instinctual, elementally *feminine* level, she knew and maybe even approved. He was manipulating her body, owning it and making certain she knew it, but he also gave her the ultimate choice. Even as he pleasured her, even as he trailed pure bliss over her nerve endings, he offered her more.

All she had to do was ask for it. *Choose* it.

Surrender.

He encouraged her with soft murmurs, well-timed between long licks and quick nips while he worshipped every inch of her skin. "Reach for my magic, love. It's yours. It's all yours."

Responding without thought, obeying the instincts screaming from her soul, she opened herself to the subtle influence of silver magic. Silviu's magic—and hers, if he could be believed. Letting her guard fall was a tentative step down a new path of trust. He soothed her and set her upright, positioning her. His cock slipped against her lips, the crest flavored with her honey and warm, as he stroked it over her mouth.

His magic filled her. Shining and strong, their connection physically manifested itself in golden cords. Georgie and Silviu were wrapped together, bound for eternity, no parts left secret if the other wanted to know.

But Georgie was beyond the wonderment, beyond the truth, beyond even herself, with her body writhing and her knees slipping on the covers. She lifted her chin and opened her mouth. Silviu guided his dick deep and Georgie moaned around him.

She sucked him the way he'd taught her to do. She cracked open her eyes, vaguely surprised by the glimmer of gold shrouding her vision but, currently accustomed to using senses other than sight, she wasn't daunted. From dark to blindingly bright, Georgie couldn't depend on what she saw, so she focused on the hitch in her husband's breath, the tightening of his thigh muscle against her cheek and the heavy, rapid pulse under her tongue. She sifted through the intense emotions streaming through the link between them.

Licking, sucking, lapping, she worked his cock as he thrust slowly. His knuckles bumped her lower lip and she caught a mental image of his fist wrapped tight around the base, staving off release. Wicked satisfaction roared through her and she pulled back, letting his crest fall from her lips with a quick lick.

"I think you're impatient, too, Silviu."

"I'm always impatient for you," he admitted readily enough. "That's not tonight's lesson."

"Then what is?" Speaking was a chore Georgie could hardly complete. Desire clogged her throat, and her brain wasn't functioning properly. She didn't know what to make of it when Silviu swung around her body, but, when he covered her back with his chest, her nerves thrilled at the heat.

"Pushing the limits," he whispered. "Trust."

"I reached for your magic."

"Then use it." He bit down on her earlobe and lodged the tip of his cock just inside her dripping entrance. "You're going to need it, Georgie."

She had no idea what he'd meant and had no breath left to ask. Roughly but slowly, he pressed into her. His pelvis rubbed her ass as he forged a path through slick tissue determined to close around him with a brutal grip, deep between inner walls that shook and contracted. Silviu's dick stretched Georgie both physically and emotionally.

She'd gotten used to her husband's intensity in all aspects of his persona, but the ferocious way he made love to her was still a novelty—new, raw and volatile. Wonderful. Georgie could only go along for the ride, though her body tried to brace itself and her hips rocked back toward Silviu's thighs. But there was no buffer. There was no way to ease the wildness or control the flow of lust.

All Georgie could control was the magic. Silviu had given it to her, and she found it malleable under the influence of her primal thoughts, the desires she held when all civility and restraint were stripped away—and they had been. The way she heaved against Silviu's body and gloried in the heavy rush of being filled while he took her from behind had eradicated all gentility. Georgie had become a ravening beast, sobbing and crying for release, pushing her husband to the edge of his control until his magic frayed and snapped.

Georgie caught it. She gripped the golden cords in tightening fists of willpower, and redirected the flow over both their bodies. Hot and electric, their magic became a new force, a new touch. Silviu hammered her pussy and Georgie bludgeoned him with his own strength. What was his became hers—and vice versa.

Pleasure built and roared through the room. Georgie burned from the inside out and caught the bedspread on fire. The necktie that bound her wrists was consumed in the blaze. She snatched at the magic with newly freed hands, newly freed senses, and buried it inside her body, saving the room in a feat of strength she'd had no idea she could— or should—perform. With the force contained within her, hot became hotter, magic grew and lust detonated. Silviu gave a strangled scream and lunged into her pussy hard enough that she felt the aftershocks in her breastbone. She wanted more.

Georgie begged for release.

"Come," he told her. "It's up to you. I give it all to you."

Magic spat and sparked, wrapped them both and cinched tight. Georgie shook the ribbons of influence running through her husband's strength and saw clear to the bottom of his soul. In those silver ropes, she found truth and love, a protectiveness she couldn't imagine—pure devotion. She found a patriarchal witch whose dominance surpassed her own.

She found her Magic Match.

And she surrendered—once and for all.

Chapter Eighteen

Costel

Costel spread jam over his toasted baguette slowly, though his fingers cramped with the hold he maintained on his knife. His thoughts were simultaneously sluggish and riotous, leaving him more confused than ever and vaguely off-balance. The relationship he shouldn't have started with Bijoux had become more than a problem.

"Good morning."

Startled, Costel looked up to see Georgeanne stepping into the dining room. He swallowed his groan and managed to smile, but he would have preferred to be left to his thoughts. At that hour of the morning—practically pre-dawn—he'd had every expectation of breakfasting alone and had come straight downstairs after he'd carried Bijoux back to her own room.

The staff had just set out a few things on a sideboard for the convenience of both the early risers and the jet-lagged. There were only a few cooks in the kitchen, and they would be busy preparing the rest of the day's meals for a great many people, as the remainder of the Council representatives and their entourages would arrive by mid-morning. The Council session would begin just after lunch.

Georgie snatched a fresh croissant from a basket and poured herself a cup of strong black coffee. Costel winced as she added a hefty dose of milk. Somewhat unnaturally, in his opinion, she chose to join him at his end of the massive table.

After a moment of swirling her spoon through her coffee,

Georgie murmured, "You seem different today."

"Me?" Costel glanced her way with raised eyebrows. With the first shafts of sunlight falling through the wide window only enhancing the softer illumination of the overhead chandeliers, he couldn't help but notice the missing lines of tension from around Georgie's mouth. The set of her lips was softer and her eyebrows weren't angled into a scowl. "I could say the same about you. Gentler, maybe."

"*Gentler?*" She snorted and rapped her spoon against the rim of her cup. "Here I was thinking you seemed less arrogant this morning, but perhaps you're only still sleepy."

Costel stiffened in his seat and retrained his gaze on the window. He groped for social niceties. "A lovely view, isn't it?"

"Of wet grass, browning for the winter?"

He smiled tightly. "Perhaps my conversational skills are best left until after I've fully awoken."

He let silence find them and lengthen around them until the weight of it filled the room. He forced a bite of his toasted baguette, but even with the generous amount of jam he'd put on it, the bread still seemed dry. It stuck in his throat.

Just as Costel was certain the awkwardness between them could not get any worse, Georgeanne exhaled and slammed her drained cup onto the table. "I'm sorry."

Her brusque tone implied anything but regret. Costel elevated his chin. "Of course."

"I'm not being fair to you," she sighed, "and I apologize for that."

"Accepted."

She exhaled roughly once again then rubbed her forehead. "I think I've never been fair to you, never given you the benefit of the doubt, and I find the knowledge weighing heavily on me this morning."

"Is that so?"

"You are oftentimes standoffish but perhaps you have a reason to be. I'm sorry I never thought of how life must have been for you."

Costel shifted in his seat to face her directly. Again, he took in her expression, the uncharacteristic torpor clinging to her. Even at rest, Georgie was a ball of energy, vitality crackled the air around her, but she sat at the table with barely passable posture and a quiet reserve Costel had never seen in her before. And yet, she looked calmer, more peaceful, and she was attempting to apologize — to him.

Mentally, he reeled. "Why?"

"Silviu...told me." She glanced up at him and grimaced. "He told me Alexandru made you the Lovasz Family whipping boy."

"Ah."

"I won't say anything, of course. That knowledge will stay with me."

"Mmm." Emotions surged, burning through his veins before ice moved in to numb him completely. To cover his reaction, Costel struggled to swallow another bite of toast, but it cost him a layer of skin from his throat. He gulped his coffee and tried to remain composed.

"It's not easy being the heir," Georgie whispered, "or heir apparent."

"No. It is a great responsibility."

"Lonely," she murmured. "Burdensome. So much pressure on you to always do the right thing and react the right way, so much resting on your shoulders. Nothing is ever for you. Everything is always for others."

"As it should be, Georgeanne. As a Family leader, you should be well-prepared to take care of your dependents." Costel hesitated only a heartbeat before adding, "I'm certain you will shine in your new role."

"It must have been worse to be the heir to the most magically gifted Family of us all, on either side of the Schism, especially when you're living in the same household as an abusive asshole like your grandfather. *And* you had to learn how to run your Family at his knee."

She lifted an eyebrow and pinned him with a look

that even his father would have found impressive—and intrusive. Stilling, and keeping still for long seconds, Costel held his muscles taut, calling on years of practice with his own Family to strain her patience and give himself some sort of leverage. He slowed his thoughts, casting about in different directions to try to figure out her game, her purpose in the conversation.

She smiled. "Relax, Costel. I'm just trying to apologize, not get Lovasz secrets out of you."

"Of course not. Why bother with an interrogation, after all?" He grabbed for his cup. "Silviu will, apparently, tell you anything you wish to know, anyway. The Lovaszes will have no secrets from the Davenolds ever again, I presume."

"He was upset. That's the only reason he told me about you—what you did for him and Ileana. He feels guilty, I believe."

Before he could stop himself, Costel let a sliver of his anger barrel through his control. He slammed his hand against the edge of the table and immediately regretted it. His action revealed too much. He tried to modify his tone but knew he had failed when he said, "That is exactly why I never told them. Why should they feel guilty for our grandfather's actions?"

Georgie's nostrils flared, but he had no idea what that meant. Her expression had closed down but still held that curiously gentle quality Costel had never seen before. He didn't understand what that meant, either. Not for the first time, he felt at a disadvantage in her presence.

When his sister-in-law rose and moved toward the coffee urns, it took nearly everything in him not to bolt for the door. Being in Georgeanne's company had always been uncomfortable, and he'd always had the idea that she was mocking him. Just then, he wasn't certain what she was doing, and he feared he couldn't think fast enough to figure it out in time to save his pride.

Then she returned to her seat and told him, "I think you're going to be a far better Father than I ever gave you credit for, Costel."

"I…" He blinked. He also tried not to sound suspicious. "Thank you."

She laughed, but the sound was slightly bitter, self-censuring. "My grandmother didn't believe I could be Mother of my Family. I've spent my life proving I was capable, but I've never been asked to take a punishment for another. I've never been tested in that way."

"You had your own tests."

"Yes." She stared down into her coffee. "I would like to strengthen the relationship between us, start fresh. I will never agree with your ideas of patriarchy, and that's where most of our tension comes from. I don't like your views on women, but if you could refrain from espousing nonsense you know will irritate a matriarchal witch, we could find a sense of harmony in our dealings."

The goodwill that had started to generate as she spoke evaporated. Costel gritted his teeth and drew in a slow breath that helped his thought processes immensely. Only when he knew he could keep his voice moderate did he reply.

"Our tension does not stem from our views on patriarchy, Georgeanne. I do not care how you feel about men or women, as I'm sure you don't care how I feel. The different sides of the Schism hold different opinions—"

"And that's where I went wrong with you," she interrupted. "I managed to work with other patriarchs without getting offended, but, perhaps because you would be my brother, I unfairly expected you to—"

"*Georgeanne*"—Costel clenched his jaw and valiantly recaptured his composure—"you and I will never heal the divide between covens, so leave it. If you've sensed any… hostility on my part over the years, it is entirely due to the way you treated my brother."

Her eyes flew wide. "Excuse me?"

Costel snatched his napkin off his lap, balled it up and threw it over his uneaten toast. "You hurt him. You keep hurting him, and the only reason I've stayed out of it is because he is a grown man."

"He wasn't the only one hurt."

"He showed up here at the Council headquarters with no spark of life in his eyes. He's desperately unhappy and abnormally touchy where you are concerned."

"We've had some issues that needed to be worked out, but—"

"And ten years ago"—Costel slashed the air with his hand—"you disappeared. He wrote you a thousand letters, but you didn't answer any of them. He traveled all over the world to find you, but you refused to see him and even blocked his entry into a country. Then, when you resurfaced, you sat at the Council table and calmly nodded to me as if we were acquaintances, when all the while, you'd shredded my brother's heart."

Costel jumped to his feet. His breath came too fast and his heart simmered with energy. He held his fists at his side and tried to examine his thoughts properly, knowing that whatever Georgie could come up with in response could be political and emotional quicksand for him. In fact, Costel was suddenly terrified he'd jeopardized too much to even contemplate.

Georgeanne turned toward the window, the gentleness riding her features that morning deepening as she nodded. "Silviu and I worked out a lot of our problems last night. And I will agree that much of the trouble was my fault. But you're wrong on some points, Costel."

"I watched my brother lose his mind for ten damn years."

"But it wasn't *my* fault. Your father was responsible for my disappearance. They sent me away." She lowered her eyebrows. "I hadn't even known Silviu was looking for me until years after the fact. I was a child, at the mercy of my Family and yours."

"You didn't see him, Georgeanne. The way Silviu... *raged*."

She searched his face. "And all that while, you covered

for him with your grandfather, didn't you, Costel?"

"Alexandru would not have approved of my brother's obsession, if he'd known the full extent of it."

"But you and Vasile hid the way Silviu felt about me?"

Costel slowly sank back to his chair. He propped his elbow on the table and rubbed his head. "Vasile couldn't know, either, Georgeanne. I don't know what my father had planned for you, but the way Silviu... My brother would never... He's a manipulative bastard, true, but he's also protective as hell—"

"Are you speaking of Silviu or Vasile?"

Georgie was smiling at him. Costel reared back in his seat, surprised and suspicious, and desperately wishing he'd never been dragged into the conversation. "Silviu, of course," he said. "I doubt my father was ever protective of anything, except himself."

Georgie cocked her head. "He knew how Silviu felt, anyway. He tried to use it against me in Poland."

"Figures," Costel snorted. "My father is set on revenge, even if he has to use his own children to achieve it."

"Look at that," Georgie teased. "Something we can agree on. I'm not your father's biggest fan either, though I do understand why he did much of what he did."

"At least someone does."

"Revenge for the life he had to live with your grandfather, who may have possibly killed your mother. Vasile felt betrayed, and he also saw your grandfather's decline and wanted some sort of barrier to protect the Lovasz coven in case—"

"In case I turned out to be a crazy despot like my grandfather?" A question Costel had pondered since they'd been given access to the Documents Chamber was answered. "I stand corrected. My father *was* protective about something besides himself, though you shouldn't overlook how that would benefit him, of course."

"He doesn't do anything without good reason."

"My father isn't a *bad* man," Costel protested weakly.

185

"Maybe not a good man, either, but he just—"

"Wants power. They all want power, Costel—every witch in this place, every witch who sent a representative here, and every witch at the mercy of another. They all want power."

"You do, too."

As Costel stared at Georgie, a thousand thoughts tumbled through his mind. He was grateful Bijoux wasn't there to see them, as they wouldn't be flattering for anyone—including his sister-in-law. She was brave and confident, courageous, intelligent and influential, in spite of her age, but she also had an agenda that would put her at the top of the witching world, along with his brother.

She lifted her chin and her eyes gleamed in a shaft of morning sun. Costel knew, in that moment, that Georgeanne wouldn't stop until she'd achieved her goals. Her success was a foregone conclusion.

"That's right," she agreed. "I want power. Silviu wants power, even you want power."

He shook his head, suddenly feeling the effects of his long, sleepless night. "I just want to go home."

"You want to go home and lead your Family. You want to go home and repair the damage your grandfather did, and I'm beginning to believe you will, too. But that's power."

Resentment waged war with loyalty in Costel's chest. "My grandfather wasn't a bad man, either."

"How can you say that?" Georgeanne threw up a hand. "I've always wondered how you could defend him—and continue to defend him—and yet, you came to my rescue in Poland."

"He's done terrible things. Many people have done terrible things. But he loves his Family and did what he thought was best. He simply couldn't learn a new way of doing things, refused to believe the world had changed. He was the last of the dinosaurs, before Silviu took his power."

Memories rose up to strangle Costel. Not all of them were bad, not all featured beatings or verbal abuse. Most were happy. There had been plenty of times where he and his grandfather would tour their land, where Alexandru had carefully taught his grandson to care for the soil, for the crops and livestock. He'd helped develop Costel's fierce love of nature, and fostered the sense of serenity Costel received from putting his hands in rich, fertile earth. There had been peaceful times and bonding times, where Alexandru had passed down knowledge and, in doing so, had given Costel a sense of Family history he otherwise wouldn't have had.

Georgie's eyes narrowed. "And what of you, Costel? What did you learn at his knee?"

"I learned how to protect my Family." He thought back to the night his brother had ripped the Lovasz magic from their grandfather, and the decision Costel had been forced to make to ensure their coven remained united, functioning and prosperous. "I learned the sacrifices required of a good Father, and how important it is to love."

"Alexandru didn't love Silviu, and Silviu defeated him." No one could ever accuse Georgeanne Davenold of an inability to follow a conversation, even one not plainly spoken. She frowned at Costel. "Is that the difference in you today? You've finally admitted you love Bijoux?"

"I would have admitted that years ago, had anyone asked."

"So would she." Georgie grinned. "In fact, she did. I was quite shocked. Asked her if she knew *another* Costel Lovasz I'd never met."

"I wish love were enough." He tried to change the subject. "But what about your new attitude? Does that have something to do with my brother?"

"I think we're getting things worked out. That's ten years' worth of lies, manipulations, distrust, secrets..."

"I'm certain you're both on familiar ground, then."

"*Ahem.* Let me interrupt before this turns ugly."

The new voice startled both of them, and Costel turned to find Christiana Davenold in the doorway. Georgie's cousin was one of the only Davenold witches Costel had ever gotten along with, perhaps because she was the one matriarchal female that had never tried to prove her superiority over him. She was gracious and kind but not intimidating like his sister-in-law.

Christiana smiled broadly. "I'm so happy your little Family power breakfast hasn't resulted in bloodshed. I know that probably took a great deal of resistance…on both your parts, perhaps. But I'm here to inform you that Daniel Levy has just arrived."

"This early?"

Chris nodded. "And he's sent word that he'll be using the gardener's entrance."

Georgie got to her feet. "The bastard was probably trying to avoid notice until the Council meeting began."

"Careful," Costel cautioned as he followed her from the room. "He's a patriarchal man, and I doubt you fully understand what he's capable of."

Georgie shivered. "Trust me, Costel. I'm completely aware of what a patriarchal male can do, but I'm not accusing Daniel of anything—yet."

He wasn't convinced. "You're stomping down the hall as if headed to war."

"He's got a point. What are you going to do?" Christiana asked.

Costel wasn't surprised when Georgie lifted her chin and said, "I'm going to find out exactly who in the Christians' Hell Daniel Levy thinks he is, to file paperwork claiming my husband should be disqualified for the High Seat."

Chapter Nineteen

Bijoux

It had been sweet of Costel to carry her back to her room, but Bijoux would have preferred him to let her remain in his warm bed. She wanted to rest in his arms, wake in his embrace, make love to him again... She rethought that last wish after reaching for a book from a high shelf. The night had been long and action-packed, but her body wasn't used to such exercise yet. She was definitely feeling twinges in private places, and thought perhaps a morning bout of sex wasn't entirely necessary for the day's happiness.

She couldn't stay put in a cold bed, no matter how heavy her eyelids felt. So, the moment Costel had left her, Bijoux had gotten dressed and headed toward the Documents Chamber. She was busy researching every reason given throughout history for one witch to accuse another of being ineligible to take the High Seat when Ileana Lovasz joined her.

Giving the woman she hoped would soon be her sister-in-law a brief explanation, Bijoux told her, "But there are only two reasons ever given for ineligibility, and only one has ever been accepted by the Council."

Ileana looked around, stroked a thick tome. "You read through all of these?"

"Of course not. My father's computer program is very organized." Bijoux hefted the only book she'd needed to page through in her search. "This had the information I required. In the history of the Council, the only reason ever found acceptable to disqualify a High Seat candidate was when a Family member had held the position before the required time limit had elapsed."

"A hundred years," Ileana murmured. "Now that Madeleine has passed, the Davenolds can't hold the position for another century."

"To ensure fairness. That's the only reason the Council has ever denied a candidate."

Ileana held up a pair of fingers. "But you said there were two reasons, in all of our history — only two. What was the other claim?"

"It doesn't matter. It was denied, and, in fact, the witch in question did become the High Seat, though not a very good one." Bijoux winced. "Of course, the only other person in the running came from a Motherhouse, and that would have made two terms of matriarchs in a row — "

"What was the claim?"

Bijoux paused at the hostility in Ileana's tone. She looked her future sister-in-law over, wondering at the expression in her metallic eyes. Her thoughts were hidden. "It was a Lovasz, actually. One of the matriarchal houses tried to thwart his rise to power by claiming he was a Reap witch who would cannibalize the magic of the combined covens."

"*What?*"

Ileana's control fractured, and it sent Bijoux reeling. She gritted her teeth as the other woman released the brutal hold she'd held on her mental wanderings, not only allowing the telepathic witch a glimpse into her head, but broadcasting them in much the same way Costel did so frequently.

Unlike her brother, however, Ileana's thoughts were overwhelming, scared and frustrated, dark and filled with danger. There was no sense of familiarity as there was with Costel or any of the other witches Bijoux habitually came into contact with. Even the thoughts of the scheming politicians currently in residence were more pleasant than the chaos streaming from Ileana's head.

Staggering under the onslaught, Bijoux caught herself against a bookshelf. "Silviu is a Reap witch?"

Ileana gasped. Her mouth worked and she shook her head but couldn't dispel the anger that covered her face. "Don't be ridiculous. Don't you know how rare that is?"

"Not as rare as a Bane-born witch, and I know one of those personally." Bijoux lifted her chin. "So do you."

She gave Ileana credit. The woman regained her composure lightning-quick. Her facial expression gave nothing away beyond a faint surprise that anyone would ever consider Silviu to be so powerful. Her body language screamed that she had nothing to hide. She would be a wonderful political hostess, in Bijoux's opinion.

Except for the thoughts Ileana couldn't seem to halt.

"There's been a baby born under the Reaping moon every few generations." Bijoux narrowed her eyes and tapped her chin. "They might not broadcast the fact, but Families are supposed to register those babies with the Council. There are harsh consequences for failing to do so, but Silviu was never documented as a Reap witch."

"Obviously, because he isn't."

Bijoux waved her hand. "You've already told me, Ileana. I can read your mind. I can *hear* it, and the truth is deafening."

"You're wrong," the other woman spat.

"It makes sense," Bijoux mused. "It makes perfect sense. Of course he's a Reap witch. It's just that no one would consider it because, as you say, it's rare. And, again, the fact that's he's married to Georgie, and I can't even tell you the odds of that happening. Reap and Bane? Nearly impossible."

"You're delusional, which isn't surprising." Ileana sat primly on the only available chair, the modern eyesore in front of the computer. "Don't confuse the past with the present. Just tell me what happened to the Reap witch who held the position of High Seat."

Bijoux pointed to the thick tome Ileana had been examining. "Coson Lovasz. I was about to reread his history."

Ileana pinned Bijoux with an uncompromising glare. "*Re*-read? You've read his history before? Why?"

191

A fresh wave of hostility sounded in Ileana's tone, but Bijoux blushed for a different reason entirely. She fidgeted but eventually admitted her curiosity to the other woman. "I've read everything we have here concerning the Lovasz coven history."

"Why?"

"I expect to marry your brother."

"Do you?" Ileana's eyebrows winged upward, nearly meeting her hairline. Animosity poured from her mouth. "What does he expect?"

Survival instincts kicked in and Bijoux took a deep breath to still the nervous butterflies swarming into her chest. "My relationship with Costel is not your business. Do you want to know about your ancestor, or not?"

Ileana jumped to her feet. "I want to know about you and my brother, first."

"I'm not discussing it."

"Because there is nothing to discuss." Ileana's expression tightened, her eyes narrowed and she folded her arms over her chest. "I see how you look at him. You think he's your ticket out of your ivory tower, but that's not going to work."

"I don't understand you. Your thoughts are confusing." Frowning, Bijoux held herself still as she tried to sift through them, with little success. She wanted to know where Ileana's anger stemmed from, and why it was directed at her. "Your memories are full of pleasant recollections of both your brothers, and the bond you all shared."

"Get your magic out of my head."

"On the other hand, however, all the times Costel has failed to stand up for you against your grandfather has caused deep scars. But I don't understand why you're so angry *now*. Are you being protective" — Bijoux cocked her head — "or do you hate Costel?"

"Of course I don't hate my brother!" Ileana took an intimidating step forward and lifted a finger toward Bijoux's nose. "But I do find it disingenuous that you, who claim such an accurate telepathic magic, could even pretend to have affection for him. *You*, who should theoretically be able to see *everything* in his head, should know the things he's done—or not done, as the case may be."

Ileana's tone was just as confusing for Bijoux as her thoughts. Part of the woman's wild accusation was made in a strident voice, dripping with contempt, while the rest rang with the wariness of a loving sister intent on vetting her brother's girlfriend. Bijoux didn't have enough experience with people to understand the volatile mix of emotions Ileana struggled with.

"You're going to marry my cousin, Eliasz," Bijoux said after a moment of deep contemplation. "Do you think he's perfect? Do you think he's never done anything wrong?"

Ileana waved a hand sharply. "That is not the point."

"Yes, it is. I see what's in Costel's head, and I know what's in his heart. Maybe that helps my opinion of him, but I know his reasons for his actions and can respect them, even when I don't agree."

"You have no idea how many times he's helped my grandfather do terrible things."

Bijoux drew herself up. The nervousness had fled, but she was still shaking under a wash of heated anger. "What makes you think he had any more choice in the matter than you? What makes you think everything he's ever done hasn't been carefully thought out in terms of costs and benefits?"

"Oh, please," Ileana sneered. "Costel doesn't have the brain power to think like that."

In a flash, Bijoux was in the other woman's face, screaming in rage. "You ran wild, uncaring of the consequences. You left him to deal with it. He was beaten on your behalf, and how have you repaid him? By using your magic to manipulate him, to get what you wanted."

Ileana, surprisingly, fell back, her eyes widening. "It's not like I knew—"

Bijoux didn't care, just kept yelling. "He had to be so careful, to keep your grandfather from figuring it all out.

He had to choose his battles precisely, and you disparage him for it. You're selfish and greedy, wanting to pick fights, then condemning Costel for not fighting them for you."

Ileana melted. The steel went out of her spine and she slumped back onto the chair, burying her face in her hands. A long moment passed, the silence between the women broken only by Bijoux's labored breathing as she struggled to regain her composure. In her mind, Ileana's thoughts tumbled and swooped, images blended and confused until they were a nearly incomprehensible stream of information Bijoux didn't feel like deciphering.

"Sometimes," Ileana muttered into her palms, "I get so mad at Costel. I wanted him to fight for me, yes. Like Silviu, though he also chose his battles carefully. But I didn't mean to put either of them into that position. I just wanted —"

"Freedom," Bijoux whispered. She saw the need in the other woman's mind and felt it in her own. That was one thing they both had in common, despite how differently they'd been raised.

Ileana glared up at her. "Sometimes, I want Costel to pay for my pain, but I don't want my brother hurt the way I think you might be able to hurt him. I've been here for days now. I've seen the way he looks at you."

"He loves me. I love him. We're Magic Matches." Bijoux lifted her chin.

"Everyone but me. Great." Ileana gave a bitter laugh. "You know Silviu specifically asked Costel to seduce you? He wanted your magic, wanted to use you to see into the Councilmen's thoughts."

Bijoux didn't deny the pang of pain the other woman's words caused, but she quickly moved past it. After all, she knew quite clearly who had seduced whom, and she'd been the aggressor in their relationship. Costel had run like a rabbit, until Bijoux had caught him.

"I owe Silviu a debt, then." Bijoux smiled. "Without his interference, Costel would never have done anything to me. I'm grateful that, this time, his thoughts have been filled with images of the seduction he would never have performed otherwise. It gave me an opening."

"An opening for what?" Ileana's eyes narrowed.

"For my happily ever after. For a future with the stubborn, foolish, prideful, *arrogant* man I love."

"He sounds like a prize, doesn't he?"

Bijoux grinned. "That's why patriarchal women were created tougher, stronger and smarter than others. We have to deal with such things from our men, and we have to be more clever to win our way."

That surprised a laugh out of Ileana. "Don't let Georgie hear you say that."

With that, Bijoux felt a bond grow between her and Ileana, a softening of her would-be sister-in-law's attitude toward her. Again they fell silent, but without the tension of before and without the confusion of turbulent thoughts. This time, the hush of the Documents Chamber was filled with the warmth of shifting emotions.

Finally, Ileana sighed. "Tell me about Coson Lovasz, my long-ago ancestor that ended up being a terrible High Seat."

"Ah, well..." Bijoux opened the thick tome she'd almost forgotten about, revealing a beautiful illumination. She stroked the heavy silver embellishments and traced the swirls of gold. The Lovasz Family crest lay inside the elaborate border, picked out with bright, bold colors. "He's the reason your coven's influence began to wane."

"But he was a Reap witch?"

"Yes. At the time of his nomination, only two houses were eligible for the High Seat. It was a volatile time. The witching wars had concluded a few generations previously, but battles continued to erupt occasionally, plus the non-witching world was a dangerous, brutal place to live."

"Right." Ileana nodded. "Life expectancy wasn't great. They probably had a hell of a turn-over rate in the High Seat position."

"At the time, they'd just lost a female High Seat and our side of the Schism wasn't about to elect another matriarch.

But there was only one eligible patriarchal Family. The Gholami tribe argued that, as Coson was born in the Reaping, his magical ability was too great to allow him access to the combined flow of magic created by the covens."

"Yet he still became the High Seat, so being a Reap witch wasn't an acceptable reason to disqualify him."

"No," Bijoux agreed. "Apparently the High Seat doesn't actually possess the magic of the combined covens. They just use it as it flows past."

"Huh." Ileana looked away, then back at Bijoux. "So, what happened?"

Bijoux grimaced. "He did try to siphon off the magic and use it for his own ends. As I said, the world was a hard place back then, and he died fairly soon after he took the High Seat. The damage was minimal, but covens have very long memories."

"They held it against my Family, I suppose," Ileana grumbled. "And subsequent generations haven't done much to change public opinion about us, either. Will that affect Silviu?"

Bijoux thought about it for a moment. "Possibly. If someone knows about this and brings the topic into light, I could see how that would make a powerful incentive to disqualify him."

"Ileana?"

The woman's head came up and a bright smile flickered across her mouth. Joy infused every line of her face as she turned toward the sound of her name. Bijoux watched as Eliasz walked down the aisle between the bookshelves, his eyes glued to his bride's, intense satisfaction wrapped around him like a cloak.

Bijoux vowed that, one day, she and Costel would be that happy.

Eliasz nodded a greeting to Bijoux as he took Ileana's hand. "I need my betrothed at my side. My esteemed cousin has finally arrived, and Ileana must stand with me to greet our Family's Father."

Bijoux clutched the Lovasz history to her chest and grabbed another, much slimmer volume concerning the mythology of Bane witches. "I'll go, too. Maybe I can get some answers to our questions directly from the source."

Chapter Twenty

Silviu

"Where is Daniel Levy?"

Silviu turned around at the not-so-dulcet tones of his irritated wife. As he did, vivid memories of their night together flashed through both his mind's eye and his cock. He would have loved to have furthered the lessons in trust that morning, but when he'd awoken, Georgie had already risen for the day. The sight of her slamming through the door onto the private, open-air patio was the first he'd caught of her all morning.

She was glorious. Silviu went rock hard at the vision she made, with her dark curls bouncing above her shoulders and her even darker eyes flashing with anger. Her cheeks were slightly flushed and her beautiful mouth was set in a thin line.

The moment their eyes met, however, Georgeanne softened — her lips, her glare, her expression. Even the set of her shoulders eased, and a hot current ran through Silviu's whole body. She took his breath away.

Gold flashed, heat sparked. Their chemistry was undeniable, and — he hoped — stronger than ever after the night's pleasures. His senses in an uproar, it took a moment for Silviu to answer. "You're just in time, my love."

He couldn't help himself. Eyes locked, unable to tear his gaze from her face, he reached out to cup Georgie's cheek. He felt the hitch in her breath when she asked, "In time for what?"

Silviu wished they were anywhere else in the world for

any other reason. Then he could scoop her up in his arms and take her to bed and keep her there until she forgot how to speak altogether. But Costel was pushing past him with Christiana on his heels, and Daniel Levy would reach them in just a few minutes. There was no time for romantic thoughts or wayward wishes.

"The final Councilman's arrival." Reluctantly releasing his bride, Silviu waved toward the garden.

The space they occupied was a good size, located at a corner, tucked under a high, arched roof and paved with massive, age-worn flagstones. Running a portion of the length of the Palace's wall and a little beyond, the patio jutted out into the garden, but the two open sides were contained by ornamental columns and thick hedges.

"An excellent location to observe the Council Administrator's office," Costel murmured. "This is one of my favorite spots on the castle grounds, as a matter of fact."

"Is it?" Silviu turned to his brother with a raised brow and a mild irritation at the idea that the man had spent time peeping through Emeric's windows, but not networking with other witches.

Costel shrugged and confronted the quiet figure leaning against the far column. Bijoux faced him with wide eyes and a peaceful expression, in spite of the tension Silviu could practically see flowing from her. She clutched two books to her chest tight enough to pale her entire forearm.

"What is she doing here, Silviu?" his brother demanded.

Bijoux's dimples made an appearance. "It's my house."

Objectively, Silviu could see the appeal she would hold for his brother. Though he suspected her mind was razor sharp, she wouldn't set out to constantly remind people of that fact as Georgie did. Bijoux was softer than that, and more accepting of the patriarchal system than Ileana had ever been. In all, she was most probably the sweetest woman Costel had ever met.

"Gods help us all."

"What was that, Silviu?"

Shaking his head, he looked at his brother, who was frowning in Bijoux's direction. "I need her help, Costel."

"I told you! I don't want her—"

"He may not even need my talent," Bijoux informed him with a hefty measure of exasperation in her voice. "Sometimes, if my father has his window open, it's possible to overhear what is being discussed inside his office from this patio."

"Ah, I see." Realization struck, and Silviu gained new respect for his brother's deviousness.

Flushing slightly, Costel cleared his throat. "We'll have to take your word for it, of course. I will, however, concede that this place is an excellent blind from which to spy on Daniel Levy."

"We're not spying. We're observing." Silviu said.

Costel leaned against the column opposite Bijoux's and twisted his body to see beyond it, toward the path Daniel would use to reach the gardener's entrance. "I have no idea what you hope to learn if you don't interact with the man."

"Who says we won't?" Silviu flicked his finger toward the lawn. "Eliasz and Ileana are waiting for him by the door. Adam is playing on the grass with the kitty."

They all looked where Silviu pointed. Adam lay on the cold, damp ground at the edge of a bed of winter-dead roses. Dressed in faded khakis as he was, he nearly blended in, though the prize for camouflage would have to go to Tulah. The Shimizu witch was in her cat form, a sleek black shadow perched between her husband's feet.

"That's no good." Georgie moved toward the edge of the paving stones, her toes nearly in the shrubbery. She put her hands on her hips and shook her head, squinting at Tulah as if she were angry, but her words revealed a different emotion altogether. "That bastard Graves revealed her secret at his wedding, remember? In fact, it was Daniel who discovered Tulah's mother was a kitsune witch, if memory serves me correctly. He knows she can change her physical form."

"So what? Like my brother said, we're not going to get far unless we ask Daniel some questions, and Adam is the only one that hasn't had some kind of run-in with him."

"I haven't either," Georgie stated.

Silviu started then stared. He thought back quickly over the events of the past several weeks and all the gossip he'd devoured about his wife before their reunion. Daniel didn't have much use for the Lovasz coven, in general, and Christiana and Milo had also riled the Father's temper. But Silviu had never heard of any problems between Georgie and Daniel, in all the years they'd crossed paths, both politically and socially.

"No, you haven't had a run-in with Father Levy," he said slowly. "Which is odd and interesting, now that it's been pointed out."

"Why odd?" she asked.

"You stand on opposite sides of the Schism."

Georgie shrugged. "It would be perfectly natural for me to greet him as he arrives, Silviu."

"I think your husband has the better strategy right now, Georgie," Christiana spoke up. She immediately grimaced. "It pains me to agree with a patriarchal male, but you should stay here, for now."

Silviu nodded. "We will simply observe. Later, we can formulate a better plan to deal with Daniel and learn who he's working with."

"I've known Daniel for a very long time," Georgie protested. "He's never been anything but kind and helpful."

"Was that before or after he accused my husband of having an affair with Suzette?" Chris spat. "When, in truth, it was him."

Silviu pinched the bridge of his nose. "I don't want you to rush in recklessly, love. I know you want answers—so do I—but Daniel could prove dangerous—"

"Oh, please." Georgie rolled her eyes.

Bijoux tried to help. "He's trying to be inconspicuous, which only makes his arrival stand out more—like coming through the gardens rather than using the door the rest of you used, or even the main doors."

"He's trying to avoid notice, coming *this* early in the morning, the very day the Council will be called to session." Silviu's words came rapidly, as the determined look in Georgie's eyes hardened and his instincts went haywire. There were times when his bride lost her senses and rushed into the fray without considering possible consequences — no doubt a result of a lifetime of dealing with witches while being immune to their magic.

"I know what he's trying to do," she told him.

"Daniel's coming up the path," Costel announced in hasty whisper.

Bijoux gasped and tightened her hold on her books. Silver light flashed and swirled. Silviu's lips quirked at the thought that the woman had never been involved in any intrigue and that perhaps their observation of Daniel Levy was the most exciting thing that had ever happened to her. He hoped she could maintain her composure long enough to help him ferret out the deepest and darkest of Daniel's secrets.

The man in question rounded the corner of the building. Dawn's light picked out orange and gold highlights in his pale hair and laid a swath of coral across his face. Though he supposed Daniel was a man of above-average handsomeness, Silviu had never bothered to pay attention to the Levy Father's looks — until he stood on a patio in the shadow of a miniature pine tree and tried to determine whether or not the man's face could give clues to his character. Unfortunately, Daniel's countenance was typically open, guileless, his blue eyes shining with warmth and laughter.

"I'm having trouble reading him," Bijoux whispered.

Georgie lifted her chin and glared at Silviu. "I know how to read his expression, his body language. I've known him for years, worked with him closely. Where Bijoux is failing, I would succeed with a simple conversation."

Silviu waved his wife to silence as Daniel stopped on the path. The faintest of greetings came to the group gathered on the patio. "Adam Davenold. I didn't expect to see you here. And I will assume the feline is your female?"

Adam gave a jaunty wave from his prone position, but Silviu couldn't hear a word the man said. Slowly, Georgie's cousin sat up and Tulah leapt into his arms. Adam held the cat protectively, close to his chest.

"Can anyone make out what they're saying?" Silviu looked around.

Everyone shook their heads.

"I can cast a spell to magnify the sound," Christiana offered.

On the path, Daniel elevated his head and stepped past Adam.

Silviu nearly growled in frustration. "I don't want to use any magic that might be noticed, and it's too late, anyway. Bijoux, what do you see?"

She stared at Daniel intently, her lower lip caught between her teeth. Her cheeks were red and a vein throbbed in her forehead. Silver blazed around her entire body. "I can't...I can't really see anything. Except what we all see with our eyes."

"Don't hurt yourself trying," Silviu muttered.

Costel stepped forward and laid his hand on his lover's back. Silver flared into gold, and even Christiana gasped as the magical connection manifested visibly. Bijoux relaxed a little but still seemed obstructed.

"Tone it down," Silviu warned.

"I can't read him," Bijoux said.

Georgie frowned. "Why not?"

"I don't know."

It didn't seem that Daniel saw the flash of gold behind the hedges, so Silviu took the chance of using his magic to enhance the others'. He added a bit of his strength to Costel and Bijoux's, then waved a hand, casting a quick spell to amplify the sound of voices as Daniel reached Eliasz. "Try again."

Bijoux and Costel were in nearly perfect sync. Silviu tried not to be jealous as a river of molten gold flowed from the couple and raced through the garden. He had no idea whether or not it was visible—as he always saw magic in use, it was occasionally difficult for him to tell if others observed what he did—but Christiana didn't gasp or appear to follow the sight with her eyes, so Silviu hoped…

Less than a heartbeat later, Daniel stiffened, and Silviu jumped for the Matched magic. His influence shot out of his fingertips, wrapping the golden stream in an attempt to hide it. "You've got to be more careful! Don't let him see."

Costel sent a questioning glance Silviu's way, but it was Christiana who asked, "See what?"

Silviu and Georgie both turned to her with carefully neutral expressions. Silviu bit his lip and let his wife take the lead. "You didn't see the magic?" she asked her cousin.

Chris shook her head. "No."

"It wasn't visible?" Silviu breathed.

"Perhaps Eliasz or Ileana said something that put him on guard?" Georgie suggested.

Silviu shook his head. "They're exchanging greetings. Chitchat, small talk. Daniel's asking if they've set a date for the Bestowal ceremony."

She turned to Bijoux. "Why can't you read him?"

The other woman shook her head, perspiration beginning to stand out on her brow. "I don't know. I can read Eliasz and Ileana, though. Ileana isn't all that comfortable right now, but Eliasz is picking his words very carefully. Apparently, Daniel expects his utmost loyalty in return for a Council seat."

"A seat he's taking for himself." Silviu waved any doubts away. "Eliasz is loyal to me."

"Are you certain?" Costel asked.

"Yes." Silviu nodded. "I don't doubt our brother-in-law or our sister."

"Daniel just sent them both on their way." Georgie tipped

her head toward the medieval arcade where the Levy witches had met up. Eliasz and Ileana turned and walked down the paved path in an unhurried stroll that would bring them to the patio while Daniel hauled open a small door set in the stone wall. The man disappeared inside. Eliasz and Ileana picked up their pace.

Adam and Tulah burst through the bushes a few moments before the other couple. As Daniel was out of sight, Silviu watched Bijoux sweat and struggle. Costel murmured words of encouragement, interspersed with pleas that she be careful. He begged her to take it easy.

Silviu didn't want her to take it easy — not while Georgie's expression grew ever more thoughtful and the set of her lips thinned in stubbornness. Silviu had a terrible feeling in the pit of his stomach.

"He's...different," Eliasz muttered, pushing past a hedge. "There's a huge difference in his demeanor since he was at my home, even since he was at *your* home, Georgie."

"Tulah's not happy, either," Adam stated. He cuddled his puffed-up kitten close and stroked her head.

Daniel appeared in Emeric's office window. The men shook hands. Christiana moved to the edge of the paving stones and squinted. "Is that just a typical greeting, then?"

Enough was enough. Silviu's instincts were going mad, but he couldn't pinpoint the source of his unease. Certainly it wasn't Daniel — Silviu's skin had never crawled in the man's presence before. Even when he'd run up against the dark magic witch in his enchanted searches, Silviu had never felt such disquiet. He feared it had something to do with his wife.

Desperation had him reaching for Costel and Bijoux. He latched onto both their shoulders and let a nearly overwhelming amount of his magic go all at once. Power rocked the three of them, but Costel was the Father of the most talented coven, and contained his brother's force with only a soft grunt to show his exertion. Silviu held back just enough to keep from hurting them. A smooth, steady river of influence wrapped their golden, Matched power and tripled the outpouring. Silviu enhanced their efforts as only a Reap witch could.

Bijoux gasped and Costel wrapped his arm around her when she swayed. The color of her face lightened. The hue of her eyes darkened. Her lower lip trembled, but she shook her head. "I'm only getting bits and pieces, flashes of insight that don't make sense."

"Like what?"

"Um…" Bijoux took a deep breath. "A blonde-haired woman. An old man, his eyes hard and dangerous. A vision of Madeleine. I don't know… There is no emotion with it, no words or thoughts beyond the image. And…there's a wall."

"Yes," Silviu hissed. "I know that wall. I've come up against it myself. The dark magic witch at work, hiding what we need to know behind it."

Georgie straightened her shoulders. "All right, then. My turn."

She stepped off the patio and Silviu finally understood the source of the nervousness attacking his ability to think, stand and plan. His wife had been coming to her own conclusions about the way they were going about things. He had known it would only be a matter of time before she threw herself at the problem, but he still tried to hold her back.

She danced out of his reach. "Stop," she demanded. "Let me do what I do. Daniel isn't going to hurt me. He can't and he won't even try in front of Emeric."

Denying his need to command her back to his side, pushing beyond his desire to keep her safe, Silviu forced himself to see merit in her words. If nothing else, proving to her that he trusted her as much as he wanted her to trust him was a powerful motive to let her go.

He still spoke through clenched teeth. "Be careful, my love."

Her expression changed dramatically. Her lips eased, her

shoulders relaxed and her eyes filled with an emotion Silviu had never seen before. The bond they shared occasionally allowed him glimpses into the heart of her—her emotions and motivation—and, at that moment, their connection shimmered with her joy in him.

Him letting her walk into danger had made her happy. Silviu cocked his head and watched her step back. No, he knew better. She was happy because he'd treated her like an equal.

He sighed and repeated himself. "Be careful."

She grinned and disappeared through the same door Daniel had used. A few moments after she reappeared in Emeric's window, her Bane shields blazed into life.

Silviu ran full-out.

Chapter Twenty-One

Georgeanne

Heart pounding, palms sweating, Georgeanne flung open the door to Emeric Laurent's office and pinned the new arrival with a cold glare. "Daniel, how are you?"

She wasn't certain why she was nervous. She'd been in much tougher situations, after all. Her intrusion of the Council Administrator's office was merely a social call, though somewhat abrupt and unscheduled. She'd known Daniel Levy for years, had always worked well with him and never had a conflict. Her anxiety could only be a direct result of the tension her friends and family had felt.

"Georgeanne." Daniel blinked, but his warm, sunny smile spread across his mouth with only a heartbeat's hesitation. This close, she could see the lines of stress at the corners of his blue eyes, as well as feel a curious prickle of energy radiating from his body.

For a moment, she thought her Bane shields had risen to the challenge, but the uncomfortable tingling subsided before it had a chance to make her fully aware of its presence. She glanced around quickly, but there was no magic in play.

Perhaps the Council Administrator had some sort of spell in place at the door, and she simply hadn't noticed when she'd walked through it.

Emeric Laurent finally recovered from the shock of her dynamic entrance. He shot to his feet behind his massive desk and cleared his throat. His Adam's apple bobbed as his attention bounced between the two witches before him.

"*Georgeanne*, please explain your intrusion."

Ignoring him, she glued her gaze to Father Levy. "I would say it's nice to see you again, Daniel, but the circumstances aren't to my liking."

"I understand," he said. So calm, so conciliatory.

"Do you? What's going on?"

He held his hands wide. "What do you mean?"

"You have a very untimely arrival this morning. I'm surprised you weren't here yesterday."

"I was delayed. There are many aspects of Family business I must see to directly."

"Ah." Georgie fought to remain relaxed. "Like after Constance's wedding."

Daniel had shown up at the Davenold estate in England after the woman's failed wedding to Graves Ngozi. As the secondary branch of the Ngozi Family was located in London, Daniel had used the proximity as reason enough to drop in on Madeleine Davenold, who'd fallen ill during the festivities. Silviu had believed Daniel was simply assessing Madeleine's chances of survival, but the Levy Father had claimed he'd had Family business to take care of before departing England and was simply offered hospitality by the daughter of the house, Georgie's cousin, Suzette.

"The Levy witches are spread far and wide," he reminded her. "It's my duty to look after them all."

"Of course. And how is your Family?"

Daniel's lips turned down. "Warner killed himself. He must have loved Graves more than I realized. I suppose he simply couldn't bear it..."

"I'm sorry to hear that." Georgie hadn't known Graves' lover very well, but he'd once unknowingly helped her out of a dangerous situation.

Daniel shook his head. "Both of us have lost people we love, haven't we?"

"Georgeanne," Emeric interjected. "Perhaps you and Father Levy could continue your conversation later? I do have business with him—"

"Yes, you certainly do." Georgie nodded mockingly. "You must discuss the complaint he lodged against my husband." She looked at Daniel. "In spite of all the duties your large and widespread Family heap upon your plate, you still had ample opportunity to file a protest with the Council Administrator concerning Silviu's possible nomination to the High Seat."

"My dear, this is a debate best left for the Council floor."

Something dark moved through Daniel's pale eyes. A cold shiver worked down Georgie's spine and clutched at her heart, poking at instincts she'd learned to listen to long ago. She blinked, and the only thing she could see in Daniel's gaze was compassion—or perhaps pity.

She went on the offensive.

"You left the Davenold estate in England before we had a chance to speak." She lifted her chin and watched him carefully.

"You'd just lost your grandmother. I didn't want to overstay my welcome."

"You weren't welcome in the first place."

"Your cousin offered me hospitality, Georgie."

"And a warm hole to stick your dick in, right?"

Daniel's cheeks flamed.

Emeric's breath left him in a sharp blast. "Is that about enough, or do you need assistance with something, Mother Davenold?"

"I do need something, Monsieur Laurent," Georgie agreed. Her veins sizzled with adrenaline. "I need to know who Daniel is working with. I need to know who is responsible for murdering my grandmother, the former Davenold Matriarch and High Seat of the Council of Covens. And I need to know just why in the Christians' Hell Father Levy ever thought I would allow him to publicly malign my husband."

"I have maligned no one." Daniel lifted his hands in the classic sign of surrender. "But I have a duty to the Council, Georgeanne. I must divulge the knowledge I have gleaned when there could be possible, and terrible, consequences for the witching world."

"What responsibility? You've only been a Councilman for a ridiculously short time and only because you refuse to nominate anyone else, in spite of assurances to the contrary."

Daniel's eyebrows winged upward. "What assurances, and to whom, Georgeanne?"

She wasn't about to confirm Eliasz's disloyalty to his own Father. As far as she was concerned, it was better all around for Daniel to believe Eliasz was an obedient little Levy. Then she and Silviu would be able to get more reliable information about the inner workings of the largest Family in the witching world.

Instead, she waved her hand sharply. "You haven't even been present at a Council session yet, but you believe you know what's best for all the covens?"

"Silviu hasn't been present, either, but he believes he should be the natural choice to fill your late grandmother's position."

Georgeanne paused on the verge of opening her mouth. She was too emotional and Daniel was responding to her verbal jabs with calm, and a reasonably well-plotted argument. She was, on the whole, thankful that only Emeric bore witness, as she knew the confidence radiating from the patriarchal male would only help his cause and hurt hers.

She switched tactics.

"Tell me, Daniel. Whatever did you hope to gain by fucking my cousin? Did you really promise her a baby?" Georgie ignored Emeric's gasp and didn't even glance his way as the man collapsed back into his chair.

Daniel, however, turned to face their host directly. "Monsieur Laurent, my deepest apologies for the turn this conversation has taken. May I beg a moment of privacy in your office with Mother Davenold?"

"Of course." Emeric jumped to his feet and hurried toward the door. As he passed, he leveled Georgie with a heated stare. "Caution," he murmured in French.

The door closed behind him and Georgie disregarded Emeric's warning. "Suzette would never have kept the Davenold Motherhood, no matter how many enhancements your black magic witch laid on her. Someone would have assassinated her with a steak knife before dinner ended that very night."

Daniel watched her with an intensity that was unsettling. "Like you?"

Georgie smiled thinly. "No. I had no need to kill her. I made her Bane instead."

"According to history, that is what Bane-born witches do," he said with a shrug. "It doesn't surprise me that Madeleine would make certain you knew how to utilize your talent, but it does make me wonder that you never used it to save her life."

For one horrific moment, Georgie's emotions threatened to destroy the dam she'd built inside her head. Confusion and shock, anguish and grief all slammed up against the barrier, causing cracks she knew she'd have to deal with soon. With so much else demanding her attention, she had no time to focus on anything but Silviu's nomination to the High Seat.

But, Goddess, it was hard. In that moment, facing a man Georgie *knew* had played some part in her grandmother's murder, with the idea that she could have—and *should* have—been able to save Madeleine's life twisting through her head, the world turned bleak. Dark and merciless. Doubts, fears and a pain deeper than any she'd ever known weighed on Georgie's heart.

She pushed it all back and raised her chin. "Look at you," she managed to croon, though, her voice was garbled and strained. "You must be an expert on Bane witches. And, dare I say, Reap witches, too?"

Daniel's eyes narrowed. "Why didn't you save your grandmother, Georgeanne? So desperate to take her position?"

"Is that why you entered into a conspiracy to kill her in the first place?" She could hardly speak past the pulsating lump in her throat, but Georgie would be damned if she let the Levy Father know of her ignorance in her own abilities. Such a weakness could not even be contemplated.

But the look in Daniel's eye told her he'd seen far more than she wanted. He responded gently, "I used to think we would have been perfect together, Georgeanne. A marriage to me would have achieved the same goals as marriage to... *him*."

His words surprised her, but they also gave her the strength to push past her own heartache. She would have dismissed his statement out of hand, but memories flooded her, all the times Daniel had taken up her cause, all the ways he'd supported her over the years. His kindness.

All an act.

She dismissed his idiocy with a shake of her head. "A marriage between the two largest covens, Daniel? We wouldn't have survived our honeymoon."

"We would have done more than that, my dear, but instead, you're stuck with a Lovasz."

"Silviu is my Magic Match." There had been far too many occurrences where the golden light produced between them had been visible in Daniel's company. The Levy Father had been there when Silviu had pulled her back from the brink of death, too. There was no use in denying the facts.

"A man could hope." Daniel smiled. "We would have been a force to be reckoned with—powerful, influential, loved by all. Who is Silviu Lovasz? The world watches him, Georgie, waiting for the moment the Lovasz madness takes over."

She finally gave in to the need to cross her arms over her chest. "Is that the reason you've been so solicitous over the years? Hoping to get into my pants, Daniel? Or into my Motherhood position?"

"You don't think I care about you?"

"Well, when you couldn't have me, you picked up a cheap

look-alike in my cousin. Apparently matriarchal witches are interchangeable to you."

"Georgie—"

"*Don't* call me Georgie! Only my friends call me Georgie, and you are no longer my friend." She yanked her arms from their folded position, lifting a finger as she lunged into Daniel's face. "Your petition against my husband will not stand."

"It's a shame you married him. I couldn't believe it when I realized what you'd done in Poland. Gods! Sex and blood, Georgeanne? There will be no getting rid of him now, which means you are of little use to me anymore."

She stumbled back. "Were you spying on us?"

Even Silviu's seemingly all-knowing father had not understood that combining sex and blood would result in a bond deeper than any mere marriage. She and Silviu had unwittingly connected their souls at Eliasz's home, though she hadn't known it and Silviu swore he hadn't realized until Adam had asked about such a connection with Tulah. It was a hard truth to face, but after the previous night, she had no more regrets about her actions.

But to think Daniel Levy had *watched*…

He scowled. "It was easy enough to see. The connection blazed between you, though it was weak and unsteady."

Realization struck, and Georgeanne didn't know whether to be relieved or alarmed at the truth. "You can see magic."

"I can see a lot of things, like the downfall of our people, if Silviu Lovasz is allowed to take the High Seat. Georgie, listen to me, I know he's a Reap witch."

"Of course you do," she spat. "The Ngozis forced my husband's hand. He had no choice but to show his strength in order to save me from the madman you would have allied your coven with."

"The last Reap witch to sit the High Seat nearly destroyed us. Another Lovasz, Georgeanne. He siphoned off the magic from the combined covens, but at least he was on his own. He didn't have a Bane Magic Match to act as a reservoir."

Daniel shot forward and grabbed Georgeanne by her elbows. He gave her a slight shake, not enough to even rattle her teeth, but his grip was strong and a bolt of fear electrified her skin. Bane shields rose and fell, a rainbow of colors shimmering for some reason she couldn't fathom. There was no magic in play.

"Whatever you think," Daniel raged, "I am doing what's best for all of us."

"Get your fucking hands off my wife before I murder you where you stand."

The door crashed against the wall in the same instant Silviu's voice filled the room. Gold light flared bright enough to blind Georgie as five points of pressure sent the nerves in her shoulder into overdrive. His grip tightening, Silviu ripped her from Daniel's hold, and she staggered back to squint up at her husband's face. Her stomach dropped. The only other time she'd seen him don such a lethal expression had been when he'd fought his grandfather to keep her safe.

Daniel bared his teeth. "Lovasz. Violence coming from you doesn't surprise me."

"Do not touch my wife." Silviu slid forward, invading the Levy Father's personal space, intimidating and dangerously serious. As always when his anger was at its peak, his voice was quiet and cold. "Ever."

As much as Georgie would have liked to have finished the discussion, to find out what Daniel knew and what he planned, and as much as she'd like to rail at Silviu for not trusting her to protect herself, she couldn't. Her husband was a heartbeat from true carnage, and Daniel looked ready to poke the bear. Though Madeleine had been fond of accusing her of reckless anger, Georgie had learned well the value of strategic retreat.

"Let's go, Silviu." She stroked her hand down his arm and caught his fingers. A gentle tug gained no results. "My discussion with Father Levy is finished. I have nothing more to say to him."

It took a moment to get Silviu moving. Georgie applied

gentle pressure, a steady draw on his hand as silent encouragement. Slowly — so fucking slowly Georgie gritted her teeth to keep from screaming — he stepped back, then took another step. Never once did he drop eye contact with Daniel Levy as he left Emeric's office.

Georgie didn't breathe properly until they were at the end of the hallway. Then she said, "I could have handled him myself, you know."

In the blink of an eye, her back was to the wall. Her curls wrapped Silviu's fingers as he buried them in her hair, his grip angling her head up to his. He held her off the floor and even flexing her toes didn't allow her to find the stone she had been standing on.

"You're mine to protect," he snarled into her face. "I will take care of you whenever I see a need, whether you like it or not. That man may be responsible for a number of crimes, and I will not allow him to get so close to you ever again."

"I just—"

With a speed that spoke of violence and frustration, Silviu captured her lips with his. Georgie gasped and he took advantage, sliding into her mouth with a hot glide that influenced nerves much lower than the ones he stroked directly. Angry, hard thrusts and sharp nips had her squirming in delight against the tightening hold on her hair.

Everything was different that morning. The sensations she'd never thought she'd get used to had tripled sometime during the night, overwhelming her completely. Her muscles quivered and shook, her bones ached and she would have sworn that golden light filled her all the way to her toes. A kiss unlike any other Silviu had ever given her set her ablaze. Rough and hungry, he ravished her lips, leaving them swollen and bruised when he pulled away, all too soon.

"I know you can handle yourself." His voice came at her like rocks rolling down a gravel hill. "I trust you to protect yourself, Georgeanne, or you would never have been in

Emeric's office alone with that man. That doesn't mean that I won't step in, every chance I get."

"This is part of the problem with us, Silviu—"

"Why should it be? You step in on my behalf whenever you see a need, as well. The two of us will just have to learn to adapt to having help." He loosened his grip and levered his body away from hers.

Georgie took a deep breath and smoothed her skirt, swiftly recognizing another truth. She had more in common with her husband than she'd previously thought, but suddenly that didn't sound as terrifying as it used to. Having someone she could depend on would be a new experience for her and, after the previous night's lessons in trust, she was willing to start fresh with Silviu.

"All right," she agreed. "We'll…work it out. We'll find better ways…"

"Yes." Silviu grinned, though it was a maniacal thing, with his temper still running high enough to color his cheeks and turn his eyes to molten mercury. Then he sighed. "As much as I would love to begin this new sentiment between us in a more intimate fashion, I believe we should focus on researching Bane and Reap witches."

"You heard what Daniel said?"

"I did." Silviu frowned. "And we must be prepared for him to repeat his accusations to the Council."

Chapter Twenty-Two

Costel

The Council Administrator banged on the table. "So begins our brief recess."

Failing to hide his impatience, Costel jumped to his feet. Pomp and circumstance was the opening act of every Council session, but the covens were outdoing themselves today, with long-winded commemorations of Madeleine Davenold. Costel stretched and grimaced, the muscles in his back revolting after sitting for so long.

Glancing toward the window, he saw how close the sun was to the western horizon and grimaced once again. Unfortunately, the Council's agenda hadn't even been read yet, and, traditionally, no official business would take place until that happened. Instead of recessing for supper, as he would have preferred, Costel would be expected back in a mere ten minutes, and the Council session would begin in earnest.

As he refilled his glass with fresh water at the table set against the wall, he noticed his brother attempting to catch his eye. When Costel followed Silviu's nod, he saw Ileana and Eliasz fidgeting in the wide doorway. With a sigh, he joined them.

"We don't have much time," Silviu murmured.

They all slipped into another room, one of the many decorating the corridor across from the long Council Chamber. Costel looked around at the little group and suddenly realized what a formidable alliance Silviu and Georgeanne had created. Powerful witches such as Ileana,

Christiana and Adam, and those with rare talents, like Eliasz, Milo and Tulah. Bijoux joined them as well, clutching the same book she'd had with her earlier, and Costel's chest warmed to think that he'd been included with such an imposing assembly of witches.

Ileana nodded. "Bane witches break dark magic. That is literally what they are born to do."

"We know." Georgie ran her hand through her curls before folding her arms over her chest. "I wish I'd known it a long time ago, but that can't be helped now. What else did you learn?"

While Silviu, Georgie, Adam and Costel had been in attendance at the Council's drawn-out memorial service for their late High Seat, the rest of the group had been occupied with other tasks. Ileana, Eliasz and Bijoux had been reading everything they could on Bane and Reap witches, while Christiana and Milo had researched black magic in all its modes. Tulah, in the form of a cat, had been sent to search Daniel Levy's room.

Costel turned to her in question. She was back in her human form and fully clothed. "What did you find, Tulah?"

She shook her head. "Too much is warded. I don't have the ability to break through and find anything of value. It was all I could do just to get into Father Levy's bedroom."

"As soon as I formally transfer the Lovasz seat to Silviu, I won't be required to attend the meetings anymore." Costel straightened his shoulders. "I'll break the wards and we'll see what we can find."

"Do you have magic powerful enough for that?" Milo asked.

Eliasz snorted. "He's the second strongest witch in the room. Trust me. I've seen him in action."

"Third strongest," Silviu protested. "Don't let the word 'Bane' fool you. You could break the wards, too, my love."

"But I couldn't put them back into place, and Daniel would know we'd been snooping." Georgie cocked her head. "Speaking of which, don't any of you find it odd that

Father Levy, a man famous for his weak magic, has wards a kitsune shape-shifter can't wriggle through?"

Everyone knew cats could get themselves into interesting places. They all stopped to digest the information before Silviu waved a hand. "The enhancement of the dark magic witch, no doubt. We'll come back to that when we have more time. Iley, what did you learn?"

"Bane witches are literally born to break dark magic," she repeated immediately. "The reason they are so rare is that a baby is only born when there is a need."

"But most Bane witches are made," Costel said slowly.

"That's just a term people used to describe witches who have lost their magic, *mon lapin*." Bijoux put her book down on the table, opening it to a place she'd marked. She pointed to the words. "Bane-born witches, however, seem to have a great deal of magic, but it is blocked from their use."

"That's what my father always claimed." Silviu leaned over to read the text of Bijoux's book. "I have reason to believe he was right. Just look at what Georgie can do."

"Not without you, though," she said. "I can't do anything without your magic."

He shrugged. "I enhance—"

"Exactly!" Bijoux clapped her hands. "That is the heart of the matter, isn't it, Ileana?"

She nodded. "Bane witches are the opposite of enhancement magic."

"Bane-born witches have only been born in the same generation as powerful dark magic witches. We have charted this until our eyes crossed, while you were in your meeting." Bijoux flipped to the back of her book and pulled out a loose sheet of paper. A hastily scrawled timeline spread across the front and continued onto the back.

Georgie reached for it.

"These are all the documented Bane witches?" Georgie glanced up, then back down. "But how could you get that information?"

Eliasz winced. "Apparently, Reap witches have to be

registered with the Council, which probably means quite a few will forever be unknown to us, like Silviu."

"My father would never have registered me. That would have lost him the advantage."

"Exactly." Eliasz nodded. "But Bane witches are a little different, in that respect. We have lunar charts and covens file a census with the Council every five years, so the records were easy enough to match up, though time-consuming."

Ileana added, "We searched through records of pregnant witches, witches who claimed stillborn pregnancies, children who disappeared shortly after birth, death records and, yes, birth records, too."

"Bane witches weren't hidden?" Adam looked around the group. "I always thought other covens would be ashamed to admit they had one in their midst."

Eliasz waved the words away. "It's magic and time of birth, not a genetic defect to show the Family's deficits, so we found a number of cases where the Family never bothered to hide the facts and even took pride in handling, uh…" He winced.

"Most Bane-born babies are killed by their covens," Georgie whispered. "We are abominations."

"More like salvations." Bijoux opened to another page. "But scary. You, *mon amie*, are a powerful black-magic witch who was born to break dark magic. Fighting fire with fire, but you are blocked from the flames except when facing the heat…so to speak."

Georgie blinked. "What?"

"A few Bane children survived into adulthood, and many were spared until their teenage years in the hopes that their magic would eventually develop."

"That's what my grandmother had hoped, too."

"Then I'm sure she was pleased to see it did develop." Bijoux flashed her dimples, making Costel's heart tremble. "You just need a key to unlock it."

"A Reap witch."

"Not necessarily," Bijoux sang. "The Bane talents unlock

with a great power, usually the witch with dark leanings they were born to defeat. You see, Bane have been born during generations where powerful black magic is being used, not always in line with Reap witches, though."

Ileana continued the explanation. "Reap witches are born every few generations, but Bane witches can be born with a millennium or more between. Read the chart you're holding, Georgie. Every time a Bane witch was born, a significant event involving dark or black magic soon followed — roughly twenty years after the birth, in fact."

"So we researched dark magic." Christiana joined the conversation by sharing what she and Milo had discovered. "Imagine our surprise when we were able to find a corresponding dark magic witch in nearly every instance."

Georgie shook her head. "Using dark magic is a choice. It's not necessarily an evil choice."

Christiana wrinkled her nose and shrugged. "Let's just say a certain type of person tends to gravitate in that direction. Plus, there is a difference in using dark magic, which is a skill, and black magic, which requires a bit of natural talent."

"Influential magic, like mine, is often considered to be dark magic by some," Silviu offered. "But I've found it to be so only when badly misused."

"Misused, yes," Milo interjected. "In some cases, notoriously misused, which is how we found them so easily in the records. Unfortunately, too many Bane babies never make it to adulthood, so there are very few cases — most far back in history — where we could see the role the Bane witch played in the dark magic event."

"Salvation?" Georgie echoed Bijoux's claim.

Christiana nodded. "On three occasions. That's all we could find because of the death rate."

Another moment passed as they absorbed that knowledge. Then Silviu blew out a breath. "What about Reap witches?"

"Reap witches are what they are." Bijoux lifted her shoulders. "Enhanced, but you are probably so very strong, from what Ileana has told me, because you are a Reap witch descended from a Reap witch and born into a magically powerful Family. And you are Matched with a Bane."

"Does it matter who he's Matched with?" Costel spoke up before he could order his thoughts. He hoped no one mocked him for his question.

Bijoux smiled, illuminating his world. "It does, *mon lapin*, so long as the bond has already been formed. Where there is affection, magic blossoms, like in your plants, yes?"

"Ah." Silviu gave Georgie a private look. "Affection can grow between two lonely teenagers faster than many adults would expect."

To Costel's surprise, Georgie blushed. Knowing what had happened a decade ago and the consequences of their actions, Costel was amazed to see a glimmer of girlishness in the way Georgie's eyes suddenly sparkled. It was plain as day. Whatever connection they'd found ten years ago had been a potent force and was even stronger now, after everything they'd gone through.

Georgie cleared her throat, but she was still breathless when she said, "Our recess is about over. Can everyone keep researching? We need as much information as possible."

Chris answered with a nod. "Hopefully we'll have more for you when the meeting ends for the day."

With that promise filling the atmosphere with determination, they all began to file out of the room. Before Costel reached the door, however, his siblings stopped him. They were alone, just the three of them for the first time in weeks.

Silviu seemed uncomfortable. Ileana fidgeted for a minute before throwing her arms around Costel's neck and hugging him tightly.

"Thank you," she whispered. "If I had known what you went through for me, with Grandfather, I would have been more subdued. I would have taken more care."

"But then you wouldn't have been you." Costel squeezed her back, then set her away from him. "It was my duty to protect you both."

Silviu and Ileana stiffened, and Costel nearly apologized for the arrogant pride even he had heard in his tone. But then they nodded and blinked their damp eyes.

Silviu reached out to give Costel a hug, slapping him on his back and only releasing him slowly. "Know that we appreciate you and what you've done. We haven't always treated you well, haven't always understood the things you've done or said or given you credit for your strengths. But we've always loved you."

"We love you," Ileana sniffed.

Costel smiled. "I know. I've always known. It's us against the world, right?"

* * * *

Costel shifted in his chair, waiting for Father Laurent to finish speaking. His turn was next, and his stomach was in knots. He hated speaking publicly — except to Lovasz witches. He knew every single witch in his coven by name and by talent. Costel could even feel them individually in the stream of Family magic anchored in his soul. They were part of him, but the witches surrounding the enormous Council table were strangers in almost every way.

"Father Lovasz." Emeric Laurent finally stood and waved to him. "Your business, sir."

Costel took a deep breath and rose on shaking legs. He hated this part, when every eye was on him. He wiped his damp palms on his thighs and straightened his posture.

And saw Bijoux standing by the doorway. She slid farther into the room, propped her shoulder against the wall and dazzled him with a smile. The nerve endings jangling throughout Costel's body stumbled to a halt, becoming utterly calm with her in his sights.

His tone of voice was smooth and composed. "I formally, and freely, relinquish my Family's Council seat to my brother, Silviu. All necessary paperwork has been filed in advance of this meeting and is in no way being coerced or compelled."

Emeric turned to Silviu, who quickly stood. "Do you accept the responsibility of representing the Lovasz coven on this Council?"

"I do," Silviu agreed.

The representative of the patriarchal Serik Family of Kazakhstan raised a finger. "But, aren't you a Davenold now?"

"Lovasz-Davenold."

"Just you?" Burkit Serik pressed. "Or both Families, as well? Who, exactly, belongs where, and who is being represented by the Davenold High Male?"

Georgie cleared her throat. "The hyphen was put in place for my happiness, Burkit. Our betrothal agreement clearly stated I was to become a Lovasz when we married, but as Mother of the matriarchal Davenold coven, that's impossible, isn't it?"

"An important distinction," Silviu murmured. "One I hope you will keep in mind while electing a new High Seat."

"Ah, the High Seat." Daniel Levy got to his feet slowly, his gaze narrowing on Silviu. "That's what this is about, isn't it?"

Tension invaded the Council Chamber. Every seated witch around the table straightened in their chairs. Costel clung to the lip of the tabletop and willed his cramping legs to hold him. Nervousness ran through him, heightened by adrenaline. He was always in bad shape before a confrontation, only gaining a sharp edge of calm once the trouble was underway.

"It's no secret we've been petitioning for the nomination," Silviu conceded.

Costel's suspicion was confirmed. Cold premonition swept through him until his stomach began tying itself into knots again, and even steady eye contact with Bijoux couldn't help. Breathing deeply, he tried not to scream in panic as she edged her way around the outskirts of the room toward him. While the other men faced off over the great expanse of polished hardwood, Costel stepped back, determined to act as her shield when she came to a stop behind him.

"You shouldn't be in here," he muttered.

"You worry too much about things that won't happen." She wound her arms around his waist and laid her head against his back.

"How do you know?"

"I see no violence in anyone's thoughts."

Costel huffed. "There are at least three people present you can't read. You could be wrong—and in danger."

With a shake of his head, Daniel spoke again, breaking into Costel's hushed arguments. "You can't be the High Seat, no matter if you're Silviu Lovasz, Davenold or some hyphenated bastardization of the two, anyway."

"I know my Council precedents very well," Georgie stated clearly. "There is *absolutely* no reason for my husband not to occupy any seat on this Council, including the High Seat."

Reflex pulled Costel's gaze toward the head of the massive table centered in the palatial chamber. The acres of stone surrounding them only enhanced the polished beauty of the throne-like chair positioned to preside over them all. It was currently empty, of course, and draped with black netting, though Representative Cen had brought a length of white silk from her Chinese homeland to lay over the back of the chair. In spite of their magical commonalities, the traditions of whatever culture witches hid within were often absorbed into their own.

Daniel grinned. "Silviu Lovasz is a Reap witch."

There were a few gasps, but many appeared to have already been aware of Silviu's strength. After hearing of the events at the Ngozi-Levy wedding, Costel could only imagine that Father Muso had busied himself spreading tales, as Silviu would never have made that information public himself. To do so would only inspire fear among the others. Reap witches were only spoken about in hushed whispers, stories of their enhanced magic used to frighten children into obedience.

"The last time this Council allowed a Reap witch to claim the High Seat," Daniel continued, "he nearly drained the covens of their magic."

"That's something of an overstatement, don't you think?" Bijoux pushed away from Costel and put her hands on her hips. "I would hardly call it *draining* and neither would anyone else who bothered to read the history."

Costel tried to push his Match behind him as Daniel's gaze landed on her. Bijoux's face flushed and a vein in her forehead throbbed. He knew she was struggling to read the Levy Patriarch. The moment he put his hand on her shoulder and tugged her back, however, her strain eased and she gave a frustrated grunt.

"I can almost see what's in there," she breathed.

"Quiet," he warned her. "Stay out of this."

"I've read the history!" Daniel's normally calm expression momentarily twisted but quickly smoothed out again. "The Reap witch tried to steal everyone's magic, and in a position like the High Seat, it's entirely possible!"

"You're wrong." Silviu waved, regaining all the attention of the room's occupants. "Madeleine herself explained to me how things were done. The magic flows past, allowing the High Seat to access it, but it doesn't reside within the witch. It can't be stolen."

Daniel's snide smile seemed pinched. "Like you couldn't steal your grandfather's magic? It takes a hell of a lot to—"

"My grandfather willingly transferred his magic to me." Costel buried his alarm under the outrage he allowed to color his tone. He'd spent his entire life protecting Silviu and, out of his depth or not, Costel wasn't about to let the Levy Father reveal such a damning fact about his brother. Anger bubbled in his veins and turned his voice to steel. "You are mistaken if you believe otherwise, Father Levy."

"I know what I saw!"

"You are *mistaken*." Costel's voice was lethal.

Silviu intervened. "It doesn't matter. I'm not running for the High Seat."

Georgie's spine straightened so fast she nearly launched out of her chair. She held her position, several inches away from the back with painfully perfect posture while she stared at her husband. Her expression was entirely devoid of emotion.

Costel took pity on her. "You're not, Silviu? After all your wife has done to get you nominated?"

"No." Silviu nodded toward Burkit Serik. "For exactly the reason he stated. In my arrogance, my blind rush toward the top, I overlooked many things." He turned and lifted Georgie's hand, kissing her knuckles as he held her wide-eyed glare. "*Many things*. But I've been thinking and making some new plans."

"Had you *planned* to talk this over with me?" Georgie asked.

"One last broken promise, my love." Silviu spoke without taking his gaze from his wife's. "As it's been stated before, a Family won't follow a different leader if one of their own holds the High Seat."

Georgie's nostrils flared. "The High Seat would overrule the Matriarch."

"When Madeleine died" — Silviu turned to face the entire Council — "the Family power came to me. I am the Davenold Mother. But through me, Georgeanne rules her coven."

At Costel's side, Bijoux gasped. Her voice was loud in the stunned silence. "Because she's Bane, she couldn't take the power. Because she's your Match, she uses whatever magic you give her."

The room erupted. Every witch present seemed to repeat the phrase 'Magic Match' at once, closely followed by a round of unanswered questions. Speaking over each, their debates raged. They wanted to know how such a thing was possible. They speculated on how a Bane witch could have a Match at all. They wondered aloud how long Silviu and

Georgeanne had known such a thing, and whether or not Madeleine had known as well.

"What do you mean?" Emeric finally demanded of his daughter.

The representatives fell silent again, eager to hear her answer.

"In my research"—Bijoux shrugged, her sudden awkwardness communicating itself to Costel until he reached for her hand, then she calmed—"Reap witches have too much magic. That's why they are feared. But as a Bane witch's magic is locked away, that can create a void, a place to put the excess a Reap would wield. Reap and Bane together would theoretically always be a Magic Match, and they would share their magic in ways the rest of us can't contemplate."

Burkit frowned. "So, what are you saying?"

Silviu spoke before anyone else could. "I nominate Georgeanne Lovasz-Davenold to the position of High Seat. She is eligible because she is no longer a Davenold or a matriarchal witch, according to the contract our Families signed twenty years ago. The magic will flow past her, but her Bane shields will keep her separate from it. There will never be any danger of her stealing it."

"And when we need it?" Burkit asked. "The High Seat has magical duties to perform."

"Then I will help her."

"Take over and steal it for yourself, through her access to it, you mean," Daniel snarled.

Silviu shook his head. "No, she's stronger than me. Ladies and gentlemen, think of the years you've known her, all the trust she's earned from you. Think of her fairness and intelligence, her compassion and diplomacy."

Silviu paused. He met every eye, took a deep breath then finished. "I think you'll agree, Georgeanne would make the best High Seat our society has ever had."

As if the shock were a bubble that had just burst, every witch in the room was suddenly on their feet and speaking loudly. Each vied for dominance. Thirty different opinions were shouted until Costel would have been surprised to know anybody had heard even one of them. Emeric swiveled, obviously trying to listen to everyone all at once. Then his face turned red and Costel knew the man had reached his limit.

Emeric banged on the table until everyone fell silent. "That is enough! We will stop for the night and reconvene in the morning. I trust by then you will all have gotten yourselves together and moved beyond this hysteria."

Chapter Twenty-Three

Bijoux

Bijoux followed Costel into his bedroom without hesitation. Not then, and probably never again—why bother with the pretense of privacy when so much had been shared between them? His thoughts, his bed, their bodies…

Costel heaved a sigh and leveled her with a glare over his shoulder. He yanked open his armoire and snatched a shirt from a hanger. "You'd better go prepare yourself for supper. I suspect it will be an unpleasant affair, and it will commence shortly."

"Why unpleasant?"

"The politics involved. Silviu's nomination has taken everyone by surprise. Georgeanne isn't someone they'd even considered, both because she is a matriarchal witch and because she is Bane."

"You believe they hadn't thought she could perform the duties of the position? I promise, it's quite the opposite."

Costel gathered more clothes and put them in a pile, along with a towel and his shampoo. "The Davenold Family can't hold the High Seat for two consecutive terms. The Fatherhouses won't let a matriarch hold the position for two consecutive terms, either, whether it's the same coven or not."

"Yes, but she became a Lovasz when she married Silviu. The Lovasz Family is eligible *and* patriarchal."

"True, but I doubt many had thought of either of them in the High Seat position before. I hadn't even known my brother wanted such a thing until very recently." Costel slowly put his razor down on his clothes pile, his thoughts working overtime in Bijoux's head. "I suppose my father always expected Silviu to lead the Council."

Some sad, dejected emotion colored all of Costel's thoughts, but Bijoux couldn't understand what or why. She only knew his pain, the way it wrapped around a thousand memories and shed new light on a thousand comments his father had made.

She came up behind him and wrapped her arms around his stiff body. "What's wrong?"

"My father. Using me to strike back at my grandfather, I'm certain. Like my brother said at the meeting, if Silviu occupied the High Seat, why should our coven members listen to me? All my authority would be stripped."

"That's not true. You're still the Lovasz Father."

"Silviu could override my decisions at any time, and he'd have a greater intimacy with our coven's inner workings than he would with someone else's Family, which means a greater likelihood of interference."

"Would he do that?"

"I don't know, but it proves my father is a sneaky bastard." Costel turned in Bijoux's arms and kissed her forehead. Then he pried her hands apart and gave her a little push toward the door. "Go on. You don't have much time to get changed for supper."

"Today's Council session took a long time." She wrinkled her nose and flopped down onto his bed. "Is it always like that?"

"No. I'm fairly certain today was one of the most unusual meetings the Council has ever experienced."

"Their thoughts were all over the place," Bijoux said. "I still can't read Daniel Levy very well. I tried so hard, but—"

"I noticed." Costel grabbed her hand and tugged her upright.

For a heart-shriveling moment, Bijoux felt as if nothing had changed for them. Costel held himself distant, aloof, as if he'd never given her pleasure or shared his own. He stared down at her with molten mercury eyes, and she stared up at him with desperation and hope. The tension between them stretched and thickened, crackling with the energy of their unvoiced desires, as it used to be — so lonely. Costel's thoughts chased each other in a confusing loop of need and fear, torn between taking her with him when he left and leaving her behind for good — forever.

Then he raised his hand and cupped her cheek. Agony streaked through him, wounding her. "You are so beautiful," he whispered, tortured.

Before she could decipher the muddled thoughts in Costel's head or the sadness in his eyes, his bedroom door flew open. The ornately scrolled handle crashed against the wall, making Bijoux flinch. Costel's body turned to marble, his muscles hardening enough to make him seem to swell as he slid in front of her protectively.

Emeric stood on the threshold, panting like a bull, his head lowered and his nostrils flared. He surged forward and snagged Bijoux's wrist. She planted her feet, but her father had the advantage and towed her from behind Costel's back.

"What are you doing in here with him?" Emeric raged. He turned his glare on Costel. "Don't touch her! Don't *ever* touch her again. She is not for you."

"I know."

Bijoux's mind filled with images of the Lovasz estate and the swooping danger Costel always pictured closing in on them. In less than a heartbeat, the fight drained out of his body and his shoulders slumped. Costel hung his head and shook it. Panic shot through her.

"No!" Bijoux pulled against Emeric's hold, but his fingers never loosened. "I *am* for you. Stop it, Costel! Stop looking like that."

"Let him go, my treasure." Emeric tried to shove her toward the door. "This foolishness is finished."

She twisted to no avail. "We're going to get married."

Costel shook his head.

Emeric's grunt smacked of sympathy. "He won't marry you," her father announced. "He knows he can't protect you, so he will leave you here with me."

"He won't. *Costel*." Bijoux fought her father's hold, gaining enough ground to peer around his body. "Tell him!"

"He's right, Bijoux. Listen to your father now."

"No!"

Costel raised his chin. When he met her gaze, his eyes were cold, shining like metal. "There is no future for us. There is no way you can survive in Romania, no way my grandfather will allow you to reside in the same place." His voice was sharpened steel.

"He will." Bijoux denied his words at the same time she denied the breaking of her heart. She had faith and optimism in spades, and she wouldn't give up.

Except Costel's thoughts had gone dark. She could still see them. She followed the twists and turns of his fears better than he did, perhaps, but there were depths she couldn't plumb. She didn't understand how he could give his grandfather so much influence over his life, how he could choose to appease the old man who'd abused him, rather than leap on the happiness Bijoux knew the two of them would find together.

"He will," she screamed again. "I'll make him. I'll remind him of all the terrible things I know I'll see in his head and make him understand that I'll tell the whole world if he does something out of line."

Costel slashed the air with his hand. "Don't be ridiculous. He'll kill you."

"You won't let him."

"How can I stop him? How can I be at your side every day, every *moment*, until he dies? It's impossible, Bijoux."

"Then we'll live elsewhere. A separate house."

Costel closed his eyes and gritted his teeth. "I must watch him like a hawk. I can't leave him to his own devices. He's too dangerous."

"But your father can—"

"I am the Father! I am responsible for every Lovasz, even Alexandru. But you are *not* a Lovasz."

She gasped as pain swept through her.

"Enough. He won't take you home with him, Bijoux," Emeric murmured. He narrowed his eyes at Costel and pressed his lips together thoughtfully. "That may be the most decent thing he could ever do for you, my treasure."

"No." The repeated denial choked Bijoux, but no more than the tears she desperately tried to swallow. "He loves me. Costel, you love me."

The agony that crossed his face nearly took Bijoux's breath. His lips twisted and his eyes dulled.

"I do," he said.

"Then take me with you."

"I can't, because I love you."

"Show her," Emeric demanded as Bijoux fought even harder to get to Costel. "Show her what will happen to her."

"I don't know what he'll do. He's...unpredictable now. After..."

While Costel spoke, images flashed through his mind. They transferred to Bijoux's head, and, for the first time, she truly paid attention—not just to the bits and pieces she wanted to see, or the bursts of surprising facts, but to all of it. Somewhere in the chaotic mess of Costel's fears was the answer to her dilemma. Sifting through his mind, she went still, barely aware of the tears that tracked down her cheeks and dripped from her chin.

She saw the abuse and the laughter. She saw the good times and the bad, the neutral, the thoughtful and the wishful. She comprehended the complex relationship Costel had with his grandfather, and she appreciated the bond he had with his siblings.

Then she saw them all in a dying rose garden, magic flying, Georgeanne standing in a swirl of silver. Bijoux watched Costel step from the bushes and fight his own grandfather to keep his brother's betrothed safe. She watched Silviu arrive and reach into Alexandru Lovasz's chest, pulling at the Family magic until it was loose and unstable, until Alexandru agreed to relinquish it to Costel. And she saw the aftermath, when Costel, Vasile and Alexandru had returned home and announced that the transfer of power had taken place.

The fallout had been nuclear.

She refused to pay the price. "Costel, we will find a way —"

"It's impossible." Costel sounded truly angry, even more than he had when she'd told Silviu about the abuse he'd taken as a child. Threaded into his wrath was a hopelessness that Bijoux wanted to rail against.

She wasn't given the chance, however. Emeric pushed her from the room and towed her down the hall. She had spent most of her life twisting her father around her little finger, but, in this, he was adamant. She stumbled and staggered, bouncing off walls and nearly tripping down the stairs, but Emeric forced her onward. He refused to release her and didn't stop moving until he reached his office.

He pushed her inside. "Enough of this, Bijoux. Costel Lovasz isn't available for you. Not now, or ever, and I can't even fault him in this."

"He's my Magic Match!" Bijoux could hardly breathe, the sobs exploding in her chest ripping through her lungs until she wondered if a woman could drown in her own tears. She choked and coughed, battling for rationality and calm, but her emotions were too frayed for such self-control.

"Oh, my treasure." Emeric tried to pet her hair, but Bijoux pushed his hand away and scuttled back toward the window. He sent a sad frown after her. "He's doing what he feels is best for you, and that is far more than I would have expected of him."

"I'm not giving up, Papa."

She managed to raise her chin, though she could only guess what she truly looked like. She'd have preferred to appear defiant and determined, but through the prism of her father's thoughts, Bijoux was a mess. Her face was a mottled red and her cheeks were stained by tears. Her lips seemed swollen and her violet eyes were nearly black with distress.

"Don't do this to either yourself or him," Emeric warned.

"I'm marrying him. I'm so close to everything I've ever wanted, and he's a part of that. My Match. I love him."

For a moment, Emeric's thoughts shifted and spun, easily read and easily dismissed, as they followed the same pattern as his words. He wanted her to let Costel go, to remain strong and serene in the face of a rejection neither of the involved parties truly wanted. Costel didn't want to leave Bijoux behind any more than she wanted him to.

"I won't allow it." Rational or not, Bijoux stomped her foot and pouted. "He won't leave me."

Emeric heaved a long-suffering sigh. "Go and pack your bag, my treasure. You will go to the cottage at the edge of the property and remain there until this Council session has concluded and all attendees have returned to their homes."

"*No.*"

"Perhaps the solitude will do you good, Bijoux. You can take stock of what you have done and what could be. You will come to understand that Alexandru Lovasz is a powerful witch who will not tolerate another threat to his status."

"How could I be a threat?"

"You would take his grandson, my treasure. Costel's love and focus would be on you, rather than Alexandru. Costel would rise to your defense, and the old man would take his jealousy out on you." Emeric shook his head. "*I* will not allow *that*, Bijoux. The Laurents would go to war with the Lovaszes."

"It wouldn't be like that."

Her father's lips pursed into lines of strict disapproval. "Now you sound like a little girl, and I know I've taught you better than that. I will make allowances for you tonight—you've had a disappointing shock—but you will get yourself together at once and face reality."

Bijoux straightened her shoulders as best she could and

237

ignored the new wash of tears in her eyes. "Marrying Costel *is* my reality."

Chapter Twenty-Four

Silviu

"Were you ever planning to tell me your true intentions?"

"You sound like my wife." Silviu glanced at his brother. Costel looked terrible. Silviu sighed. "The farther I go down this path, the more I realize how much I've hated it. Having power no longer seems as important as it once did."

"So you have no plans to undermine my authority as the Lovasz Father?"

"Neither yours, nor Georgie's as the Davenold Mother. I just want to protect the people I love and maybe regain their trust."

Costel narrowed his eyes. "Is that why you're over here, pretending your cognac needs a great deal of inspection before you'll take a sip?"

"Partly." Under the guise of refilling his snifter, Silviu took an opportunity to catch his breath. The undercurrents at supper had been dangerous enough, but the after-dinner mingling was proving lethal. Silviu found himself a bit out of his depth, unprepared for the challenge he'd set himself with his nomination of Georgie to the High Seat.

He relished the game, but Georgeanne played it better. All night, she'd been simultaneously gracious and sly, cool and composed. Silviu had been a mass of nerves, struggling to hide the full extent of his anxiety. Georgie had sailed through the parlor with smiles for everyone and diplomatic answers for every pointed question.

As his brother walked away, Silviu thought even Costel was doing better than him that night. Silviu was the only one who seemed close to rabid — understandable, considering he'd been forced to make a huge sacrifice, trading the one thing he'd worked for to save the one thing he treasured. He couldn't be the High Seat and keep Georgeanne's love. Something had to go.

"Do you think the Matriarchs will allow you to keep your new position as Davenold Mother?" A man from the Castillo coven approached and reached past Silviu to snag a bottle of brandy. "You are, after all, a patriarchal man."

"Not anymore." Silviu sipped his cognac and let the smooth, dark fire work over his tongue as he thought about the consequences of his actions.

There was no telling how the other covens would react, but he was betting a great deal on their ability to get used to the notion quickly. His whole life, he'd been associated with the Davenolds. Madeleine's training over the years had also provided a basis of matriarchal understanding other men on his side of the Schism would never achieve. He just hoped the Motherhouses saw that, as well.

"How did the Davenolds react to the news?" the Castillo man asked.

Not having confessed to his new Family yet, Silviu shrugged and lied. "Georgeanne and I have bonded on a level that goes far beyond what most Magic Matches find. We share our abilities fully and completely. The Davenold Family knows this and still recognize her as their Mother, because she is an extension of me."

"Sounds…vulnerable, if you ask me."

"On the contrary. It is a strength that can't be weakened." Silviu stared at the other man, watching to make certain his message was received and fully understood. "It would be pointless to even try to test the bond we share. Ask Graves Ngozi how it went for him."

"He's dead."

"Exactly." Silviu smiled over the rim of his glass.

The other man pointedly lifted an eyebrow. "By Muso's hand."

Silviu leaned toward the aggravating Castillo witch. "I own Muso."

He spun on his heel and walked away before the Lovaszes began another quarrel with the Castillo Family. Years ago, Ileana had been betrothed to one of their lesser-ranked sons, but when Alexandru had broken the betrothal, the chaos that had ensued had been spoken of in every level of witching society. Silviu couldn't afford to antagonize the Castillos again.

He'd only taken a few steps when Mei Lan Cen stepped into his path. Silviu immediately bowed—a short movement giving her just enough respect and not a dollop more. "Councilwoman," he said.

Like many of the matriarchal Cen witches of China, Mei Lan had a powerful talent for working with gemstones, and her fingers were dripping with diamonds, emeralds and sapphires. They flashed in the light as she waved her hand. "Silviu Lovasz, please allow me to congratulate you on coming to your senses and switching sides."

"I'm sure that's exactly what Madeleine had envisioned," he grated out, irritated with the woman's comment, in spite of himself.

Mei Lan smirked. "It is an interesting strategy. Georgeanne is matriarchal, no matter what any agreement between your Families state. She is more staunchly matriarchal than any other witch I know, as a matter of fact. However, without you, she would be ineligible for the High Seat."

"I am aware of all this."

"The patriarchs will insist on a witch from a Fatherhouse to lead this time."

Silviu gritted his teeth. "Georgeanne is now a Lovasz."

"Yes, of course." Mei Lan rolled her eyes. "And yet, she is hobbled by her defect, isn't she? So, by the two of you sharing power... You did say you share power?"

He struggled for calm. He fought for tranquility in the face of Mei Lan's insult to his wife, not to mention such a blatant interrogation and disbelief—but he'd prepared for it. Though he didn't like it — and he was growing frustrated by the repeated questions and the constant explanations — Silviu had faith that his strategy would prevail, and his arrogance couldn't help but thrill to the notion. "We unlock each other's full magical potential."

"How...messy that sounds." Mei Lan gave a delicate shudder.

"Will you support my wife, madam?" He prepared himself for more insults concerning the supposed defects of Bane witches.

To Silviu's surprise, the woman laughed and nodded. "Of course! *Yes*. There is not a Motherhouse who will deny her. The patriarchal covens want a patriarchal leader, which we all understand. They have spent a number of years under the leadership of Mother Madeleine, and, if the situation were reversed, the Motherhouses would ask for the same limitations."

"Yes." Silviu elevated his chin in agreement. "The two sides of the Schism have always traded, in terms of leadership. Traditionally, the next reign would be patriarchal, as Madeleine was matriarchal, but—"

"But you have found a way to put a matriarchal witch on the throne, once again. Georgeanne is, of course, the matriarchs' only hope of a second term in a row." Mei Lan grinned. "It is not *our* side of the divide that will object to this scheme."

"Well then"—Silviu cleared his throat, suddenly unsure of himself or his plan, though his optimism rallied quickly—"thank you, madam. Have a good evening."

He left her to her laughter and made an unsophisticated dash across the room. He was growing increasingly uncomfortable, feeling in desperate need of fresh air and a silent moment to think. Instead, he found his wife in the middle of a knot of witches and joined her.

Georgie was luminous, radiant from within. Her joy and excitement reached out through the crowd around her and her words came fast and sharp — witty, urbane and diplomatic. As he slid his arm around her waist, Silviu had to admit that she was far better at politics than he was or might ever be. She'd once made such a claim and he'd dismissed it, disbelieving that his charm could fall so far short of her own.

"I'm glad to see you enjoying yourself, my love."

She was in her element. The environment she'd been bred for, all of Madeleine's machinations over the years bearing fruit and all of Vasile's manipulations paying off. Georgie had learned at the knees of the very best the witching world had to offer — the most ruthless, cunning and conniving.

Silviu's cock hardened in a rush. Pride burst in his chest and it was all he could do to remain politely at his wife's side without growling, beating his chest or throwing her over his shoulder to haul her away and ravish her in the closest bed he could find.

"I'm having a wonderful time, of course," Georgie replied. "I'm among some of the best company in the world."

Smooth and suave. She was his Match in every way and the knowledge rooted deeply in Silviu's soul. She was the public face. He was the manipulator behind the scenes. She was the one with the honest eyes and the quick response, while he was the bastard that would ferret out all the secrets other witches held close. Two sides of the same coin, joined through blood and pleasure — and love.

Just thinking such thoughts had a golden sheen growing brighter between their bodies. Silviu gritted his teeth but refused to hide the intensity of their union. Several of the witches around them blinked and gasped, finally confronted with the bond they hadn't believed in.

Not for the first time, Silviu heard the question, "How can a Bane witch have a Magic Match?"

Georgie's smile froze on her face, but she turned toward the one who'd asked with all the considerable charm at her disposal. "We've had the opportunity to look into that very thing while we're here," she said. "I'm learning truths hidden in the archives of time."

"Like what?"

Silviu held on to his smile and allowed Georgie to answer. As much as he would have liked to offer some glib half-truth, or, better yet, demanded nosey witches mind their own damned business, they had to hear Georgeanne. The patriarchs had to see her in—and acknowledge she occupied—a place of power, even with her husband by her side. Besides, Silviu knew, if either of them ever hoped to alleviate the fears so many held about Bane and Reap witches, Georgie would have to explain what she felt was necessary.

One of the men from the Njele entourage turned to Silviu and humphed. "Your wife speaks for you, does she?"

For a moment, Silviu was floored by his new reality. All his life, his father had pushed for him to reach the top of the witches' hierarchy. Every moment of his childhood had been spent in pursuit of one goal, regardless of what he had to do to achieve it. No wonder his father had helped send Georgie away so long ago. He'd known Silviu would give up everything for her.

He already had. And he would do it again.

Madeleine must be cackling with glee from beyond the grave.

"There is no one I'd rather have at my side," Silviu told the Njele witch, making certain his words carried to everyone in their little group. "No one I trust more. My wife may speak for me whenever she takes the notion to do so."

The Njele man surrendered a lifetime of tradition with the simple act of apologizing to Georgie. The action renewed Silviu's optimism. He'd been surprised at how well the Council representatives and their entourages had responded to the new information he'd dumped on them, but they knew Georgie. They'd worked with her and trusted her, to some degree.

Silviu still worried the rest of the witching world would not see things in a similar light.

Georgie smiled at those gathered. "Apparently, Bane

magic is a natural talent totally inactive unless triggered by a threatening dark or black magic."

"Really?" Burkit Serik drifted into their circle with raised eyebrows and wide eyes. He gestured with a glass of clear, pungent liquor. "I had no idea Bane witches were black magic witches, but it does make a macabre sort of sense."

Georgie stiffened slightly. "Just Bane-born. Apparently, we come about when the universe decides a great threat is imminent."

"And what threat would that be?" Burkit asked. "Bane or not, it seems to me that *any* black magic witch would be a problem, especially one that can break another witch's magic."

Silviu and Georgeanne both froze. Very few people knew about Suzette, and all of them were either Davenolds or Silviu's most trusted allies — except Daniel.

Silviu caught the other man's eye with a glare that promised retribution. "Breaking magic. And where would you have gotten that notion, I wonder?"

"Are you saying it's not true?" Burkit did not back down.

"I'm asking where you heard such a thing."

"A little Levy told me." Burkit smiled at Georgie, all teeth. "Is it true? You broke a dark magic effigy, then broke a dark magic witch? You made another Bane?"

Again the crowd gasped and Silviu gritted his teeth. Protectiveness surged. Defensiveness clogged his throat with harsh words. Swallowing heavily, he dug into his reserves of patience and diplomacy to answer the smug, patriarchal bastard, but Georgie beat him to it. Silviu bit his tongue and let her respond.

"I first learned about my talent after Graves Ngozi targeted my grandmother with an effigy. There were extensive enhancements on the doll, and I'm still surprised he was able to utilize such strength in the spell. But, of course, he had help. Was it you, Burkit?"

"I would never help that pig," he snarled. "Graves Ngozi — as far as I'm concerned — should have been executed decades ago, perhaps in his mother's womb."

"Animosity can so easily hide a secret alliance, however." Georgie smiled.

"I would rather leave my Family and join a Motherhouse than work with that whoreson." Burkit spit on the ground, causing many to leap back from the point of impact.

With only a slight pursing of her lips to show her distaste, Georgie shrugged. "Then perhaps you and I feel the same way about the man. Oh, that's right" — she snapped her fingers — "I did leave my Family and switch sides in the division."

Her humor smoothed a bit of the tension, as several witches laughed, but the pressure skyrocketed again when Burkit asked, "But you joined a patriarchal Family after you stole your cousin's magic and made her Bane, correct?"

"A little Levy told you that, too, hmm?" Silviu drawled.

"Maybe not so little." Burkit's eyes flashed with perverse humor. He held his free hand up around head-height. "About this tall. Very little magic but plenty of authority."

"He's wrong on the timing, as Silviu and I were married long before my cousin suffered her...*breakdown*. Unfortunately," Georgie shook her head, theatrically disappointed, "Suzette wielded dark magic. After she'd begun an affair with Daniel Levy in the hopes of bearing his child that was, apparently, supposed to take over and unify the witching world, she challenged me for the Davenold magic."

"Which, according to your husband, you don't have," Burkit stated, ignoring the murmur moving through the crowd at Georgie's news.

"Which I don't have," she confirmed. "However, my cousin attacked me while the rest of my Family was present. I, of course, am immune to such magic, but my Family is not, and I fear the Bane talents also took exception to the events."

"I heard you broke her magic completely."

Georgie lifted her chin. "Correct."

"You simply couldn't help yourself? Your magic got away from you?"

"I knew what I was doing, Burkit. I was in complete control."

Silviu refused to gainsay her in front of their audience, but he was forced to quell a shudder as the memory streaked through him. The entire event had been nothing but black, roiling chaos, with magic surging and spiking hard enough to throw the Davenolds against the walls. It had taken every ounce of his ability to force Georgie's magic back under control.

"What about mine?" the other witch pressed. "Can you break my magic?"

"You don't wield dark magic." Georgie winked. "As annoying as I currently find you, Burkit, you are safe. While I can assure you I would never underestimate either your abilities or your intelligence, my talent doesn't recognize yours as a threat."

"I wonder if I should be offended by that." Burkit sipped his drink. "And your cousin? Was she the great threat you were born to defeat?"

"No," Silviu answered before Georgie could. "We've found evidence of a black magic witch stronger than anything else I've ever encountered. This witch has already caused a great deal of trouble and is very dangerous. Whoever leads this Council from the High Seat will have to deal with the situation, and Georgeanne is the only one among you that has the ability to stop the villain."

"Hmm," Burkit murmured. "Food for thought."

Chapter Twenty-Five

Georgeanne

Georgie slipped off her shoes, kicking them in the general direction of the closet. Silviu yanked at his tie and collapsed onto their bed. He pushed himself high enough to prop his shoulders against the headboard, leaving his chin angled down awkwardly. As she watched, the tension drained from his face until his eyes sparkled like newly minted nickels from between his thick, dark lashes and his mouth relaxed into a soft smile.

"You seemed oddly uncomfortable tonight, Silver." She reached up and took the clip from her hair. Curls sprang free, making the roots pull a bit where they had been confined. She dug her fingers into her scalp. "Didn't you expect these results from your announcement earlier?"

"I expected it. It was a calculated move, my love."

"Seemed to me that you panicked. Blurted out the truth before you could think better of it."

"No, the truth was simply the best way to move forward." Silviu shuffled a little higher and wriggled his shoulders. "I realized that my father was extremely short-sighted. Not as brilliant as I'd thought he was."

Georgie disagreed. "He expected my grandmother to be alive to help ease you into the position of High Seat. He expected you to use your talent against the Councilmen, too." She cocked her head and watched him carefully. "Why didn't you? You could have been elected this afternoon."

For a minute, he held his silence, and Georgie started bracing for a lie. Then she realized what she was doing and shook herself. They were starting fresh, and that meant giving her husband the benefit of the doubt. He didn't disappoint her.

"This time we do it together." He took a deep breath. "No more secrets, no more manipulating each other. We'll talk about it, share all the power we can manage to grab for ourselves and make this work."

"But you wanted to be the High Seat."

His eyes flashed. "I wanted you."

"You could have both," she whispered.

Silviu shook his head. "Only if I choose you above everything else. And that's how it should be, my love. I'd give all the rest of it up right now, if I thought the two of us could be safe."

Georgie thought of the expressions stamped on every Councilman's face that afternoon. Their fake smiles couldn't hide their thoughts. The fear and speculation of the most influential people on either side of the Schism didn't bode well for the future, unless she and Silviu could prove their strength and their fairness. Only then would the threat others saw in them be diminished.

"Hiding is not an option anymore." She moved toward the bed, only stopping when her knees hit the mattress. Deep inside, she felt a glimmer of magic rise up at her proximity to her husband, but she willed it away. She wanted something different that night. "Even if we could ignore our own safety, find some deserted island somewhere, what about any children we might have? I won't let them be hunted."

"Neither will I."

She heard the promise in his voice and trusted it. Something warm and confident curled through her, reassurance from his actions and reaffirmation of her emotions. In that moment, Georgeanne realized that Silviu would hurt her again, that couldn't be avoided in any relationship, but beyond the passion they shared, they had a better foundation than most witches—not because they were Matches but because they were equals.

Somewhere along the way, she'd earned his respect and he'd earned hers. And they loved. It was enough.

"You could have had everything you've worked for." She hiked her skirt up to her thighs and lifted her knee onto the bed. "But you gave it to me. I bet Vasile never saw that coming."

Silviu focused his attention on the sliver of leg still covered by her skirt. "Oh, I think he did. I think Madeleine would have been surprised, though. Well, maybe, maybe not."

"I don't want to talk about them, Silver."

"Good. Neither do I." He reached for her, clamping his big hands down on her hips and tugging her forward. "I loved seeing you handle the room downstairs. Those witches didn't know what hit them. They still don't, and tomorrow they'll all vote for you."

"I'm a good politician."

"You're authoritative, commanding" — he squeezed her waist before sliding his hands to her ass — "sexy."

"They're still afraid that we'll be too powerful together, like the legends say."

"We will be." Silviu sat up and kissed the sensitive spot just beneath her jaw, making Georgie shiver. "There is no use in denying it."

"It was" — her breath broke when her husband licked a hot trail over her collarbone — "an excellent idea to make everyone think our combined power could work *for* them, though."

"Knowing you, it will." Silviu went to work on her blouse buttons. "You are much more generous and fair than I ever learned how to be."

"I had better role models."

The soft pressure of Silviu's knuckles moved down her chest as, one by one, he tugged each button free. With the cool air sweeping over her skin, Georgie closed her eyes and tipped her head back. The silk blouse slipped over her body in a smooth caress, warm and supple, before being brushed away to reveal her to the room's slight chill — and the heat in Silviu's gaze.

It struck her that he'd always looked at her with fire in his cool silver eyes. Sometimes his emotions blazed, as they were doing then, and sometimes they smoldered, banked for a more appropriate time of expression, but they always burned for her. She hadn't always understood it, and she hadn't always trusted the emotion she encountered in his gaze, but with the intention of moving forward with him, of strengthening their bond and working together, of allowing herself to love him as much as he loved her, Georgie let herself fall into it.

He must have seen something of her thoughts on her face. Silviu's eyes narrowed. His lips tightened sensuously. As a faint flush crossed his high cheekbones, he lowered his head and dropped soft, roaming kisses over the tops of her breasts. Inside the lacy cups of her bra, Georgie's already peaked nipples hardened in a rush that came close to being painful.

She gasped and arched, encouraging Silviu to kiss more of her skin. He gave her what she wanted, dragging his lips over the tops of her breasts until sensation tumbled through her chest in a ceaseless wave. She rolled her shoulders and rocked on her knees, silently begging for more.

Silviu snaked his tongue under the top edge of her bra. Wet heat impinged on her senses and nerves all around Georgie's nipple started dancing, crowding closer for maximum advantage. She hardly noticed when he peeled her bra off her body, but she couldn't miss the roll of sleek velvet over her needy flesh as he licked her. With her lungs locked in pleasure, she was getting dizzy, her thoughts flying off, only to circle home again, reminding her of her original intent.

"Stop," she panted.

He lifted his head, surprise widening his eyes. "Why?"

"I was trying to seduce you, and you took over." She pushed at Silviu's shoulders. "Sit back."

For a moment, she thought he would refuse. His biceps

bulged beneath his shirtsleeves and he appeared to quell a fierce shudder, but then he inhaled and released her — slowly.

Silviu arranged himself on the mattress, arms and legs spread wide. "I'm all yours."

"I know." Georgie examined him, experiencing such satisfaction that her lower stomach clenched and her pussy flooded.

Tall, lean and hard, his body was a work of art — fatal to a woman's resistance, dressed in a rumpled suit, as he currently was. Silviu exuded sex appeal, though his face bordered on pretty until Georgie got her hands on him, then his full lips would thin and his narrow nose would widen with deep inhalations. His body would tense and his eyes would damn near glow.

For her.

He was hers and she was thrilled with her possession. As dominant as he ever was, Georgie leaned forward, placed her hand at his throat then dragged her palm down the length of his body. She never took her gaze from his. Through touch alone, she catalogued the rough silk of his clothing and the hot man beneath, the smooth disks of the buttons she encountered along her way and the hard bulge she found at the end of her journey.

The gleam in Silviu's eyes was priceless — and hot.

She palmed his erection, watching his eyes grow ever more mercurial and loving it. He was always so reserved and cool, almost never showing his true feelings to anyone except her. She'd learned to read him in public, but in private she looked forward to the moment he softened and lowered his guard as he only did with her.

Georgie opened his fly and ventured inside. Hot, silken flesh rose to her touch, his pulse pounding in the length of his cock, a single eager drop of pleasure decorating his crest. She smiled and stroked as best she could, her hand still hidden within the tight confines of his trousers.

"This is mine," she declared.

"All yours," Silviu immediately agreed.

"Just so you know." Georgie pulled his cock free of both his pants and underwear.

She cupped his balls and leaned down for a leisurely lick up his shaft. Silviu grunted, one hand lifting to clench in her curls and draw them away from her face. Georgie tugged against the sensual prickle, the tingle of need that worked over her scalp and somehow plunged straight to her pussy. Tensing her thighs, trying to alleviate the ache between them, she then mimicked the action with a tightening of her lips over the head of Silviu's dick.

Groaning, he arched up. She swallowed him, letting his shaft slide through her lips and his tip push to her throat. Working her mouth over his cock, remembering how he'd taught her to suck him and applying everything else she'd learned since, Georgie licked over the crest and drew hard on the top of his glans, relishing the broken noises he rewarded her with.

She teased him for as long as she could, but fire seemed to lash the inside of her veins and her pussy was squeezing itself almost painfully. Urgency took on new meaning as Georgie procrastinated in favor of pleasuring her husband with her mouth. Her panties were uncomfortable, sticky and wet, and her clit ached with neglect.

She rocked on her knees and tightened her thighs, but there was only one cure for the madness she'd developed. Reluctantly, she let Silviu's cock pop from her mouth and attacked her own panties. They were in the way and she wanted them gone, but too many pairs had been sacrificed to lust and she couldn't afford to lose another. Taking them off only teased her further and made her hotter.

Georgie yanked her skirt to her waist and straddled Silviu's hips. She was spread before him, her folds fully exposed to his sight. Silver gleamed between his lashes and Silviu bared his teeth.

"Fuck," he growled. "Do you have any idea what you look like? How wet you are?"

"No, I don't." Mischievous and willing to instigate, Georgie touched herself, pushing two fingers along her folds to rub at her entrance. "I'll find out, though."

He groaned as if in agony, but Silviu never looked away. Watching her husband's reaction while she played between her legs added to Georgie's joy dramatically, jolting her body with energy and pleasure. She liked the glazed look that came to his eye and the heavy breaths he took. She loved that his cock flexed every time she pushed a little deeper, as if feeling the same pleasure vicariously.

Less than a minute passed before Silviu snuck his finger into action beside hers. Georgie's clit throbbed as he circled it. Her pussy gushed once he slipped his finger lower. He met her at her entrance, stroked it and dipped inside, stretching her just a little, making her shiver with a sense of the forbidden. Her fingers and his, working together.

"Let me do it," he whispered. So tempting.

Georgie struggled to deny both him and her body. "I can do it myself."

"I'd like to help." He thrust his finger deeper, then withdrew. Disobedient and sly, Silviu began a rhythm that had Georgie unable to catch her breath. She writhed and arched, desperate to bring him closer, even as she fought to make him stop.

"It's my turn." Her protest came out too winded, too much like a plea.

"I want to taste you, love." Silviu brought his other hand up to clamp down on her hip, rocking her forward and guiding her back. Georgie didn't know if he was helping her ride his finger or if he was trying to lead her up his body.

Especially when he said, "Just let me have a taste."

"No." She shook her head, her spine flexing as her clit pulsed and Silviu's fingertip hit a spot that sent streamers of pleasure into her abdomen. "I'm taking you this time."

He gave her a dirty smirk. "Please? Just a little taste. Come here."

"No," she repeated. Forming words was difficult, but it was too important not to try. "You'll get me up there and I'll lose all my power to you. Tonight, I want it. I want to take you, pleasure you. I know you, Silver. You'll pull me up to sit on your face and fuck me with your tongue, and the only thing I'll know anymore is how damned good it is to ride your mouth."

He blinked his glazed eyes, his lips fell open and the flush deepened over his cheekbones. "That sounds perfect."

"I'm in control this time. You want a taste?" Georgie chased his finger with her own, gathering her juices before offering him her hand, wet and shining with her pleasure. She rubbed her fingers over his bottom lip. "I'll give it to you."

He didn't miss a beat. Silviu opened his lips and drew in her fingers. Hot, wet suction lit nerves Georgie never could have guessed were so sensitive. Tingles rose to her elbows. Her body clenched around Silviu's still-thrusting digit. Urgency became immediacy.

With a strangled groan, Georgie pushed Silviu's hand from between her legs. As much as her pussy protested the loss of the intrusion, it celebrated when she grasped Silviu's cock and notched it against her entrance. Stretched by something much larger than a finger, much smoother and hotter, her body wept in gratitude.

Teasing them both, letting them both grow slick and slippery, she held him there another moment. The sensation of his dick's head just breaching her body had her lungs locking. Georgie loved that her thighs felt too tight and relished how it took all her willpower not to sink down and capture her husband in her hot, wet hold. Anticipation was addicting.

Only when she imagined that neither one of them could breathe anymore did she take him into her body. In a slide just short of a greedy rush, Georgie welcomed her husband, her pussy stretching around him, opening for his intrusion as nerves trembled and honey welled up, sucking him deep. She filled herself with him and the magic they shared threatened to break free of the control *someone* had over it. She didn't know who and she didn't care—the only thing claiming her focus just then was Silviu's iron-hard cock and the bliss transferring to her from it.

Georgie arched and gritted her teeth to hold back a scream. She wanted more and she wanted it *now*. She'd hardly adjusted to Silviu's thickness within her when she lifted and plunged back down. Her muscles went haywire, jumped from her control before she could stop them, undulating Georgie on her husband, forcing her to ride him hard and fast.

Silviu gripped her ass to help her wild dash to climax. His other hand fisted in her hair, dragging her low to his chest. The silk of his shirt abraded Georgie's skin and the buttons rasped uncomfortably, so she gripped the material and ripped it open, ignoring the ping of the offending buttons against the floor and tables, shoving his tie over his shoulder. Her nipples bounced, brushing his dark mat of hair with every thrust of her hips, making Georgie moan at the pleasure bearing down on the tight peaks. She leaned even closer to Silviu, grinding on him, working her ass until the small of her back ached.

She licked his chest. The flavors of sweat and sexy man redefined Silviu's unique taste, the scent of him that Georgie always carried in her nostrils. Struggling to elongate her back, damn near dislocating her spine, she reached farther, licking toward his clavicle, where she gave him a nipping bite.

Silviu sat up in a fast move that managed to shove his cock deeper into her body. Georgie wholeheartedly approved. Breath trembled from her on a sound that spoke volumes of the thick, heavy pleasure coursing through her. Silviu's face echoed the sensations Georgie felt—his eyes were shiny platinum, his lips thinned, teeth bared.

She bit his lower lip and licked the sting away. "You're mine, and I'm keeping you."

"Yes," he growled. Clamping his arms around her, he helped her ride faster. He lifted, thrusting his cock as deeply as possible, running his shaft over the same needy, greedy, *aching* place until rapture caught and exploded.

Georgie gripped Silviu's hair and captured his gaze as she flew off the edge of the world. Her pussy clenched down on his shaft, and only then did she feel the magic bubble up within her soul. Roaring, finally set free from whoever's hold had kept it contained, the force blew through them both, burning them to ash. Turning the world to gold.

Waves of sensation pulled all her muscles taut, but a single sentiment made it through the mind-destroying bliss. "Love you, *love you*," she groaned.

"I love you, Georgie." Silviu tucked his face into her neck and surged deep. He held still and blasted her with heat and magic. "So much."

Georgie knew it would be like that forever between them. Wild and tempestuous, forgiving and passionate, loving as only they could. Together, they would reach every height — magical, political and pleasurable. Only with her Match.

With the golden light pulsing around them, Georgie and Silviu found their fulfillment together, as they were meant to.

Chapter Twenty-Six

Costel

The breakfast rush had ended and the coven representatives were occupied with their business downstairs. Still, Costel held his breath as he followed the black cat down the corridor. Everything was quiet and, in spite of his current mission, he rolled his shoulders, relishing their lightened load and enjoying the peace stemming from his freedom. Having transferred the Lovasz seat to Silviu, Costel didn't have to attend the Council meeting—and never would again, if he could help it.

Unfortunately, the gossip around the breakfast table hadn't given him much hope. Whether or not Silviu could remain in the position was up for debate, but it was out of Costel's hands. Silviu would have much better odds of influencing everyone else's vote than he would, so Costel had made his own plans for the day

He and Tulah were on their way to investigate Daniel Levy's bedroom.

Subterfuge was better than sitting alone in his own room, feeling sorry for himself. Without Bijoux in his bed, the previous night had been too long, cold and miserable to bear. Costel was amazed at how quickly he'd gotten used to her presence—and he could only hope he would forget the way she felt against him, warm and naked, just as quickly. He hoped the lavender he grew back home didn't remind him of her eyes at the peak of her orgasm or how lovely she always smelled. He would banish all thoughts of her, because he couldn't spend the rest of his life suffering the agony he'd felt all night long — without her.

He had to let her go. He *would* let her go.

It was for her own good.

Up ahead, Tulah stumbled to a halt. She squatted down on her haunches, ears and whiskers twitching, before slinking forward. She whined — a drawn-out sound filled with such premonition that he shuddered. Costel slowed his steps and glued his gaze to the cat, reminding himself to breathe as Tulah's fur fluffed up. He tensed too, preparing himself for nearly anything.

Tulah arched and hissed. She moved erratically, stepping back and forth as if she wasn't certain which direction she preferred. She jumped, landing somewhere around the corner, out of sight. Costel's heartbeat spiked and he took off after her, terrified that some dark spell had just taken hold. He skidded on the runner, knocked against the wall and nearly fell over.

Tulah crouched next to a woman lying unconscious on the floor. The cat's whiskers twitched and she yowled hauntingly, but Costel couldn't understand the feline. He focused on the woman, instead.

She was face down, the runner bunched beneath her. One arm was thrown wide, the other curled protectively around her head. Blonde hair flowed in every direction. Like her arms, her legs were uncoordinated — one knee bent, the other straight. One beige high heel was several feet away, while its mate still clung tenaciously to the woman's toes.

Tulah yowled once more and threw in a hiss for good measure. Costel carefully rolled the woman over, unsurprised that he recognized her but shocked at who he revealed.

Constance Gage-Levy.

She was breathing — shallowly, but steadily — taking one worry off Costel's mind. Seeing her chest rise and fall, he didn't bother checking for a pulse, though he did send a questing tendril of magic over her body to evaluate the extent of her injuries. She seemed relatively unharmed, no bones broken, though she remained unconscious.

Tulah arched and hissed again. Costel gently placed Constance on her back, thinking of the short conversation they'd had while they'd both been in Poland, at Eliasz and Ileana's betrothal celebration. Costel hadn't believed they had much in common, and he'd been put off by Constance's cold silence. She also should have displayed more respect for the men of Eliasz's branch of the Family, but her warmth had been strictly reserved for the matriarchal guests. She'd focused nearly all of her attention on Adam Davenold, if Costel's memory served.

He glanced at Tulah, wondering how much she knew about Constance. With the way the cat fluffed up and growled, Costel assumed she knew a great deal. He wished she would change into her human form so he could understand what she was trying to say, but he had no clothes to offer her — and, considering Adam's relationship to the downed woman, Costel wasn't willing to irritate the Davenold male any further than he suspected Adam would be when he discovered the arrival of the newest guest.

He tapped Constance on the cheek, slightly alarmed to feel how cool her skin was. "Wake up. Wake up now, and open your eyes."

Her lashes fluttered but didn't rise. He chafed her hands. "Come on."

Slowly, too slowly, her lids lifted to reveal dull blue eyes, groggy with pain. Constance winced and panted, red circles appearing in the paleness of her cheeks. Her throat bobbed. She shuddered.

"Easy," Costel cautioned. "Take your time."

"Have to tell…" Constance wheezed. "Came to tell Silviu… He's got to know!"

"Know what?" Panic fluttered through Costel's chest. "What does he have to know?"

"It wasn't me," she coughed. "I wasn't the one —"

Constance cut her words off abruptly and her eyes flew wide, locking on something over his shoulder. Tulah screeched. Costel, still crouched, spun on his toes and struggled to keep his balance, but he was nearly knocked over by the blinding explosion of onyx light.

He'd had no idea that darkness could be so bright.

His retinas burned. Tulah shrieked again. Constance screamed and adrenaline flooded Costel's system in a hot rush. He surged to his feet, his hand rising as silver magic hurried to his command, filling his palm—cool and clean and strong. So strong.

Silver light met black and peeled it away with a heavy surge forward. Costel felt the wobble in the other witch's magic, sensed the surprise at his strength. Everyone underestimated him, but he was the Lovasz Father, the sole possessor of the greatest combined talent any coven could boast. And that was on top of his personal magic.

But the black rolled in, crashing over the silver stream in an angry tide. Costel felt the impact in his thighs and his spine. He grunted and braced his feet, lifting his other hand to counter the renewed assault. Concentrating until sweat popped out on his forehead, he ignored the pounding of his heart and chanted a spell to put the two weaker women inside a protective, shielding bubble.

That freed him to focus an offensive strike against the attacker. Costel pushed at the air with both hands. A shockwave of silver spiraled down the corridor. The runner carpeting the floor flapped beneath their feet. The revealed stone shone as if coated with ice.

An answering sphere of glittering black magic rocketed toward Costel. He tossed out his own shield, but the attacking magic blasted through it in a soft explosion of deepest purple. Pain pierced Costel's head, something in his chest twisted and he felt blood slide from his nose.

He glanced at the women behind him. They cowered in the bubble he'd created, but he wondered how long it would hold under the force of the black magic. He guessed only moments.

"Go!" he commanded.

The moment the magic he'd placed around them fell, Tulah jumped free. Costel hoped she would run to her husband and get help—preferably before it was too late. Determined to hold on for as long as possible to give the women a good chance to get away, he feared he wouldn't still be alive when the cavalry came, but at least his brother would finally find the villain he'd been searching for.

But Tulah didn't make it a single step. Smoke roiled from the darkness gathering in the corridor and wrapped around her tail. It yanked her back. Her scream echoed off the stone.

Constance scrabbled forward on her knees. Clearly acting in reflex, she snagged Tulah by the scruff of her neck and pulled her from the smoky grip of magic. The feline wobbled and fell, grunts and growls pouring from her mouth as she used her claws to drag her body away from the attack.

Costel was already moving, bracing his legs against the hazy magic and throwing up new shields to hide the women. Protective instincts welled up, incinerating his muscles, forcing them to move faster than he would have thought possible. But he couldn't move quickly enough. Constance didn't get free in time. Even as he lunged to physically shield her with his body, black light walloped her in the head. She fell and lay still.

Costel screamed. Rage and fear ripped from his throat in a battle cry recognized only in the deepest parts of his patriarchal soul. Light blazed around him, cool metallic fire flickering in the gloom. Teeth bared, he snarled at the darkness, willing it to part so he could see who the attacker was.

Costel had no delusions. The black magic witch stood before him somewhere in the blinding darkness and he didn't stand a chance against the greater force. Swirls of ebony, purple and green obscured his vision and jet crystals seemed to decorate the air, but Costel could *feel* the villain, somewhere just beyond the cold, slick magic. He wasn't far, maybe a few feet.

Costel wanted to spit in the bastard's face before he took his last breath.

Bending low, he forced his legs to carry him onward. He pushed through the magic. A step, then another. He raised his hands and gritted his teeth, forcing his own magic to work, to part the black wall holding him back. Silver flared, cleaving the darkness, but the onyx light rushed in every time a cut was made.

A ball of deepest purple sailed past Costel's head. He dodged it and threw a spell of his own, the magic swirling like mercury on glass. He grunted and shoved forward, pressing closer in spite of the bone-cracking tension. Sweat poured down his face, his legs cramped and his back spasmed, but Costel pushed on.

A dim shape formed from the shadows. A little closer and he would see. Costel squinted and threw another spear of magic, then held out his hand to catch a responding attack. His palm burned, blistered with cold fire. Blood dripped from his nose and his ears popped. All noise was cut off, except the alien sound of his own breathing whistling through his aching head.

A little closer.

Then he saw.

Just before the darkness became complete and dragged him beneath crashing purple waves, Costel identified the dark magic witch.

He wasn't surprised at all.

Chapter Twenty-Seven

Bijoux

Bijoux opened the Council Chamber door as quietly as she could, but the silence within didn't penetrate her awareness until she poked her head inside. She'd expected a full room and a rowdy table, with debates or arguments raging, as they had the day before. Instead, she found her father setting out water glasses.

"What are you doing sneaking around, Bijoux?" He slammed a glass on the table and glared at her.

Immediately casting off the cloak of stealth she'd employed, Bijoux threw the door wide and stepped in. "Where is everyone?"

"We've been delayed. A few of the Councilmen sent down requests for the meeting to be postponed for a bit."

She looked around the empty room. "I see everyone got the message."

Emeric shrugged. "Everyone who needed to know. I am well aware of how to do my job, and very cognizant of my responsibilities, unlike you."

"Papa—"

"Why are you still here, Bijoux? You are supposed to be packed and on your way to the cottage by now."

It was bad enough her father had locked her in her room until after breakfast. The night had passed in a maddeningly slow torture, taunting her with the many tasks she wouldn't be able to accomplish until morning. She lifted her chin. "I'm not going to the cottage. I am going to Romania—with Costel, as his wife."

She kept her shoulders straight, showing her father the determination she'd held on to throughout the long, lonely night. She wouldn't waste the few, precious moments she had to change Costel's mind by pretending to pack. She needed to speak with him and explain again—then he would see that they were better together and would not leave her behind when he returned home.

Emeric's nostrils quivered. "I've given you too much, surrendered too often in an attempt to make you happy. I know how lonely you have been here, with just me and a handful of servants to occupy your time. I know this, but I couldn't risk letting you go to be used against me."

"What are you talking about?" Her father's words were accompanied by a slide of discomfort down Bijoux's spine.

"I am the Council Administrator, and you are my one child. Do you think someone wouldn't have used you against me, if given the opportunity?" Emeric waved his hand sharply. "They are vultures, greedy and power-hungry, looking for every advantage over one another."

Bijoux was surprised at the bitterness in her father's voice. "But Madeleine protected me."

"I am powerful, with a powerful role. Greedy fools will always make an attempt to manipulate such a man, Bijoux." Emeric sighed and shook his head. "A man such as Alexandru, for example, who is already believed to have murdered his daughter-in-law ages ago. Do you think I'll allow you to live in the same place as that monster?"

"Costel would protect me." With the memory of how he'd protected his brother and sister stark in her mind, Bijoux knew it would be true.

"Is it fair to ask him such a thing?" Emeric raised a hand and cupped her cheek. "He is doing the best he can by leaving you here, where you will be safe."

"But not happy." She shivered as a depressing weight settled on her mind. Perhaps it was her own sadness, though it felt almost as if it came from somewhere else.

"Oh, my treasure, one day you will understand and find

peace."

"No, I won't."

She would have argued further, but the door opened and Silviu's voice came through. He was already in conversation with Burkit Serik, who entered the Chamber on his heels.

"I don't appreciate you playing devil's advocate," Silviu said. "You know you'll vote my way."

Burkit raised his eyebrows. "You want me to vote on many things, however. You want me to approve your nomination to the Lovasz seat as well as Georgeanne's nomination to the High Seat, which also means a new nomination to the Davenold seat. So much to vote on these days."

"Georgeanne will replace herself with Adam Davenold. He'll represent the Family. You've known him for years, Burkit. He's been attending these meetings as long as Georgie has."

The other man laughed. "What is the witching world coming to? A man representing a matriarchal Family at this table and a woman leading a patriarchal coven, lording it over us all. This is most unusual."

"These are unusual times." Silviu refocused his attention on Emeric and Bijoux. "The meeting wasn't postponed again, was it?"

"No, no," Emeric rushed to assure him. "We will begin in just a few minutes. You are simply the first to arrive."

Again, Bijoux's spine became chilled. She rubbed her arms and stepped back toward the wall, hoping her father forgot her presence in the Council Chamber. She hoped to catch Costel's eye when he arrived and somehow signal her desire to speak with him. He wouldn't make a scene in front of so many witches and would surely agree to meet with her in private, if only to maintain his composure in front of the other Councilmen.

She took a deep breath and willed away her growing unease. Surely she was simply nervous, and her unyielding optimism would make a resurgence at any moment. She just had to wait.

Her father had different ideas, however. "Go, Bijoux. The car is available to take you away."

She lifted her chin and rubbed her arms again, as another icy quiver snaked through her. "Just let me say goodbye to Costel, at least. I can wait here until he comes and—"

Something was wrong. She didn't need to see Emeric shaking his head to know some unplanned thing had taken place beyond her awareness. Her father's thoughts had become erratic and confused, but Bijoux could have sworn he didn't believe Costel would attend the Council meeting.

Silviu confirmed it. "Costel gave his seat to me, Bijoux."

"But we have not voted on that yet," Burkit muttered.

"My brother hates his Council duties." Silviu glared at the Serik representative. "He won't be attending the rest of this session unless he's forced to."

Bijoux looked between the three men she faced. "Well, then, where is he?"

The answer was imperative. Bijoux was shocked at her own impatience to find him.

Silviu's face didn't change. He didn't blink, flinch, flush or grimace. His voice remained even and the pulse didn't throb in his neck. There was no overt sign that he lied when he said, "I'm sure he's packing to go home."

But Bijoux knew he told an untruth. It took a heartbeat to realize and accept the subtle indication that she'd only recently learned to look for—the metallic hue of his eyes darkening for just a moment, the way Costel's had on the rare occasions he'd lied. She couldn't read Silviu's mind, and, even in the shadows of her own, Bijoux realized her suspicion could be nothing more than wishful thinking, but she stepped forward and tried to call his bluff anyway.

"No, he's not. Where is he?"

For a minute that seemed to stretch into eternity, Silviu simply stared at her. Bijoux ignored the disquiet that streaked along her nerves, the chill that seemed to grow as time went on. She held Silviu's eyes with a narrowed gaze that she hoped he would think meant she could read his thoughts. She really needed to know where Costel was at that very moment.

He stepped close to her and lowered his voice to a murmur she strained to hear. "We spoke of this yesterday, Bijoux, remember? Tulah needed his assistance."

"You mean…" Her eyes flew wide. "Now?"

"Yes, because…" Silviu lowered his eyebrows then immediately reversed their direction. "Good God, where is Daniel?"

Behind him, Burkit Serik asked, "Why would you care where Daniel is?"

"I don't know," Bijoux whispered, ignoring the question. She shivered under another arctic blast of unease. "I didn't know the meeting had been postponed, so I doubt Costel did. Papa said he told all the Councilmen. That would include—"

"Of course Daniel knew about the delay," Emeric snapped. "He was one of the witches who requested the time!"

"Why did he need it?" She glanced at her father, but an aura of purple light flashed in front of her eyes and she became too lightheaded to focus. An image of Costel zipped through her mind, but she thought that might only be because she'd been thinking about him.

"Bijoux"—Silviu lifted his hand to her shoulder—"are you all right?"

Another picture assailed her. Costel and a blonde woman Bijoux had never seen before, surrounded by smoke and darkness. The image was there and gone, teasing her memory and her senses. She thought she'd heard the howl of a cat.

"Something is wrong." She shook her head, but that made her feel ill, so she stopped. She swallowed the thickness building in her throat and clutched at Silviu. "I'm not sure…"

His fingers tightened on her shoulder. "Where is Costel, Bijoux? Where is my brother?"

"I don't know. Too far away for me to read him. We might

be a Match, but there are still limits — "

"Shh. Listen to my voice…"

Silviu grabbed both of Bijoux's shoulders at the very moment she feared her lungs would cave in. The constriction around her chest didn't ease much, but his hold was enough to slow her breathing. Once she regulated her oxygen intake, the brilliant flashes of light dancing in front of her eyes receded. Slowly, Silviu's words began to make sense to her.

"Relax and let me help, Bijoux. Just let the sound of my voice guide your talent."

Bijoux nearly scoffed. The sound of Silviu's voice was strained, undercurrents hinting at anger, though she realized he might be feeling panic. She certainly was. Her instincts were screaming that something terribly wrong was happening.

"Let me enhance your ability." Silviu became monotone. "Reach for your Match. Find him and him alone."

A cool sweep of magic brushed Bijoux's senses. With her mind as open as her fear would allow, she couldn't miss it. She leaped for it and pushed her own abilities out into the world in a way she rarely needed to do. She was used to a certain level of intimacy associated with her talent, but then she'd never tried using it from such a distance before, either.

Costel had always been easy for her to read, and the boost of Reap magic closed the distance between them. Pictures came to her, images and hints of his location, the trouble that had found him. Bijoux hardly knew what was happening, but her stomach twisted with premonition. She broke out into a cold sweat, the panic she'd barely managed to contain breaking free of her control.

Costel was hit, the magic burned. His head hurt. Then every thought and perception winked out, leaving Bijoux with a final impression of her Magic Match hitting the floor and remaining still. Then nothing… Costel was gone from her awareness.

She screamed.

Silviu shook her, yelled in her face, but Bijoux hardly heard him. She fought against his hold, pushing him until he released her. She barely glanced past him, didn't care at all about the stunned expressions of the crowd that had joined them while she'd connected to Costel. She screamed until her throat seemed to rip in two and she lurched toward the door.

"Bijoux!" Silviu commanded.

"No. *No*. He's dead!" Tears streamed down her cheeks, her heart shriveled. Without a plan, Bijoux sprinted from the room.

Bijoux flew down the corridor and stumbled up the steps. A hard hand caught her elbow and pushed her on when she fell. Somewhere within the ringing in her ears, she heard Silviu ask where they were going. She thought Georgie answered.

She staggered from the stairwell and sped down the corridor she knew to be the last obstacle between her and Costel. A black cat lay on the runner before her. Behind her, a man shouted. The cat dug its claws into the rug and used its hold to inch forward. Bijoux was pushed to the side as Adam Davenold raced past her.

She jumped over him when he crouched and gathered the animal to his chest. Bijoux was vaguely aware of Georgie hesitating before following her around the corner. Then all Bijoux knew was the man on the floor.

Her lover, her Match. He looked broken on the stone, his hair obscenely dark against his awful pallor and his mouth slack. His shirt smoldered. Bijoux had no air left in her lungs when she collapsed next to him. She lifted a shaking hand, beyond devastated at the coldness of his skin.

Georgie and Silviu moved down the hall with lethal intent. Bijoux barely spared them a glance as they investigated the scene, and yet the danger they posed to whoever had committed the crime was easily felt. All the small hairs on Bijoux's body stood up, though she folded over Costel's chest.

He lay cold and still beneath her. Bijoux sobbed without breath, feeling as if her soul had cracked in half, one chunk utterly disintegrated, gone. Pain as she never knew existed ripped through her.

"Stay there." Georgie crouched next to her and planted a hand on her back. "Just like that, Bijoux. Help him heal. That's the benefit of being a Match."

She jolted, confused and angry, wondering why Georgie would mock her. But, as she lifted her lashes and squinted through her tears, she saw a golden glow between her and Costel. As she watched, he shuddered and drew a great breath. Hope nearly undid her completely.

"What do I do?" she gasped. Her heart felt close to exploding. "How do I help?"

"Keep touching him." Ileana fell to her knees on the other side of Costel's body, surprising Bijoux, as she hadn't known the woman had followed. She briefly patted her brother's hair and said, "His magic makes things grow. I'm sure there is some healing benefit that goes along with that."

Bijoux sobbed. "He makes the flowers bloom."

"I've seen him make them bloom in the dead of winter from a dried up stick growing out of rock." Pale, lips trembling, Ileana seemed to struggle for the strength to wink. As she did, a tear dropped free. "He's strong, and he's got a Match."

"He's got all of us." Silviu joined them, and a blast of pressure made Bijoux supremely aware of his magic. He was actively using whatever talent he had for his brother, and his strength only grew when Georgie reached for his hand. Gold light flared between them as well, enough to fill the hallway.

"He's going to make it," Georgie declared.

"What about Constance?" A few feet away, Eliasz Levy held the unfamiliar blonde in his arms.

"She's the least of my worries," Silviu snapped. He

grimaced. "I presume she's breathing?"

"Yes," Eliasz confirmed. "I want to know why she's here, though. It would be nice if you could spare a small sliver of magic to help her, too."

"No." Silviu turned back to his brother. "Costel gets it all right now."

Eliasz's tone hardened. "I have some questions for her."

"Well, then, let me see the hussy," Christiana called out, indecently loud in the hush of the corridor.

Bijoux glanced up at the woman striding around the corner, closely followed by her husband, as well as her brother. Adam was shirtless, his button-down wrapped around the woman he carried in his arms, though it couldn't hide the wicked bruise stretching the length of her leg.

"Tulah?" Georgie looked up, clearly demanding an answer.

"I'll be all right," the woman whispered. "Adam and Chris worked some magic."

"What happened here?"

"Costel and I came this way and we saw Constance. She was unconscious and Costel tried to wake her. When she opened her eyes, she said she'd come to talk to Silviu, and that's when the attack came."

"The black magic witch?" Silviu elevated his eyebrow.

"Yes." Tulah turned her face into her husband's neck for a moment. Then she took a deep breath and continued. "I couldn't see. It was all so dark. There was magic everywhere, and I got caught, but Constance grabbed me and pulled me free. Costel jumped in front of us, but it was too late to stop us from being hit. He took the brunt of the attack, though."

Bijoux moaned and pressed her forehead to Costel's sternum. She prayed to any deity listening, begged all the gods to make her lover wake up. She needed Costel to be all right, even if he left her behind forever. So long as he was alive, she wouldn't complain.

"Please, please come back to me," she whispered brokenly.

"Costel is strong," Silviu reminded her. "He's also stable

now. We're just waiting for the last of the dark magic to wear off."

"Unfortunately" — Georgie's lips twisted — "we've got experience with this now. If the spell follows the same pattern it did with my grandmother, Costel will be awake in a short while."

"Let's get them out of the hall," Eliasz suggested, then nodded, unable to point as his hands were full. "Daniel's room is just down there and I'd prefer to be away from it."

"You'd better get going while you can," Christiana told them. She waved her hand over Constance's body one final time and nodded to herself. "There's quite a crowd at the top of the stairs, but Milo worked his calming mojo and now they're all milling around like lost sheep. Make it quick, before the spell wears off, and no one will realize you've slipped past them."

Silviu hefted his brother and commanded Georgeanne to lead the way. Though it proved awkward, Bijoux refused to let go of Costel's hand and ended up walking pressed to Silviu's side. She was surprised to see her father standing quietly at the edge of their sad — and determined — little group. As she passed him, she declined to look his way, unable to handle the emotions she feared she'd glimpse in his gaze.

Chapter Twenty-Eight

Silviu

Halfway to his bedroom, Silviu surrendered to the need for magic and levitated his brother the rest of the way. Levitation spells were complicated and draining, but, with a man hefted over his shoulder, long corridors and curving stairs were even more so. It was with a groan of relief that Silviu finally laid Costel on the bed.

He staggered back, wiping his forehead as he leaned against the dresser containing Georgie's clothes. The rest of their group trooped in behind him. After a moment, Eliasz stopped glancing around the room with a seemingly panicked expression and reluctantly put Constance on the bed beside Costel. For just a moment, she tensed—Silviu narrowed his eyes when he saw the muscles of her body react—but then she relaxed again.

Eliasz straightened and grimaced. "I don't know what else to do with her."

"That's fine," Georgie told him. She tugged a chair from the corner, so delicate Silviu had assumed it was merely decorative. "Here, Adam."

He eyed the chair and tightened his grip on his wife. "That won't hold me."

"I meant for you to let Tulah sit there."

Instead, Adam dropped to the floor, keeping his wife on his lap. He tugged his shirt around her, adjusting the hemline to be assured of full coverage. "I'm not letting her go. We're fine here."

Georgie sighed and turned to Silviu. "Are *you* all right?"

"Costel's not that heavy," he scoffed. Then he added, "With magic helping carry him."

"That's not what I meant."

"Ah. In that case, no."

Silviu couldn't help the edge that sharpened his tone. Tension suddenly filled the room, and he wondered if it all stemmed from him, considering how murderous he felt. His anger was frighteningly close to the surface and he fought to moderate the effects by speaking softly, but that seemed to alarm Georgie and Ileana. The two women glanced at each other, sharing some private thought, making him feel excluded.

On the bed, Constance stirred then settled. Costel slept on.

Silviu studied Bijoux, her tear-stained face pale and her wet eyes nearly black in her distress. Occasional silent sobs still racked her, jolting her body until the mattress shook. She sat on the edge of the bed next to Costel's hip, but she'd turned herself awkwardly and folded herself over her lover's chest. She looked pathetic and near to breaking. Behind her, Emeric seemed about the same, as he bore witness to his daughter's anguish.

She clearly loved Costel. Watching her, Silviu's rage notched impossibly higher. Not *at* Bijoux, but at the possibility that his brother had found something special—and had deserved something special far more than anyone had known—yet might never have had the chance to immerse himself in it. Happiness, love, a simple connection with someone who believed in him—whatever Bijoux offered his brother, Silviu had come to endorse it. She brought out the best in Costel.

And he'd almost died.

"This is the second sibling I've almost lost in less than two months' time," Silviu said slowly. "I don't care for the experience of knowing my loved ones are in harm's way. I particularly dislike when I am not around to help defend them."

"Something happened to your sister, too?" Emeric tore his gaze from his daughter to evaluate Ileana, who'd wrapped her arms around Eliasz's waist. A tear slid from her eye and soaked into the fabric of her fiancé's shirtsleeve.

"In Poland," Georgie murmured.

Emeric lifted an eyebrow. "The same thing?"

"No," Silviu drawled in a dangerous tone. In Poland, his sister had been targeted by a pair of witches desperate to get revenge against Alexandru and keep Iley from marrying Eliasz. "This is far more disturbing. The black magic witch is here and about to implement his plan."

Emeric's gaze bounced between all the occupants of Silviu's bedchamber. "How can you be certain?"

"He targeted my brother." Just speaking the words sent a new wave of wrath through Silviu.

"He targeted *Constance*," Tulah suddenly spoke up. She lifted her head from Adam's shoulder, wincing as she moved her swollen, bruised leg. "We just stumbled onto it, and Costel had no choice—"

"But he did have a choice." Bijoux also lifted her head, long enough to pin Silviu with a stare. "You remember that the next time you feel so damned superior. He could have walked away, and whatever Constance had to say to you would remain unsaid forever."

"You are correct." Silviu elevated his chin. Her words were sandpaper over his wounds, but that was the nature of a painful truth. Feeling a measure of shame, he looked away from Bijoux to focus on the stiff figure on the opposite side of the bed. "Perhaps Constance would care to speak to us now? Will you tell me your message before something else delays you?"

For a moment of time that aggravated Silviu to no end, the woman held herself stiff and silent, pretending to be unconscious while time was of the essence. He gritted his teeth and prepared to challenge her again, but something in the tension singing through the bedroom must have prodded her into action.

Constance sighed and opened her eyes. "I didn't think I'd have a crowd."

"Too bad. Speak your piece," Georgie ordered. "What are you doing here? You didn't arrive with Daniel."

Constance barked a bitter laugh and covered her face with her hands. A sob tore free from between her fingers and her shoulders shook. "I need help. You're the only ones I know of who might have a chance... After what I saw in England, at my wedding..."

Silviu looked the woman over. He'd been so utterly focused on his brother that not even Tulah's sorry state had registered fully. But now, Silviu took note of Constance's appearance — her lack of makeup, her ripped clothes, her bare feet. They'd left her shoes in the hallway. The side of her face was turning purple and her left wrist was close to black with bruising. There were red marks crossing her neck.

But she was alive and her posture was revealing.

Silviu snapped straight. "You know who the dark magic witch is."

"I want a promise of protection." Constance repeated herself in a surprisingly strong voice, but when she lifted her head, her eyes were red and running with tears.

"Protection from who?"

"I know you hardly know me," Constance ignored the question, "and my wedding was awful. That wasn't my fault and I told them—"

"*Who*," Silviu growled.

She took a deep breath. "Let me start at the beginning, so you'll understand."

He wanted to protest. Hell, Silviu wanted to shake the truth from the woman's mouth immediately, then hunt the dark magic bastard down and kill him in the most gruesome way he could think of. He glanced at Georgie, however, and saw that she wavered at the outer limits of her patience, and Silviu knew *someone* had to be the voice of reason. He decided to give Constance enough rope to hang herself.

"Go on," he encouraged.

She licked her lips and turned her gaze to the ceiling. "The former Levy Father was a monster, but almost no one knew it. His son fell in love with my mother, and she returned his feelings, but the former Father refused to allow them to marry."

Silviu folded his arms over his chest as he listened to a tale he'd already heard. The information Constance offered was little better than the gossip spread through the Levy Family in Poland, where he'd first learned of how Anne Gage-Levy came to marry her Magic Match, Warner. He was a man who had been sleeping with Constance's fiancé, Graves Ngozi, and Anne had been rumored to have been in betrothal negotiations with Daniel years ago. According to the gossip, she had spurned Daniel and seduced his father instead. Consequentially, she'd been punished with a marriage to a man far beneath her rank in the Family.

"The Levy Father," Constance continued, "was furious when he found out my mother was pregnant." She took a deep breath and turned her gaze to Eliasz. "With his son's child, me."

Eliasz pursed his lips. "Because your father shouldn't have been able to have another child after Daniel was born. Our Family's patriarch would have known—"

"I am my father's only child." The muscles of her neck rippled as Constance swallowed. "My father was Daniel's *brother*."

Silviu froze. Witches could have only one child—an unbreakable law set forth by nature. Only Magic Matches wielded enough of a connection between them to have multiple children without resorting to vile curses and dangerous enchantments. The former Levy Father had never had a Match.

Eliasz cursed. "Daniel once told me you were born of a dark spell and that you were his sister."

Constance shook her head very slowly, her eyes never

leaving Eliasz's. Silviu didn't take offense—Eliasz was, after all, the strongest witch in her Family, and probably much easier to face than he was, at that moment. She spoke directly to Eliasz, as well, when she said, "Not me. Daniel. My uncle."

"*Someone*, though." Eliasz mimicked Silviu and folded his arms. The disbelief in his eyes was easy to read. "Someone was born of dark magic."

"Power is passed to the grandchildren in the hopes of creating long, stable reigns, but my grandfather had no confidence in my father's ability to produce a future leader." Constance seemed to choke on her whisper. "And I turned out to be a girl, which vindicated his belief, in his own eyes."

"Constance." Silviu commanded her attention in a quiet voice. "Who was born of dark magic?"

"Daniel." She breathed deep and met Silviu's stare. "My grandfather cast a spell so dangerous, so forbidden, that there's hardly any record of it anymore. He peeled off layers of Levy magic. He added his personal strength into the mix, and he stripped my father of all he had too, leaving him Bane-made. Our patriarch used all the stolen power to create a child, which he forced a female to bear for him."

"Levy magic is notoriously weak." Silviu glanced at his brother-in-law apologetically, but he did not soften the truth. "How strong could such a child have been?"

"The Levy Family is *extensive*," Constance argued quietly. "No matter how weak those of us born to the bloodline may be, there are many of us. And you forgot to include the women who have joined our Family through marriage. Look how strong Eliasz's mother is."

Georgie shook her head. "But Daniel's magic is too weak for what you're claiming."

"No, it's inverse." Constance glanced at Silviu, then away again. "Daniel *is* the Levy magic, but like…a shadow side of it."

"All of the dark and none of the light. The result of the

black magic spell," Christiana mused, "if you're telling us truth."

"Spells like that leave a deformity," Adam protested.

"Is being a psychopath enough?" Constance lifted her chin. "Daniel has no remorse. He feels no guilt and he can't use even a drop of magic that isn't dark or black in origin. That's why so many believe he's weak, when the opposite is true."

"But therein lies the problem." Georgie cocked her head and watched the Levy woman carefully. "I can see whether or not someone is using magic, Constance. I can verify that Daniel's magic is weak and has always been so. What you say can't possibly be true."

"He hides it!" The woman sat up in a rush. Her face drained of color and she clutched her head, but Silviu wondered just how good an actress she might be.

"How can he hide from me?" Georgie asked. "I am Bane, born to fight dark magic, apparently. I've never felt a hint of such a thing in Daniel's presence."

Constance rubbed her forehead. "He was very careful around you. He never uses magic in your presence and said if you, of all people, knew what he could do, it would ruin everything he was working for. I always thought it was because of how much he wanted you to be with him, but then I saw what you and Silviu did at my wedding and understood."

"No, I would have known," Georgie argued.

Silviu thought back to Daniel's arrival at the Council Palace. Remembering the sight of Georgie and Daniel framed in Emeric's office window still triggered fear and anxiety, the heat of adrenaline in his veins. At the time, he'd thought he'd seen a glimmer of rainbows around Georgie's body—the subtle light show that always occurred when her Bane shields rose in response to a threat.

"What if you simply hadn't realized?" he suggested. "My love, you've worked with Daniel many times over many years. Perhaps that had an impact on what you sensed. A dulling of your perceptions."

"Don't be ridiculous. I've never gotten so used to someone else's magic that I stopped being aware of its use."

But Constance leapt on Silviu's suggestion. "Daniel has a natural enhancing talent, but the shadow side — the inverse — to such an ability is *hiding* magic."

Silviu considered her words. He was intimately acquainted with enhancing magic, having the ability himself as an extension of his talent to influence, and he knew well how often he'd successfully, and purposefully, hidden from others. Most of the time, Silviu hid his magic instinctively, so others wouldn't know he was a Reap witch.

Having already confessed in front of the Council, however, there was no longer any use in pretending to be something other than what he was. "I can do such a thing as well," he admitted.

Georgie gasped, but Tulah surprised everyone. The Shimizu witch jumped to her bruised feet. "Don't tell me you believe her!"

"Every word is the truth!" Constance's eyes widened. "Daniel is the witch you're looking for."

"How convenient that you show up just in time for the dark witch to attack." Tulah planted her fists on her hips. "It's even more convenient that you're already awake when Costel is still out cold."

Silviu frowned. "You said he took the brunt of the attack, Tulah."

"Yes, but Constance was attacked twice, and came 'round awfully quickly when Costel and I first found her. You can't believe her. Look at everything she's tried to do!"

"Find a way out?" Shaking and sweating, Constance got her feet, swaying a moment before glaring at Tulah. "That's all I wanted, and you have no right to judge me. You did the same but succeeded where I failed. You found a man to take you away from your Family, to save you and protect you."

"Protect you from what?" Christiana demanded.

"From Daniel!" Constance put her hand to her head. "He forced me into his scheme. I had no choice."

"That can't be true." Adam slowly got to his feet. "You're smart and resourceful."

"I'm a patriarchal woman, clinging to the lowest rung of my Family and forced to do whatever the leader asked of me." Constance's eyes spilled over with tears again. "And I would have refused. I would have let him kill me, but his punishment would have been far worse than death. It would have affected everyone I loved."

"Then why tell us now?" Tulah struck an aggressive pose. "We're on the verge of the dark magic witch doing *whatever* it is he's planning, and you pop up to reveal all in the nick of time. I hardly think so!"

"It's true." The woman turned to Silviu. "Please believe me. I need your help."

"She needs redemption for her plan to work, more likely," Tulah said.

Constance gripped her hair. Her legs wobbled dangerously and tears dripped from her chin. "I have no plan but to get away."

"You have no plan, but Daniel does." Silviu wondered again how much of his own eyes he could trust. Constance was a mess and unsteady on her feet, and her bruises were darkening as he watched. But he'd seen desperate witches go to far greater lengths to pretend their lies were truth. "What is Daniel's plan, Constance?"

"To take over the Council." No hesitation.

"Why?"

"I don't know. Insanity? Ego?" Her knees gave out and she sat on the edge of the bed heavily enough to shake Costel's prone form. "I know he thinks he can do better than anyone else, at everything. He thinks everything would be improved if he controlled it. He believes he can make the world a better place by ruling over it all."

"How was he going to do this?"

Constance rested her forehead in her palm and stared

up at Silviu. "I don't know. He never trusted me with his whole plan, just the part he needed me for, like marrying Graves. Except we found out Warner would have made a more suitable choice, but it was too late to change things. Then Daniel set me up to be a whore for his information."

"And that's why you latched on to me?" Adam's voice held only curiosity.

"No. That was just for me — for freedom. Daniel believed otherwise, though."

"You could have just asked for my help."

She never looked away from Silviu as she answered Adam. "I thought I had to offer you something first, like anyone else would demand. But, trust me... Daniel didn't need my input into the Davenold coven. He had someone else for that."

"Suzette," Georgie declared.

"She was his backup plan," Constance admitted. "He'd spent years trying to woo you, Georgeanne. He'd been so confident that you would join him, that you would see what he was trying to do and understand his vision. He thought you might even marry him, but then you married Silviu in Poland and Daniel got so angry. Everything sped up — all his plans, my marriage to Graves."

"Ah." Silviu glanced at his wife. "I'd wondered at the timing. How did he know when we didn't?"

"Daniel told me he could feel it, that he could see it between you." Constance slouched a little more.

Silviu sighed. "I wish we'd known that earlier. I would have employed different strategies where he was concerned."

"He was so angry." Constance shook her head carefully. "Everything changed that night. He started pulling everything together, certain that the two of you would come after him. He said he needed to be prepared, that time was up. He thought Madeleine had figured out what he was trying to do — "

"Which was what?" Georgie interrupted.

"Take the High Seat from her," Constance said. "Take everything and reunite the witching world under the banner of patriarchy. He thought she'd deliberately brought the two of you together to fight the threat he posed."

Georgie closed her eyes. "She didn't. We didn't even know."

Constance shrugged. "That's why my wedding was thrown together so suddenly, and why Daniel invited you all. He demanded Madeleine's presence. Poor Graves, Daniel mistreated him as badly as he mistreated me."

"He deserved it," Georgie spat.

"Perhaps, but he didn't have a choice, either. We were all just following orders and hoping our loved ones weren't killed in the process." Constance blinked back tears and bravely raised her chin to meet Georgeanne's eyes. "I'm sorry for your grandmother. I'm sorry for what he did to her. I would have tried to contact you sooner but Daniel—"

Her voice broke and she folded over her own lap, sobbing into her hands. She painted a compelling picture of misery, and Silviu was inclined to believe her. No one could act so well. No one had so many false tears inside them. The emotions rolling from Constance were raw and real. They had to be.

"Why now, Constance?" he asked. "Why not a week ago, when we could have saved Madeleine? Why not come clean at your wedding?"

"He killed Warner." Her words became choked, nearly impossible to understand, but Silviu heard. "And he hurt my mother. I don't know if she'll survive. I have nothing left to lose now."

Constance fell back to the bed and curled into a ball. Costel shifted. He gasped and blinked, then groaned the most beautiful sound Silviu had ever heard. All eyes turned toward Costel as he lifted a trembling hand and cupped Bijoux's wet cheek.

"Are you all right?" she asked.

"Don't cry," he whispered to her. She lowered her head to

his chest and bawled.

Silviu felt like doing the same. He had no words to describe the heat that swept through him, the shakiness that threatened his stance. He braced his legs as best he could and struggled to remember how to breathe. He cleared his throat and blinked, grateful when Georgie stepped into the silence.

"Costel," she asked, "did you see the dark magic witch?"

"Yes, and I knew it. I told you, Iley. Told you it was him." He shivered and lifted his head to meet Silviu's stare. "Daniel Levy tried to kill me with a magic stronger than my own."

Chapter Twenty-Nine

Georgeanne

Georgeanne was the only Council representative standing. Even Emeric sat in his ornate chair, a seat only slightly less ostentatious than the High Seat. The Council Administrator had called the meeting to order — chanting the traditional words then quickly reminding the others of the agenda, as well as the events that had resulted in the previous day's adjournment. He'd said nothing of Constance, Costel or the dark magic witch.

Positioned at the very center of the long side of the table for maximum drama, Georgie stood in front of her chair. After much manipulation and the agreement of several others on the Council, the Lovasz and Davenold seats were positioned the way Georgie required — directly across from the Levy seat. Butterflies filled her stomach until every nerve in Georgie's body seemed to be affected. She stood still as a statue, however.

Emeric gestured toward her. "Representative Mother Davenold, one half of the recognized leadership of your matriarchal coven, I call upon you to make your statement."

"Members of the Council..." She took a deep breath and glanced around. Georgie noted her surroundings in less than a heartbeat of time, the training her grandmother had given her serving its purpose just as much as the real life experience she'd gained in the Asian witch hunts. She was quick to take in the details and adrenaline made even the minutiae obvious.

Silviu sat like a lazy jaguar in his chair, dangerously

deceptive. She felt both his magic and his lethal anticipation beating at her senses, demanding free reign. Against the wall behind the Levy seat, to the right of the wide, double doors, sat Eliasz and Ileana. To the left, Christiana, Milo, and Bijoux. The telepathic witch was flushed, staring at Daniel with an easily discernible intensity. Considering the arrogance riding the Levy Father's face, Georgie was grateful for Adam's presence at her back. Though Tulah wouldn't be much help, at least Georgie had allies on her side of the table.

Another deep breath fortified her as much as was possible. "We have gathered to discuss a great deal of business. Our world has changed, and changes must be made. My grandmother was a woman who had her finger on the pulse of the witching community, working tirelessly to ensure safety for us all, not just the matriarchal side of the Schism." Georgie looked at the Castillo representative. "Isn't that correct?"

The man's throat bobbed, but he nodded. "Y-yes. Th-that's correct. She was impressively fair in that regard."

"No matter where they take place, the witch hunts hurt us all." Georgie looked beyond the Ngozi representative to focus on the Family Father, Muso, sitting in one of the chairs lining the walls. "Wouldn't you agree?"

It was well known that Muso had married a woman from the rival Njele Family to cement an alliance necessary for the African covens to succeed against the terrible hunts spread across that continent. If anyone in the modern day could understand the full scope of atrocities committed against suspected witches, it was Muso Ngozi.

"Of course," he agreed.

"No one," Georgie pinned a glare on the woman representing the Marsh Family, long-ago transplants to the South Pacific, "would actively campaign in favor of instigating witch hunts anywhere. Would they?"

The woman shook her head. "We are being executed in Asia, just as they are in Africa. And the lower ranks of my coven live in fear of the hunts reigniting in their home countries."

"So many of us are killed every year," Georgie agreed. "And what is matriarchal and patriarchal ideology in comparison to the brutality found in the non-witching world? How important would it be to hold on to your particular dogma in the face of bonfires and beheadings?"

"We live in dangerous times," Silviu intoned.

Georgie touched his shoulder briefly, then said, "There are events happening in territories ruled by Mothers that will prove detrimental to all if we don't attend to them now. Someone is behind these events — instigating them, enflaming them."

"Who would be so foolish as to support chaos that would bring witches back to the forefront of the world's thoughts?" Mei Lan Cen demanded. "We've only just managed to be dismissed as a mere story or some neo-pagan religion honoring plants and animals."

"A good question." Georgie looked at Daniel. His eyes were hooded, one corner of his lips curled up in a smirk. He was calm, though, sitting at ease in his chair with his hands resting on the arms, his fingers relaxed. Comfortable. "Who would do that, Daniel?"

"Who indeed?" he asked. "I suppose only a man who could hold us all safe would attempt change that some might consider inflammatory."

"Sounds like a delusion of grandeur." Burkit Serik waved his hand carelessly. "No one person on Earth could hold such a large community safe."

"Some are arrogant enough to try, however," Silviu drawled.

"Like you?" Daniel challenged.

Georgie shook her head. "I was about to ask you that very question, Father Levy."

"As the Father, I have a duty to protect my Family. That includes advancing our interests."

Georgie nodded as if in agreement but didn't fail to

notice his evasion. "Yes, you are the leader of the extremely prolific and widespread patriarchal Levy Family, the only coven large enough to withstand war with the non-witching world. The only coven weak enough to escape their notice and hide in plain sight."

"The opposite would be true, surely?" Daniel elevated his chin. "Wouldn't the Levy weakness suggest a different culprit? One who had the means to *influence* others. One with a great deal of magic, like a Reap witch from the powerful Lovasz coven?"

"You've spent a great deal of time outlining, in writing, exactly why Silviu Lovasz-Davenold should never be considered for the High Seat position." Georgie tilted her head, watching for any hint of what the Levy Father was thinking, but she found none. His political mask was firmly in place. "You're still arguing, even after he bowed out of the running, but I assume that's because you've nominated yourself to lead us all, haven't you, Daniel?"

"I will admit to believing I'd do better in the position than your too-powerful husband."

"Many witches sitting at this table owe you a favor. Will you call in the chips today? Or attempt more drastic measures?"

"Georgeanne?" Mother Choudhury called from a chair behind her representative. "Are you accusing Father Levy of crimes of provocation? My region is also conflicted with witch hunts, so I have a vested interest in this argument, but I do wonder whether you've gotten off track."

Georgie glanced at the woman who'd taught her so much for so many years. She could have answered straightforwardly, as she knew the woman expected. She could have stated her accusation, baldly placing the facts before the Council and allowing them to make the final decision, but Daniel was well-liked and people would not turn against him easily without a sound argument and a proper foundation for their suspicion.

So she said, "I'm still trying to figure out the details of

the plan and how someone could expect to come out of it unscathed. As best I can tell, a witch has deliberately instigated trouble for our people, including confusion and regime change in this Council. Perhaps he will point out the failures of whoever you elect to the High Seat and challenge for it, or perhaps he has finagled his way into the position already. Whatever the case, he is willing to sacrifice countless witches to achieve his goal, which seems to be absolute power over us all."

"Do you speak of Daniel, though?" Mother Choudhury pressed.

"I speak of *someone*," Georgie told her vaguely.

Silviu shifted in his chair but did not tense or rise, and never elevated his voice above the soft slide he used when he was at his most lethal. "Only someone who wanted to lead at any cost would do such a thing—undermining our traditions, our independent authority and our safety in the name of a greater good, perhaps? A promise that he, alone, could keep us safe."

"One witch can't achieve all that," Father Laurent called out.

"They can if they're powerful, intelligent, charismatic and sit the High Seat." Emeric lifted his hand. "But let us hear where Representative Mother Davenold is going with her statement, please."

Georgie looked down at Silviu. Without glancing up at her, he took her hand and pressed a quick, light kiss to her knuckles. His presence soothed her and strengthened her. Knowing he was by her side and that his love for her was deep and true, she felt more than ready to face any obstacle.

It also helped that her husband didn't stand, that he didn't try to continue on for her. She'd finally come to understand that he was strong enough to let her lead, and he set out to prove it by letting her take charge of the accusation she'd come to make.

She glanced around and took note of the suspicion in everyone's eyes. She hoped it was directed where she'd intended, but she had no time left to strengthen her case. With enough evidence to pin at least one crime on the man, Georgie laid her cards on the table.

"I would object to your nomination to the High Seat." She straightened her shoulders. "Daniel Levy, you are not fit to lead this Council. You have instigated war and backed policies and programs around the world that put witches in a vulnerable position. You have targeted Motherhouses in the most destructive and unforgivable of ways."

"Where is your proof, Georgeanne?" Daniel shook his head.

"Allow me." Clutching a large envelope, Milo rose and approached the table. Though he tried to hide it, his expression was too smug, but Georgie understood — the Levy Father had threatened to ruin both Milo's business and his marriage if he didn't keep his mouth shut about the affair with Suzette. The vindicated man pulled out a single piece of paper and placed it in front of Daniel before taking the envelope to Emeric.

"Proof," Milo said. Satisfaction rang in his tone. "These documents outline Daniel Levy's business dealings, account transactions and political manipulations. He has thrown money at a variety of projects, predominantly in matriarchal strongholds, that have resulted in a destabilization that may easily lend itself to a resurgence of witch hunts on a level we haven't seen since the middle ages."

Gasps came from all around the room. The representatives fidgeted in their chairs. Those whose Mothers or Fathers had attended the meeting with them turned to share speaking glances with their leaders, a wealth of direction passing between blinks, while the others murmured among themselves and with their entourages. At the foot of the table, Emeric's eyes raced over the pages Milo had given him.

"Good gods," he breathed, sending a new round of noise circling the room.

Georgie could see the hostility his reaction garnered.

291

Everyone turned to stare at Daniel, who sat quietly shaking his head. Georgie didn't doubt he was plotting his next lie. Behind him, the massive doors opened, any noise they made lost in the murmurs of the crowd. Eliasz, Ileana, Christiana and Bijoux got to their feet. Bijoux smiled as if she'd just witnessed the greatest of glories and held out her hand.

Costel stepped into the room, Constance Gage-Levy on his heels. Their entrance was observed by everyone but Daniel, whose back was to the door. But Father Levy stiffened, and Georgie knew he was well aware of who had just arrived. Slowly, he got to his feet, but never took his eyes off Georgeanne.

Silviu also stood. Hackles visibly rising, he put his hand on Georgie's lower back in support and encouragement, and she needed it. Her emotions threatened to give way and drag her under. For so long, she'd been strong in the face of every fear she'd ever held in her heart. The loss she'd felt was too enormous to contemplate, the betrayal she'd been dealt had ripped her wounds wider.

But she'd forced it all back and concentrated on her mission, the end-goal. She would find the black magic witch and expose him. She would help Silviu get into the leadership position and figure out how to deal with the consequences later. She would take care of her Family. With everything seemingly drawing to a close, her endurance was quickly wearing out, leaving her shaking and dangerously close to tears.

Georgie swallowed the lump in her throat. She blinked and raised her chin, focusing on the predatory glint in Daniel's watchful gaze. She would not fall apart before him, before she achieved her goal. She would not surrender to her emotions.

Not yet.

"You have instigated war." She made her accusation in a clear, strong voice. "You are guilty of using black magic against those in leadership positions. You are responsible for the death of Mother Madeleine Davenold, the former

High Seat of this Council."

"I will stand witness," Costel called out as he let go of Bijoux's hand and moved toward the table. "You should have made sure I was dead, Daniel. What stopped you?"

"I heard the others coming." Daniel grinned.

Murmurs filled the room once more.

"You are hereby charged with magical murder and mayhem." Emeric slammed the papers in his hand down. "What say you, Representative Father Levy?"

"I demand a trial." His blue stare was unflinchingly centered on Georgie.

Satisfaction gripped her. "That was my intention, exactly."

"I'm sure," Daniel taunted. "Trial by jury? Or *by fire*?"

He lifted his hand and a black corona exploded from his palm. Georgie gritted her teeth as her Bane shields flared to life, but she stood her ground, trusting in her natural immunity to keep her safe. Then a black flash shot from Daniel's finger and whipped through the air.

At Silviu.

Costel yelled and jumped onto the table. He leaped in front of Silviu without a moment to spare. Purple light blazed, the air crackled and the scent of burning hair twisted in Georgie's nostrils.

Anger saturated her senses. The room turned black as pitch.

Chapter Thirty

Costel

He saw the attack coming. Costel knew exactly what Daniel Levy would do as if he were the telepathic witch, rather than Bijoux. In a flash, he saw the magic build, compressed and pressurized, ready to lash out with a strength the others couldn't yet imagine.

But Costel knew. He knew what it felt like to stand under the impact of that force, and he knew he couldn't allow Silviu to suffer such pain. And not just because he was the witch who could see everyone else through, not just because Georgie and Silviu would need to work together to take down the threat damaging the entire witching world, but because Silviu was Costel's baby brother, and old habits died hard.

Costel jumped into the line of attack. Purple fire stole his breath and he felt as if he'd been electrocuted. He thought his muscles had liquefied and his bones had turned to rubber. His brain blanked and sparked like a blown fuse, gold and silver swirling somewhere in the terrible darkness that suddenly overtook his senses. He slid off the table and slammed onto the floor.

For a minute, Costel thought he had died or, at least, that his eyeballs had ruptured under the bone-creaking pressure that had swallowed him whole. But then he realized the smoky, swirling onyx mass in front of him was magic — as he'd never seen it before. Impenetrable, flashing with gold and silver flares, the raw, elemental force was unlike anything Costel had ever encountered — but with the darkness skewering his body, he couldn't deny the impact.

Pain shot through him in a hot current. His muscles spasmed, but he was unable to tense, unable to brace himself against further assault. The magic moved through Costel like water through a sieve, with little impediment, and he flopped on the floor helplessly as the current jolted along his neural pathways and pricked every one of his nerves. The rushing sensation sweeping through him galvanized his body, though his paralysis wasn't ready to let go yet.

A shocking, terrifying contradiction.

In slow increments, Costel's vision stopped tearing up and wavering. Oxygen came back in sharp bursts that made his lungs burn and twist. The room cleared of the blanket of darkness and instead filled with long cylinders of pitch black magic, shot through with the deepest hues of purple and green. Costel wasn't certain whose magic it was, but it was dangerously energized and swooping through the room erratically.

Silence reigned until Bijoux's scream seemed to puncture the sound barriers that had taken up residence in his ears. Woozy, Costel grimaced and searched for his Magic Match, hardly able to see through the haze. Then she was there, next to him, reaching for him before recoiling. She hissed in pain and a flash of rainbows swirled over Costel's body as if it shielded him from her touch.

He couldn't feel her physically. Somewhere in the deepest parts of his soul, Costel was aware of their shared connection churning in anger, but he couldn't feel Bijoux's touch in the moment she'd tried. The lack provoked the irrational need to drag her into himself, consume her magic as his own and use it to keep her safe. She seemed too far away, and the sensation was its own kind of pain.

Then the colorful glimmer faded and the rest of whatever bubble had consumed Costel popped. The room and all the screams within it jolted into sharp clarity. Next to him, Bijoux wailed and reached for him once more, throwing her arms around his neck as Matched magic rose in a heavy tide. Costel's confused nerves finally began working again.

Relief came to him with a cooling flow of golden light, but so did panic, as his brain rebooted.

Immediately Costel rolled, putting his Match on the hard floor and curling his body around hers. His muscles balked and felt as if they were tearing from his bones, but he forced them to work before Bijoux could be hurt. A streak of black magic sailed past his ear and he ducked his head, covering Bijoux's with his hand, as if that could save her.

"Are you all right?" She clutched at his back

He breathed her in, felt her body along the length of his and tried to contain his fear. "Are you?"

Costel felt a hard hand on his arm and glanced over his shoulder.

Emeric's face was stern and pale. "Come!" he demanded.

Emeric tugged with more physical strength than Costel would have thought possible. He let the man haul him to his feet, then leaned down to help Bijoux. He tucked her into the crook of his arm and hunched over her.

"Get up and get moving!" Emeric pushed the couple toward the edges of the room. "Get out of their way."

"What happened?" Costel staggered, put a hand to the wall. The stone was beautifully cool against his burned palm.

"I don't know what Georgeanne did." Emeric shook his head. "Daniel tried to use his magic and she made some sort of shield around you. I don't think she was fast enough to stop all of it" — Emeric squinted at Costel — "or was she?"

"I'm alive. It was enough."

"Good. Can't have my treasure disappointed again. She's got her heart set on seeing Romania." The man shook his head, a terrible expression haunting his eyes. "I'll never get the image of her draped over your lifeless body out of my head. Her heartache... I am glad you didn't die. Try to keep it that way."

"You know I can't take her —"

"I think your grandfather will love living at the Council

Palace." Emeric steamrollered Costel, both with words and by shoving him closer to the door. "Get out and get to safety. Take care of my treasure, Father Lovasz."

But Costel wasn't about to leave his brother. He pushed Bijoux behind him and drew on the powerful Lovasz magic to keep them both safe from the dark enchantments snaking through the room. Sinister fingers of purple, green and black coalesced then spread out, unfurling to flick at the unsuspecting. Witches dodged or suffered, falling to the floor with agonized screams.

Christiana and Milo ran toward Costel, dragging Constance with them. Adam and Tulah soon followed. Costel waved and took them all into his barrier but, though Christiana and Adam added their Matched strength to his spell and tightened the protection, they denied its safety.

"We need to stop this." Christiana squinted in Georgie and Silviu's general direction. "Daniel must be held accountable for his actions."

"Georgeanne and my brother will kill him. I know they will prevail." Costel firmed his voice until he was certain that none would realize the doubts he held.

He knew how strong Daniel was. Costel wasn't, however, certain how strong his brother and Georgeanne could be. Taking down Alexandru was one thing, but Silviu now faced a witch more powerful than himself and lacking any morals. Costel was terrified at the potential outcome.

"Death today would be too easy," Christiana spat. "That bastard killed my grandmother and I want him to pay. I want him to face what he's done and have to face others and know *they* know what he's done. I want him to live in a world where his reputation has been shredded, and he is shunned."

"Then let me help, *krasavitsa*." Milo took his wife's hand.

Costel watched in mute astonishment as the couple left the safety of his shields. A heartbeat later, Adam also decamped.

Costel turned to Tulah. "What are they doing?"

"Milo has the talent to calm. I suppose that's what they'll do."

The trio moved through the room slowly. The twins held hands while Milo spoke, but whatever the matriarchal man said was lost on the other side of Costel's magical barricade. He could see some spell being cast, even if just in the dazed stupor descending upon the witches who had previously been rushing for the doors. There were a few holdouts — witches who were casting their own attack spells at Daniel or others who seemed lost in blind panic, but, on the whole, Costel was impressed with how such calm could be brought about so efficiently.

He glanced at his brother and witnessed the moment when Silviu pitched in with his allies' effort. Costel could practically see his brother peel a portion of his magic away from the main fight to help Milo achieve calm in the chamber. He obviously needed it, too. Milo's face dripped with sweat and his body shook. The twins were more than vulnerable, standing behind the man with linked hands, moving in complicated patterns, their Matched magic glowing obscenely, a brazen target. Silviu gritted his teeth, his pale skin losing nearly all its color. Georgie alone looked unaffected, calm and composed and wholly focused on Daniel.

Who had stopped fighting.

"You will cooperate," Georgie informed him.

Costel could just barely hear her through his shields.

"By my own choice," the man replied. He waved and much of the dark haze dispersed. "Not because of his magic."

"I know how Milo used it against you at my Family's English estate, and I will allow him to use it so far as to make you a drooling zombie, Daniel, if you get out of line again."

He laughed. "You want to kill me yourself? Gods, how I wish you hadn't married Silviu. You're smart, so powerful. You and I would have ruled the world together."

"I am the one thing on this planet that can bring you down." She shook her head as if she couldn't believe her own ears. "I would never have joined you. I would never have been with you against the agreement my Family made two decades ago. My Match with Silviu is far too important, as is the alliance that spans the Schism."

"A relationship with me would also have spanned the Schism."

"I would never be with someone like you, Daniel."

"You think I'm evil?" Seeming to switch tactics, he raised his hands. "Look around. Have I harmed anyone? My magic isn't a force for evil, Georgie. I can enhance things, people and policies and magical elements. My only goal has been to strengthen the witching community and put us in our rightful place—ahead of those without magic, where we belong. Let the Council decide whether or not my abilities would be useful."

"You're charged with murder and mayhem—"

"Which I did not commit except against Father Lovasz, who interfered while I disciplined my own Family member." Daniel looked around the room. "I'm sure everyone here can understand the predicament he'd placed me in."

"What you did to Constance was far more than discipline," Costel shouted. The memory of the hallway attack was stark and haunting, as was the way Constance had appeared when he'd first rounded the corner. Costel knew abuse when he saw it.

He turned to the woman, who huddled against the wall behind Bijoux. "I won't let him hurt you again."

She smiled sadly. "You can't help it. This is a ruse. A way to either buy time or get everyone exactly where he wants them."

"It doesn't matter. Christiana's right," he told her. "He needs to face people who know what he's done and be judged by them. Not for his sake, but for my brother's, because otherwise Silviu and Georgeanne will be stuck with a reputation they don't deserve."

Bijoux sighed. "You're afraid that people will always wonder about the truth, and begin to suspect Georgie and Silviu of rushing things to hide their own...deficiencies, or greed or…"

"Yes, exactly." Costel noticed Georgeanne staring at him. He met her eyes, and she winked. He wondered if she could read lips.

"Why don't you give me a chance to explain?" Daniel looked too innocent in his appeal, especially after throwing dark magic spells around the chamber. "Surely you can listen to my side of the story."

"An excellent idea." Georgie lifted her chin and smiled, dominance and manipulation coloring the air around her.

In another flash of insight Costel could hardly credit, he once again saw exactly what would happen before it occurred. He understood Georgeanne's goals and motivations.

She hurt, and soon, Daniel would, too. They knew so much that could bring him down, but he hadn't yet realized. They hadn't even begun to share his story with the Council.

Georgie narrowed her eyes. "Let's start with the dark magic spell the Former Levy Father, your proud papa, cast in order to give you life."

Chapter Thirty-One

Bijoux

"The sins of the father must fall to the child, I suppose."

Bijoux held her breath as Daniel picked up the verbal gauntlet Georgie had thrown down. She didn't believe the Levy Father was as calm as he appeared—after all, he'd just used black magic with the intent to harm—but Bijoux couldn't fault Georgie for going along with the man's pretense. She understood the need to make him answer for his crimes. He'd caused too much damage and hurt too many people to face a quick end, and so long as he was reasonable, there were few options in how to handle him.

Christiana and Adam used their Matched magic to keep him in his chair. Bijoux wondered if their spell could really hold Daniel, if he decided he didn't want to be held anymore, but let them worry over that detail. As she looked around at the representatives slowly returning to their seats, though some tugged their chairs away from Levy's central position, Bijoux realized she had a role to play as well.

She pushed at the magic encasing her. "Let me get closer."

"You've lost your mind if you think I'm letting you get anywhere near Daniel." Costel folded his arms over his chest.

"I want to stand with Georgie and Silviu, as a matter of fact." Bijoux prodded his shoulder. "Let me out of here, Costel. I can help."

"What can you do?"

"Read his mind."

Costel shook his head. "You've tried and failed already. This time won't be any different."

"Every little bit helps." She pointed at Milo, standing behind his wife with both hands raised. His lips moved as if he were keeping up a constant stream of words—a calming spell, no doubt. "Like him, your brother has helped me, too. I became more effective."

Costel stared at her, considering. His silver eyes darkened with a worry Bijoux could read easily, even without the validation of his thoughts. Images flashed in her mind, however, and told her she'd won her way.

He glanced at Tulah. She shrugged. "I will become a cat and hide."

Costel groaned. "Don't leave my side, Bijoux. Stay close." He gripped Constance's elbow and lowered his shield. "You're coming with us."

The three of them crossed the room to stand with Silviu at Georgie's side. Bijoux allowed Costel to steer her so that she could observe the Levy Father without dividing her attention. Her Match made certain she didn't trip over any of the chairs that had been overturned.

"You can't hold me accountable for a spell cast by the former Levy Father," Daniel protested. "I didn't ask to be born."

Georgeanne pursed her lips. "But you did take advantage of your talents—"

"Who here hasn't?" Daniel shrugged. "We are witches, and we use the gifts nature has given us. Even you, Georgie."

"You lied, though. You told Eliasz Levy that Constance was your sister and that she was the one born of a dark magic spell."

"She's like a sister to me." Daniel scowled over his shoulder at Eliasz, who refused to meet his Father's eyes. "As for which one of us was born of a dark spell... Well, you can't expect a man to share all his vulnerabilities with a witch he barely knows."

Bijoux caught a flash of knowledge that wasn't a memory.

It was similar in both appearance and weight to the times the women in the kitchen had gossiped about far-off witches or Family history they hadn't been an express part of. It was an ingrained perception without having been perceived directly.

A brother had been passed over for leadership. One of the brothers wore his honor like armor. The other engaged in questionable activities. One was strong, the other easily led. Bijoux had difficulty understanding exactly who was who but knew the choice of inheritance had caused deep scars and a rift that would never be healed.

The thought had come from Eliasz. Bijoux glanced his way, noting his forbidding expression. Even his eyes had lost their sparkle. Ileana stood behind him—close, but not touching—casting several nervous glances at her fiancé as Bijoux watched. He was beyond angry at Daniel and couldn't care less what consequences the man faced.

"You lied to him," Georgie said, "but you expect us to believe you now?"

Daniel spread his fingers in an innocent appeal. "What have I lied about here?"

"A very good question." Bijoux saw her opportunity and reached for it. "Perhaps I can help with that?"

Daniel's features closed down, his impassive mask tightening until there was no hint of emotion on his face, not even the manipulative innocence he'd donned a moment ago. "What do you think *you* can do?"

"He knows I can't read him on my own," she whispered. Bijoux leaned into Silviu and went to her toes, speaking directly into his ear so that hopefully no one else could hear her. "You can enhance my ability, can't you?"

Silviu blinked but nodded. As close as they stood, his voice was nearly inaudible as he turned to Bijoux. "Of course, but when Daniel first arrived, it didn't seem to make a difference."

"We're closer now, just steps away. And he's under stress, giving me a little advantage."

Silviu glanced at his wife "Georgie should have a greater ability to...help me, now, as well."

"Then try again."

Silviu nodded once more and bent toward his wife. Bijoux watched as he whispered to her but couldn't hear a word. She didn't need to. Georgie nodded, took his hand and bit her lip. A flash of gold sparked between them.

Magic reached for Bijoux. She wasn't certain who directed the flow, but she stretched for it, ignoring the strange, disconnected sensation that accompanied the action. She'd never done such a thing before. The closest she'd come had been with Costel, and his magic had simply been there without her trying to capture it.

Bijoux's skin prickled and pulled to the point of pain. The pressure from even such a small amount of Georgie and Silviu's Matched magic was uncomfortably high, and it gave her a clue as to how it might feel to be on the bottom of the ocean. Then Costel put his hand on her shoulder and the dizzying influx of power ebbed.

She reached up and gripped Costel's hand, pushing his fingers harder against her collarbone. "I'm all right."

"What can you tell us, Bijoux?" Silviu asked.

She closed her eyes momentarily to better evaluate what was happening inside her head. "I can see, but I have to concentrate, I think. I'm getting quick flickers of memories, perceptions, but not the whole story like I do with others. He's still hiding. Gods, he's strong."

"He uses dark magic. How has he used it, Bijoux?" Georgie asked loudly, for everyone's benefit.

Though their audience couldn't have heard their whispered conversation, no one seemed surprised that Bijoux now stood at the table, staring at Daniel. They knew what her talent was. She ignored her father's glare, the unspoken demand that she stay out of it and keep her mouth shut, the piercing thought shuttling from his mind that warned her not to show the full extent of her talents to the crowd.

She had no choice.

"He has taken things he had no right to. Someone's…" Bijoux sank her teeth into her bottom lip and squeezed her eyes shut again, digging into the shadowed landscape of Daniel's mind. "I don't know. I see a silver light coming from a man and sinking into Daniel. I can feel it, too. It's cool and electric."

"Magic," Silviu announced. "Anyone who has inherited a leadership position has felt such a thing."

"That's what that was." Daniel lifted his hands shoulder height, palms out but devoid of magic, just as Bijoux opened her eyes. His was a guiltless and conciliatory gesture she didn't believe for a second. "When power passed from my Father to me."

Bijoux frowned. "And when it happened again with a woman?"

"That was a gift."

The woman taking shape once again in Bijoux's mind was also connected to others, men and women Daniel knew, liked, cared for or had use of. His memories of them streamed out in a line longer than she would have hoped. "He has allies. More than you thought, from nearly every coven."

Silviu looked around the handful of Family leaders in attendance. "That is a problem for the Mothers and Fathers, the branch leaders and house managers, not the Council. Each Family can root out its own defectors."

A murmur of agreement ran through the crowd before Georgeanne put an end to it by clearing her throat. "Did they give him their magic, Bijoux?"

"Some did. Some seemed…reluctant in his memories. Others were given tasks they'd need magic to achieve and so there was no transfer from them."

"Like Graves Ngozi?"

Having never met the man, Bijoux couldn't say. She turned to Constance and looked inside her mind, where the vision of a tall, charismatic psychopath took shape — a misunderstood hero to Constance, simply because he'd offered her some sort of protection from Daniel on several occasions. They'd both been roped into the Levy Father's schemes before they'd been able to figure out how to save themselves.

"But Graves enjoyed himself too much," Bijoux muttered, staring at Constance and wishing she'd paid more attention when the woman had explained her role in things to Silviu. "You were held hostage. There is someone you're protecting, but Graves liked the power he received."

Constance licked her lips. "I know what everyone thinks, but—"

"Graves cared for you because he loved..." Bijoux reached a little farther and found the image of a man Constance cared for as well. "Your father?"

"My father was the son of the Levy Father."

"No, not that one." Bijoux tapped her chest. "The father of your heart."

Constance sighed. "Graves was in love with Warner. Warner raised me, yes. Daniel made us keep tabs on Graves by getting very *personal* with him. Friendships developed between the men."

"Daniel had a *friendship* with my cousin, Suzette, as well," Georgie murmured. "Somehow, all of this is connected— Graves and Suzette, what Daniel wanted, needed and tried to achieve. I want to know how."

Bijoux looked at the Levy Father. "Well?"

"Well what?" He laughed. "You're doing a marvelous job and saving me a great deal of trouble. I don't even have to speak. Here. Tell them this."

The stream of knowledge suddenly widened into an overwhelming flow. Bijoux's brain seemed to expand and contract, a sharp pain curling over her scalp and pinching in the base of her neck. She gripped Costel's hand. A small explosion went off between her eyes and a drop of blood fell from her nose as she gasped.

Her knees buckled, and Costel clutched her to his chest.

"Bijoux!"

The images cut off. As if through miles of water, Bijoux thought she heard Daniel apologize, but she ignored him and fought to piece together what he'd shown her.

"Graves wanted money. Suzette wanted a baby. Both wanted to lead, wanted more than their share or what they were promised. Others want power, justice, revenge. There are a hundred different reasons why they've joined Daniel. Some follow simply because they believe he'll win. He wants it all, believes he can do better. Thinks he can make a difference in the world."

Daniel shrugged. "You didn't expect me to believe I could do any worse, did you?"

"And the policies he's supported all over the globe?" Georgie glared at the man. "Is that how he thinks to achieve world domination?"

A confusing jumble filled Bijoux's mind, though softer than the torrent that had come before. The contradictions were hard to follow, but she gritted her teeth and sought to rifle deeper into Daniel's thoughts. "In some places he would support one thing, but in another he would support the opposite. I don't understand why."

"He supported whatever would rile the group he targeted." Milo stopped chanting his spell long enough to offer insight. "He wanted chaos, because he could claim power in the resulting turmoil."

"Yes." Bijoux nodded. "His thoughts agree."

Representatives shifted, whispered and grumbled.

Daniel smiled. "See how cooperative I'm being?"

"Perhaps," Georgie said. "Or, perhaps your thoughts lie as well as your mouth."

Bijoux shook her head. "No, he's thinking lies also, but they feel different and come through sharper than the truth behind them. He may be harder to read, but that doesn't mean I'm not learning how to do it."

"Very good. You're amazing." Costel's praise warmed her straight through.

"What lies is he thinking?" Silviu asked.

Bijoux told him, "He is not calm and he did not want Georgeanne. Suzette was in line to inherit the Family when he recruited her, and he didn't approach Georgie later because she's Bane and he hadn't done the proper research on Bane-born witches until recently."

"You've been leading my cousin on for that long?" Georgie tsked. "No wonder she's such a mess."

Bijoux continued, "Only later did he realize what Georgie might be able to do. Then they met, became friends. He was trying to woo her, but she was blocked to his influence and refused to be seduced."

Silviu smirked. "Because she loves me. Because she's always loved me, and no other can *ever* compete against our connection."

To everyone's surprise, Burkit Serik spoke up. "But what would Daniel have done if he'd gotten Georgeanne as an ally?"

Appalling thoughts filled Bijoux's mind like a cancer. Hazy and incomplete though they were, and as hard as Daniel tried to snuff them out, Bijoux had already learned how to see the facts. She nearly gagged and hesitated to answer.

But, in the end, she told them the truth. "He wanted to bring Georgie to the point that she could break all magic, not just the black. He wanted to use her abilities to steal the magic from anyone who opposed him. Only he would be left with any, cementing his sovereignty."

Everyone on the Council spoke at once. Questions and statements, opinions and ideas. They were angry and scared, betrayed. It seemed no one remembered to hold on to the reserve Bijoux had previously hated so much. Their ability to compartmentalize their thoughts and hide them from her talent was lost in their emotional upheaval. She now understood just how necessary their distrust of her had been to her sanity. Voices lifted and ideas were tossed around until Bijoux felt dizzy and sick, bombarded and blasted. She pressed against Costel's chest and let him hold her tightly. She concentrated on breathing as he whispered soothing encouragements in her ear.

Queries came at her from all sides.

"Could he enhance Georgeanne to that extent?"

"He believes so," Bijoux replied, swallowing against her nausea, "but I doubt it."

"Has he stolen magic from other witches?"

"Yes." Bijoux panted.

"Has he donated money to causes in my region?"

"Yes."

"He would truly strip the matriarchs of their power? Their authority?"

Bijoux pressed her sweating forehead to Costel's shoulder. "Yes. He dreams of uniting our community under the banner of patriarchy. One house — his."

"Why? Our system works well."

"To avoid another war." Bijoux was nearly blind with all the images assaulting her brain. When someone pressed a cup to her palm, she grasped it gratefully and let Costel help her take a sip. "The opposite of what you thought, Georgie. The Levys won't survive another witching war."

"Witching war?" someone asked. "Between covens, you mean?"

Bijoux groaned. "Yes."

"What war? There is no war. We have a Council to settle disputes now."

"He's paranoid," Bijoux moaned.

Georgie's voice cut across the din, silencing the noise Bijoux heard in her ears, if not the racket in her skull. "They won't survive a witching war, but they would survive a witch hunt. The Levys aren't strong enough for the one, but they're certainly weak enough for the other."

"He once shared a similar fear to me," Eliasz called out. "Daniel and I discussed the *trouble* we had at my betrothal celebration. Daniel suggested the danger to Ileana and you, Georgie, could be a ploy of a more magically powerful house than our own, specifically the Lovasz coven, to instigate conflict. If another witching war came about, the Lovaszes would be in prime position for victory."

Bijoux gasped. Against her, Costel stiffened. "I assure you, the Lovasz coven is too small to have such grand plans."

"And why bother anyway," Georgie asked, "when we've gone about gaining power legitimately, unlike Daniel? Marriage and politics, not secret alliances and magic theft."

"The Lovaszes *were* at fault. Alexandru tried to kill Georgeanne, and he's insane enough to have carried on his destruction, if he hadn't been stopped." Daniel swiveled in his chair to look at Eliasz. "Is it so wrong of me to want to protect my coven? You are also one of mine, and I did this for you, too."

"Next time," Eliasz spat, "don't do me any favors."

Mei Lan Cen shot to her feet. "It is you who is bringing about war, Father Levy!"

"He's too dangerous," Burkit shouted. "How far will he go? We can't afford leniency, especially with his allies still unknown to us and free to create havoc."

Bijoux shuddered as the representatives began shouting again. Several of the matriarchs called for Daniel's death. One of the patriarchs wanted to let him go with a warning and a hefty fine. They had precious little physical evidence to hold against him just then, but Bijoux was confident they could find it, with her help. Unfortunately, reading Daniel's thoughts wasn't enough, and the Council majority refused to consider the interrogation they'd just listened to in the same light as a formal trial.

Mei Lan banged on the table to get everyone's attention. "I suggest we bind his magic pending our next meeting. In the meantime, we shall investigate these claims, each of us looking for evidence of Father Levy's misdoings in our own covens. When we meet again, we will be better prepared to conduct a formal trial."

Georgie and Silviu had stayed out of the discussion, but Bijoux didn't need to read their thoughts to know Mei Lan's suggestion met with their absolute approval. Coming just a minute after Silviu had said a few quiet words to the woman, Bijoux could understand why.

The idea was agreed upon unanimously. Widely renowned as two of the best spell-casters in the witching world, Christiana and Adam were given the task of placing limits on Daniel's abilities — how he could use them and to what aim. They redirected their Matched magic into a binding spell. As Bijoux watched, golden ropes became visible between the twins and they sent the coils to wrap around Daniel's body.

Around and around, as the spell was chanted. The ropes seemed to pull tight.

Then they blazed black and caught fire. Daniel laughed as dark light spread out around him.

"You fools can't bind me. I've had enough of this nonsense." He leaped onto the table in a single, athletic move. "You will either support me, or you will die."

Chapter Thirty-Two

Silviu

"*Move*. Watch out!"

Silviu shoved Georgie out of the way of a dark magic blast. He had no idea if the spell would hurt her, but the last time she'd been hit with an enhanced enchantment, she'd been dragged to the brink of death. He had no intention of simply watching to see if that happened again.

Georgie staggered sideways. Her chair tumbled toward Silviu. With a stream of churning black magic between them, they were effectively cut off from each other. Silviu knew that had been on purpose. The Levy Father was trying to divide and conquer the whole Council, starting with the two witches who posed the largest threat to his goals.

"He meant for this happen quickly." Bijoux's voice trembled as she staggered to Silviu's side. Her face was ghostly pale and her violet eyes were too large in her face. A river of blood ran from her nose to drip from her chin. "I can see... I can see."

A pulsing purple ball rocketed toward her. Costel threw up a shield that barely held long enough for him throw Bijoux to the side. The ball slammed into the stone wall behind them. Cracks formed and chunks of rock hit the floor.

"What?" Silviu caught Bijoux and shoved her into a chair. Time was of the essence, but he needed to know. "What do you see?"

"He lured us here. Let us lower our guard. No trial." She shook her head. "Never a trial. Then he attacked, like he meant to."

Standing on the table, Daniel laughed like a madman. He raised his hands and onyx lances sailed through the air. Around the room, nearly every witch dodged the renewed attack and raced for the door, stampeding each other.

There was no exit. The door was blocked with magic. A few tried, anyway, and fell for their trouble. Their screams rang out in warning and they dropped to writhe on the floor. Unlike last time, Daniel's newest assault was meant to destroy. Mass hysteria spread as witches pressed to the walls and Silviu saw the Levy Father's intent as clearly as if he were Bijoux—perhaps because their magic was still partially linked.

"Shit." He realized he'd been continuing to enhance her telepathy and abruptly stopped. It was too late to prevent the damage that had occurred in her head, but he used the bottom edge of his shirt to clean her face. "Daniel bought himself time with our hearing today, then took us by surprise."

Bijoux made an attempt to wipe her nose herself. "Before, he was simply showing his power. A test and a taste of what was coming."

"Now he means to win against us."

"Would have, anyway," Bijoux slurred. "His plan."

"Of course it was." Silviu glared at the chaos erupting around them. Two witches had dragged Daniel from the table, but his magic was getting the best of them on the floor and he'd hardly begun to breathe heavily. "He got us right where he wanted us. He would have come out of this the sole survivor, blamed anyone he wanted and taken over completely. He could have claimed to have been elected to the High Seat. Who could gainsay him if we're all dead?"

"You can't stay, my love." Costel stumbled toward them, hand outstretched for Bijoux. "We've got to get out of here. Silviu, I'll be back as soon as I find a safe place for—"

"No one can leave." Silviu pointed at the door, iridescent with visible magic. "Daniel made sure of it."

Costel's eyes widened and he looked around in obvious panic. "I've got to find a safe place for her."

Silviu looked around, too. Georgie was farther away than he'd realized, almost to the end of the table, not just on the other side of her chair. Beyond her, witches had sprung forward from their huddles against the wall and sliced through the crowd, creating havoc, attacking their friends and Family.

Silviu cursed. Daniel's henchmen had infiltrated the Council.

"Milo!" Silviu spun to find his own allies. He spotted the man, standing across the room with his wife. Christiana and Adam were glowing gold, throwing up as many shields and spells as possible, but they were under attack by three other witches. Milo chanted rapidly.

Silviu cursed again and, as Milo glanced his way, threw out his own magic, a cold silver stream that caught Milo's warmer, soothing talent in a fierce grip. He didn't wait for permission. As he'd done several times before, Silviu manipulated Milo's magic boldly, using it to blanket the room with calm.

The wrong witches were affected. Representatives and their entourages stopped and stared, their eyes glassy and their lips lax. Silviu studied the shimmering silver haze as quickly as he could, searching for defects in the spell, but there were none. Daniel and his allies were shrouded with a deep purple shield.

"He pretended," Bijoux whispered in a dazed sing-song behind Silviu. "He can stand against Milo's magic, and so can his people. He charmed them so it would be, after Suzette succumbed to Milo's talent."

A bolt of black lightning flew across the room. It hit Milo squarely in the chest, sending him sailing back against the wall. Christiana screamed. Her Matched magic wavered. Milo slid to the floor and lay still.

"*Fuck.*" Silviu turned to find Georgie.

She punched a man in the eye. Part of the Serik entourage,

Silviu noted darkly. Murder rose in his soul as he watched the man lash out at his wife. Adrenaline enflaming his heart, Silviu jumped over Georgie's fallen chair, reaching for her. A deep green squall stopped him in his tracks. He reeled, jumping back before the toxic spell could hit him.

Daniel's laughter boomed. He laughed harder when Eliasz tackled him. They rolled a moment before Daniel sprang to his feet. Eliasz was sent flying by a dark blast of magic, but with Milo's calm broken, others rushed the Levy Father with deadly intent as well. He didn't seem to care as he gathered his power. Silviu spun back to his wife.

The Serik witch raised a long, straight-bladed knife over his head. Both edges of the sharp kindjal dagger shone in the light of the overhead chandeliers and though magic swirled through the ornate designs carved into the handle, the blade was un-enchanted. Bane shields would not stop it. Georgie kicked out, but the larger man barely flinched as her foot sank into his abdomen.

Silviu leaped forward again, only to meet a transparent wall of flashing black light. He pushed against it, and the skin of his palm sizzled. Still, he pushed harder, ignoring the scent of his own burning flesh, desperate to get to his Magic Match and save her from the blade arcing down toward her heart. He threw himself at the obstacle.

"Georgeanne!"

Love and loss and mindless desperation filled Silviu's scream. His brain blanked on a cold tide of horror. Fear choked him. Magic rose and shuddered through the room, reverberating off the walls and smashing the crystals in the chandeliers. Witches fell under the power of the Reap witch.

Daniel's dark magic didn't even wobble.

Georgie lurched back. The blade shimmered in the light. Burkit Serik's battle cry halted Silviu's heedless drive against the magical barrier before him. The opinionated Councilman proved himself a courageous warrior when he leaped onto his cousin's back. Muscles bulging, Burkit wrestled the man to the ground

The blade proved as deadly as Silviu had feared. Burkit turned to his next opponent.

Panting, Georgie met Silviu's eyes. A moment in the midst of chaos, a connection. Golden light flared to life around both of them.

"*Reach*," he demanded. "Break this fucking wall between us!"

She stared at the wall in surprise, but he was aware of her tugging on the invisible tethers connecting them. Deep in his soul, he sensed her presence, her life and her spirit, and the energizing stream of the magic they shared. He felt it unwind as if from a spool, following her guidance, coming to her call — him to her.

Gold light blazed and washed over the glimmering, transparent wall separating them. Georgie rushed toward it from the opposite side, dodging the few dark magic strikes sent her way.

Silviu risked a glance at Daniel. He and his henchmen fought the crowd from the center of the melee that had formed. Christiana and Adam were gaining ground against the Levy Father's allies, her wrath flavoring the attack spells they used. Daniel was momentarily distracted.

"*Now*," Silviu ordered. "Break the wall down."

Georgie took a breath deep enough that Silviu practically felt it himself. She lifted a shaking hand to the barrier. Magic tugged deep inside him as her fingers moved, unharmed, over the surface. Hazy and dim though his vision seemed, Silviu saw links in the spell break under Georgie's fingers. The wall fell.

He reached for her physically. His grip was too tight, but his need was too great and he had to get his hands on her. He clutched her shoulders and hauled her to him, knowing he'd leave bruises. He drew breath through gritted teeth and tried not to hurt his wife too badly as he absorbed the feel of her, safe for the moment, in his arms.

"Come on," she whispered, wriggling from his hold.

"There's too much to do to lose control now."

"We've got to stop him." Silviu knew she was right. He let her go and tugged her toward the group attacking Daniel.

On the opposite side of the table, half the Council battled. Magic flew, spells exploded. Fists launched. Silviu saw a woman beating one of Daniel's henchmen with her shoe — blazing silver with some enchantment that left the man's shirt smoking.

It would have been comical, if it hadn't been so terrible.

Around the battle, fallen witches littered the floor. They sprawled. They flopped. Blood oozed from noses and ears. A few had holes blasted into their chests and stomachs, already cauterized under pitch black flames. Some could be saved if they acted quickly, others were beyond hope.

In the center of the melee, Costel's magic flared brilliantly. All the power behind him, all the combined strength of the Lovasz coven erupted in a silver blaze that left Silviu squinting. Costel was shrouded with writhing black magic, his dark hair in spikes and his clothing tattered. To Costel's credit, Daniel looked nearly as bad.

Panic surged and squeezed Silviu's heart. His stomach twisted. Fear and adrenaline pulled him apart until his nerves seemed too stretched to feel anything at all, but he pushed his own magic — joined to the impressive Davenold force — toward his brother, helping him in his attack. "Georgie!"

She was there. "You need a plan!"

"Bind him," Silviu ordered.

"You still want him to stand trial?"

"I want everyone in the fucking world to know he'll face judgment for his crimes." Silviu stopped at the edge of the fighting group and shoved Georgie behind him. "And I'll make certain they know what happened. The truth."

"He won't make it easy. He won't submit while we bind him."

"We can hold him." Silviu straightened his shoulders and lifted his hands, letting the full force of his magic free. "We have to."

"Then let me be the shield." Georgie stepped in front of him.

He would have argued. His instincts were screaming. Alarms were ringing in his skull and his muscles were already bunched to put her behind him again, where he could protect her. But he knew he couldn't. She was born to shield them all, born to face Daniel's threat.

Silviu had to be worthy enough of the promises he'd made to let Georgeanne do what she must.

"Let go," Silviu encouraged her. He slipped his hands around her waist, holding on to her, even as he demanded she release her reservations. "Let go of everything, no doubts between us. No secrets or manipulations, just love."

Gold light blazed. Their connection solidified into a force Silviu felt in every part of his soul, but it was unstable.

Gold light turned black. Daniel spun toward them, a maniacal grin spreading across his face. His magic came to his command easily, with years of practice behind him, while Georgie and Silviu struggled to handle their newly combined strength.

"Give me everything, Georgie. All of it," Silviu begged. He held her hips in a grip that had to be killing her, as his fingers cramped and ached. In a heartbeat's time, the shared flow of their bond — something Silviu had previously thought was strong enough — distended into a raging, dangerous inundation of magic. Black light consumed all trace of gold and the whole mess wavered erratically.

He tried to hold it. Sweat poured down his back and his muscles felt as if they were peeling from his bones. Every inch of his scalp burned. Silviu braced his legs as more magic rushed in — always more, without limit. Too much, more than he'd ever known before. Witches dropped to their knees and clutched their skulls. Only Daniel and his henchmen remained standing.

"Georgie," Silviu croaked. The taste of copper in his mouth gagged him. He spat out blood.

She tilted her head back. From where he stood behind her, Silviu couldn't see her face. He could hardly see anything past the black flashes expanding in his vision, but she must have donned some terrible expression because Daniel stumbled, his eyes widening.

Then the Levy Father's eyebrows lowered and his lips thinned. He paused for just a moment more before stepping forward. He grabbed his own ally by the throat and dark purple light flared, streaming from one witch to the other as Daniel stole the man's magic for himself. He dropped his ally to the floor and reached for another.

"Please, love." Silviu could hardly make his mouth move under the enormous pressure bearing down on him. His joints popped and his muscles tore. Whatever Georgie was doing dragged immeasurable power through Silviu's body, and he wasn't certain how much longer he could hold out.

"It's you," she told him in a tone of voice he'd never heard her use before. Her words echoed with magic. Power. Ignoring Daniel, Georgie turned to Silviu. Her eyes shone gold, illuminating the air in front of her face. "Reap witch, with all the power of the universe at your command."

"With the right key," he gasped, unable to believe what he saw, half-afraid and half-proud of his wife and their Match. He had no idea how others would react. "You've got to focus it, Georgie. Stable, my love. We need stability."

She spun back to look at the Levy Father. Georgie raised her voice. "I bind you, Daniel. You will not cause more harm. You will not instigate war. But you will stand trial, and the whole world will hear of your crimes and know what you truly are."

Pressure ripped into Silviu's bones as magic surged over him. Perhaps *from* him, as Georgie had stated. It wobbled and wavered, gold threads flashing in the darkness, a brutal wind picking up along the edges of the stream. Black cords enveloped Daniel and pulled tight.

Silviu gritted his teeth. Pain became the center of his world, and his thoughts dwindled to the narrow focus of making certain Georgie completed what she attempted. He wrapped his arms around her waist, pushing his chest to her spine and willing his legs to support them both as Daniel shrugged off the Bane witch's command.

Magic rebounded with a roar. Georgie staggered. Silviu despaired, wondering if his wife could pull them through, yet he held on to his faith as the only lifeline they had left. Failure wasn't an option.

"Everything," he demanded. "I want it all! Give me all of you, Georgeanne."

"I am. I did!"

"Stop holding back on me!"

With the last of his strength, Silviu did the only thing he could think of. He speared his fingers into Georgie's hair and pulled her around to face him. As Daniel shook like a wet dog, dislodging the binding spell they'd tried to contain him with, Silviu kissed his wife, his Magic Match.

He took her mouth, conquered it. Potent and wild, tender and fierce, the caress left their breath merged and their lips clinging. He tangled his tongue with hers, leading her in the sliding, gliding dance of hot, wet friction. Sleek velvet against tempting satin. Magic and love interwove into a new force and Silviu felt Georgie's final reserves crumble. She'd given him so much that he hadn't realized he was waiting for anything more until the power that grew between them still hadn't been enough to stop the Levy Father. But Matched magic was influenced by emotions.

They'd suffered heartache and anguish. They'd lived through trials and tribulations. They'd discovered something rare and pure in spite of the resistance of so many. The love they shared had been forged in the heat of their first passion and tempered by a decade's worth of loneliness.

There was no fairy tale, no myth and no legend that could compete with what Silviu and Georgie had created. Their love was a magic all its own.

And the power of true love's kiss remade the world.

Light exploded. Gold and black twisted and turned. Tunnels whipped through the room, knocking the rest of the furniture aside. The double doors catapulted open. Witches that had fallen to the floor arched and gasped, once-stilled chests rising as new life filled them.

Daniel screamed in rage. He charged. Silviu saw it all with his eyes closed, his senses expanding to fill the universe, everything known at once, and forgotten the moment he ended the kiss.

Gasping, Silviu jumped in front of Georgeanne — reflex, instinct. Daniel's magic barreled toward them, obscenely illuminated in comparison to the seamless force produced by the Bane and Reap Match. The power of its flow swarmed the pair, streaking past and circling around to find a target.

They were distracted. Silviu focused on the magic, rather than the man. Daniel flung himself at them, caught Georgeanne to his chest. The Serik witch's kindjal blade was clasped in his fingers, hurtling down.

"No!"

Silviu dove onto his wife, smashing her harder against Daniel, protecting her between their bodies. Daniel's arm came down, stabbing Silviu in the back. The double-edged blade was as sharp as it had seemed, slicing through skin and muscle to lodge in bone, spreading fire through his ribs and shoulders. Daniel's elbow dug into his collarbone as Silviu wrenched free.

He slid to the ground with Georgeanne's scream ripping through his head. Silviu panted and gasped, searching for enough oxygen, but his lung felt deflated. His blood seemed too warm as it coursed down his back and his heart stuttered alarmingly. But Silviu barely had the ability to think about it.

All he had the energy left to do was send the rest of his magic to his wife, who would surely need it.

She was a vision of rage, pain and loss. Wavering though she was in Silviu's sights, Georgie was gorgeous. With her fingers twisted in his shirt, she kneeled by his side, staring up at the patriarchal leader bearing down on them with wild defiance in her glowing eyes. Curls flying, black and gold light rioting around her body, power pulsing steady and strong—not like Silviu's heart at all.

It was no wonder he loved her so much.

"My love," he whispered.

"You *will* live." She turned her eyes back to Daniel. "But you will *die*."

Not a prophesy or a wish, but a command, cold and calmly given. Magic rushed to do her bidding. Silviu felt his body lifted, intense heat sweeping his spine, and he struggled to keep his eyes open when the golden light blazed brighter than the sun. Energy poured through him, using him as a conduit to her, his Match. Pain pulled every one of his nerves taut.

All around Daniel, a network of dark cords was revealed in the blinding illumination of Georgie's full power. *Their full power*, Silviu thought giddily, just like the effigy that had targeted Madeleine and just like the questing spell that had challenged Georgie after her grandmother's death. Appearing as a net, Daniel's magic was formed of individual threads that met at intersections, twisting and linking the dark spell of his birth together.

In a rapid wave of motion, the cords snapped, one by one, under Georgie's direction. In the blink of an eye, Daniel's dark magic had been dispersed.

Eradicated.

He fell to the floor. The Levy Father did not gasp or grunt. He didn't speak or stir. He was utterly still.

Fire engulfed Silviu, the rushing, jolting energy knitting him back together with a tenacity so far beyond pain there was no description of the sensation. Silviu hung in suspended agony until the ability to breathe returned to him. His collapsed lung inflated. His heart stopped leaking down his back. As he healed, Georgie's glow began to diminish, leaving her slumped against him in exhaustion.

Silviu was stiff and sore, but he rolled over to poke at the fallen dark magic witch. "He's not dead."

"He will be," Georgie said. "Daniel was born of dark magic. Without it, he is nothing."

"Not nothing." Silviu pushed up to his knees and looked around at the dazed and frightened faces of the crowd. He focused on Eliasz and Constance, kneeling together at the end of the table. "He's your Father. What about the Levy magic?"

Constance shook her head. "He can only use dark magic. The Levy power has been held hostage."

"But where is it? What happened to it? Did you break that, too?" Silviu turned to Georgie.

She shrugged, clearly not knowing any more than he did, but then she angled her chin toward Daniel's body with a tired jerk. "Look."

The man gasped—a terrible rattle from deep within his chest. His eyes widened and his mouth opened, but he moved like a puppet, making Silviu wonder if there truly had been any life in him after Georgie had broken his magic. It could have been the Levy Family's power, housed inside a corpse and fighting its way free, because silver light rushed from between Daniel's lips and soared into the air.

And shot into Eliasz. Having just gained his feet, he dropped back to his knees, grimacing, obviously holding back a scream Silviu could understand all too well. Claiming power hurt.

"The Levy Father is dead," Silviu announced. He continued ironically, "Long live the Levy Father. I have confidence he will prove better than the last."

Emeric stumbled toward Eliasz and helped him back up. "And who better to lead the Mothers and Fathers of our community than a Matched pair to share the power of the High Seat? As much as I loved Madeleine, I do believe our new sovereigns will also prove better than the last. Better than them all."

The Council representatives raised their voices as much as possible in their tired, battered states. Their agreement was unanimous.

Chapter Thirty-Three

Georgeanne

"It's a great compromise, Georgie."

"Mmm, yes." She hugged Milo tightly, her relief so overwhelming she could hardly comprehend his words. He'd been badly hurt in Daniel's attack, but he would pull through. Almost everyone would pull through, after Georgie and Silviu had released so much magic. Formless, wild and raw, it had swept through the Council Chamber and healed so many.

Milo relaxed back into the chair he'd been pushed into a moment after he'd been helped to his feet. "Look around. They're all happy. Each side of the Schism feels they will be represented with the two of you in power."

His words finally penetrating the turmoil in her mind, Georgie did as he suggested, turning to scan the room. The Council Chamber was a mess, the aftereffects of battle stark and disturbing. Chairs were strewn about, the side-tables that used to hold water pitchers and carafes overturned, glass and crystal from the overhead chandeliers sprinkled across the stone floor. Dark streaks of soot and magical residue were left on the walls. Blood stained the floor.

Witches from every coven were in various states of disarray—clothing ripped, with burns, bruises and bloody wounds showing through the tatters. They were tired and scared, more subdued than she'd ever seen them. Georgie could understand completely. Sometimes there was simply too much to process. At least most had survived the ordeal.

Christiana and Adam, the strain of their mission heavy on

their features, were finishing the last of the spells they had cast. From fighting Daniel and his henchmen, to cleaning up the room and healing the survivors as best they could, their abilities had been in high demand. The golden light between them began to fade, signaling the end of their task.

Christiana came toward Georgie and Milo, and sank to her knees in front of her husband. Georgie stood awkwardly, watching a moment too intensely private for the location. Christiana gazed up at her husband adoringly, tears tracking down her cheeks, while Milo stared back, hungry for some indefinable thing. Emotion was a tangible force between them.

"I was so scared," Chris whispered.

"So was I, *krasavitsa*, but we came through."

Georgie left them alone. A few feet away, Adam nuzzled a black cat. Georgie was happy that Tulah had changed forms when the fighting had broken out. The woman wouldn't have stood a chance of survival otherwise. Georgie moved past the pair with only a nod.

She walked around the table slowly, doing and saying the things she imagined a sovereign should do or say after winning a battle — shaking hands, dispensing words of wisdom she didn't feel adequate enough to share, thanking witches for their bravery. Georgie checked on wounds without knowing how to help them beyond the simple first-aid she'd learned during the Asian witch hunts. She assisted a few trembling witches into chairs and bowed her head over those who had fallen and would never rise again.

"Georgeanne."

She turned to find Burkit behind her. "Thank you for saving my life," she told him.

He waved her words away. "I wouldn't want to see your husband's heart broken by your untimely death." Burkit winked. "Besides, you are a patriarchal witch now."

"That means men should take care of me?"

"A good man always takes care of his allies, doesn't he?"

She knew what assurances he was after, and she gave

them freely. "You are definitely an ally, maybe even a friend."

"Ah, a good day, then. My coven will be pleased with my success."

Mei Lan and Mother Choudhury approached. "Everyone is settling down after the ordeal," Mei Lan said. "Many of us would like to bestow the High Seat powers as quickly as possible, before another egotistical bastard tries to take over."

"There is no telling what Daniel's allies will do, once they hear news of his death," Mother Choudhury added.

Burkit agreed. "Let me talk to some of the men around here and see what they think. I believe the sooner we get things done, the more efficient we'll be at cleaning this mess up. It sounds as if we all have been invaded by Daniel's people."

"It's best we get started, then." Mei Lan nodded.

"Tomorrow is soon enough. There is still much to do here, and I think we could all use a good night's rest." Georgie wanted peace and quiet, a moment where she could finally indulge in all the emotions she'd been shoving back for far too many days. She couldn't have it immediately, but she fully intended on claiming a minute for herself soon. The transfer of powers to the High Seat was a long-winded ceremony she couldn't contemplate just then.

Once again, she began moving around the table. On the far side, Silviu and Costel continued to work over Bijoux, but Georgie could see their worry was unnecessary, as the woman was faring much better. The blood had been cleaned off her face and she sipped a glass of orange juice, though it obviously didn't hurt her ego to have two protective patriarchs caring for her health. Or three—next to her, Eliasz rested in a chair, also giving unasked-for medical advice, with Ileana curled onto his lap, her face tucked into his shoulder.

Silviu immediately opened his arms for Georgie. She slid into them, against him, resting her cheek on his chest to better hear the steady thumping of his heart—a heart she'd felt slowing, dangerously close to stopping.

She'd almost lost him. It had been in his eyes—the fading life, the flickering magic. Georgie had felt it.

She pushed the thought back, unable to face it yet. There was still too much to do. Georgie looked up at her husband. "They wanted to perform the ritual now, to make us the High Seat."

"You'll be the High Seat," he informed her. "I'll just be the conduit to the magic."

"They want us to share power."

"And we will." He dipped his head and brushed his lips over hers. "But you'll claim the official title."

"I told them tomorrow was soon enough."

Silviu smiled. "That was an excellent idea. We still have a lot to deal with, removing the bodies and preparing for their return to their Families. We need to clean things up, get everyone healed as completely as possible. I'm certain many of us could use a stiff drink…"

Georgie watched his lips move and the rogue notion that she might never have seen such a thing again struck her hard. Fear, a tragic horror, shot through her and tied her stomach into knots. She blinked, but it did little to hold back the moisture suddenly blinding her. She couldn't hold on another moment.

"Silver—" Her voice broke.

His arms tightened around her. "Costel's very good at handling crises. He can see to the cleanup, can't you?"

"Of course," his brother answered. Gently, he helped Bijoux to her feet and kissed her temple. "I'll start by sending Bijoux to lie down and rest. Perhaps the two of you should do the same? You expended an awful lot of energy. I'll tell everyone you're checking on the rest of the building, making certain it's still structurally intact."

Grateful, Georgie nodded against Silviu's shoulder. Her tears wet his shirt and thickened her voice. "Yes, I—"

"One more minute." Silviu pulled her closer and

whispered into her ear. "Stay strong for one more minute. Don't let them see weakness." Louder, he said, "Have you spoken to Emeric? He's inviting Alexandru to stay here with him for the foreseeable future."

"It's lovely." Bijoux's voice still held a slur of exertion. "I will go with Costel to Romania and my father will have the company of a houseguest."

"I must agree. I believe my grandfather will love to have the chance of sneaking into the Documents Chamber and discovering all he can about everyone."

As he spoke, Silviu led her out of the room. Georgie kept her face turned down, as if she were listening raptly to every word, all while blinking desperately. She let him handle their goodbyes, the murmured assurances that the Council would meet in the morning and conclude the business they'd all come for. He got them out of the Council Chamber with speed and diplomacy, a combination Georgie appreciated with her whole heart just then.

He picked her up. Georgie found herself held to his chest, cradled and cared for, as he took the steps two at a time.

"Put me down! You were hurt."

"And now I'm healed."

Georgie surrendered. There was no sense in fighting him and she was where she wanted to be, where she *needed* to be. Putting her arms around his neck, she held on, breathing in Silviu's scent, absorbing the feel of him against her, his warmth and his magic—his life.

She cried. There was no sense in fighting tears, either. She'd been strong when Alexandru had attacked her, strong while Graves had poked and prodded, and she'd held it together when her grandmother had fallen ill. Georgie had stood firm when Madeleine had died and had still found a way forward after Silviu had taken her inheritance.

Daniel Levy had not and *would* not bring her down, but sometimes a woman's soul needed cleansing.

Silviu kicked open their bedroom door and laid her down. Never loosening his hold on her, he kept her against him as he climbed onto the mattress, caging her protectively, impressing her senses with the knowledge that she wasn't alone. She'd never be alone again. He stroked her back for long, long minutes, until her tears stopped flowing so fast and her quiet sobs grew scarce.

"Don't let me go yet," she whispered.

"Never. Haven't you figured it out yet? I'll never let you go, Georgie."

"You almost did." Fresh tears took her by surprise. She'd thought she'd be dried out by then. "You almost died."

"But I didn't. You wouldn't let me."

"No." Georgie took a shaky breath. "I need you too much."

Silviu held her tighter, and, when her tears still didn't stop, he rolled over her, pinning her to the mattress with his body. He levered his weight up on his elbows and stared into her eyes, his own molten nickel, shining bright with love.

"So many times I lost you," he said. "To your Family, to the witch hunts, to Graves' spell. My own desperate ambition. So many times you almost slipped away forever. I think I know how you feel right now."

"How?" Georgie had no idea what she was feeling. Too many emotions, too much sadness and relief were crowding her chest. Her brain was silent, but her muscles remained tense. She was sick to her stomach, yet she felt as if she could sleep for a week.

And all she wanted to do was lie in Silviu's arms and let the world burn down around them.

"You love me." Silviu kissed the corner of her mouth, then dragged his lips over hers. "You're my Magic Match — my heart and soul, my torment and my joy. Sometimes, there are no words to express that depth of feeling. But we'll be all right, my love. We're in this together."

"Always." Georgie sniffled and shifted against him, losing herself and her fears in the heat of his body and the strength of his arms. "Forever."

* * * *

The morning dawned cold and sunny. Beautiful, in a prophetic way, leading the witching world into a new era, one of healing and hope but also of grief. A contradiction, just as Georgie knew she and Silviu were.

They stood together at the head of the table, but only Georgie would sit in the High Seat. Immediately to her right, a chair similar to Emeric's had been positioned for Silviu. They'd occupied their places for the entirety of the Council meeting, as lesser business was handled before the pageantry of the High Seat ceremony began.

Eliasz was the new Levy Father and was approved to take the Levy seat at the Council table. He swore he'd find a new representative, though, as he would be kept busy with his leadership duties, including routing out all those who supported Daniel's schemes. The Levy Father had a daunting task before him, but Ileana was at his side, ready to help however she could. Her magic would be useful — Georgie didn't doubt — but her love for Eliasz would see them through the hard times they all knew would be coming.

Georgie gave the Davenold seat to Adam. He would serve as the first male to represent a matriarchal coven in the Council's history. His was a unique position, having married in a way that allowed him to remain with his coven rather than joining his wife's. Tulah stood next to him, chin lifted as she watched the proceedings. Georgie knew the woman would see everything, remember everything. The perfect spy. The Shimizu Family representative was over the moon, believing his coven had an advantage with Georgie, as Adam's devotion to his wife was plain to see.

Milo would be an official advisor to the High Seat. Georgie had already been fond of him, but his sacrifice during the battle had gone far beyond anything she'd expected. He'd repeatedly held firm in the face of Daniel's manipulations and had fought valiantly to restore calm during the conflict.

That talent, as well as his understanding of economics, made Milo valuable beyond measure. Christiana agreed, though she was happy enough having her husband alive and well and even more devoted to the family they'd created between them. Milo had accepted his new role with a quiet nod as he positioned himself behind his wife, the very image of an obedient matriarchal husband, his big hands cupping her belly, protecting the life within.

"So much has happened in these past several weeks," Georgie murmured.

New love had been planted and a love that had taken years to develop was finally in full bloom. She looked down the length of the table to where Costel and Bijoux sat together, hands linked. Emeric had given them permission to marry, and Costel would take Bijoux home with him as soon as Vasile arrived at the palace with Alexandru. Emeric planned to make the old man's life a living hell, along with Georgie's suggestion of banishment to the cottage at the edge of the property whenever the Council was in session. The other representatives agreed.

Costel's future was settled, and Georgie was grateful for that. They might never see eye to eye, might never be friends, but she'd discovered a new respect for her brother-in-law. Watching Costel and Bijoux, finding him at peace and her radiant with joy, a golden glow humming between them, Georgie was happy.

For so many things.

She looked at her husband and knew he felt the same. Sometimes, it was as if they each inhabited the other's soul, but the sensation that triggered was becoming less alien and more comforting. Silviu smiled back at her and reached out. Georgie took his hand and held on. She'd never let go again. His magic thrummed in her heart, along with the additional tug of the power of the combined covens. Emeric, at the foot of the table, was winding down his speech.

Once he finished, Georgie would be the High Seat, but Silviu would be the one who drew on the magic. It was a fair divide of duties. She trusted her husband to not misuse his authority.

Powerful, ancient words swirled with sparks of rainbow colors, indicative of all the magic each coven could wield. Even through her Bane shields, Georgie felt the weight, recognized the enchantments. The strength of the witching world was in her hands, entrusted to her care, and she vowed to never let them down.

"I do so promise to hold our magic in trust," she said when prompted. "To never let our community fall, to do no harm that would instigate war or mayhem. I swear to uphold our laws in all fairness, show mercy whenever possible and avenge those who have been wronged with the purest justice."

Silviu nodded. "I swear, as well."

Emeric raised his hands and silver nets gathered the rainbow magic, directing it toward Georgie and Silviu. "Then so shall it be. Take this gift of our magic to keep and uphold, to protect with your lives and serve with the utmost loyalty."

Silviu sparkled. Inside her own soul, Georgie felt his claim on the magic in a way similar to his taking of the Davenold power. They were connected. Once all guards were lowered, once trust was established, everything between them had strengthened and condensed. What had been his had become hers, and what had been hers had become his, just as Silviu had promised.

The power of the combined covens moved past him, all around him and through him in a constant current that would not be stilled. Georgie felt the rush of cool magic, felt her husband soaking it up and adding it to his reserves before he let it out slowly. As golden light blazed and the pressure of the air became tasking, Georgie closed her eyes and let her husband fill her.

She was a vessel that had been crafted to hold his overflow. She was the Bane witch to his Reap. She was his Magic Match.

And they would rule together.

"Together," Georgie whispered.

"In all ways," Silviu promised.

Motherhood

Excerpt

Chapter One

Silviu

"Blood me as your heir." Silviu Lovasz let his magic rise and weave into the tone of his voice, sending it out with his words.

"Why should I?"

Mother Madeleine Davenold nearly blended in with her pillows, pale and frighteningly motionless. Only her eyes still held evidence of the fierce woman she'd been a week ago, before dark magic had infiltrated her defenses. A woman who prized the concept of Family above all else. Family was everything to the old lady.

Silviu had experience dealing with such a sentiment, however, having often manipulated the same driving emotion in his older brother. Influencing others was a talent

Silviu wielded ruthlessly, and in Madeleine's weakened state, it would be easier than it had ever been before to gain a foothold.

"I will take care of them." Silviu pushed a little harder. "Trust me."

Silver light spread out over the woman's fragile skin, shimmering brightly before sinking in. Her eyes glazed. Silviu felt his magic meet the Davenold strength and slip through. With the dark spell poking holes in her resistance, Madeleine couldn't stand against him.

Burrowing deeper, his talent took hold as the woman's breathing turned ragged. Magic set down roots and reached farther. Silviu had a vision of tendrils curling out—only to meet a snarling black wall that surged up to reject the influence with a violent expulsion.

Madeleine screamed softly, clutching her chest. Silviu was knocked back as the silver light retracted into his soul with a painful snap.

The dark magic had blocked his efforts.

The two witches stared at each other in grim astonishment. Madeline rubbed her chest with a shaking hand. "What was that?"

"Dark magic." Silviu refused to elaborate. There was no way he'd admit that he'd tried to gain influence over her. He rushed toward her to evaluate the damage he might have done.

Madeleine's pulse was weak but steady under Silviu's fingertips. The magic coursing through her veins was cool and smooth, nowhere near the raging river it used to be. There wasn't a trace of the dark magic energy that he'd felt, but that didn't mean it was gone.

"How do you feel?"

The old woman's eyes flashed with amusement. "Terrible."

"Then why do you look as if you're enjoying some private joke?"

Madeleine smiled. Her pale, papery skin stretched taut

over her cheeks, lifting the sagging flesh until she appeared almost beautiful. A pang shot through Silviu's chest as he realized his betrothed would look like the Davenold Mother when she reached the same age.

Madeleine's voice was a thread of sound. "Because you've been doing all you can to save my life when it would be in your best interest to let me die."

Something inside him rebelled at the thought. "That's not quite true."

"I suppose you think I can still be of use to you."

Silviu closed his eyes and again searched for the spell draining Madeleine of strength and life. He couldn't find the origins, couldn't even feel its presence, but he could sense the changes within her. Every day she was weaker, every day a step closer to death.

"I expected to have your guidance when I joined the Council." Silviu released Madeleine's wrist and eased a hip onto the bed next to hers. "I haven't even been formally named to my Family's seat yet. I need your influence over others to further my cause."

"I doubt that." Her black eyes, still sharp with intelligence in spite of her ailment, narrowed. "You'll do just fine on your own."

"If I have to." Silviu's shoulder rose and fell as his mind busied itself with modifications to the plans that had been in place since he was four years old. "You taught me well, but it would be easier to have you at my side."

"You'll have Georgeanne."

He nodded, satisfaction racing through him at the old woman's simple statement. "Yes, you've trained her well, too."

Madeleine studied him for a long moment, a hint of suspicion in her eyes. Silviu met her gaze calmly, years of practice supporting his serenity in the face of such a thorough examination. His own father had a habit of watching him in the same manner.

"She knows how to handle herself in politics," Madeleine

finally said. "I've made certain she was an asset to you and your rise to power. And vice versa."

"I know. We'll work together to achieve our goals. She'll cement your Family's influence over the other matriarchal houses and extend your reach over the patriarchal witches when I lead the combined covens."

"That was the plan."

A plan that had been concocted twenty-three years before, when the matriarchal Mother had agreed to betroth her infant granddaughter to the youngest son of a patriarchal coven. Reap and Bane were the rarest of witches—one with too much magic, the other with none. Silviu's Reap magic merged into the blocked Bane magic Georgie contained within her, making them the strongest Matched pair the world had ever known.

Silviu considered it their right to rule over the combined covens.

Legend suggested the pairing was able to join their talents into a force that could fell every witch before them. Together, Silviu and Georgeanne wielded a power that could pull each other back from the brink of death—a fact they'd learned when Georgie had nearly been injured by the same dark magic targeting the Davenold Mother.

"A thousand generations ago," Madeleine mused, "our community was torn apart by countless wars. The witches who walked the traditional, matriarchal path versus those who wanted to follow Fathers."

"I know the history very well," Silviu reminded her.

She frowned him into silence. "And when the war eventually dwindled down, they all saw how devastating it had been. To the world and especially to our community. The truce resulted in the Schism, Silviu. Motherhouses to one side of the divide, Fatherhouses to the other."

"With a High Seat to lead them all," he said impatiently. "A position you've held for half your life, a position I intend to hold for the rest of mine. What is your point?"

"You've been trained to take that position. Every tutor I

sent to you and every burden your father heaped on your shoulders has all been to get you to the top of the covens' hierarchy." Madeleine's eyes flashed and a secretive smile played at the corners of her mouth. "But you won't get there without Georgeanne. Witches respect you, Silviu, but you are still a Lovasz."

More books from Totally Bound Publishing

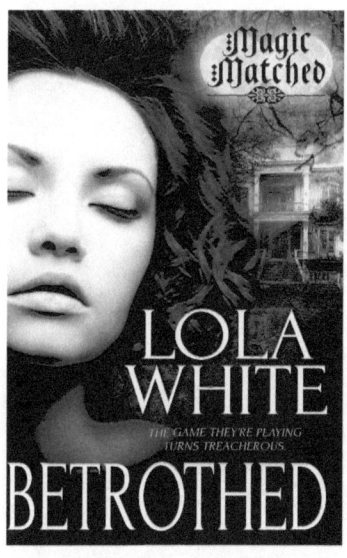

Book one in the Magic Matched series

*In witching society, magic and politics are the only things
that matter, and marriages are arranged for advantage
rather than love.*

Book one in the Vamp Hunters series

Her life on hold for a decade, Meghan's ready to take it back and move forward. Valor is ready too. The Vampire Master won't let her disappear, not ever again.

Book one in the Sisterhood of Jade series

*Within Derrick's hot embrace, Samantha discovers being
the hunted just might not be as bad as she thought.*

Book one in the Arcanium series

He's the reason to be careful what you wish for.

About the Author

Lola White

Delve into the emotions, dive into the erotic.

An extensive traveler who loves to incorporate various legends from around the world into her tales, author Lola White likes to twist reality at its edges in her stories. She likes delving into the emotions of her characters, finding their strengths and weaknesses, and seeing (and showing) how they get themselves out of whatever trouble has found them—if they can.

Lola White loves to hear from readers. You can find contact information, website details and an author profile page at https://www.totallybound.com/

Home of Erotic Romance

www.ingramcontent.com/pod-product-compliance
Lightning Source LLC
Chambersburg PA
CBHW020212260626
47156CB00002B/349